"Malcolm Devlin di
individual tragedies, and summons the m...
other selves are out there living alternate lives, and in doing ...
he offers the reader an unexpected and surreal consolation."
Anne Charnock, Arthur C. Clarke Award-winning author of
Dreams Before the Start of Time and *Bridge 108*

"Devlin writes intelligent, profound and perfect short stories.
A brilliant collection."
Aliya Whiteley, author of *The Beauty, Greensmith* and many more

"Acutely strange yet deeply humane, Devlin's stories are slippery
in all the best ways. This collection is a perfect demonstration of
his range, wit and skill."
M.T. Hill, author of *The Breach* and *Zero Bomb*

"I've been an admirer of Malcolm Devlin's fiction for years. He
writes with compassion, intelligence and precision, not just crossing
but obliterating genre lines with joyful abandonment. His newest
collection moved me deeply with its imagination, lyricism, and
gorgeous prose—a terrific book to knock you off your jaded feet
before landing you in all sorts of unexpected places."
Usman Malik, author of *Midnight Doorways*

"Themes of fate and free will, choice and contingency thread
through these twelve luminous and lyrical stories. Frequently,
as I was reading, I had to stop, my breath taken away at the
sheer quality of the writing, the ease and craft with which the
narratives unfolded, the compassion brought to each individual
character, the strange beauty found in the everyday. Malcolm
Devlin is one of our most gifted and perceptive writers."
Una McCormack, *New York Times*-bestselling author

"Devlin is a master of the new new weird, bending the genre
into wild new shapes. Pay attention or be left behind."
Gary Budden, author of *Hollow Shores* and *Judderman*

Also available from Unsung Stories

UNEXPECTED PLACES TO FALL FROM, UNEXPECTED PLACES TO LAND

MALCOLM DEVLIN

UNSUNG STORIES

Published by Unsung Stories

3 Rosslyn Road
London E17 9EU, United Kingdom

www.unsungstories.co.uk

First edition published in 2021
First impression

Paperback ISBN: 9781912658169
ePub ISBN: 9781912658176

Edited by Dan Coxon
Proofreading by Jonathan Oliver
Cover design by Vince Haig
Text design by Cox Design Limited
Typesetting by Vince Haig

Printed in the UK by Clays Ltd, Elcograf S.p.A.

CONTENTS

To Mum & Dad
For helping me take off.

To Helen
For helping me land.

"Nevertheless so profound is our ignorance, and so high our presumption, that we marvel when we hear of the extinction of an organic being; and as we do not see the cause, we invoke cataclysms to desolate the world..."
— Charles Darwin, *The Origin of Species*

"I know death hath ten thousand several doors
For men to take their exits; and 'tis found
They go on such strange geometrical hinges,
You may open them both ways..."
— John Webster, *The Duchess of Malfi*

WE ARE NOW
BEGINNING OUR DESCENT

I have always dreamed I would die in an aeroplane crash.

It will be a big plane. A commercial flight. I will be seated in economy as normal. On this flight, the dice will have rolled against me and I will be trapped in the middle of a row. There will be a businessman on my left: he will be portly, balding, busy with a briefcase. His tie will have been loosened with a nervous tug of a crooked finger, and beads of sweat will have started pebbling his forehead before the cabin doors have even closed. To my right, there will be an elderly woman who will spend the majority of the flight tottering up and down the aisle to the bathroom and chewing the teeth that do not quite fit. Reading her complimentary tabloid, she will tut over the stories of benefit frauds and immigrants; she will linger over the nudity with a mournful fascination.

We will attend to the ritual incantations of the air stewardesses as they perform the hallowed sign of the emergency exits and direct our wandering attention to the airline safety catechism located in the rear pocket of the seats in front of us.

In the unlikely event of loss of cabin pressure, oxygen masks will fall from the overhead compartments. You use them like this, like this, like this.

It will be too late for all of us, and I'd like to think that somehow, we will know all of this in advance. Terrible events don't need portents; we retrofit them afterwards, as though by making them inevitable, we can make them digestible. Accidents have always been a part of the world, we will tell each other. This is unavoidable. This is *written*.

As we fall, we will see the engines blossom into fire, lighting the cabin with a private sunset. Our heads will be pressed deep into the foam of the seats and even without looking through the windows we will know the plane is pointing downwards. We will give ourselves to gravity and the rush of it will be delicious. Together, we will cast ourselves at the brittle sea with such a force, it will make salt of us all.

❯ • ❮

A dream, then. One I have had many times during my life, since before I ever set foot on an aeroplane in person. As a child, I would cast my toys down the stairs or into the bath, until they fell apart and were confiscated from me. It was not because I was tired of them, as my parents believed, but because it seemed a more fitting conclusion to the games I played. It would end with fire, with twisted metal, with broken parts skittering across the kitchen floor.

Through my dream, I have always known how to fly. Because I knew it would be the end of me, there was peace in that understanding.

My wife always promised me she understood.

'Sometimes we only appreciate the places we are,' she said, 'once we've determined the manner by which we can escape them.'

My first flight was a shuttle from London to Edinburgh, barely an hour in the air. I was fifteen and we could have taken the train, but I had begged for the opportunity to fly for the very first time. My father had agreed, because he believed he might be the one to show me something new.

I let him pretend the experience was his to teach. Even at that young age, it felt known and unsurprising. The ritual of it reassured me while my father tried to mask his fear. He had been born soon after the war and had grown up among the ruins of cities razed by the enemy's aircraft. He flew infrequently if at all.

For me, the plane was as warm and familiar as the womb. The dip in the gut as the plane lifted its nose from the runway, the thick, granular roar in the ears, the sharp and sinus-scratching coolness of the processed air. I had dreamed all of it, and even as the plane bucked in turbulence prior to landing, making my father clutch at the arms of his chair, I was never afraid.

I should be clear. My dream has never been a nightmare.

There is comfort in the perception of five hundred people enacting the exact same emotions at the exact same time. There is comfort in being part of something greater than yourself. There is comfort in dying in company rather than alone.

Those who die in aeroplane accidents are granted famous deaths, but also anonymous ones. For a brief time, your flight number will be on the front page of every newspaper back home, and there won't be a single member of the informed public untouched by the news. But your face will be lost in a grid of casualties and no one will see it unless they are looking. No one will see you unless they know who they're looking for, tracing their fingers over the matrix of blurry portraits like an old woman working her way through the Sunday wordsearch. There you'd be, surrounded by strangers. A smile intended for someone else, a photograph you'd have been too embarrassed to share when you were alive, but one that someone, somewhere, thinks represents you in the way they want to remember. Perhaps there'll be a memorial? That must be a consolation. Who hasn't dreamed of leaving their name carved in stone in a public square, open letters weathering the human years, outlasting us all?

I grew up and flew up as much as I could. Business and pleasure, long weekends away. At first my wife was flattered by my extravagance, then frustrated by my excess. We flew too much, she would tell me. Think of how much it's costing us. Think of the environmental impact.

She was a patient flyer. She would sit in the light of the cabin window and read one her paperbacks, unmoved by the alien tilt of the horizon beyond the glass. She would smile flintily at the security staff and avoid eye contact with the passport officials. It was only when we landed that time would catch up to her. She would sigh with impatience by the baggage carousel and check her watch as though it might hasten our belongings. Air flight was never more than transport to her. For a time, she would humour me, but that did not last.

'Perhaps we should take the ferry next time,' she would say, or, 'How about the train?'

This was after she had read the newspapers, covers blackened with the photographs of remains. She would cluck her tongue at the outrage, and when she had gone to bed I would find the grid of casualties within the paper, using scissors and glue to add myself to their number. Just so I could see.

I followed the exploits of terrorists in the news with an enthusiast's interest. Please don't misunderstand, I did not support their causes. For the most part, I didn't quite understand them, but their appreciation of the aeroplane as a form of sacrifice, a burning Viking vessel to bring down an empire? Well there, perhaps, I admired their invention.

It was never about ethos. I mourned those they murdered as everyone did, but somewhere deep and private and buried, their atrocities *excited* me at a personal level. By making air travel more dangerous, they made my dream more achievable. I could remain apathetic to their wars and their casualties, because their atrocities glimmered with a self-serving light.

'You're more likely to die in the home than in an aeroplane accident,' my wife told me once, while outside in the world other people's crusades fought to redress the balance.

〉 • 〈

A bomb would be no good. There would be no beauty there, because a bomb would be too quick to *know*. How would any of us appreciate our final moments in the sulphurous seconds between trigger and release? I longed instead for the cruel longueur of an accident. A crack in the hubris of rocket science, the laws of physics snatching us from the air.

A bomb was a fruit plucked too soon; an accident ripened on the vine. It deserved to be relished.

Nevertheless, as the bombs sang their baritone chorus, and the airports darkened one by one, I flew more than I ever had. Seeking out the remaining flights that criss-crossed the globe, intersecting with the news feeds and column inches with spots of brilliant light.

When the news cycle quietened, I learned that budget airlines fly with limited fuel. Enough to get them from one location to another but with no reserve to keep them in a holding pattern. It's a dangerous practice, but it means they have to land on time or risk the safety of the passengers and ground crew. I mortgaged the house when I learned that. I booked every flight I could find. It felt like a promise.

My wife flew less frequently. I would call her before each flight I took and tell her that I loved her. I did this because it was true, but also so that after the accident, she would have a story to tell the paper when they called.

'My husband called me before he boarded the flight,' she would say. 'It was almost as if he knew.'

The media adored that sort of thing. Love stories cut short, last words delivered in tears before the final curtain. A perfect bittersweet ending. They weren't interested in sequels. They didn't care how the loved ones were left behind at the departure gates, playing their messages over and over again.

I was spending more and more of my time in the air, wondering each time if the next flight would be the one that would take me. I would reserve seats in the middle of rows and wait for the businessman and the old woman to join me. Every time I landed, the plane thump-thumping onto the tarmac, the shriek and holler of shredded atmosphere outside, I felt disappointment that the flight had done only what it was supposed to do. It was upsetting that the pilots had done their job; that the journey had been routine. Among the clatter of released seat belts and the whistle of mobile phones returning from blackout, I would sit back in my seat, dejected, until the plane had cleared. This time, at least, the journey had not transcended its purpose.

My wife left me somewhere between flights. One moment she was by my side at the check-in desk, the next she was gone. I don't remember where that was. I don't remember when.

The phone rang and rang and rang. The papers wanted to know if she'd told me she loved me.

'Do you know why they make you wear seat belts on planes?' I told them instead. 'They won't save your life. It's so they can identify the bodies if something goes wrong.'

I won't bore you with the particulars of how I died. Only that it wasn't what I had in mind. There was no aeroplane crash for me. No glorious company, no memorials or front pages. My death was an embarrassment. It was rushed and incomplete, and if you'll forgive me, I intend to leave it at that.

My days are now spent in transit, hurriedly moving westwards down the concourse, my hand luggage rattling behind me on its tiny little wheels, my coat draped over my arm, my passport in my hand.

The airport is familiar, as all airports are. An international space, culture shaved down to the basics so it has become something bland and palatable. The signs are written in international glyphs. Stick men and symbols, yellows and blacks. The windows to my right show a tarmac ground and a matching tarmac sky, each punctured with red and yellow lights moving in preordained lines.

I don't remember landing here. I don't really know where I'm going, but I know I should head westerly, always westerly. The signage indicating the boarding gates clocks upwards one by one as I walk. Double figures, treble figures. More. I know that despite the fact that I have been walking for days, months, years, I have a flight I must not miss under any circumstance.

The concourse stretches onwards to a distant point, my bag clatters behind me. I feel the tug of the weight of it at my shoulder, a roughly drawn stress line, thick across the muscles of my back.

Everyone is rushing to go somewhere else, I have the sense that no one really sees each other. We are all trapped within the borders of our discrete groups. There are businessmen, families, couples linked arm-in-arm. Sometimes they jog past me, sometimes they're heading the opposite way, sometimes they're lingering by the concession stalls and the duty free. They talk idly in languages I don't recognise, let alone understand. This, too, is comforting in a way.

Sometimes the gates I pass are full, with great crowds of people sitting together under storm clouds of impatience and exhaustion. I know it's impossible to get comfortable on those seats and my heart goes out to them. People pace back and forth. They lie on the cold thin carpet as though it might let them sleep.

I see the way they look at the information boards for updates about their progress. A child cries, a couple argue. I walk on.

Every now and then, I see someone I recognise, alone in the ranks of seating beside an otherwise empty gate. I never remember their names. I don't seem to remember anyone's names, and they don't look up as I pass by; they stare into the middle distance instead, preoccupied by something private I have no wish to interrupt.

There is one woman in particular. I have seen her before, but I couldn't tell you where from. She always sits at the end of the row of seats, closest to the aisle. Her coat is arranged neatly on the chair beside her and her small cabin bag is tucked between her feet. She has a paperback open in her lap, which she reads intermittently as though she is saving it for the journey ahead. She seems to know I'm coming because she always looks up from her book as I approach and she smiles at me.

I don't know how she moves from one gate to another. She's always there before me. I have come to look forward to seeing her again. I look forward to her smile lighting the path as I go on my way.

I have spoken to her only once. She smiled at me as she always did and this time I stopped beside her. She lifted her coat and set it on her lap, her hand touching the seat beside her, inviting me to join her.

We talked mostly about air travel, but I have always found it remarkable how it's a subject that can connect to nearly everything else. Politics, culture, love. Its roots stretch broad and deep, it touches all of us in some way.

We talked for hours, as though we had only just met. There was so much we had missed.

She told me how she had always dreamed she might have a family, and I told her about my dream in turn. I told her how I always expected to die in an aeroplane collision, but how I was disappointed.

'I died in an aeroplane crash.' She said this simply, as though it was a fact of little or no consequence. It meant nothing to her. Not any more.

'Was it beautiful?' I said.

She smiled at me again and there wasn't judgement there, nor pity, nor anger.

'I don't remember,' she said.

She glanced at my luggage.

'They're not going to allow all of that on your flight,' she said. 'They have restrictions.'

I told her I wasn't ready to leave any of it behind and she nodded as though she understood. I checked my watch, even though I couldn't read the time on it. I told her I should be on my way if I was going to catch my flight.

I haven't spoken to her again, but she still smiles at me when I pass. She lowers her paperback and moves the coat from the chair beside her and I smile back, wave, and pass by.

> • <

Some time ago, I thought I saw the businessman. The portly gentleman I dreamed sat to my left as our plane crashed into the sea.

I saw him disappear into the lavatories outside one of the gates, and I waited outside for three days, expecting him to come out again.

I haven't seen him since. I haven't seen the old woman at all, but I find it reassuring to think that they're both here somewhere. It gives me a certain purpose I might otherwise have lacked. It was my first sense that things were moving forward, the first time I understood I wasn't simply going round in circles after all.

I hurry down the concourse, my luggage skittering and skuttering behind me. The gate numbers clock up, but now I know they're converging to a point. The woman with the paperback smiles at me and I salute her as I pass. My flight is ahead of me. They will call my name and I will be there.

We will take off, launching expansively into the night. How arrogant it is to fly! How beautiful! How absurd! And when it is time, we will all fall together, unified and exhilarated and finally complete.

THE PURPOSE OF
THE DODO IS TO BE EXTINCT

1. THE SINGULAR DEATH OF PRENTIS O'ROURKE

When Prentis O'Rourke was ten years old, he read a book about the last words spoken by the famous and historically significant, and wondered what he might say himself when his own time came.

For the most part he was not a morbid child, certainly no more so than any other boy his age. To the extent it was relevant to him, he knew what death was, but the thought and manner of it had never consumed him. Instead, it was a subject he merely found interesting. It was something worth bearing witness to if not investing in.

Beyond that, death was by no means his only concern. It was interesting to him in the same way it was interesting that you could make a rainbow with the hosepipe on a sunny day, or the way his mother would slice an apple into eight neat little pieces before she would eat it. Death was just something else that happened, and given that there were so many things that happened, it seemed strange to waste too much of the life he had left on one thing at the expense of the others. It was a postcard from a far-off land that he did not intend to visit for many, many years. It would happen, it would happen to him, and it would happen last.

His family had never been dishonest with him about death. When Breadbin, the family cocker spaniel, had died last year after chasing the wheels of a Peugeot 305, there were no euphemisms to shield him from the truth. He wasn't told that Breadbin had gone to a retirement home for dogs, or that he had taken off in a rocket back to Planet Dog, or that he now lived in a magical meadow, full of rabbits and squirrels to chase.

Breadbin had died, he was told. These things happen, he was told. It was okay to be sad, he was told.

Prentis had helped his father dig a trench at the end of the garden and together they buried the remains of the dog. Breadbin's funeral shroud was the same old Martini-branded beach towel that had previously lined his plastic bucket-bed. They filled the hole and planted a cherry tree in the grave, and Prentis was satisfied that some degree of completion had been achieved. He missed the dog, of course he did. He missed the movement of him about the house, the warmth of him as he curled up at his feet while they watched television, but he didn't need to believe in Planet Dog; the arrival of the cherry blossom in the spring was more than enough to help him understand.

Prentis's second experience of mortality came with the death of his grandmother only six weeks later. His parents took the opportunity to reframe Breadbin's passing as less of a tragedy and more of a lesson to prepare their son for what they imagined must be the greater loss. They needn't have concerned themselves. Prentis's grandmother had been eighty-seven and claimed she had been dying of one thing or another since her own son, Prentis's father, had moved out of the family home in Galway some thirty years earlier. At the funeral in Ireland, Prentis stood next to his father again, and while only a few other people had taken the time to attend – his grandmother's neighbours, her brother, an elderly cousin Prentis had never met before – the atmosphere was surprisingly upbeat. It was hard to be completely miserable, he reasoned, given the general feeling that this was what his grandmother would have wanted all along.

As he read his book that bright afternoon, the ten-year-old Prentis O'Rourke considered what his own last words would be. He hoped they would be important, because he hoped that by the time he finally died, he might be important too. Being important meant that people would listen to him no matter what he said, but even so, he felt he should say something pithy, witty and clever. A phrase that would be debated endlessly after he had gone, recasting the magnificent life he had led into one more valuable still. He wrote lines on the backs of used envelopes and rehearsed them in front of the bathroom mirror, giving each syllable a painful gravitas and then swooning theatrically onto the bathmat. He stared into the light fitting on the ceiling until it dissolved into rainbows and forced him to close his eyes. He would be known, he thought. His words would be known.

Thirty-one years later, just after a quarter past eight on the morning of 16 October 2019, Prentis lay on his back on the corner of Laburnum Road and Heathcote Avenue, staring up at the afternoon's clouds coalescing and darkening above him. His blood unspooled into the cracks of the tarmac beneath his head, unknitting his being across the intersection, and Prentis struggled to summon the will to say anything at all. But despite the pain, despite the fact his jaw no longer felt like his own, despite the fact his consciousness was already slipping from him by degrees, he did manage to achieve two distinct and final things. Firstly, he worried dreadfully about his thumbs; and secondly, he managed to speak.

'If only,' he said to no one at all. The brightness of the sun made colours dance before him, making him smile at some half-forgotten memory. They were colours he could still see when he closed his eyes and then died.

If only.

In this instance, there was nobody there to hear him. There was no one there to question how the sentiment might have concluded. Not even Janet Baskerville heard him speak. The woman who had killed him, the only witness to his death, sat in the front seat of her Saab 98 and all she could hear over the whine of the radio was the stiff percussion of her own heartbeat. *Thump, thump, thump*, the same distinctive concussion the car had made when it had struck Prentis O'Rourke only moments before. It taunted her, re-enacting the scene over and over and over again. The man flying from her bumper, and then flying again and again. As her airbag deflated in front of her, as her shoulder started aching where the seat belt had bit her and held her firm. She could see colours too, but most of them were red and black and white and grey.

At the very moment Prentis O'Rourke unpacked his life across the tarmac on one side of town, Laura O'Rourke hesitated in the act of packing her own into a matching three-piece luggage set on the other. She stopped suddenly, a towel half folded in her hands, and looked to the window in a moment of unbidden introspection. It was a bright day, a clear one, and there was nothing but the even blue of the sky within the open frame to distract her. There were no sounds from the street outside, no birds at the bird box Prentis had installed on the silver birch the previous summer. She could barely even hear the hum of traffic on the bypass.

Later, when she was told the news about her husband's accident, her husband's death, she would recall this moment and question it. Later still, she would come back to it and argue she had sensed that something, somewhere was wrong with the world. It was a moment of uncertainty that she would come to believe was concrete proof of the intuition she had always suspected she possessed. The intuition her husband had once dismissed as another example of her *bullshit superstition*. Her conviction that she had sensed her husband's death would ultimately unbalance her confidence for a long spell and lead her to some very dark places, some unreliable literature, some questionable professionals. Responsibility rather than loss would keep her awake at night. If she could have sensed it, why couldn't she have stopped it? What was the point of intuition if it only made sense when the time to act upon it had passed?

Laura had taken her time running away from her marriage. She certainly wasn't concerned that Prentis might come home too early and catch her in the act of leaving him. Prentis wasn't and had never been a threat to her; he had never really been an equal. He was ineffectual, he was dull, he was – God help him – *well meaning*.

Her father had been a warrant officer in the British Army, and they had moved frequently during her childhood. As a consequence, she knew only too well how to fit her whole world into her hand luggage, and her mother had been no different. Laura's mother had always struck Laura as being on the verge of leaving her father for good, so it came as something of a surprise when Laura's father died before she had the chance. The abrupt loss left her mother unanchored, and Laura reasoned that ultimately, her mother had needed someone she could leave, without ever having to. These days she rarely left her room in the nursing home, as though she had chosen to step out of the world instead. She didn't read books and she didn't watch the television. Instead, she sat at a card table and played endless games of solitaire, dealing out the cards in neat little stacks, ordering them carefully and packing them up again. She played countless games each day, identifying obscure patterns Laura would miss. She would use each deck until the corners began to curl, then she'd slide the cards back into the box and file them away with the other used decks on the bookshelf.

Whenever Laura would visit, every subject was filtered through her game, as though the deck of cards now not only defined the way she lived, but represented her philosophy on life itself.

'Not all lives can be won,' she told Laura after Prentis died. 'Some of us start with good hands, some start with bad ones. A single decision early in the game can undo your future in ways you simply can't foresee.'

Prentis had been different when Laura first met him. He was the promise of something stable, something reassuring, solid and static, the complete opposite of the life she'd grown up with. It was an outcome she thought she had always wanted until she sensed how it had begun to trap her. The walls of their new-build two-bed semi slowly closed in on all sides, and all she could picture was her mother's green baize card table, sparsely arranged with doll's house furniture. The same motions repeated over and over again. Deal, play, lose, repeat. The thought was suffocating to Laura, but Prentis, who had lived in the same place for most of his life, without the imagination to consider escape, seemed oblivious.

Prentis's father had always hoped he might be an engineer. He bought him a poster of Isambard Kingdom Brunel to put on his bedroom wall, and on his birthdays took him on field trips to places like Iron Bridge or the Thames Barrier.

'Engineers reshape the world,' his father said, unaware that his son was content to be shaped by his environment instead. Prentis preferred to devour history books, looking backwards rather than forwards. He marvelled at the ways people could persevere to survive the unsurvivable. How they pushed on through everything the world threw at them.

Perhaps it was no surprise that the Prentis Laura met taught history. His final job title was head of department, but that still mostly involved negotiating with bored teenagers at the Bridge Road Comprehensive. He told her how, whenever the class got rowdy – as they often did on a Friday afternoon – he would bring up his slides about mass extinction. He concentrated on the big five. The times when life on Earth had turned itself off-and-on-again and the planet had carried on, scarred but persistent into the future. His point – that some form of status quo would be maintained, no matter whether a species failed or not – was lost on the noisier sections of the class, but the illustrations of giant trilobites, ammonites and dinosaurs invariably captured their attention in a way Agincourt, the League of Nations and Neville Chamberlain did not. On a good day they would grant Prentis O'Rourke enough grudging goodwill to coast through the final hours of the afternoon until the bell marked the end of the day.

Prentis believed in free will rather than fate. The history he taught was too chaotic, too arbitrary, too cruel to bear the fingerprints of a guiding hand. After he died, Laura would come to believe the opposite was true. Every action she would take, she decided, must have been preordained. Everything she touched was part of some cosmic plan she didn't ever need to understand. Every choice she made was to position a switch on some unimaginable array of celestial circuitry. Together, she and everyone else on the planet was writing the subroutine that would ultimately reveal God; that would bring about the glory of the end times; that would lead them all to transcendence. It didn't really matter. She knew the outcome wasn't for her generation to witness. She understood her own singular purpose and with that, she was content.

That was Laura's future. While her husband died barely half a mile away, the Laura of the present checked through the house twice for things she might have forgotten, briefly arrested by the notion that her momentary pause was enough to reconsider her action. But the room had always been draughty, and without the benefit of hindsight Laura O'Rourke was more practically minded and rational than she might otherwise have admitted. She took her toothbrush from the bathroom. She took her running shoes from the closet. She folded each item of clothing and tucked them away with the same delicate care her mother might, in earlier, better days, have employed to put her daughter to bed.

2. A NEW MASS EXTINCTION

The coroner would rule that Prentis O'Rourke's death was accidental. He wasn't looking where he was going as he walked up Laburnum Road and he wasn't paying attention as he stepped out in front of Janet Baskerville's speeding car. This was all true and the thoughts that distracted him were pitifully trivial. In his mind, he was composing something witty that he would likely never have written. A rejoinder to something he had seen on *The Guardian* website's opinion section. A nonsense article crowdsourcing recommendations for a list of favourite (not best) science fiction movies. Prentis was going to nominate John Frankenheimer's *Seconds*. Not because it was one of his favourites, but because none of the other commenters had mentioned it yet, and this seemed like a grievous oversight. Good teacher that he was, he had every intention of explaining why in despairing detail.

Therefore, perhaps, Prentis O'Rourke died because of *The Guardian* website. Therefore, Prentis O'Rourke died because he had once seen a 1966 science fiction film and felt a little bit pleased with himself when given the opportunity to introduce it to others. Therefore, Prentis died because none of the other users of *The Guardian* website saw fit to champion the same film.

Prentis O'Rourke died because Janet Baskerville was also distracted. As she had turned onto Laburnum Road, Jefferson Airplane's 'White Rabbit' had come on the radio and she caught herself singing along with Grace Slick's breathy vocals. The song had always reminded her of a brief holiday affair she'd endured aged nineteen. His name had been Stephen T. Something-or-other and they'd met at the themed bar in a beach resort in the Seychelles. He had been handsome in that plastic 1980s way, all teeth and jaw and improbable fringe, and by 2014 she could no longer tell how much of their affair was real and how much had been filled in by the excess of eighties nostalgia, which had permeated popular culture since. In truth, she could no longer remember much about Stephen T. at all, and what she could remember seemed too much like a music video to be taken seriously, but she could still picture herself kissing him against a gloriously airbrushed sunset as they stood ankle-deep in the surf-washed sand.

Since the accident, her association with the Jefferson Airplane song had been forever rewired. Now, when she heard Jack Casady's ambling bass, the military thump of Spencer Dryden's drums, she saw only the last flight of Prentis O'Rourke, vanishing into that same glorious sunset that had never been there in reality.

She too has often tried to imagine how things could have been different. She has tried endlessly to identify the junction in causality where things went wrong.

If only she had been going slower.

If only she had applied the brakes harder.

If only she had followed Stephen T. back to his home in Southport all those years ago.

In the version of reality where Janet had indeed braked in time, diligently screeching to a halt mere inches from Prentis O'Rourke's knees, the gangly pedestrian stopped to stare at her owlishly, shocked and adrenalized by her screaming approach. He offered her a brief apologetic smile before collapsing where he stood, as a brain aneurysm took him down instead.

The Prentis who had been aware enough of his surroundings to observe how the driver of the Saab 98 was not paying attention to the road had stopped on the pavement to wait until she passed. He was brained by a falling tree branch, loosened by the previous day's gale, while Janet drove past singing along to her radio, completely oblivious to his slapstick exit from the world.

In the version of reality where Janet had followed Stephen T. back to Southport – inevitably breaking up with him between four and six months later, because there was a very good reason why she didn't remember anything about him other than his looks – she would have been completely absolved of Prentis's death, but Prentis O'Rourke would have died anyway without her intervention.

Janet Baskerville killed Prentis O'Rourke, but she didn't kill every Prentis O'Rourke.

The Prentis who stopped for a coffee on the way to work choked on a small piece of plastic that broke off the lid of his travel coffee cup. The Prentis who took the scenic route through the park was hit by a reversing tractor. The Prentis who followed the footpath down the river was spooked by a pair of hissing swans protecting their nest. He wasn't really scared of swans, but their sheer size and lurching aggression was enough to make him lose his footing on the bank; the current of the river strong enough to trap and drown him in the weir before he could understand what was happening. The Prentis who waited at the top of the road for the bus was mugged by a man named Kieron Boone, a not-quite-clean junkie who wasn't armed, but did a good enough job of pretending he was to make Prentis run under the wheels of the bus that was supposed to be taking him to work. The Prentis who decided to skip work entirely and stay in bed never woke up at all.

In a rare cosmic anomaly, at sixteen minutes past eight on 16 October 2019, Prentis O'Rourke died in every reality in which he had survived until his forty-second year.

The event's consequences were seismic, ricocheting through all versions of reality, forking through each and every permutation of each and every existence like once-bottled lightning, shaken and set loose. A hairline fracture spidered through the filigree webs of all possible worlds and every thread was severed in the exact same place.

In that one moment, millions died, but as only a single death was recorded in each reality, it was an event only observed and mourned by a tiny minority in each. A small, personal tragedy consigned to a few lines in the local press, if it was covered by the media at all.

It was only in a handful of realities, those where the Landry Institute had established a foothold, that the incident was observed, recorded and studied with the same solemn reverence that global disasters are traditionally afforded.

Here, the manner of Prentis O'Rourke's deaths was documented, catalogued and investigated; chains of causality were extrapolated, traced and analysed. Questions were asked, studies were prepared, countless theses were written. To those who study such things, the sheer quality and quantity of data provided by the billion deaths of Prentis O'Rourke was quite unprecedented.

The last recorded personal extinction had occurred some seventy-three years earlier, in 1941. Less than a year before that, the first Landry Institute had been established in London as an experimental means to test the outcomes of various military strategies in the field. Not yet a cross-existence concern, its preliminary ideas were theoretical, but when Mrs Caroline Buchanan of Des Moines, Iowa (verified in approximately 59 per cent of cases), died en masse, having reached the age of sixty-two, the Institute came to realise how her many and varied deaths served as the map they had been missing, the sheer scope of which no one among their number had the vision to fully anticipate.

They also learned how the cartography of reality can only by complicated further by war. The mass of conflicting decisions made during the years of World War Two were tangled and scrambled in a shocking and chaotic fashion. Compared with the sober, ordered pencil lines that had come before, the sheer volume of realities born from conflict were best understood as a desperate, palsied scribble across the pages of the ledger. Not all realities survived, proving once again how the true cost of large-scale violence is never adequately itemised.

Within this nightmarish scrawl, a single casualty per strand of existence was easy to overlook, and with no one yet trained to identify such patterns, the Landry Institute took many diligent years analysing the fragments of salvaged data before Caroline Buchanan's fate was identified.

Ultimately, they discovered that her extinguished lives exceeded the sum of all other casualties in each reality she existed in, but the executive council members of the Landry Institute were at pains to make clear Caroline Buchanan's deaths would not be in vain.

From here, the Landry Institute took some time to establish itself. It built resources over the intervening decades, expanding exponentially through each plane of existence. It remained patient and poised, waiting until a comparable event occurred. This time, they would be ready. This time, they would witness the event in real time. This time, they would capture it all.

There were near misses: Clifford Yant died nearly a million times in 1971 as a branch of his existence was inexplicably culled during an existential quake. Ashish Gupta died 20 per cent more frequently, for reasons still under debate.

The data collected thanks to the deaths of Prentis O'Rourke was considerably more significant. This, it was argued, was what the Landry Institute had been preparing for since its very inception. If the map provided by Caroline Buchanan had charted the coastline of a new world, the data provided by Prentis O'Rourke was a geological survey, a 3D model, a dashboard-mounted GPS device.

Thus, although he was never aware of it, Prentis O'Rourke had achieved immortality in one sense, even as he ceased to exist in another.

> • <

There are countless ways to die, and considered as a group, the variety of deaths of Prentis O'Rourke represented an even sample of every possibility. The only omission, it might be argued, was that none of the Prentis O'Rourkes who died that day died of old age.

Some were murdered. Debts owed came back to haunt them, things once said had repercussions, characters with whom they'd once had dealings proved not to be who they claimed. There were crimes of passion: some Prentis O'Rourkes were killed by their wives or husbands (the collected Prentis O'Rourkes' diverse variety of sexual orientations would prove something of surprise to those who thought they knew him well, and a number of bestselling books would be written debating the subject); some by their lovers, some by their children. Others sacrificed themselves to save loved ones, or were sacrificed by those they thought they loved. Many were simply in the wrong place at the wrong time: collateral damage to someone else's crime. A stray bullet, a wandering blade, an out-of-control getaway? Prentis O'Rourke would become a crime statistic, blinking into the darkening sky.

'If only,' he said and nobody heard.

Some died in hospital. Minor ailments turned bad, diseases contracted long before the event made all other diagnoses moot. Even those whose outlooks had improved were faced with a sudden, unstoppable downturn.

'These things happen,' their loved ones were assured by their doctors. They were right, but perhaps not in the way they thought. These things do happen, but they are so rare, they remain almost unimaginable.

The Prentis O'Rourkes who found themselves at war, either by choice, by career or by accident, found their individual ends lost among the chaos and horror which surrounded them. They fought on all sides: military, mercenary, rebel, civilian. They committed acts of atrocity, of cowardice, of heroism. Lives thrown away by circumstance and idiocy. Some did not fight at all, but found themselves consumed regardless.

Some Prentis O'Rourkes died by their own hand, their reasons many and varied. Cuckolds, lovers, bad investments. Others were simply consumed with sadness, hopelessness, anxiety or fear. They took pills, they took poison, they jumped from buildings, in front of trains. They leaped away from everything that made sense. Perhaps, in their final moments, they had time to regret the choice they thought had been theirs all along.

'If only,' they said.

Beyond all else, though, Prentis O'Rourke died by accident. If the many different worlds have anything in common, it is a cruel and unforgiving sense of humour. Things fall, things crash. Something misplaced sets off a chain of events: an escalating sequence of 'what-ifs', leading to the alarmed expression on Prentis O'Rourke's face as he suffers his final indignity.

There are so many ways for a life to be extinguished, and on that afternoon in his forty-second year, Prentis O'Rourke experienced them all.

In one curious moment of concordance – one that would be debated endlessly over the subsequent years – across the multitude of realities, each and every Prentis O'Rourke who was capable of speaking said the very same last words.

Granted only three final syllables in their respective lives, they each failed to say anything more significant before they died.

'If only,' they said. '*If only.*'

An enterprising intern at one branch of the Landry Institute took it upon herself to trace and clean up sound files of each recorded occurrence of Prentis O'Rourke's last words from across the spectrum. She brought them together and collated them, observing how their modulation and inflection matched perfectly from one to the other. It was a single voice, she concluded, playing back the combined recording on a loop. Not a scream, but a sigh, resigned as though the collective speakers were entirely aware of the situation they found themselves in, entirely aware of what would come next.

3. EDITED EXTRACT FROM *OFFICIAL CATALOGUE OF THE DEATHS OF PRENTIS O'ROURKE*, CONCISE EDITION (THE LANDRY INSTITUTE PRESS, REF: 825-159-884/T & DEPENDENCIES)

(1) <u>Category: Accidental</u>
    (Definition: Deaths caused by unmotivated
    circumstance, unattributed to conscious thought of
    subject or other party [See: Terms of Reference].)
    (1.1) <u>Articles fallen upon subject</u>
    (Definition: articles struck subject at force, directly
    OR indirectly causing physical trauma which led
    directly to death.)

ANIMALS
Domestic*

Including: Birds (including cages), cats (including travel cases), chinchillas, dogs, fish (including bowls/tanks), hamsters (including travel cases), garter snakes, gerbils, newts (including tanks), pythons, rabbits, salamanders, squirrels, stick insects (including tanks), tortoises, weasels.

Other*

Including: Alligators, badgers, bears, cows, coyotes, crocodiles, dogs (farm), deer, dodo (stuffed), dolphins, ducks, elephants, fish, flamingos, foxes, kangaroos, giraffes, goats, hares, hippopotamuses, horses, iguanas, insects (including tanks), Komodo dragons, lemmings, lions, lizards, monkeys, newts (wild), pandas, pigs, porcupines, rhinoceroses, sea cucumbers, sharks, sheep, sloths, snakes, squid, stoats, swans, tigers, turtles, walruses, whales, zebras.

* NB: This category is for articles which fell upon subject, leading to death. For animals which CONSUMED, PURSUED, POISONED or triggered ALLERGIC REACTION in subject please see relevant category.

BATHROOM ACCESSORIES*

Including: Baths, bath mats, cleaning products, electric toothbrushes, hot water tanks, plungers, razors (electric/manual), shampoo bottles, shower fittings, sinks, soap (liquid/bars), sponges, toilets, toilet brushes, toilet seats, towels, towel rails.

* NB: This category is for articles which fell upon subject, leading to death. For bathroom accessories which DROWNED, WOUNDED or led to ELECTROCUTION of subject please see relevant category.

BOOKS
Physical books

Including (most commonly cited ONLY): *2666* by Roberto Bolaño (paperback), *Angela Carter's Book of Fairy Tales* (Virago edition, hardback), *The Bible* (Old and New Testaments), *Building Stories* by Chris Ware, *Testament of Youth* by Vera Brittain (hardback, Bodley Head), *The Complete Sandman Box Set* by Neil Gaiman, *The Complete Works of Shakespeare* (RSC edition), *The Illustrated Lord of the Rings* (three-volume slipcase edition) by J.R.R. Tolkien/illustrated by John Howe, *Jerusalem* by Alan Moore, *The Infinite Worlds of Antonia Landry* by Sandoval, Malik, Bell et al. (Paperback, MIT Press), *The Luminaries* by Eleanor Catton (hardback, Viking), *The Riverside Chaucer* (second-hand, hardback), *The Wind-Up Bird Chronicle* by Haruki Murakami (paperback, Harvill edition), *Ulysses* by James Joyce (all editions, unread).

eBook Readers, crate of.
‖ See also: FURNITURE > BOOKSHELVES.

FURNITURE
Beds
Including: Day, doubles, kings, queens, singles, superkings, futons.
Bookshelves
Including: Fitted, flat-packed, freestanding, wall mounted.

Chairs
Including: Armchairs, dining, garden, kitchen, Laz-E-Boys (TM).

Garden accessories
Including: Dustbin, fences, fence posts, gates, gnomes, parasols, pond liners, recliners, rockeries, recycling bin, sheds, slides, statuary, swings, swing seats, water features.

See also: MASONRY, PLANTS and TOOLS.

Piano
(see: INSTRUMENTS, MUSICAL)

Sofas

Storage
Boxes, chests, cupboards (kitchen).

Tables
Including: Bedside, coffee, , dining, display, kitchen, occasional (stackable), side.

HOUSEHOLD ITEMS
Including: Air conditioner units, ashtrays, bookends, candles, candlesticks, computers (monitors/printers/scanners/sundry peripherals), curtain rails, desk fan, desk lamps, fire axes, hi-fi (stereo/sound equipment/speakers/turntables), iron, ironing board, marble bust of Mr Gladstone, mirrors, novelty bookends (left/right), oil lamps, pictures, remote controls, ropes, shoeboxes filled with ephemera, television (games consoles/media players/sundry connected boxes), vase of flowers, Venetian blinds.

See also: FURNITURE.

KITCHEN APPLIANCES

Including: Baking tray, bottles, bread bin, bread board, bread knife, bread maker, bowls, cake tins, chopping board, coffee maker, cups, deep-fat fryer, food processor, forks, glasses, jars, mugs (see cups), ovens (electric/gas/microwave/solid fuel/other), pans (frying pans/griddles/saucepans), pasta press, pestle and mortar, plates, kettles, knife block, knives (all types), rice cooker, rolling pin, salad spinner, slow cooker, spoons (large), teapots, tin opener (electric), toasters.

MASONRY

Building materials*
Building fittings

Including: Banister rails, carpeting, doors (external/internal), flooring, windows (frames/glass) stair rods.

Electrical fittings**

Including: Cables, electrical sockets, junction boxes, light bulbs, loose wires.

Plumbing fittings

Including: Pipes, tubes, water tanks.

* NB: This category has been determined too wide for the purview of this document. For more detailed analysis, please see appendix II in the report 'Prentis O'Rourke and Relationship to Deconstruction of Property'.

** NB: This category is for articles which fell upon subject, leading to death. For electrical fittings which BURNED or ELECTROCUTED subject please see relevant category.

METEOROLOGICAL EPHEMERA*

Including: Hailstones, meteor fragments, snow.

* NB: This category is for articles which fell upon subject, leading to death. For meteorological ephemera which BURNED, DROWNED or FROZE subject please see relevant category.

ORNAMENTATION

Including: Bowl of potpourri, ceramic miniatures, decorative light fittings, family portraits, figurines, fire guards, fire pokers, novelty set of coasters, vases.

* NB: This category is for articles which fell upon subject, leading to death. For ornaments which BURNED or IMPALED subject or were used as sundry MURDER WEAPONS please see relevant category.

OTHER SUBJECTS

Including all other subjects (people) who may have landed on subject (Prentis O'Rourke) resulting in at least sixteen fatalities.

PLANTS

Including: Boxes of seeds, bushes, cacti, cut flowers, plant pots, pot plants, seed trays, shrubs, trees (and portions of trees).

SIGNAGE/STREET FURNITURE

Including: Billboards, bollards, drain grilles, dustbins, gates, hoardings, kiosks, loose kerbstones, market stalls, newspaper boards, recycling bins, scaffolding, signs, signposts, street lights, telephone boxes, traffic cones.

See also: MASONRY and VEHICLES.

TOOLS
Manual tools*

Including ALL KINDS of: Anvils, bradawls, chisels, clamps, crowbars, cutters, drills, forks, hammers, hoes, knives, machetes, ladders, loppers, planes, poles, rakes, saws, screwdrivers, scythes, spanners, trowels, shovels, spades, steps, vices.

Power tools*

Including: Angle grinders, band saws, chainsaws, circular saws, drills (hand-held/pillar), hedge trimmers, lathes, lawn edgers, lawn mowers, leaf blowers, log splitters, nail guns, pile-drivers, sanders, staplers, strimmers.

* NB: This category is for articles which fell upon subject, leading to death. For tools which DISMEMBERED, IMPALED or WOUNDED subject please see relevant category.

TOYS

Including: Arcade games, bagatelle, balls (various) blocks, board games, bricks, cars, ceramic dolls, clowns, collectable card games, dice, dolls heads (crate of), Hello Kitty, inflatable snoman, fruit machines, Gerald the Happy Giraffe, jigsaws, juggling balls, juggling clubs, Lego (various), Meccano, model railway, puppets (finger/hand/string/miscellaneous), rag dolls, robots, shove ha'penny, snooker balls, snooker cue, snooker tables, teddy bears, Transformers, train set, variety of stuffed bears in a sack, very large stuffed rabbit, video game console (and accociated peripherals), water pistol.

VEHICLES*

Including: Aeroplanes, articulated road freight, bicycles, boats, buses, cars, canoes, motorcycles, penny farthing (vintage), scooters, ships, steam roller, tanks, trains, trucks, unicycle, vans.

* NB: This category is for articles which fell upon subject, leading to death. Please see ACCIDENTS > VEHICULAR, MURDER > VEHICULAR and SUICIDE > VEHICULAR for alternative relevant listings.

Next category:
(1.2) Articles subject fell off or from.

4. A DIGRESSION INVOLVING THUMBS

Laura asks what's keeping me awake.

I tell her about the dream I had the previous night and she pushes herself up on her elbow, her head resting in her cupped hand. It's too dark for me to see her face, but I can feel her watching me from a familiar silhouette.

'I dreamt I was at Lou's wedding,' I say. 'Lou Bishop. Remember her? Remember that? How many years ago was that?'

'Five years,' Laura says. 'No, six. We'd just come back from Spain. Lou… I haven't spoken to her for years.'

I kick the covers away and pull myself to sitting position. The night feels warm but the painted brick wall is cold against my back.

'So there I am,' I say, 'it's a wedding and it's exactly as it was as far as I remember. But they don't have the disco they had that night, they've got a band instead. Nothing big, just this guy in a hat, sitting there on a stool. He's got a woman with a bass on one side of him, another guy with a clarinet on the other. And they're playing in a way that says they're doing it as a favour.'

'Was I there?' she says.

I don't look at her.

'I don't know,' I say. 'No. I don't think so. It was a dream, you know.'

'Charming.' She repositions herself to get more comfortable. 'So what does this band do?' she says.

'They're a covers band,' I say. 'Not the sort of thing you'd expect to hear played at weddings. Hipster shit. Mopey stuff. Leonard Cohen and Bob Dylan, Patti Smith. I don't remember exactly, but that sort of thing. And there's Lou dancing in front of them. Eyes closed as though she's totally consumed by the music. It was her and... what was his name? Jack? It was her and Jack's first dance, remember that?'

Laura's amused.

'Jack was a lousy dancer,' she says and there's that twinkle in her voice. 'I remember that, at least. God.'

She's right, but I don't reply to her. 'There's something about the guy,' I say instead. 'Something that bothers me.'

'Which guy? Jack?'

'No. Well, yes – *obviously* Jack bothered me, but in this case it's the singer. The guy in the hat. He's sitting there on this stool, white shirt, black hat – pork pie, you know? Like Gene Hackman in *The French Connection*. He's strumming chords on his guitar and he's singing in this... this *voice*—'

'A good voice?'

'Yes,' I say. 'God yes. But... raw. You know? He has one of those voices you only get if you've been smoking since childhood.'

'Is that what was wrong with him?'

'No, it's his hands,' I say. 'There's something about the way he's holding his guitar. He's got blue-black tattoos snaking all the way up his forearms, disappearing under his rolled-up shirtsleeves, and he's clawing at this guitar in a way I've never seen before. There's something primal about it. It's like he's compensating for something, only at the time I don't realise what it is. Every time he repositions his fingers it's like it causes him pain, but every time, his voice just gets that much richer, that much more... I don't know.'

'Stronger?'

'More powerful. It was extraordinary.'

I push myself out of bed and pick my way across to the window. The room is overdue a tidy, our clothes are strewn all over. The window is open a crack. I push it so it's open all the way. There's a pack of Golds on the ledge; I light one for myself. I light one for her.

'So,' Laura says, joining me and accepting the proffered cigarette. 'What happens?'

I shrug, exhaling smoke into the night sky. It disperses, dreamlike.

'I don't know,' I say. 'It goes on for a bit longer, I suppose. I don't remember what happens next. Usual wedding stuff. Relatives and kids. The next thing I do remember has me at the bar. This must be later in the evening. I've lost my jacket by then and I've got an open collar and I'm sitting next to the guy in the hat.'

'Gene Hackman?' she says. 'The singer?'

'Yes, and you know what I'm like in situations like that. I can't talk to anyone. I mean, I admire this guy and I can't even compliment him on the set he's just finished. I'm all gummed up like a kid meeting a pop star, it's pathetic.

'But then he turns to me. He starts talking to me. He buys me a drink and we just talk.'

'What about?'

'Oh, I don't remember most of it. About him, I suppose. It's awkward to start with, but he gives me room to loosen up like he knows how bad I am like that. He talks about where he first learnt the guitar, his time hitching rides abroad, people he's met. I think there was some time in jail or something.'

'He spent time in jail?' Laura says. 'Where on earth did Lou dredge him up from?'

'It's a dream,' I say. 'It's not supposed to make sense. It didn't really happen. And it's not as if he's boasting about it or anything like that. It just sort of comes out in passing. I don't remember everything he said to me, I only remember that he seemed like a guy who had lived. And all the time he's talking, he's holding one of his hands cupped inside the other like this.

'And he catches me looking. And he says: "You looking at my hand? You want to see my hand?" And so he shows me. His right hand, he shows me.'

'And?'

'No thumb,' I say, indicating my own. 'Just a mess of scar tissue where there should have been one. It was ugly. Really ugly. A real horror movie sort of deal.'

Laura whistles. 'And he could play the guitar?' She's impressed.

'I don't know how,' I say. 'It's a dream, right? But he could. Really though, he could and he was great at it. And he's got this incredible voice. And the thing is, that's when I recognise him and he knows it. It's what he's been waiting for.'

'Who is he?'

I look at her beside me. She's standing in black and white, the contours of her face half-lit by moonlight. The way she smokes, she looks for all the world like Lauren Bacall if Lauren Bacall ever got her hair mussed while sleeping.

'When I was twelve,' I say, 'I snuck out of bed one evening and took the carving knife from the drawer in the kitchen. I held it over the top of my right thumb like this and I started to cut.'

I see her eyes widen.

'You never told me that,' she says.

'Well, no,' I say. 'Can you blame me? I didn't do anything. I freaked out. I broke the skin – only barely – but it was more than enough for me to change my mind. I skulked off back to bed and cried myself to sleep.'

'Why on earth would you want to do something like that?' she says.

I take a while before I answer. I look at my right thumb, older, plumper, bonier. It doesn't look like any kind of survivor.

'I felt,' I say eventually, 'as though it was holding me back.'

It sounds so foolish and she agrees with me.

'That's crazy,' she says.

I take a moment to finish my cigarette. There's an empty plastic water bottle on the window ledge already half-full of fag-ends. I add to it like a kid saving pennies. Laura is watching me closely. She looks like she's waiting for something special, something epic. Like the kid who stuck his thumb in the dyke and saved Denmark. I manage a small laugh as though I might prepare her for the disappointment.

'When I was small, I used to suck my thumb,' I say. 'Nothing unusual there, but I was still doing it when I was twelve.'

'That's not massively abnormal,' she says.

'In fact,' I say, 'I only eventually gave up sucking my thumb entirely because, when I was fifteen, sixteen, I found something to replace it with.'

I light another cigarette pointedly and hold it up to her: Exhibit A.

'And remember what I was like when I tried giving these up the first time?'

Her eyes roll.

'Don't remind me,' she says.

'It was like that,' I say. 'Only worse. It was like trying to give up with a kid's impatience. It's supposed to be only a phase you grow out of, but for me it was an addiction, and I didn't really understand that back then. I knew it was wrong and I knew I wanted to stop. I read a lot of history books, when I was a kid. Famous people, heroes. You know? Don't laugh, but I always dreamed I might end up in one of those books one day.'

'In a history book?' She's smirking at me. Not unkindly, but she's definitely smirking at me.

'Yeah, well you know. I was at an age when I thought that was how you knew if you made it. So I wanted to be famous. Important. Only none of the famous people in my books sucked their thumbs like kids did, and so when I was twelve, I got out of bed and held the carving knife over my thumb, like it was all the thumb's fault.

'Like Struwwelpeter, remember that? Those creepy German stories for kids. Little Jimmy who sucked his thumb: the scissor man came and *snip-snip-snip*. Serves him right. I'd look that book up in the library and look at the picture of that little forlorn kid with stumps where his thumbs had once been. Not in pain, not frightened, not even angry; just this expression of regret. Kids don't feel regret, I'd tell myself. Not like that. His anchor had been cut, in some strange way; he'd been set free.

'Anyway, I didn't cut, but this guy. This other guy? He did.'

'Pork pie,' she says. 'The guy in the hat?'

'Yes. He steeled himself and cut through this thumb, flesh and bone. Sawed through with the carving knife. And that's not easy. I mean, look at it, most domestic kitchen knives would be blunt before they even reach the bone. But still he kept going. I can't imagine the strength it must have taken. He said he could feel the bones splintering. He was cracking them, not cutting them. He said the pain almost made him sick, but he kept going until he was all the way through. Sawing away.'

I stare out the window into the blackness of the back garden. She's staring at me in horror, but I don't need to see her face to confirm it.

'He said he nearly passed out before he was done but he was terrified that he would be found, and they'd take him to hospital and put it back on. That overtook the pain, he told me: the fear of failing. In some ways, he needn't have worried. He'd done so much damage to it, they couldn't have fixed it back if they'd tried. He almost lost the entire hand, but by some miracle—'

'God,' Laura says, halting me from saying any more, her hand touching my arm, feather-light, insubstantial. 'That's horrible.'

'I told you,' I say.

She takes her hand away and looks out the window, her expression thoughtful.

'He was you?' she says eventually, gesturing at me with her cigarette, a spot of burning red bouncing before her.

I bob my head, indecisive.

'He was the me who had gone ahead with it.'

She frowns, then shakes her head. Amused again.

'So,' she says, 'if you'd sawn your thumb off at an early age you'd be able to play the guitar by now?'

I laugh at that.

'Yeah,' I say. 'Something like that.'

'And that's why you can't sleep.'

'Yes,' I say.

Laura sighs and kisses me on the cheek.

'Prentis O'Rourke,' she says. 'I love you, but you're a fucking idiot at times.'

She stubs her cigarette out on the outside edge of the window and drops it into the bottle. Trailing her hand over my shoulder, she turns back to the bed. I watch her reflection in the open window. By some trick of the optics, she looks like she's walking away from me: down the street, into the dark.

'Close the window a little when you're done,' she says. 'It's starting to get cold out there.'

I tell her I will and gesture with the half-smoked cigarette in my hand.

'You don't mind if I finish?' I say.

I hear her chuckle from across the room. Already distant.

'You should really give those up,' she says. 'I'm serious.'

I stare out the window into the darkness. The nicotine will keep me awake, it'll make me resent the morning when it comes. But I can live with that.

Because I don't tell her the rest of the dream. I don't tell her about how – every time – the guy leans towards me, so close I can smell the whisky on his breath, and he says: *We've led the same lives, you and me. But everything you've wanted to do, I've done. Everything you wanted to say, I've said. Every place you wanted to go, I've been. Everyone you've fallen for, I've fucked.*

I don't tell her how he holds up his ruined hand to me and says: *This is all it takes. Not the thumb: the act. The following through. This is all it takes to reshape the world.*

And I can't shake the way he played. The beautiful pain in that voice of his. And the image of her – not Lou, it was never her in the dream, but Laura. *The* Laura. My Laura – looking at him like she will never look at me.

And she's dancing for him.

She's dancing.

Dancing.

Dancing.

5. EXTINCTION SOLITAIRE

The Laura who worked in the Analytics Department of the Landry Institute was no longer the same person as the Laura who had married Prentis O'Rourke. Their worlds had diverged early in their respective lives, thanks to a single reckless decision made not by Laura, but by her father. Thus, one father died in a pointless brawl when his daughter was only eight years old, the other went home without getting involved. The former established a different causality chain, one that steered Laura well away from the life of Prentis O'Rourke rather than pitching her headlong into it.

This particular Laura – still named Laura MacNee – sat at her desk where she worked in the Landry Institute offices and scanned through the report she had requested from the Repository. She was disturbed how, in many of the documents, Laura O'Rourke was referred to simply as The Widow or The Wife, as though she was nothing more than an adjunct to the man who had died. She was troubled by the tone in which her counterparts were described. She came across as shallow, she was cold and uncaring, treating her marriage with a similar glibness to that which the report's author used to describe her. It simply didn't seem fair that history – history being the Landry Institute's central concern – should treat an individual, a witness, with such ambivalence. Prentis O'Rourke was gone and his blast radius had caused all kinds of collateral damage. Surely someone should be paying attention to those he left behind?

The Repository was the Landry Institute's central database interface. Beyond the inappropriately cute cartoon logo in the shape of a fluffy dodo wearing a baseball cap, it was a remarkably sophisticated and rather unlikely piece of equipment that – by means Laura had never troubled herself to understand – collated data from all known realities, sharing resources, processing requirements and occasionally dividing costs across the gamut of viable existences.

During her induction, Jack, her new line manager, had run her through the bespoke systems she was unfamiliar with, and Laura had questioned the choice of the dodo icon for the Repository.

'I think it's supposed to serve as a reminder,' Jack had said, double-clicking on the icon with surprising force as though he were punching the poor bird between the eyes. 'It was something someone said once. It's in the welcome documents somewhere. This idea that if we could go back in time, many of us would give anything to save the last dodos from extinction, but the truth is we've probably learned more from them all being dead. That sort of thing.'

Employees of the Landry Institute were not forbidden from tracking how their alternates lived in different worlds or how decisions they sweated over might have taken them on a different path, but they were not encouraged to do so either. To work at the Landry Institute was to become hyper-aware that every decision made, no matter how small, would extrapolate a whole universe, a fresh green shoot which would grow and expand. New staff made a concerted effort to appear more decisive, believing that by doing so, they would be more efficient. Older hands knew that the more realities were created, the more Institutes would exist and therefore – potentially – the more processing power the Repository would possess to handle them.

It was a contradiction, a paradox, but it didn't take long working at the Landry Institute to become ambivalent to such magical thinking.

A typical Monday morning would see many of the staff running quick reports about their weekend's activity, to confirm the suspicion that the decisions which had seemed like a good idea while drunk on Friday, and a terrible idea while hungover on Saturday, had fewer consequences on Sunday than they might have feared.

For Laura MacNee, tracking the lives of her alternates felt too much like spying. And if she thought that, then the women who shared her name, the women who shared her whole life up until one specific moment, would think that too. Many of her alternates, who it was reasonable to assume also still worked for the Landry Institute, might already have glanced at her own data in return, and the thought of all those eyes upon her, judging her decisions, made her nauseous. It was as though her every move and thought was being recorded on surveillance cameras by those who knew her better than anyone.

Laura MacNee lived alone. When someone asked, she would tell them that she was 'between dalliances', which was true to an extent.

It was something to do with working at the Landry Institute. She had seen so many relationships fail in so many different ways, there didn't really seem to be much point in pursuing one of her own. She knew others had become addicted to keeping tabs on how their other selves were thriving and failing in their love lives, and they would adjust their own courses to suit, but Laura felt that using the Repository in such a way was a form of cheating. To begin a relationship under the eye of the Landry Institute, she thought, was to open a book, one with the perception that there was only one real path through to success. This idea felt claustrophobic to her, as though she would be trapping herself in a frustrating and narrow band of possibility, continually under stress from the fear that she might be veering off the perfect racing line.

This wasn't free will, she decided, but it wasn't fate either. It was a mean path that ran somewhere between the two.

The news about Prentis O'Rourke had come as a surprise. Late on the morning of 16 October, Laura had arrived in the office and became increasingly aware over the course of the first few hours that her colleagues were treating her with a deference she was unused to.

'I'm so sorry,' her friend Janet said to her, leaning over her shoulder so she could view her screen.

'I didn't even know him,' Laura said, paging through the preliminary press release. It was a strange feeling. Global disasters came and went in her news feed and she would read each with an appalled diligence. She had never felt as though she should be invested before, and she realised she felt guilty because – despite all evidence to the contrary – she still couldn't find a way to connect to the vastness of the tragedy.

In all cases of major disasters, the employee handbook advised, there was a high probability that members of staff would have alternates who were personally involved. It published a series of recommendations advising how staff might distance themselves psychologically from the events and carry on working as normal. In the case of Prentis O'Rourke, Laura was in deep. Nearly 64 per cent of the Prentis O'Rourkes who had known Laura had been in a relationship with her when he died, and her name cropped up remarkably frequently in a wide variety of the subsequent analysis.

The Wife, The Widow, The Woman in his life.

She tried to understand why so many of her had ended up with so many of him. She scoured his profiles trying to understand what she might have seen in him, what about him could have made so many of her go all in. Had she met him in a bar in her current life, would she have fallen for him? Would she have had a choice?

She searched for a trace of his charisma that might translate through the terse language of the Landry Institute's paperwork, but what she found was relentlessly unexceptional. He had dreams, but not the ambition to fulfil them; he was kind, but too easily distracted; he was liberal in thought, but conservative in deed. He had a crooked smile and a self-deprecating manner, and until he came to the forefront by dying in such spectacular quantity, he was the sort who would fade into the background at the expense of all others.

She paged through the document, the words and figures blurring into nonsense before her. Was that it? Was he really the best she could do?

She thought of all the news stories of fires and bombs, air collisions and terrorist atrocities. All the witnesses who would show up afterwards explaining how they should have been there themselves. That they should have died, only they were saved by some quirk of fate: a lie-in, a hangover, a phone call from a stranger with a wrong number. She always thought it was strange that people should need to explain themselves on television in this way. It seemed so tasteless. A way for someone to make a stranger's tragedy more personal, to claim it as their own. The Repository made such speculation concrete and real. There was something exhilarating, people said, about learning how one of their alternates had perished on the way to work.

'Still,' Janet said. 'It could have been worse. In around 5 per cent of cases, apparently, I killed him. Me! I know! It's hilarious. I killed Prentis O'Rourke, if you can believe that.'

Janet was from Luton originally, but her vowels were still softened from the years she'd spent living in Lancashire. She smiled broadly, as though by doing so she might eclipse Laura's frown.

'Well,' Laura said. 'These sorts of things happen—'

'More than you'd think,' Janet said. 'I know, I know. But look at that.' She pointed to a cluster of dots at the top of the scatter graph on the screen. 'In these realities, here, here, here, I killed your husband. Imagine that.'

'Janet.'

'Accidentally,' Janet said. 'I'm not one of the ones who murdered him. Lloyd in requisitions, though? Apparently one of his alternates killed Prentis in a knife fight. Lloyd! You wouldn't think he had it in him.'

'Janet, *please.*'

Janet tapped her on the shoulder, a comradely gesture. She backed away to the office door, pausing to throw a smile back to Laura before she exited.

'Listen,' Janet said. 'Whenever I get vertigo from all of this, I look at the mirror reports. I'm serious. It helps, really.' She fluttered her fingers in a wave and walked away, humming something passingly familiar as she rounded the corner.

That evening, Laura visited her mother in the retirement home overlooking the river on one side and the meadow on the other. The receptionist glanced up at her as she came through the door and smiled briefly in acknowledgement before returning to the paperback romance she had open before her.

Laura followed the familiar corridor to her mother's flat, tapping on the door once before opening it with her own key.

Her mother barely acknowledged her as she came in. She was sitting, folded over her card table in the middle of the lounge, her glasses propped on her nose, an expression of utmost concentration on her face. A game of solitaire was laid out before her, blue-backed cards ordered in military ranks. The advancing second hand of the clock on the mantel loudly counted an insistent marching time.

Laura slipped her bag off her shoulder and sat on the edge of the sofa to wait for her. There was the thick smell of boiled cabbage from the kitchen and, fidgety with impatience, she got up again to open a window, to pace across the carpet. Her mother worked silently and swiftly, her eyes darting around the table before her, the remaining deck of cards clasped in her knuckles like a pack of cigarettes.

Laura returned to the sofa and glanced up at the shelves which lined the room. All the decks of cards her mother had already used, lined up like the spines of tiny books. There were so many of them, and for a moment it struck Laura that they looked familiar. In the foyer to the Landry Institute offices there was a mural intended to illustrate a million lives, each stacked and filed on shelves like library books. There had been a time when she had looked her mother up in the Repository, but all her paths seemed to straighten out into something similar, as though in every life she reached a point where she stripped her own options bare. Her father would die and her mother would stop. It was a simple as that and it was all too much. She followed the mothers who had not reached this point yet, but she couldn't read their reports without seeing signs – real or imagined – that told her this future was inevitable for each of them. Perhaps this was what Prentis O'Rourke was to her. A beacon on a horizon that she doggedly made for. Something unavoidable, a gravitational well that would spin her off course if she came under its influence.

'Have you been crying?' her mother said. She wasn't quite looking at her. She had collected all the cards back into the deck and was holding them tightly in her fist, staring at the empty green of the table as though she could still perceive things in its design that no one else could.

'No,' Laura said, wiping her face anyway as though she had been.

'You look sad.'

'Someone died,' Laura said. 'I didn't know them.' For some reason, it felt like a lie.

Her mother nodded. That made sense to her. She shuffled the deck of cards, an instinctive gesture, her hands moving quickly and confidently, her eyes unfocused.

'That is sad,' she said.

Laura stood up and crossed to the other side of the table. She knelt on the floor and reached across the green baize, taking the deck of cards from her mother's hands.

'Let's play something together,' she said.

She dealt out ten cards to each of them.

'Rummy,' she said. 'We used to play Rummy sometimes, didn't we?'

She set the remaining cards upside down and removed the top card, placing it face-up beside them. The ten of diamonds.

Her mother remained silent. Her hand was still raised from where Laura had taken the cards from her, her eyes stared at the table as though it was still empty.

'Mummy,' Laura said.

Her mother raised her head slowly to meet her eyes. She reached out a hand and started gathering all the cards on the table towards her in a broad, sweeping motion. Cards jumbled, blue backs and white fronts. There was a quiet desperation there as her mother fought to restore the order.

'This isn't how it works, Laura,' she said.

Laura watched as she resolved the cards into a deck again and started shuffling. She dealt the cards out again. Another game of solitaire, this time orientated away from her, facing Laura. When she was done, she reached across the table, passing the remaining cards to her daughter.

Laura looked at her. She imagined the version of herself that took the cards and obediently played. She imagined the version of her mother who had accepted the game of Rummy and played with her. She imagined the version of her who stood too soon, flipping the table and scattering cards across the floor and making her mother howl in grief. She imagined herself running back to the Landry Institute and starting fire after fire after fire.

'It isn't how it works,' her mother said again.

'I don't think that's true,' Laura said.

> • <

That night, Laura dreamed of Prentis O'Rourke. He was giant, bloated, blimp-shaped, drifting above the city street, creaking and turning on some unseen tide. He was eclipsing the bright summer sun like one of the alien spacecraft in a science fiction film she had once seen. His shadow passed over everyone as they went about their daily lives, and while most ignored him, Laura couldn't look away.

Don't they see how he's affecting everyone? she thought. Don't they care?

In her dream, Laura stopped in the middle of the street to stare up at him as he passed. Time lengthened as it often does in dreams and she watched as he slid lazily overhead, his body ballooning, his eyes closed, creased, a flicker of a frown as though he was troubled by dreams of his own.

The shriek of brakes and the desperate, angry car horn distracted her enough to see the bright face of Janet Baskerville at the wheel of her car, veering towards her both too fast and too slow. It was cartoonish and absurd, with poor Janet pulling all kinds of faces as she tried to master the brakes of her Saab 98 before it was too late for either of them.

6. THE MIRROR REPORTS

If, for any self-contained universe, gravity creates a point where the distance between particles is minimal, then when the particles expand outwards, they do so in two temporal directions.

Therefore, on the other side of the Janus point, in the exact mirror of reality ref. 785-157-894/N (assuming that everything that can happen does indeed happen), the story of Prentis O'Rourke will be substantially different; here there will be fate but there will be no free will –

and in these circumstances it will not be poorer for the reversal.

In this world, Janet Baskerville is escorted to a wrecked Saab 98 on the corner of Laburnum Road. As the airbag folds itself up, the steering column seals itself, she looks through the windscreen to witness the man lying in the road before her open his eyes and then leap joyously into the air, throwing himself at the bonnet of the car as she stamps into reverse. He walks off down the street, a smile on his face. She will never see him again, but it is an event that will colour the rest of her life; gone is the sense of guilt and disappointment which has hounded her days and rendered her nights sleepless, gone is that ache at the base of her neck which has nagged her for as long as she can remember. She drives home immediately and fiercely embraces her husband and daughter.

At the home she has moved into while Prentis has been away, Laura will unpack her clothes and place her toothbrush in the bathroom. She will put her luggage away in the attic and it will not be touched again until her honeymoon, six years later. Her sense of contentment will grow as the years progress. Laura and Prentis will become closer over time, their passion will increase, everything will seem so right, so perfect, so new.

Their relationship will end on a glorious high, beyond which parting seems logical and effortless. They will not cry when they go their separate ways, they will not need to.

Prentis O'Rourke will live out his life in reverse. Whenever he reaches a turning point, his world will become bound with those of every outcome of every experience: the threads of reality will plait together to form one stronger, unified world in which every decision has been dissected, considered and learnt from. As Prentis O'Rourke becomes younger, he becomes stronger. He becomes more knowledgeable and more experienced.

Ultimately, all the possible worlds which have been created by decisions made by every Prentis O'Rourke will converge into one single reality and one final Prentis O'Rourke.

But before this happens, when the cherry tree in his parents' garden stops flowering and withers to a stem, he and his father will dig it up and exhume the remains of Breadbin, who they will place gently on the road and watch from the kerb as he is resuscitated by a passing Peugeot 305.

A year before that, when Prentis is ten years old, he reads a book; a chapter of which discusses the last words spoken by historical figures who do not yet exist.

Prentis will roll onto his back, his hands folded beneath his head, and he will stare up at the clouds coalescing in the sky above him, watching the bright colours of the morning dance and whirl.

Here, he will consider his own last words. He will know what he said when every version of him died, and he alone will understand what each version of himself meant when he spoke those final words in each of those different realities, all that time ago. The thought will make him smile, and that, he decides, is enough.

Prentis O'Rourke will have ten years of his life still to live, and he will be content.

WALKING TO DOGGERLAND

(1)

Across the road from the bus stop, a young man was working a sculpture free from an upturned sack of builder's sand. The unpromising pile had been worked over with care, built and stacked, smoothed and carved with such patience and precision that it had adopted the shape of a melancholy-looking Labrador, slouching to its side while a trio of fat puppies suckled at its chest.

Penny hadn't meant to stare, but as she waited, she had become trapped in her fascination for what the man was doing. It was late in the morning and the street to the station was mostly quiet. She knew it was arrogant and this knowledge embarrassed her, but she was struck by the dizzying sense that the artist was working for her benefit alone. By inches, she shifted her small day bag closer to the edge of the road so she might steal a better perspective.

Overhead, a chevron of geese barked across the dirty white of the sky, and somewhere in the town centre an alarm hollered then snapped silent. There was a tense greyness to the day that made the street feel primed and faintly unsafe, and even the usual squabble of gulls she had always associated with Bryhanton sounded to her like late-night drunks spoiling for a fight; but the artist ignored them all, concentrating only on the work ahead of him.

He was young, but then everyone seemed young to her now. He was possibly still in his twenties, which made him *very* young, with cropped black hair and a charcoal dusting of beard emphasising the leanness of his jaw. He wore an oversized blue and white anorak like a football manager and black tracksuit trousers with a white sports company logo repeated down the outer seams like police tape.

Penny checked the traffic before crossing the road, her knees complaining with the sudden movement. Closer, she could see he was working with what looked like a tablespoon, using its rounded side to smooth the sand into an even surface, turning it around to use the narrow end of the handle to carve deeper, more detailed work. There was a water spray bottle beside him. One like Sister Beryl used to wield to mist the herb garden, much to the consternation of Sister Agatha, who would insist that the plants be properly watered or else they'd start to moulder in their pots.

Penny watched in fascination as the sand dog's features came into focus. The mother dog's big, sad, watery eyes, the distortion of folds where its jowls spread across the ground, puncture marks where its whiskers would be. With a practised *flick-flick-flick* of his spoon the man worked on the front paws, and the balls of sand took on shape, then texture, then claws.

It was miraculous in a way. An act of creation, an illusion of life born from the basest of materials. Not that she would have admitted anything so naïve and blasphemous out loud.

Penny smiled instead.

'What's her name?' she said, and the sound of her voice in the silent street surprised her almost as much as the childishness of the question itself.

The man stopped his work and looked back at her. He looked older than she had thought he was. His skin rough and worn, his dark eyes wary and tired.

'You say something?' The morning's cold made his voice rattle.

'I said, what's her name?'

The man shrugged.

'It's just a dog,' he said. 'It's not real.'

'Oh, I know.' She *did* know, but even so close, the weight and the shape of the sculpture had something convincing about it. There was an uncanny sort of life to it, as though if she were to turn her back, it would push itself to its feet and shake itself off. 'It's beautiful, it really is.'

'Thank you.'

'You should call her Oscar,' Penny said. 'I know it's a boy's name, but I don't think that matters for dogs, do you?'

The man didn't reply, he just watched her, waiting.

'When I was little, I had—' she stopped to correct herself, '—I *knew* a dog just like her. Oh, this was long ago. Years and years. She was a sandy coloured Labrador. She was called Oscar. She was beautiful too.'

Penny smiled again and felt foolish. She didn't know why she had said anything at all, and now she felt herself reddening with embarrassment. The man looked away as though he was impatient for her to leave, and Penny glanced at her feet, where she noticed a detail she had overlooked. A simple paper plate with the words 'THANK YOU' written across it in marker pen.

'Oh, I am sorry,' she said. She flustered with her bag and retrieved her purse, pooling through her change with a fingertip. She glanced up at the street and saw shuttered buildings and looming doorways. The coins were all coppers, so she fished out a note instead, thrusting it at the artist and making him blink.

'I think she's beautiful,' she said again. *Beautiful.* The word came unbidden and she felt afraid of the magnitude of it. Was it beautiful? Was she even qualified to judge if it were? She waved the note at the man, mortified by the lurch in gravity as the status shifted between them. The man stared at her but didn't take the offered money. Penny stooped and laid it on the plate instead. A breath of wind lifted it, testing it to see if it could snatch it away, but the man caught it with a sharp *clack* of the spoon.

'Thank you,' he said, not looking up.

'I'm so sorry,' Penny said. She stepped backwards, turning her heel and then catching herself, saving her from an inelegant moment of slapstick.

A hand took her elbow. It was Veronica, looking furious.

'Not today, thank you,' she said in a tight voice to the man. 'She's not interested.' She steered Penny away, marching her down the pavement at a brisk pace.

'Is that your bag?' She gestured to the canvas carry-all Penny was clutching with both hands.

'Yes.'

'Is that all you brought?'

'Yes.'

Veronica frowned, taking the bag off her. Her car was parked by the kerb, a broad silver-blue hatchback in need of a clean. She unlocked it with the electric key fob. It beeped and whistled and the lights flashed on and off.

'How much did you give him?'

She opened the boot and slung Penny's bag inside without much ceremony. There were a pair of suitcases there already, a red gingham two-piece luggage set.

'What?' Penny said.

'The beggar. How much did you give him?'

'He's an artist.'

'It was a twenty, wasn't it? A *twenty*? Jesus, Penny.'

Veronica opened the passenger-side door and ushered Penny inside.

'You have to be more careful with your money, I'm serious. You're in the real world now. Sorry about the mess.'

The footwell on the passenger side was full of food wrappers, paper printouts and brightly coloured magazines. Penny cleared a path for her feet and sat down, putting her hands between her knees and holding her shoulders in while Veronica slammed the door shut on her so the world went abruptly silent.

The car was a little stuffy, the windows clouded. There was the soft smell of biscuit crumbs and a sharp one of ripened fruit. The blurry ghost of Veronica's shape disappeared around the back of the car, and for a moment Penny panicked, craning around in her seat to track her movement.

The driver-side door clattered open and Veronica plumped in beside her, shutting the door after her with a practised thump.

She glanced at Penny briefly.

'Seat belt,' she said, plugging the keys into the ignition.

'I thought...' Penny tailed off.

'What?' Veronica connected her own seat belt and juggled the gear stick. 'That I was going to go and get your money back?' She shook her head. 'It's your money. You really should be more careful.'

She turned the key and the engine rumbled and settled. Veronica glanced at the rear-view mirror, then cranked the window open and stuck her head out to see behind her.

'Besides,' she said, putting the car in gear and easing away from the kerb, 'I'm not going to slog out there and demand money *off* a beggar, am I? Can you imagine how that would look?'

'He's an artist.'

'Honey,' Veronica said. 'It's a scam. A racket.'

Penny shook her head. 'It's not,' she said. 'It was beautiful.'

There was that word again. It felt softer this time. Deployed on the defensive, it fitted better. It sounded more fully earned.

'Well, perhaps it is, but he's over here illegally,' Veronica said. 'They're smuggled over in shipping crates or whatever. And they're all over the place, making dogs out of sand. All the same. Dogs lying down, looking sad. Last year it was miniature kites, the year before it was duck whistles. This year it's sand dogs. Someone's teaching them all this. They've got handlers, the people who smuggled them over, who profit off them. Modern-day slavery. Poor bastards. A van comes round at the end of the day, shovels those dogs back into their sandbags. The handlers take the money, they go back out again the next day. Make more dogs.'

Penny stared out the window. She could see the concrete fortress of the amusements on the seafront. It looked shuttered, abandoned, but there were still lights on, and the late-morning sunlight made the facia gleam against the gunmetal of the sea in a way that made it look more exposed and bleak.

She'd always been a little afraid of the pier when she'd been young. It had felt too noisy, too brash to her. Everyone had seemed older than her in a leering way and their raucous laughter had a meanness to it. It didn't help that she'd never had anything to spend there, it was all promise, no delivery; all sin, no purpose. Now that she was older, comfortably in her late middle age — older — the place felt frightening for the same reasons, except that the laughing people were now younger than her.

It was a blessing when the car turned inland and out of the town, following the cliff road. Green lawns papered over the coastline and evenly spaced birch trees strobed the window like a kineograph machine. Beyond them was the cliff edge, and below that the thin line of the main beach. She thought of Oscar running across the sand, that joyous, full-body run of hers, eyes wide and tongue lolling.

'Why dogs?' she said. 'Why do they all make dogs?'

'We're in England,' Veronica said. 'The English give more money to animal charities than human ones. Turns out that dogs are cuter than refugees.'

Veronica shot her a glance.

'Don't fret about it,' she said. 'It's terrible and *someone* has to do something about it. But you? Me? Who has the time? You're not the only one who falls for it. But god, it's a miserable thought, isn't it?'

She risked another glance, then reached out to touch Penny's knee gently.

'You're looking thin,' she said. 'Are you eating enough.'

'I'm fine.'

'And how's work?'

'It's okay,' Penny said. 'Thank you for asking.'

Veronica shook her head.

'I can't believe you just managed to walk into that job,' she said. 'There's me fretting about my CV nearly all the time? And you just walk straight in with a blank bit of paper and—'

'Ronnie, you're a teacher,' Penny said. 'People will always need teachers.'

Veronica shot her a dark look.

'Oh, you are so delightfully naive,' she said. 'Besides, I'm nearly seventy, if you can believe it. They would much rather I retired so they can recruit a bunch of young men in my place. Honestly, I think this government thinks that education is one area where hiring fewer women can be seen as progressive.'

'The gnome,' Penny said, pointing ahead.

'I know, I know.'

Despite her confidence, Veronica stamped on the brakes, hanging onto the wheel so the car lurched in a broad arc to the left, swinging past the statue of a man with a fishing net that demarcated the otherwise hidden entrance to Wallasey Row.

Technically, the statue wasn't a gnome at all. Originally, it had served to point the way to Pinner's, a line-and-tackle shop that had once stood a few hundred yards down the road, hidden from the traffic by the thick knots of blackthorn hedgerows.

Pinner's was long gone, Penny had never been inside it. Dark and run-down, it hadn't looked anything like as inviting as the gnome had advertised. The entire shop had been demolished and replaced by a new development of boxy-looking flats, but the statue remained, standing sentry at the side of Clifftop Road, hand raised in greeting to the generations of traffic that rushed past. Lulu said there had been a minor uproar when the council had considered removing it, as though unlike Pinner himself, whom no one really spoke of, the statue was one of the most well-loved residents of the town. There had been petitions and a protest against the eviction. Someone had wrapped him in a sash inscribed with the slogan 'Save the Pinnerman', and for a good week the passing traffic would sound their horns as they passed in support until the council backed down. If anything, Lulu said, they went a bit too far in the other direction, which was why you could now find his face on souvenir key rings and tea-towels.

Pinnerman. That's how he was known locally, but as a child Penny had always assumed he must have been an oversized garden gnome because he resembled the one their grandmother had kept on the window ledge of her downstairs bathroom. That gnome had been a fisherman too, one who held a rod rather than a net, an expression of jovial patience belying the fact that his line was connected to an old boot. Penny had always thought he must have been quite lonely and frustrated, being confined to quarters in her grandmother's house. Little wonder he couldn't catch anything more substantial. When she was eight, she had demanded he be released into the garden. It was quite the tantrum she threw, and her grandmother had acquiesced with benign bewilderment. They planted him beside the fishpond at the foot of her garden and Penny fussed until he looked like he belonged there.

He lasted until the first rains, and then cracked and collapsed overnight. He was never cut out for the climate of the Norfolk coast and was better suited to the indoor life after all; his confrontation with reality had been unsparing.

Wallasey Road cut downwards through the cliff, curling in a hairpin to the left and then the right before emerging on Stove Causeway, which was no longer a causeway at all and now only ran a mile or two along the coast. There were a number of houses here, tucked away from the road, the cliff flattening to dunes behind them as the road ran eastwards. To the west, the beach connected to the one at Bryhanton, and when the tide was out it was an easy walk back to town. At high tide, the water came all the way up, swallowing the sand, and while there was still a pathway of sorts, there were all kinds of bright-red capital-letter signs erected at each end to warn people off.

'I phoned the hospital,' Veronica said. 'They moved her to a larger ward this morning. We can visit until around eight.'

She shot a glance across at Penny.

'We can see what needs doing in the house until then.'

Penny nodded, distracted by the view from the window.

The houses along Stove Causeway were a chocolate box assortment of desirable holiday properties and most looked deserted so late in the season. There was Bluebell Cottage, a wooden bungalow, painted mauve and propped on stilts; there was Stove House, a narrow twin-gabled Victorian red-brick that had probably been there the longest. There was Bay View, built during the seventies as something abstract and adventurous in which all the windows faced north. And there was the Royal Coronation Guest House, still pretty with all its window boxes and painted shutters.

It had been more than forty years since Penny had last been here, and yet each landmark was familiar to her. Not just the buildings, but the stones, the shrubs, the kink, turn and twist of the road. Certainly, the houses had changed – new paint jobs, the occasional extension – but the route aligned itself almost seamlessly with the one in her memory and she found herself catching her breath as the chimneys of Breakers slid into view.

Breakers was the last house on the causeway. Beyond it, a small sign indicated a further footpath along the coast leading to the cliffs and Barrow Hill, but the road itself terminated in a cramped turning circle.

Veronica pulled to a halt on the opposite side of the road and the two of them stared at the house without speaking to each other.

It was a small, whitewashed cottage with blue wooden trim. In some ways, it looked like a child's drawing of what a cottage should be. The door was in the middle, a window on each side. Upstairs, three dormer windows broke out of the black roof-tiles and faced the sea. The woodwork around the eaves was decorative like lacework, and the whole thing looked as though it had been transplanted wholesale from a German fairy story.

A narrow strip of garden was boxed in with a low stone wall and parked in front of that was Lulu's sky-blue MX5 convertible.

Penny stared at the house and smiled. As children they'd spent nearly all their summers here. Every year, the three of them would take the train to Bryhanton, then take a taxi from the station to the house using the envelope of money that Lulu had been entrusted with. Every year, Mrs Kaye would be standing on the doorstep waiting. She would be wearing her housecoat and her hands would be on her hips as though, each time, they had arrived later than they should have.

Veronica sighed.

'Oh my god,' she said. 'What *has* she done to the place?'

'What?'

'The garden is a ruin, look at it. And the bedroom window. Oh. If Mother saw this it would break her heart.' She unbuckled herself and clattered out the door.

Penny hesitated a moment before following. She was aware that the sheer force of Veronica's perception might reshape her own, and she was reluctant to succumb to her sister's cynicism. Besides which, bringing their mother into the equation felt like a false note. Antonia Landry had lived in the house when she was young, but throughout Penny's childhood she didn't think she remembered a time when her mother ever showed affection for the place.

She unfastened her seat belt and let herself out of the car. Turning back to the house, she saw everything Veronica had seen, but she was relieved to see the warmth of the cottage was still present. Despite this, the front garden was thick with yellow grasses, the bins overflowed beside the front door. The window frames upstairs were cracked and peeling. Blackened wood behind the broken blue paint. Closer, there was a weight to the house that had never been there before. The recognition of it whirled inside her and made her fretful.

Veronica was inspecting the bins. She had adopted a business-like demeanour that Penny imagined served her well in the school she worked in. All outward purpose, minimal engagement unless absolutely necessary.

'She's been knocking it back,' Veronica said. 'God. Look at all these bottles.'

She kicked the base of the bin and it clinked like a musical instrument. She shook her head and explored her handbag until she found a fist of keys.

She turned back to Penny before opening the door.

'This might not be pleasant,' she said. 'Lulu hasn't let anyone come in for I don't know how long. So.'

'I know.'

'Well, then,' Veronica said. 'Just...'

She turned the key and opened the door.

The hallway was much as Penny remembered it. The staircase lurked as it always had at the back of the room to the right. The textured glass of the lounge door threw scattered leaves of daylight across the big square flagstones, forming a fat chequerboard across the floor. The geography of the house came flooding back to her, and with it the smell of the wood stove with their swimming clothes hung up around it, the *rattle-rattle-hum* of the boiler coming to life in the evening, the faint slapping sound the floor made as they ran across it, barefoot.

It was dimmer than her memory allowed, older and dustier and more worn, but everything looked familiar. The same picture was mounted in the hallway – the landscape of a royal hunt, bright figures and animals diminishing into the trees. There was the same copper plate mounted above the bathroom door in the shadow of the stairs, the three figures in relief, military or royal, she had never really been able to tell. In the centre of the ceiling there was the same glass lampshade with the blue crystal tears. It was all exactly the same as it had been all those years before.

It was only when she stepped inside that she understood this was the problem. How old had she been the last time she was here? Fifteen? Sixteen? Still young enough to fall under the spell of a place that wasn't quite theirs, and perhaps it was that very distance that explained the trick of it. Now, it felt smaller, and there was something stagnant about the way it had dug its heels in and tried not to change.

It had been a surprise to learn that Lulu had bought the place fifteen years ago. Penny had only heard when Veronica came to visit her in Liverpool one summer, the brightness and energy of what she had to say filling the small concrete visitor's room even before she had the chance to say it.

'Lulu's bought Breakers,' Veronica had said, her face flushed with weight of the gossip. Adult disbelief co-existing with the spectre of her childhood excitement.

'Breakers?' Penny hadn't heard the name for years. 'I don't understand.'

'She's back in the country,' Veronica had said. 'She'd come back from one of those trips of hers and she's ended up in Bryhanton, of all places. She wandered down to see the place for old times' sake and saw it was for sale. Either that or she found the owners and bullied them until they sold it to her.'

'Why did she do that?' Penny said. 'Buying the cottage, I mean?'

'Why does Lulu do anything?' Veronica said. She shook her head. 'I don't know. She's having a mid-life crisis, perhaps. Do women get those? Still. It's nice in a way. I could take the boys down there for the summer, maybe? Show them the view of Doggerland. It would be like the old times.'

Penny smiled in encouragement, but didn't say anything.

'Do you think that would be strange?' Veronica said. 'Taking the boys for a holiday to our childhood? Would that be strange?'

'It's what Mother did to us,' Penny said, and Veronica's face fell a fraction.

'God,' she said. 'I hadn't thought of that.'

She never did take the boys to Bryhanton. Lulu might have bought the cottage, but she'd proved maddeningly elusive when Veronica had tried to schedule in time to visit. She'd been away, she was having work done, the timing just wasn't convenient. 'The place is crawling with builders and plumbers,' she told Veronica over the phone. 'It's really no place for children.' Eventually Veronica had given up, capitulating to the likelihood that the idea had been a lousy one anyway.

What was clear now, standing on the threshold, was that Lulu hadn't had any work done on the property at all. As they walked in silence from room to room, it was apparent that stagnancy had infected the air of the place. A strong sense that the cold lingering there had been there long enough to put down roots. There was a noxious smell of damp, of vegetable products on the turn; of soured milk and rotting meat; of something too sweet and cloying to be palatable.

'Oh, Lulu.' Veronica raised her hand to her mouth.

The ceilings were dusted black with mould, the furniture was tattered, stained and unkempt. The kitchen was cluttered with abandoned and filthy dishes, the sink dark with globular matter that Penny couldn't quite identify. A mason jar of preserved fruit sat open beside the sink, a sturdy blanket of grey fuzzy mould tucked in neatly around the edges. The work surfaces were cracked, plywood corners fraying like the pages of paperback books left in the rain. The window frame above the sink was black, paint peeling.

The bin was full and shrouded with a stained tea-towel, and the fridge door had swung wide open and inside a milk bottle lay on its side, its contents clouded and nearly solid. Beside it, a plate of ham, barely covered, had become furred with flies.

Penny pushed the door closed. It would need attention at some point, but that was for later and Veronica didn't need to see it. Her sister looked pale enough as it was.

'Upstairs?' Penny said.

Veronica nodded.

Upstairs, the sloped ceilings were circled with fringed contours of damp and the dusty spiderwebs were thick as citadels in the cavities between the furniture and the walls. The bed was bare of sheets, the mattress stained, the uncovered duvet was bunched to one side. All the whites had become yellow and grey. The books on the bedside table looked swollen as though they'd been dropped in the bath.

Boxes were piled high on the landing, and while Veronica moved from room to room, tutting loudly, Penny opened the box at the top of the stack and was surprised to find a collection of Lulu's portfolios and exhibition catalogues. There were multiple copies of each, some still shrink-wrapped in plastic. Some of them Penny hadn't seen before. Galleries she hadn't heard of in Seattle, Melbourne, Cape Town. She paged through the book on the top and lost herself briefly in her sister's work. Candid shots taken in city streets after dark. Partygoers leered at the camera, tall women navigated in improbable heels. There was a vibrancy to the black-and-white images. A neon sheen that made everyone faintly unearthly. There was grit to the subjects, but there was beauty there too. It was a world away from the confines of Breakers, and it wore a carefully controlled sort of beauty, framed sharply against the blurred edges of the ugly and the real. She paged through the pictures and realised how alien the people in them seemed. Her distant student days in Liverpool had been brief, but the city then had seemed so much more ordinary and grounded than the ones Lulu had captured. For a moment, she felt guilty that she hadn't followed her sister's career more closely. She set the book back in the box and closed the flaps with reverence.

Other boxes were filled with framed photographs, all Lulu's work, none of which she had found the time to display on the walls; some of them had slipped from their mounts leaving them squint and off-centre in the frames, faces hidden behind the edges. The damp had got to them, coffee-coloured stains encroaching from the corners. A sweaty gloss to the emulsion.

Penny had to stand on tiptoes to see the window ledge behind the boxes. The sailing boat figurines were still there as she had remembered them. Three identical little boats: one blue, one red, one yellow. They had been overrun with the cobwebs, a fat little spider's nest stitched between the sails. Even the net curtain behind them was familiar but changed: the same little pinwheel designs, the tessellated symmetry that had fascinated her when she was small.

Further boxes filled the two spare rooms, including the one Penny and Veronica used to share when they were young. She managed only a cursory glance in each room before returning to the top of the stairs.

Veronica was waiting for her. She shook her head and sighed.

'This is why you should never go back,' she said.

'Back where?'

'Anywhere. I mean, look at the place, she's… It used to be so lovely.' She glanced at Penny, there were tears in her eyes. 'It used to be so special. Do you remember?'

Penny nodded.

'We were very young,' she said. She looked back at the window, where a shaft of sunlight caught the model boats and, for a moment, made them shine. Sometimes it was better not to see every detail of them. Sometimes an impression was all that was necessary to salvage a moment. 'It still could be.'

She knew she sounded uncertain and Veronica ignored her, her own indignation mounting swiftly to eclipse any positives.

'She said she'd done all this work on the place,' Veronica said. 'I was so angry at the time, can you believe it? I thought of her ripping out all the things I loved about the place and making it modern and expensive. Some BoHo New York loft or some bullshit like it. It was so… so *her*, you know? Lulu takes charge. Blows on through like a thunderstorm. But she hasn't done anything. She's… she's just let it rot.'

She hugged herself against the cold.

'She hasn't put any of her pictures up,' Penny said.

'What?'

'Her photographs, they're all in these boxes. She hasn't put any on the walls.'

It seemed quietly wrong to Penny but Veronica only nodded, half paying attention.

'Listen,' she said. 'I'm going to open the windows. All of them. You go and get the heating on or we're both going to catch our death in here.'

Penny nodded and made her way down the stairs.

When she reached the bottom, she glanced up to check that Veronica had disappeared into one of the bedrooms, then she stooped down to slip her shoes off, placing them neatly at the foot of the stairs where Mrs Kaye had once left a small rug for the purpose. She rolled her socks into balls and set them neatly inside each shoe. The floor across the hall and lounge were paved with the same wide, grey flagstones. The cold of it was razor sharp under her feet, but it was bracing too – deliciously so. She almost laughed at the shock of it, but swallowed the sound down and settled for a wide, slightly manic smile. She crossed the lounge and the dining room, smiling as her feet made the same *pat-pat-pat* noise they had done when she was a child.

In the kitchen she could feel the muck on the floor from its texture, the graininess and stickiness and oiliness beneath her feet, its shift in temperature from tile to tile. This too was familiar; she remembered how Mrs Kaye used to make such an extravagant mess when she was cooking and then polish the whole place up to a shine when she was done. She remembered coming in barefoot and standing on tiptoes at the counter to try and reach for one of the rock cakes left on the rack to cool. Then, of course, there would be the sharp thwack of the wooden spoon when Mrs Kaye caught her in the act.

The boiler was in the cupboard next to the sink. It did look as though it had been replaced within the last forty years, but it still looked old. Penny's experience of boilers was limited. There was a simple combi unit she'd learned not to disturb in her flat in London, but the convent had relied on an archaic wood burner which was only lit for a couple of months of the year, and that was to keep the water pipes from freezing. Even then, Sister Agnes had refused to let anyone else near it, and the way she treated it anyone would have thought she was guarding the gates of hell itself.

Penny found a likely looking power switch and jabbed it with her thumb. A thread of red lights lit up but nothing else happened. She punched a few other buttons on the control panel but there was no other sound, no other indication that something had come on, certainly not the *whoosh-click* sound her own made when it was working.

'I've opened all the windows,' Veronica said. She pushed past to the sink and unlatched the window there, shoving at it. 'They're mostly all swollen in their frames. I don't know what she's done with the place.'

She gave up trying to move the kitchen window and glanced at Penny.

'Any luck with the boiler?'

'I don't think it's working.'

'Shit.' Veronica looked down and stiffened when she saw Penny was barefoot.

Penny waited for her to say something.

'Is this...' Veronica said. 'Is this a nun thing?'

'Not really, no.'

'Okay.' She looked up again. 'Only, the place is... it's really dirty. I mean...'

'I know.'

'And it's giving *me* arthritis just thinking about how cold you must be.' She collected herself. 'So the boiler's not working?'

'I don't think so.'

'Shit,' Veronica said again. 'Half the lights in the place aren't working either. She just hasn't bothered to replace the bulbs. I don't know what she was thinking.'

She opened a cupboard door, a tall broom cupboard just behind the kitchen door. It was full of cleaning products. Bleaches, cremes, cans of polish, scourers and Brillo pads and shrink-wrapped slabs of sponges. Everything was pristine, unused.

Veronica sighed and closed the door again.

'Listen,' she said. 'We're not staying here tonight.'

'We're not?'

'No! God.' She shivered at the thought. 'No, I've booked a couple of rooms in The Corrie. It's off-season, so...'

'The Corrie?'

'The Royal Coronation. I mean, we'd get hypothermia here. Or lung disease? Have you seen how much mould covers the place? It's probably killing *us* right now. I don't know. I'm amazed she only had a bit of a fall. The whole place seems to be conspiring to kill *someone*.'

She looked about her, hands on hips. 'I thought it would be bad,' she said. 'But this...'

She paused for a moment, her expression unfocusing. The moment stretched until she broke it with a sudden, decisive movement, flustering in her pocket for her mobile phone.

'I'm going to call the boys, they told me to check in when we got here,' she said. 'And the social worker, I'm going to call her too. And maybe the hospital, check it's okay to visit. Okay?'

Penny nodded.

'Okay,' Veronica said again. 'I'll be in the car.'

She turned away and stalked back through the lounge,

her running shoes making a *squit-squit-squit* sound on the tiles, punctuated by the slam of the front door.

The cold of the floor was making Penny's feet ache, but it was bearable. It felt like a connection and the connection felt important and necessary. She realised she was still wearing her winter coat and felt suddenly ashamed. She shrugged out of it and arranged it carefully over the back of one of the kitchen chairs, where the cracked varnish felt tacky and a little damp.

Mrs Kaye had always had strong thoughts on wearing coats indoors.

'You'll not feel the benefit when you go out,' she'd say, waiting, hand outstretched for them to shed the layer. As a child, Penny had never thought to question the logic, said as it was with an adult's confidence in the truth of it. Now, it felt faintly ridiculous, but the cold had never bothered her that much, certainly not since leaving the order.

The order had been cold. Properly and punishingly cold and not the sort of cold a British winter coat would have alleviated. It was an old building and came with all the draughty stone corridors and ill-fitting doors you might expect of its vintage. The habits were little compensation. Wool, yes, but starchy and scratchy, they were built for modesty above all else. Penny had always thought she'd get used to it, but through all the years she had lived there she never had. Sister Agnes had always seemed immune. Strutting across the frozen quad on a bitter February morning, her purpose undulled even by the blueness of her lips and fingertips.

For Agnes, everything was God's plan. The cold and the discomfort were bearable because nothing else was necessary. The calling was a path, she said. If you followed it diligently and avoided the distractions along the way, it would take you where you should go.

When she had still been a novice, Penny had asked her if everything was God's plan, why did Agnes spend so much time tending the plants in the garden? Agnes had glowered at her.

'God granted man dominion over his garden,' she reminded Penny. 'It is a small responsibility compared to His.'

It was not until Penny had left that she realised her skin was perhaps a little thicker than others, that her requirements for central heating and hot water were not quite as essential. In the office job she had taken in London, she was surprised by the younger members of staff sitting at their desks in the open-plan office, wrapped up in scarves or with hot water bottles nestled in their laps. The warmth of the office's automated temperature-control system had always seemed needlessly decadent to her. Perhaps, in some strange way, she needed the cold now. She needed a sense of it to clarify the limits of her experience.

Penny opened the cupboard door again and inspected the cleaning supplies. Alone in the house, the task she had set herself felt overwhelming. Where should she start? How should she move forward? She opened a packet of dusters and took a can of polish. Making a decision based on sentiment rather than anything more logical, she returned to the room she and Veronica had shared when they were children.

Working quickly and patiently, she set to rearranging the boxes that filled the room until she had forged a narrow corridor through to the window at the far end. The glass was clouded, the net curtains pulled across it yellowed. Among their fraying hems, the corpses of a handful of flies were scattered across the still. Their legs in the air like something out of a cartoon. Sitting nearly square across the ledge like a Bible on an altar, she found a small-format paperback book with dogeared corners. It felt clammy to her touch, but she recognised her mother's face on the cover, and for a brief moment it felt like a sign that she had made the right choice to begin where she had.

The photograph of her mother was a familiar one. Antonia Landry standing on a beach, looking seriously into the camera lens. There was something about her expression that was very Lulu. A way of looking deeply into someone, sizing them up, pressing for a weakness that might be exploited. Her hair was tied back in a business-like plait that looped over one shoulder, but stray and careless strands curled across her face, softening it just enough to make it edge closer to accessible than aloof. Blown up to fit on the cover, the photograph looked a little blurry and indistinct.

The book's title was fitted around her, white letters against a grey sky: *The Infinite Worlds of Antonia Landry*. Penny had never heard of the book before. She turned it around in her hands. It was published by an American university's in-house press, and the text on the back was packed tightly, less a marketing exercise and more an abstract of the book's thesis. She scanned it, briskly enough to get the gist. It was an overview of her mother's research, a collection of essays and responses by contemporary theoretical physicists and the usual biographical notes, bibliographies and references. Penny paged through it idly. The damp had infiltrated the meat of it and there were tide lines marbling the edges of pages.

The centre pages were taken up with a block of thicker, glossier pages printed with photographs and scans of handwritten diagrams and chalkboards. From the contents page, Penny didn't recognise any of the contributors, but she hadn't expected to. She turned to the biographical notes and scanned through them briefly enough to note that her mother's family and home life weren't mentioned at all.

She closed the book and sighed. It smelled of something dank and wasted, but she slipped it into her pocket anyway. A keepsake, a recognisable map-pin in the memory of the place.

Penny unhooked the curtains and set them aside and the room brightened a fraction now the window was unfiltered. She rested her elbows on the window ledge and leaned close to the glass.

She didn't know what made her smile. Maybe it was the memory of the place. With the room behind her, everything seemed more vivid. The view was better maintained than the house. She could see Veronica in the driver's seat of the car outside. She could see how the roof of Lulu's car was spattered with bird droppings which hadn't been cleaned. But beyond both there was the familiar corrugated edge of the dunes, the jagged grasses bending in the breeze. She could see the short scrub of the beach, and beyond it the silver of the edge of the tide. A ragged chalk line drawn and redrawn across the sand.

They had come here every summer when she was a child. Perhaps not every *single* summer, but every summer that had mattered. At first, it had been the whole family. Mother, father and the three girls. But as the years had gone by, their mother's work kept her at the university. For the first few years, their father had remained attentive, but then he had bowed out as well – unhappily citing work he needed to pursue instead – and so Penny, Ronnie and Lulu would be left alone in Mrs Kaye's capable hands for six whole weeks of the year.

It hadn't all been perfect, but memory had a way of making things glow warmer with hindsight.

Back then, the beach along the causeway had been theirs. They knew every inch of it, every inlet and chase, every sign of permanence in a shifting landscape. They could have drawn the currents in pencil lines on a map. When the tide was out, they could run down the sand to Bryhanton, where the beach was broader, busier and combed with groynes. There were caves along the cliffs that they'd raided for pirate treasure, there was a path up to Barrow Hill that afforded the best of views. The town was menaced by gangs of laughing gulls, there was the smell of fairground food and fish and chips. During the later years, they would meet up with the kids who lived in the town. Lanky Matthew who strutted along with his shoulders high and his hands deep in his pockets; Faye-with-an-e and a withering look reserved for any perceived idiocy; little Francis with the crew cut and the wicked laugh. Each group envied the other; they circled, didn't always get on, but it was always good to know they were there.

A noise from downstairs broke her into the present, and she assumed it must have been a memory until it happened again. A gentle *click-click* noise, as though something small and sharp was striking softly against the flagstones. Through the window she could see Veronica was still in her car. She was gesticulating with one hand, holding her phone with another. When she turned, the room felt darker, the illusion of the view gone, the cardboard-box canyon felt close and claustrophobic.

The sound again, something downstairs. Footsteps? Maybe. Not Veronica, not Lulu. Someone else. Some*thing*.

Penny pushed herself away from the window and retreated to the top of the stairs. She stooped low, pushing her hair back behind her ear. She waited, but she saw no movement in the room below.

> ● <

The summer she found Oscar had been one the tabloids described as being the hottest on record. She was thirteen, and the distance between her own age and that of her sisters felt as though it had grown over the course of the year. She remembered allowing herself the expectation that things between them would go back to normal over the summer, that the familiar rhythms of the holiday period would slowly return, but as the weeks had passed that hadn't happened. Lulu was no longer interested in the games they had once played on the beach together, preferring to spend more time with Matthew and Faye in town. Ronnie, who worshipped her older sister, fell into a mood, declaring that it was unfair of Lulu to leave her *babysitting* Penny and deciding to stay in the house to read, much to the consternation of Mrs Kaye, who had very strong opinions about the upstairs rooms being used during the morning and afternoon.

'It's a bright, sunny day,' Mrs Kaye said. 'A girl your age has no business being cooped up indoors.'

Penny had made her own attempts to encourage her, giving it her very best in doe-eyed desperation, but Ronnie had seen it all before and she refused to fall for any of it.

'You'll just have to look after yourself,' she said, turning the pages of her book. She made a show of reading furiously until her younger sister left her alone.

Penny had been on the beach on her own before, but it was the first time she felt as though she had it to herself. The stretch along Stove Causeway was shorter and less popular than Bryhanton Sands. Many of the summer tourists never made it out so far, and the little car park used by those who did was empty so early in the morning. The barren stretch of sand felt vast to Penny. It felt extravagant, too much. With her sisters, she had always enjoyed the sea, but on her own, she could admit to herself that she was wary of it. She stood well back from the line of the surf and studied it as though it were an animal held captive at a zoo. It certainly felt like a living thing, a muscle expanding and contracting. It was restless and hungry. It roared with an insatiable violence. It clawed for desperate purchase on the beach, but every time, it lost its grip on the shifting sand and slipped away.

This was why beaches were as they were, Penny thought. They were loose, intangible fringes between one world and another. If they weren't there, the sea would be free to pull itself up, to stand tall on torrential limbs and tramp across the landscape forbidden to it.

The tide was out enough that the narrow run of sand leading to Bryhanton sparkled like the Yellow Brick Road. Penny walked along it. She hadn't really wanted to go into town. It brought its own risks, primarily that she might run into Lulu, who would only resent her presence even more than Ronnie. So, she was in no rush as she picked her way across the rocks, keeping a good distance from the reach of the water, a good distance from the fall-line of the cliffs.

She'd read stories about people being trapped on the causeway path when the tide turned. She even had a dim memory of the coastguard being called to retrieve someone who had fallen asleep in the lip of one of the caves. She hadn't ever seen who it was that had been rescued, in fact she hadn't been able to see anything other than a distant bobbing light, but it had felt like an adventure nonetheless. It would teach Lulu and Ronnie some sort of lesson if anything happened to her, she thought. Maybe she could stay there, sit cross-legged right *here* and wait for the sea to swoop up the beach and claim her. She could imagine the worried looks on their faces when the coastguard brought her back home, a blanket draped across her shoulders.

She stopped to study the line of the surf. Was it going in or coming out? She frowned. The leading edge did seem to be gaining ground, or was that just a stronger wave than the rest?

She glanced up the beach towards Bryhanton. The town was just out of sight around the corner. She might make it, but if the tide did come in, she might end up trapped there and Mrs Kaye liked them walking along the Clifftop Road even less than she liked them taking the causeway.

In the distance, she could make out a dog on the path ahead of her. A hazy yellow shape, standing to attention as though it had spotted something of importance. Then it moved, jumping into the surf and then running back away from it again. Its tail whirred like a propeller.

Penny couldn't see the dog's owner. She supposed it had one. Perhaps they were just around the corner? If nothing else, it was reassuring that someone else was in the same predicament as she was.

Her foot suddenly went cold and the shock of it made her look down to see the seawater peeling back across the beach. It *was* coming in, then.

She didn't stop any longer to consider her options; she turned around and started running back towards the Stove. Ahead of her, the path was worse than she had feared, as though the sea had been closing in behind her, ever so silently, like a creeping monster in the night. She ran, veering around the larger rocks, away from the inrush of the tide.

She heard the dog before she saw it again. A yapping bark somewhere behind her, the drumming of footsteps and then a yellow shape speeding past. She felt the brief fuzzy warmth of it as it passed her. It was a young rangy Labrador; maybe a retriever, she had never been able to tell the difference. It loped past her and turned as it did so, giving her a view of its tongue lolling, its jowls grinning. It wheeled clumsily and ran back to her, circling.

'What are you doing?' Penny said, her voice hoarse from the effort of running. The dog barked in reply, then hammered off ahead of her, vanishing around the corner. Penny hurried onwards, her feet splashing through the rising water.

Around the corner, on the safety of the beach, the dog was waiting for her. Its head cocked as though it had been wondering what had taken her so long. It barked at her again and then circled her, its tail a happy blur. Penny had never been scared of dogs. She put her hands down for it, her fists clenched so the animal could sniff them.

'What are you doing, you silly thing?' Penny said, reaching to scratch behind its ears. 'You'll get lost following me.'

She looked back and saw the causeway was almost completely under water now.

'Where's your owner?' she said. 'Where is he? Humm? Now then...'

She reached deep into the dog's fur at the thick of its neck and found the collar buried there. A silver-coloured coin hanging from it read 'OSCAR' on one side and what looked like a phone number on the back.

'Oscar?' she said and the dog sniffed her hungrily, its expression still both dopey and happy. 'Oh, Oscar. What are we going to do with you?'

Oscar's expression snapped to attention as something caught his eye. He bunched up and sprang away from her, charging across the beach to where a gull had settled. The bird lifted itself back into the air before he could reach it. Penny took off after him, calling his name.

With the bird gone, the dog's attention returned to the running girl. They ran together in the way that children and dogs do. When Penny threw herself onto the sand, the dog landed beside her, rolling to skid along the sand so it ended up with its back against her, its head arching around to grin at her.

'Where's your owner, Oscar?' Penny said.

They had been running around the sand for a good hour, but no one had come, from either the causeway or Clifftop Road.

'Where do you live? Are you hungry?' She made a decision and got to her feet. 'Come on,' she said.

Oscar followed her back to Breakers. Mrs Kaye had the front door wedged open, the mop and bucket planted in the aperture, a warning that she had just cleaned the floor. Penny followed the path along the front of the house and tapped on the kitchen window. The movement of the shadows inside corresponded to Mrs Kaye's size and demeanour.

'Not now, girl.' Mrs Kaye's voice sounded easily through the glass. It always did have a way of cutting through things that should have been impenetrable.

'I found a dog,' Penny said, raising her own voice to be heard, raising a hand to the window as though she might be able to open it from the outside.

'Well, put it back where you found it and leave it there.'

'It's lost. It got trapped on this side of the headland by the tide.'

'Penelope, child, it's not our business.'

'I think it's hungry.'

'All dogs are hungry.'

'Can't we feed it something?'

There was no reply.

'Mrs Kaye!'

Still there was no answer. Penny leaned in close to the window, cupping her hands around her eyes. The room was dark and still. She turned back to the door in time to see someone appear in it. Not Mrs Kaye, as she had expected, but Ronnie, leaning out and peering around. Her sister's expression held the ruffled irritation of someone who had just got out of bed.

'What's going on?' she said. Penny knew the sleepy nonchalance was an act. She hadn't been making that much noise, and it was unlikely that Mrs Kaye would have let her sleep at all, but the word 'dog' had been mentioned without caution, and Penny didn't doubt it had been enough to raise her sister from her apathy.

'I found a dog,' Penny said. 'He followed me down the beach before the tide came in and now's he's stuck here.'

Ronnie stooped to examine Oscar, while Oscar examined her in return.

'It's a girl dog,' Ronnie said.

'It's called Oscar.'

'Then it's a girl dog called Oscar.'

The answer didn't quite seem satisfactory to Penny.

'Maybe it's someone else's collar,' she said.

Ronnie didn't say anything, she was preoccupied scratching Oscar's ears. Oscar, for her part, seemed preoccupied with Ronnie, leaning in close to nuzzle her, huffing her nose as though she was mining for the deepest scents of an unwashed hand. Penny waited with impatience, alone and dogless.

'Well, she's hungry, anyway,' she said.

'There's a number on the collar,' Ronnie said.

'I know.'

'We should call it.' She bundled up to her feet and ran back into the house, shouting Mrs Kaye's name. Excited by the burst of energy, Oscar followed, her feet slipping on the hallway floor.

'Oscar!' Penny said, hurrying after them.

The hallway was empty already, but she could hear where Ronnie and Oscar had gone. There was the clatter of a door, the shout of Mrs Kaye, and beyond it all, the *click-click-click* of the dog's claws on the tiled floor.

'Get that animal out of my kitchen!'

'We need to use the telephone.'

'There's no telephone in the kitchen, get away with you!'

Ronnie appeared again, Oscar close by her heels. Ronnie reached the telephone table and snatched up the receiver.

'Read out the number,' she said.

Penny shot her a look. She resented the fact that Ronnie seemed to be trying to take control of the situation, but she appreciated that she was the one who got to hold the dog.

She crouched low and dug out the collar again. Oscar licked her across her cheek, making her squeal with laughter.

'Pen! The number!'

'Sorry. He… *She* licked me.'

She read out the number and Ronnie dialled it into the phone, repeating each number back as she did so. They waited patiently, but Ronnie was already frowning.

'It doesn't work.'

'What?'

'I don't think there are enough numbers. Read them again.'

They tried twice more, but with no more luck.

Ronnie put down the receiver and crouched to join Penny and Oscar.

'I suppose we'll have to keep you, then,' she said. 'Would you like that? I bet you'd like that.'

'You're not keeping it.' Mrs Kaye was standing in the kitchen doorway, drying her hands on a towel and staring at the dog.

'But she's lost,' Penny said. 'She ran all the way here along the causeway.'

'And it can run back when the tide's out again,' Mrs Kaye said. She shook her head. 'I'll call Murray at the police station. Let him know it's here.'

'She!'

Mrs Kaye cast them a dark look. Oscar ignored her and padded around the house, nosing open the lounge door and disappearing inside. Mrs Kaye craned her head as though she might be able to follow her.

'Take *it* out the front,' she said. 'There's a planter out there you can fill with water from the garden tap. I'll see if we've got any scraps we can spare.' She fluttered her hand. 'Go on, now. Get it out of the house before it gets all over the furniture.'

Outside, they watched as Oscar polished off half a bowl of water, then made good headway on the food Mrs Kaye had prepared. Bread crusts in milk and egg, prepared in the cracked bowl she usually kept by the sink for food waste the girls had left neatly at the side of their plates. Oscar wolfed it all down, licking the stoneware cleaner than it had ever been before and snuffling around the ground where the bowl had been for anything she might have missed, making the bowl rock and clatter on the flagstones.

They spent the afternoon on the beach. Rushing across the sand, taunting the sea. They threw sticks and Oscar ran after them, barking and dancing in the surf. She was egalitarian company, favouring neither of the sisters over the other. She ran from one to the other, circling them, binding them with an invisible thread and pulling it tight. There was a simplicity in her joy that Penny and Ronnie could not help but capitulate to. For the precious hours of that summer afternoon there was no one else but the three of them. They ran together, screaming across the sand, chasing the waves as they had done when they first started coming to Breakers.

It was Ronnie who suggested they go to Barrow Hill.

'We can show her Doggerland,' she said, her eyes bright with amusement.

It was the first time Penny had made the connection.

'Do you think that's where dogs come from?' she said.

'I don't see why not,' Ronnie said. 'Come on.'

She ran up the sands and Oscar followed happily.

Barrow Hill rose from the headland at the opposite end of the beach from the causeway. It was a bulbous fist of landscape, an unexpected roundness pushing up from the sheer and torn peripheries of the cliff faces that fringed it. A small cleft near the foot of the beach led to a zigzag path which climbed to the cliff top, where the landscape flattened a little. From there, a more conventional track carved a wavering line to the summit of the hill itself. The path up the cliff was steep and narrow, the reddish clay crumbling to sand at a number of points along its length. A series of chains had been bolted into the rock faces to act as handholds, but there were a few corners where a small leap needed to be made to get from one chain to the next. For those who paid attention it wasn't dangerous, and in good weather it was a popular route for tourists. For the sisters it was forbidden, and therefore it was essential.

When they reached the base of the cliff path, Penny stopped for breath.

'Eyes closed,' she said, but Oscar bounded ahead.

'Oscar isn't closing her eyes,' Ronnie said and ran after her.

It was steep, hard going, but it was a path they'd taken often enough to know well. Even though they weren't taking the route with eyes closed, Penny made a conscious attempt not to look at the growing view as she pulled herself upwards, hand over hand along the chain guiderails. At the top of the cliff, Oscar rushed off towards the round of the hill and the sisters barely had time to catch their breath before they took off after her.

They caught her at the summit. Ronnie took her collar and they all sat down together. Oscar was panting, her big red tongue was hanging like a pendant, but her eyes were wide with excitement.

'There,' Ronnie said, once she had got her own breath back. She pointed out to sea, to the horizon. 'Out there is Doggerland. It used to be an island. Before that it was this land that joined Britain to Denmark. It sank, but it's still there. Look. You can see a different colour in the water, as though there's something just underneath it. Do you see?'

Oscar licked her face and Ronnie squealed.

'That's where you come from, Oscar,' Penny said. 'Or your mummy and daddy. Or their mummy and daddy. That's where dogs come from.'

They sat there together for a long time.

As the sun finally began to slip in the sky, they picked their way back down the path to the beach, sliding on their backsides while Oscar waited for them with her tongue still lolling. As Mrs Kaye stood in the doorway and hollered at them to come home for tea, a man appeared at the edge of the causeway, which had cleared now the tide had retreated. The man did not approach them, but waited, a leash hanging in his hand.

At first, they paid him no attention. There were often figures on the beach, tall willowy silhouettes whom they had never seen before. Penny offered the stranger only a glance and saw nothing but its shape, a shadow standing on an empty beach, and behind it the sea churned.

But then there was a whistle and Oscar's attention was scrubbed down to a single point. She turned to stare, ignoring the girls completely, and then she was away.

They didn't have time to say goodbye. She ran like a bullet towards the silhouetted figure, running across the sand in that full-body movement of a dog in flight, a yellow mark circling the distant figure's legs. They watched as the stranger stooped down to clip the lead to her collar and Oscar waited, her tail wagging furiously. Oscar didn't look back, her afternoon already eclipsed, but the stranger did. They raised a hand in a wave, but that was all before they turned away and led Oscar back along the causeway towards the town.

Penny had wanted to chase after them. For a brief moment, everything was clear to her. She didn't want to run to say goodbye, to ruffle her ears a final time; she wanted to run with her. To follow her up the causeway path and away. She had never really entertained the idea of running away from home before, and being at Breakers, she wasn't sure if this counted. But at that moment the feeling was a strong one, as though a door had been left open to her, inadvertently revealing the scope of the world outside. She juddered forwards, but Ronnie held her back.

'It's too late,' she said. 'She's gone home. So should we.'

'Home?' Penny was surprised by the strangeness of the word. Ronnie smiled at her, not understanding. She looked tired, but her happiness made her glow.

'It was fun, though, right?'

Penny nodded, the strange dream of escape fading almost as slowly as it had consumed her.

'Maybe we can get a dog of our own?' she said.

They both knew that such a thing would never happen, but Ronnie smiled anyway.

'Maybe,' she said.

That night they lay awake in their beds and Penny wondered what would have happened if they *had* run away together. In that moment, she hoped that Ronnie would have followed her. And so Penny, Ronnie and Oscar would have run together, on and on until they'd run out of land to run through. If they had taken her up the headland, away from the beach. If they had taken a bus and travelled far away. She could imagine Oscar sitting between her knees, the movement of the vehicle making her impatient, excitable. She would glance at Penny to make sure things were alright and Penny would reassure her, palming the velvet of her ears. She would hold her and love her and never let her go.

It was a choice, she was sure. One she *could* have taken, one she *should* have, but one which had slipped away from her and faded completely.

> • <

Upstairs in Breakers, Penny held her breath and waited. Before long, she was rewarded by the sound again.

Click-click-click.

This time, it sounded as though it was in the lounge. It sounded as though something was moving at leisure around the room, exploring the geography of it, understanding its chimney stacks and alcoves. She waited in agonising patience, looking for a shadow, shifting against the wall. She imagined she might hear something sniffing as well, that exploratory snuffle she remembered, but instead the house fell quiet. Resolving to get closer, she edged down the stairs, remembering to avoid the sixth step from the bottom which had always creaked. She was nearly at the door when the sound came again. *Click-click-click*, this time just on the other side of the wall, somewhere in the lounge, near the fireplace.

If she took one more step and turned to face the doorway, she would see...

The front door clattered open and Veronica came in.

'What *are* you doing?' she said.

Penny stood straight, collecting herself.

'I thought I heard something.'

Veronica nodded as though she hadn't really been listening anyway.

'So, I called the social worker.' She slammed the front door and pushed the door open into the lounge, disappearing inside. 'I told them about the state of this place. The fact the boiler isn't working. The lights and so on. She agreed with me that Lulu can't be sent back here again, so they might be thinking about putting her into care. At least for a little while. I know, I know, it sounds awful, but I don't know what else we're going to do.'

Penny hesitated before following her into the lounge. When she did, she wasn't surprised to find it as it had been. She looked to the fireplace, where she thought she'd heard the footsteps, and frowned.

'Anyway,' Veronica said, 'when we go visit her later on, I'm going to have to grill her about her finances. I always thought she was loaded, but she's spent nothing on this place at all. Nothing. She's either saved it all or blown the lot of it.'

Penny stopped by the fireplace and ran her fingers along the floorboards. The dirt was grainy and solid, she could feel it collecting on her fingertips, under her nails. She lifted her hands to the light to inspect them.

'What is it?' Veronica said.

'Sand,' Penny said. 'It's all over, look.'

'Well, it does blow in, I suppose.' Veronica searched through her handbag. 'Oh, and the boys send their love.'

'Oh?' Penny's smile was faint and hesitant, as though she couldn't quite believe it. 'Tell them I said thank you.'

> • <

They spent the afternoon cleaning. Ronnie found an old plastic radio that only tuned to a local station. She set it in the stairwell and it felt better now the house was full of noise. Ronnie volunteered to work on the bathroom while Penny took the kitchen. She bagged up as much of the filth as she could. She emptied the fridge, she took out the bins. Removing the topmost layers of the mess only revealed the damage to the kitchen left behind. The surfaces had swollen and become uneven with damp, and the yellow-brown discolouration and black streaks of mould were not something that could be easily scrubbed away. The cupboard doors hung poorly, the screw holes where the hinges were fitted scored furrows in the wood, and the shelves were bubbled with sticky circles of residue from old cans and jars. Even when six bin bags sat outside, ready for collection, it was difficult for Penny to look at the room and see that progress had been made. It made her think of a series of illustrations she'd seen in a copy of *National Geographic* in a dentist's waiting room. They were speculative images showing what might remain of cities if their human populations were no longer present to maintain them. They showed a vast forest on its way to reclaiming the concrete and glass of conventional habitation, breaking down the straight edges and perfect corners, making them soft and organic, bringing them closer to the more chaotic geometries of nature. The illustrations had fascinated her, almost to the point that she missed her appointment. The changed cities looked so green and beautiful, the remains of tower blocks rising above the canopy like Aztec ruins in the jungle. It was comforting, in a way, to see how the world might restore itself in the absence of civilisation. In this context, Lulu's kitchen seemed to be halfway there. On a human level it was a near-unsalvageable mess, but there was the suggestion of something beautiful in the way it was breaking itself down.

She set down her cleaning equipment and stepped back. Her memories of the room had a picture-book clarity. Mrs Kaye in her housecoat scrubbing everything until it shone. Pies and cakes cooling on wire racks. A red gingham tablecloth, continuous pots of tea. There was a warmth to this perception of the room's history, but there was a fabricated quality as well. In a sense, Penny thought, they had learned to preserve the past too cleanly. Too respectfully. There was heat here, but vinegar as well, and perhaps it was the right thing to do to allow the house and its memories to succumb to entropy. The dog and everything else were made only from sand. They served to prick a certain sentiment but they weren't built to last, before time evened everything to a flat and endless plain.

FINISTERRE

FINISTERRE

Jorgen stood on the outcrop, his arms outstretched. The lighthouse beam swung unhurriedly, spotlighting him as it passed. Far beneath, white-fringed waves boomed against rock with a violence that cut the air with salt.

He turned around and grinned with matinee idol teeth.

'Welcome to the end of the world,' he said.

We'd met him a few days earlier in Santiago de Compostela.

I was due home within the week, having spent three months walking the pilgrim route from Le Puy-en-Velay in Central France. Nicole was a schoolteacher from Roquefort I'd met at the refugio in Leon, where she'd nursed me back to health after a bout of sunstroke. Now she joked that we'd seen the worst of each other, so the only way to go was up. We'd spent the subsequent month living as part of a shifting group which gathered along the well-worn trail like a wave. We'd managed to enjoy only a handful of small, rushed moments of intimacy, and we were both looking forward to a little time alone together once the community that had swept us along had broken against the city.

Jorgen had been staying in the same hostel in Santiago. He'd completed the pilgrimage some time before us; he was cagey when we asked him exactly when. He told us that he simply didn't want to leave, he wanted to extend the buzz of accomplishment instead, to prolong the sheer brightness of his spiritual high.

Preliminary conversations with our fellow pilgrims invariably began with the same two questions, and things were no different now we were done.

'Where are you from?' I'd said as we shook hands.

'Norway,' was Jorgen's answer.

'And why did you walk the Camino?'

'Because it's awesome,' Jorgen said, and that was the first time I was subjected to that smile of his.

My own motives had been more economic than spiritual. The cynical truth was that the pilgrim route, with its purpose-built refugios and church-funded bunkhouses, was an inexpensive way to travel the continent and see it up close. While my own Catholic education had floundered once I'd left my local RC primary school for the secular comprehensive, I liked to imagine it had equipped me with a thin veneer of authenticity that wouldn't make me feel like a complete fraud.

When I explained as much to Jorgen he was convinced I was suffering a crisis of faith, and Nicole had known me long enough to think this was funny. I had found the pilgrim route beautiful, challenging and fascinating, but it hadn't reignited anything I might have believed when I was younger.

'But there are other kinds of faith,' Jorgen said to me one evening. We were outside a bar on the Rúa do Franco, roughly halfway between the Cafe Paris at one end of the street and the Dakar Bar at the other. 'It is the drive that makes us succeed, no? Art. Music.' He waved his hand from me to Nicole and back again. 'Love. Yes? No? You have to believe in it. You have to have *faith* in it.'

'Right,' I said and drank my beer.

'So you're English, yes?' Jorgen said.

'Yes,' I said.

'So you walked the Camino Inglés?'

I bristled. 'Christ no,' I said. 'I walked from Le Puy. Camino Frances, like everyone else.'

Nicole elbowed me in the ribs. I set my glass down on the crowded table and tried to clarify myself.

'I came for the walk,' I said. 'The Camino Inglés is, what? A hundred miles straight down from A Coruña? I've been walking for three months, not three days.'

Jorgen dropped a hand on my shoulder, his face creased with guileless sympathy.

'I don't think it would have any impact on your plenary indulgence,' he said, misreading my concern. 'It's the traditional way from England, after all. You come by boat from Plymouth; you walk what's left. There are so many ways to begin. It's not about where you come from; it's not about what transport you use. It's about where you end up. Where everyone ends up.'

He raised a finger as though he was making a proclamation.

'The cure for purgatory,' he said, 'is good company.'

He sounded so serious; I couldn't tell if he was making fun of me.

'Well, maybe if I had my own boat,' I said.

Jorgen sighed and stared across the street.

'I had a boat once,' he said. I didn't doubt him. He was tall, Nordic, charismatic. Of course he had a boat as well.

The night proved to be a spiritual one in the sense that tequila was involved. By morning we'd hooked up with Jack and Lou, an Irish couple we met well on the way to the Dakar Bar, and Jorgen had talked all of us into accompanying him to Cape Finisterre at the far north-western tip of Galicia.

'The end of the world should be the end of our journey,' he said as we stumbled up the steep road back to the hostel.

'He sounds like a fortune cookie,' Nicole said.

'*There is such faith in love!*' I tried to mimic his accent but failed.

Nicole snorted with laughter and leaned in close to me. Supporting each other, we followed after Jorgen at a safe distance.

If he'd heard us, he made no sign. He was leading the way on unsteady feet, shouting effusive greetings to everyone who crossed our path.

> • <

Later, Nicole and I sat alone on the steps of the hostel, watching the sky turn from velvet blue to velvet black and back again.

'Why did you walk the Camino?' she said.

It was not the first time she'd asked me, but I'd never liked the question and had yet to provide her with an answer that satisfied us both. *Because it was cheap* sounded too flippant; *because I might meet someone like you*, too sentimental; *because I wanted to believe*, too Jorgen.

'Because it was there,' I said.

She shook her head.

'Do you think that's arrogant?' she said. 'Just because something is there, doesn't mean it has to be conquered.'

I shrugged. 'It's something some mountain climber said once,' I said.

She smiled, but didn't look at me. Her arms were folded over her knees and she stared out across the lights of the city below us.

'I believe,' she said, 'that the only reason to climb a mountain is to see what it looks like from the top.'

'*Faith in love!*' I was drunk enough to imagine my Jorgen voice was improving.

This time she didn't laugh.

'Be nice,' she said.

> • <

With its bright whitewashed walls, red roofs and narrow streets, Fisterra was a small harbour town recalibrated to net tourists as well as fish. We couldn't get into the hostel, but the summer sun was fresh and warm, and the air was still, so Jack suggested we all sleep on the beach, where a thumbnail of sand nestled beneath a horseshoe of cliff.

When a campfire was proposed, I volunteered Jorgen to help me find firewood. For some ill-considered reason I'm still not proud of, I didn't want to leave him on the beach alone with Nicole. My rudeness went unnoticed. He agreed with an enthusiasm that left me ashamed, and noted that we could visit the lighthouse on the way.

> • <

On the rocky promontory on the edge of Europe, we watched the precarious-looking sun hang above the Atlantic.

'You know the pagans used to come here?' Jorgen said. 'Before the Christians came along with their saint-in-a-box? The pagans used to come to Finisterre because it was the end of the known world. They came to see the sun melting away into an infinite ocean.'

He grinned.

'They called it *La Costa de la Muerte*. They would burn their clothes to symbolise their death and renewal.'

He slapped me hard on the back.

'We should all totally do that,' he said.

I laughed, uneasy. 'Well, maybe some socks or something…'

Jorgen nodded. 'Socks,' he said. 'Totally.'

We looked out across the sea. The sun had dropped to the horizon. It looked angrier; it had ignited the surrounding clouds.

'They came here and believed this was it,' Jorgen said. 'This was the outer limit of all there was to know. They believed there was nothing else out there. It's crazy, isn't it? Just because you can't see something, doesn't mean there's nothing there.'

He looked so sincere it was exasperating.

'If you're still talking about faith—' I began, but he cut me off, gesturing at the stars which had shyly begun to emerge now the light of the sun was on the wane.

'I'm not talking about God,' he said.

> • <

The road back was lit only by the intermittent sweep of the lighthouse, and after a clumsy, half-blind search along the verges we found enough wind-fallen branches to drag back to the beach.

We returned to find the others had bought food and wine from the village store. We prepared a fire and gathered around it. We stayed up talking into the night and, with Jorgen's encouragement, we each burned a piece of clothing with a certain degree of mock solemnity. Jorgen burned a pair of jeans, a shirt, some shoes. I could only assume he had spares. I burned my socks. They bubbled and melted into the flames.

Maybe it was because the rest of us coupled off and neglected him, but a little later Jorgen seemed to tire of all the talk and trivia and wandered off down the beach alone.

'There walks the enigmatic Viking,' Nicole said.

Jack pulled a face. 'I don't think he's from Norway.'

I asked him what he meant.

Jack held the wine bottle up to the fire to gauge what was left.

'I was telling him about this trip I took to Stavanger some years back,' he said, passing the bottle to Lou. 'He just looked at me, grinning blankly like he'd never heard of the place. Maybe I can't pronounce it. Maybe he's Swedish.'

Later, while the others pulled their sleeping bags into position around the fire, I found Jorgen standing ankle-deep in the surf. He was staring up at the infinite density of stars, the multitude of suns melting into the black.

'You never said which route you took,' I said. 'To Santiago, I mean.'

He didn't look at me, but I saw him smile. Not that big toothy Hollywood smile, but something smaller, something sadder.

'Camino Inglés,' he said.

WE CAN WALK
IT OFF COME
THE MORNING

It was New Year's Day and the standing stone was a disappointment. Planted deep in the middle of a sheltered field on the eastern flank on the hill, there was an undeniable scale to it. It was a good fifteen feet of stark grey granite, eight foot wide and eight foot deep, reaching up out of the mud like a pointing finger. Despite this, there remained something industrial about it, something prosaic. Its faces were too smooth, its edges too defined. It felt crudely at odds with the soft and sodden landscape that surrounded it.

'Is that it?' Jack said. He sounded resigned. It was unreasonable to be angry when they had been promised no more than a point on the map. Still, it was anticlimactic. It was just a stone, standing in a field, brusquely surprised that anyone should have searched for it at all.

Aleyna didn't answer. She approached the stone and regarded it with the reverence she assumed such a monument must deserve. The shape of it was certainly monolithic: its uppermost edge a dark, straight line against the unvaried grey of the sky. As an afterthought, remembering something her father once told about how she would press her palms against the ragged bark of trees when she was a child, she slipped her hand from her glove so she could feel the texture of the stone without impediment. For some reason, she expected there to be an inexplicable warmth to it, some mechanical hum to set it apart from the muted chill of the afternoon; but it was cold beneath her fingertips, made stark and frigid by the rain and the wind. The texture was barely perceptible beneath the growing numbness of her hands. A gentle lunar landscape of shallow contours but no more than that. She stepped back again, disappointed more with her own perception than with the stone itself.

Jack waded back into view.

'I read a book once, when I was a kid,' he said. 'And in it, there was this stone up on the moor somewhere, and if you walked around it three times, it would summon up a rabble of little goblins who would chase you down and stab you with spears.'

'So don't walk around it three times.' Aleyna took another step back. The field was heavy with the rain, and if she didn't keep moving she had the sense she might sink into the mud and never move again. A hell of a way to start the year.

Jack lifted one foot, planted it back, then lifted the next. He looked absurd, like he was treading grapes in wellington boots. 'Thing is,' he said, 'I know the moor the book was talking about. And they've built a road around it now. All the way around it like an island. So whenever I pass by that way, I always wonder if driving around it would count as walking around the stone? Or do you have to be right up close? Maybe distance itself didn't matter at all. Because these days, there must be thousands of commuters going one way or another around this thing, and at some point they'll have to have gone round it three times, right? Maybe not all at once, but eventually, right? Thousands of them. So do they all get chased? Do the goblins come out and go:

"Fuck me, traffic's bad today," and then just get on with it anyway.'

He joined her in front of the stone, reaching out to it with his gloved hand.

'I can just imagine them. All broken and dying at the side of the road. These armies of goblins throwing themselves into the traffic and getting killed like all the foxes and deer and badgers. Goblin roadkill. What chance does something from a fairy tale stand against a rush-hour's worth of Transit vans?'

Aleyna laughed despite herself. 'Well, I don't fancy my chances outrunning anything in this,' she said.

Water pooled around the base of the stone, and even in the grey light she could see the faint green of the grass beneath it, rocking in a gentle current like pondweed.

She glanced back down the field where they had come and saw how the edges were now completely lost in the fog.

'We should go back,' she said.

Jack nodded.

'Might be able to catch the others up,' he said. 'Tell them what they missed.'

He plunged his hands into his pockets and jutted out his elbow, inviting Aleyna to take his arm. She rolled her eyes before complying. He leaned over to kiss her but she pushed him back with her free hand. He felt stubborn and solid, not quite standing-stone solid, but immovable in his own way.

'If they see us...' she said.

'They'll have damn good eyesight,' Jack said.

They set off down the field, heading back to the corner from which they had entered. The mud was marshy underfoot, the standing water rushing in to fill the heavy footprints they left behind. Joined together, the going was awkward, but neither saw fit to go it alone.

'So what do we tell them?' Jack said.

'We'll tell them we saw the standing stone,' Aleyna said. It had been the whole point of the expedition, after all. They'd pored over the map at the kitchen table, searching for something to mark the day, something to clear their heads after all the drink the night before. It was Kevin who had spotted the monument, marked in blackletter script in the middle of an otherwise unpromising looking pasture. The walk had been longer than anyone had anticipated, following the narrow, minor roads up the hills which rose deceptively steeply on the opposite side of the main street from the cottage they'd hired. While it wasn't exactly raining, the clouds had lowered to envelop the landscape and the air they walked through felt dense with poised moisture. It lingered before them, allowing them to drench themselves just by moving through it.

Lou had given up first, complaining of a headache and the likelihood she might wind up sick as well. Kevin had gone with her, measuring his own gallantry against Jack's like they were drawing straws. Turning back down the path, the two had diminished into the blankness and Aleyna had watched them go, a faint notch of panic opening up within her. They disappeared with such a gentle precision it looked like the climactic scene fading out at the end of a film, and she had to fight the urge to run down the path after them to make sure they were still there.

'We'll tell them it was magnificent,' Jack said. 'A secret Stonehenge, lost from view in the beautiful *Oirish* landscape.'

The accent made Aleyna wince. Jack might have looked local, but he certainly didn't sound it.

'They won't believe us,' she said.

'They will. We'll tell them that when we stood in the middle of the circle, the stones made the wind sound like it was singing to us.'

'There isn't any wind.'

'Then maybe the stones themselves were singing to us.'

'You're full of shit.'

'So's this field, and yet here we are.'

'Jack.' She broke away from him so she could vault the stile, casting him a dark look as she did so.

He grinned at her. The rain had plastered his fringe to his forehead, making him look younger. He had his holiday beard on: a week's growth of red whiskers that gave him a pleasant and scruffy nonchalance she couldn't quite square with the clean-shaven and office-suited Jack she was more familiar with.

'Kidding,' he said. 'I'm just loath to admit they might have been right about turning back.'

'We could just say it was nice,' Aleyna said.

Jack shook his head, clambering over the stile after her. 'There's no magic in nice,' he said.

The path down the hill was mostly gravel, ground deep into the mud. Hazy shapes of demarcated farmland ascended in steep embankments on either side, knotted cords of hedgerows and low stone walls frayed into the whiteness. They walked onwards and the dogged clouds followed them, water running freely down the path in a steady stream.

Aleyna's coat had long since soaked through. It was woollen and heavy and completely the wrong sort of thing to wear for a walk of this nature, but then the weather hadn't seemed quite so miserable when they'd started out from the cottage, and by the time they were halfway up the hill it would have been far too much of a fuss to ask to go back for something more sensible. Worse still, it would only have cemented the second thoughts about the enterprise that Lou had already started to entertain.

Jack started whistling through his teeth. The tune almost recognisable, but out of reach until he spoke again.

'Do you think these are the actual Cork and Kerry mountains?' he said. 'I always figured they were different things. Like the guy was walking through one and then the other. It never really occurred to me the county border might run through them.'

He didn't wait for an answer, just carried on whistling as before, but something struck Aleyna about what he had said.

It felt appropriate they should be walking along a border in the hazy, hungover gap between the years, having left one behind and yet not quite committed to the next.

'Borderlands.' She spoke the word aloud, and while Jack didn't reply, Aleyna smiled to herself as though there was something satisfying, something spell-like about the phrase.

The cottage was by the sea, halfway down the Beara Peninsula. They'd spent the best part of the previous day jammed alongside each other in the rental car; Lou and Jack had taken it in turns to drive the coast road, passing through a succession of tiny communities pinned to the edge of the Cork landscape.

'Michael Collins country,' Jack had said as the road twisted through the rocky outcrops. He pointed out signs to Clonakilty as they passed, and gestured to where he thought Bealnablath should be through the rear-view mirror.

Aleyna hadn't risen to his guide-book wisdom. There was more to history than coordinates marking where something began and where something ended, it was the tangle in-between that resonated. She leaned against the window, watching the landscape roll past them. There was a beauty to it but it felt stark to her, an untamed rawness that made her think of the sea.

They'd spent the night of New Year's Eve in the cottage, eschewing the local bars to drink together undisturbed. It had felt strangely decadent, making all that effort of flying somewhere new just to ignore it and drink indoors like they so often did back home. They were the last of their circle of friends to succumb to the designated responsibilities of adulthood. They didn't have kids, they didn't have dogs, and only Jack could claim to have a mortgage. Everyone else had peeled away as their thirties had eroded, their youthful priorities gently realigned to adult expectation, social calendars hijacked by nappies and inoculations and schools and savings schemes. Aleyna had looked around at the four of them who were left and allowed herself the private suspicion that given the choice, they may not have been the friends she would have chosen to be marooned with.

Even so, they had a shared purpose for the evening. They worked their way through the wine and rum and whisky they'd stocked up on at the local shop; they'd smoked the weed that Jack had smuggled through the flight, packed tightly in a talcum powder tin and still smelling slightly of roses and old ladies. Although Kevin had tried to intervene, they had dined on the sort of junk food that holidays make acceptable: pizzas and crisps and those sugary cakes that come off a production line in neatly sealed plastic. They watched midnight arrive on the local television station and they had stepped outside in the rain to toast the new year. They had come all that distance, but they could have been anywhere really. Time found them, ticked them off, and moved on, the passing year's departure both momentous and anticlimactic. They stayed up until four in the morning, drinking and smoking and playing cards.

The following afternoon the sky had remained grey, but the hills looked sharp and distinct and the landscape surrounding them seemed brighter and more alive after the rainfall. The greens and browns and yellows were richly saturated like raw and unmixed paints applied in great round swatches to a fresh blank canvas. There was a beauty to it, certainly, but more than that there was the promise of something verdant, something vital and alive.

'Is this the way we came?' Jack said.

The landscape had evened out as they descended the hill, the path rising a little so the embankments shallowed and hazy moorland stretched upwards on their right, and downwards on their left. The views on both sides were foreshortened by the mist, but there was a sense of unbounded space nonetheless, a hint of the infinite, hidden just out of view.

'Yes,' Aleyna said. 'I think so.'

'Okay, then.' Jack kicked a loose pebble and watched it skitter ahead of them, coming to rest in the middle of the path, splitting the current of water into a pair of plaited streams. Perhaps unconsciously, he quickened his pace as though impatient to reach it again. 'Has the fog got worse?' He held his arm in front of him as though it might help him judge.

'A bit, maybe.'

He glanced back up the path at her, squinting with concern.

'Listen,' he said. 'I know it's probably too late, but do you want to swap jackets? That old thing is going to give you hypothermia or something.'

That old thing.

He started unzipping his Karrimor overcoat, slow enough that she could stop him before he was done.

'It's fine,' she said when he was past halfway. 'Doubt mine would fit you anyway.'

She smiled.

'But I'm fine,' she said again. 'It's not cold, it's just wet.' And horrible, she would have added, but she didn't want to say it out loud in case it might make things feel worse. It wasn't that bad. Not really. And the cottage wasn't far away, and if Kevin had got there already he'd have the fire lit...

'Well, if you change your mind.' Jack zipped his coat up again and hunched into it. 'Sorry I didn't think of it earlier. We're getting way too old for expeditions like this.'

'Speak for yourself.'

'Hangovers make me feel older.'

'Don't drink so much then. We had lots of fruit juice. Coke.'

'Fruit juice makes me feel like a kid. How are you feeling?'

'I didn't drink as much as you did.'

It was true, but only just true. It had been a long time since drinking had felt so illicit to her. Back then it had been the last fluttering ends of her childhood faith nagging at her with stern disapproval, but this was different and felt more transgressive in its way.

Before they'd arrived, Aleyna had promised herself she wasn't going to drink at all, but once plump little Mrs Leachy had unlocked the cottage and briskly shown them around, Aleyna had accepted a glass of prosecco from Jack without a thought. After that, she found herself engaged in a game. If Kevin offered her a new drink, she would refuse; but if Jack did, she would accept. Three glasses of wine in and she remembered how Jack didn't really ask. He just leaned in and topped up her glass when he judged it to be low. She had smiled. She had polished off everything he had given her. It would be his fault either way.

They passed a row of three small houses, low-slung roofs and whitewashed walls; each had the appearance of being buried halfway into the hillside. A fourth house at the end of the row looked unfinished, and a wide aperture in one wall was masked by a canvas sheet that the wind had loosened so it flapped and snapped at them like a chained dog as they passed.

'Where is everyone?' Jack said. 'Everywhere looks deserted.'

'They probably think only idiots would go out for a walk in weather like this. Mad dogs and Englishmen.'

'Which of those am I?' he said, turning back to her.

'Mad Englishman.'

'Half English.'

'No one's half English. When you're brought up in England, it blots out everything else.' She tapped the side of her head. 'Shadow of the Empire, fitted as standard.'

He snorted, glancing up at her as though he was gauging a retort, but then he looked away again, losing his nerve as he always did. 'They all looked empty,' he said instead. 'Every house we passed looked empty. No lights, no movement.'

'They're all sleeping in. Nursing their heads like normal people.'

'Even so.'

'It's fine.'

Perhaps she sounded more confident than she felt, because before they rounded the corner, she glanced back. The houses didn't seem so empty to her; in fact, she was struck by the clear impression that there really was someone there in the unfinished house at the end of the row, standing just out of sight behind the flapping canvas, watching them pass.

Figures moving through the fog, she thought, imagining the homeowners glimpsing their forms emerging from the whiteness like spectres. No wonder everyone had their doors firmly closed.

'Holiday homes, maybe,' she said.

Jack winced, staring ahead unfocused.

'My mum used to come to these parts in the holidays,' he said. 'Back in the fifties, sixties. Near enough, anyway. Had cousins round near Bantry, but best I can tell, she spent most of her time being shuffled from one relative to another over the holidays. She said she remembered seeing kids around these parts walking into school barefoot, holding their shoes to save the wear on them.'

He shook his head.

'Seems crazy it should be all holiday homes now. Doesn't seem right.'

Aleyna touched him on the shoulder and he stopped in surprise.

She leaned forward and kissed him. His lips were edged with a fierce cold, but there was warmth in there too and her hunger for it both surprised and embarrassed her.

It was his turn to push her gently away.

'They could be just ahead of us,' he said.

Aleyna shook her head, but her look remained uncertain. 'They'll be home by now. Lighting a fire. Putting the kettle on.'

Jack laughed. 'They won't be moving that fast. If we pick up the pace we'll likely catch up with them before we get back.'

'They're not that slow.'

'Lou is, trust me. And if she's complaining – and by God, she will be complaining – it'll slow her down further.'

'You should be nicer to her.'

'I'm a gentleman with her.'

'But behind her back…?'

'In the fog…'

They kissed again, longer, deeper, until Aleyna broke away, sensing some distant movement beyond Jack's shoulder, a flickering motion like a bird, perhaps, or an animal. She looked back the way they had come, hidden now by the whiteness that had closed behind them like a curtain. Again, she had the distinct sense there was someone there, just out of sight, barely invisible.

'Could they be behind us, maybe?' she said.

'Only if they took a wrong turn.' Jack turned to see where she was looking.

Aleyna called into the fog. 'Kev?' she said. 'Lou?'

The words felt stunted, abrupt. Cast into the whiteness, they didn't sound like names to her at all.

'There's no one there.' Jack turned back to her, his hand came up to her cheek but she flinched away.

'That last junction,' she said. 'Maybe they went straight when they should have turned left? Maybe they backtracked when they realised their mistake?'

'There's no one there,' Jack said. 'If we carry on, we can catch up with them. Hey.' Again, his hand was at her cheek, but its gear had changed: this wasn't seduction, it was concern. 'Look at me,' he said.

He looked at her, serious as a father.

'You stare into that fog,' he said, 'you're going to see whatever you think you're seeing. Doesn't mean it's really there, though. Trick of the eye. It's full of shit.'

'I didn't see anything,' Aleyna said. It was mostly true but still discomforting.

'Come on, you're cold and soaked through.' She felt his hand on her shoulder, pushing, steering her back down the path. 'Let's get you back to that fire. I'm sorry for delaying us at all.'

'Such a gentleman.'

'Only to your face.'

'Asshole.'

'Cow.'

The path gave way to a tarmac road that descended gradually, zigzagging between the fields. There were drainage ditches on either side, but the roadway was crosshatched with sparkling rivulets of water, chasing their way downwards.

The air felt thicker, denser, and from somewhere Aleyna imagined a faint smell of woodsmoke drifting across on an intermittent breeze.

'You know what this reminds me of?' Jack said.

Aleyna shook her head, but didn't look at him; turning would only move her coat and it already felt colder and heavier around her. She could feel the dampness had soaked through to the lining and the wool of the jersey she wore beneath. It felt like cool fingertips tracing down her arms, hooking around her chest from behind.

'Volumetric fog,' Jack said.

'You're waiting for me to ask what that is, aren't you?'

'That game Kevin and I worked on back in the late nineties. It was called Something Invasion… *Mutant Invasion*? *Mutoids*? Shit, I don't know, I've tried to block it out. It was one of those first-person shooters, trying to cash in on *Goldeneye* on the N64. Only it was awful. You were walking around this planet, shooting insurgents – you were invading the whole planet single-handed, you know how those computer game plots used to be – and it looked terrible. Crap textures, low poly count. Terrible.

'But the thing with that sort of game is that you're only shown the landscape your character can see. Nothing else really existed, the hills were all hollow. And even more so than other games of its type, it was completely unstable. There was this weird sense that, without warning, the player might break free from the point of view and the illusion would fold up just like that. You'd turn around and there'd be nothing there at all. Just blackness.'

He stared out into the fog, his grin only loosely pinned into place.

'The hills were hollow,' he said again, thoughtful. 'Anyway, the system was so slow we could barely show any of the landscape at all, and if we did, everything just ground to a halt like you were wading through treacle.

'So time was short and we cut corners. We cranked up the volumetric fog to hide the fact the scenery was popping up in the distance and being redrawn when you turned around.'

'What happened?'

'Everyone hated it. Went straight to the bargain bin in Woolworths. Remember Woolworths?'

They walked on in silence for a while.

They had all worked together once. Aleyna had arrived, youthful and enthusiastic from some Lancashire backstreet, flushed with the colours and variety of the capital. The company was one of those little start-ups that grew too fast, too bright and too eager. Before they knew what was happening, before their feet even touched the ground, the company was already gone, snapped up by a bigger fish, scattered to the winds. But the four of them circled each other still, the same workplaces, the same bars. Constantly cycling, over and over and over.

'Is that why you stopped writing the games yourself?' Aleyna said after a while. She'd heard versions of the story before, different variants with different villains, as though whoever asked got someone else to blame.

Jack sighed.

'I wasn't even supposed to write most of that one. In one way, I fucked things up by compromising; in another, I saved the day by actually finishing the bloody thing.' He shrugged. 'In the future, I figured I'd leave the coding to the Kevins of this world.'

Aleyna stopped.

'Be nicer,' she said.

'That's not what I meant,' Jack said. 'I mean, he's better at that sort of thing than I am. I bluff my way through, he absolutely gets it. I'm better at the other stuff. Managing, getting funding, talking to people, you know? I'm good at that.'

'Sure. You're doing a bang-up job.'

'You know what I mean. Kevin's smart. The man's an artist. But if he didn't have me watching his back, people would be fucking him over at every turn.'

They walked onwards in silence. Aleyna didn't write code, she wrote copy. Back then she had written documentation and manuals, newsletters that no one read. These days, she worked freelance for a catalogue company, spending her hours coming up with different ways to describe the same things: a dozen ways to say 'carry cot'; one hundred ways to say 'pushchair'; one thousand ways to say 'child, baby, bairn'. She tabulated her work in spreadsheets that from a distance didn't look so different from the pages of code that Kevin would trawl through. Editing, debugging, refining, releasing. The day-to-day dance was familiar to both of them.

On their right, Aleyna and Jack passed the gate to a farm, and like the other buildings they had seen it was a dark and cold-looking place. The farmhouse, a low building at the far end of a muddy concrete forecourt, had a melancholy quality accentuated by the collection of faded plastic children's toys gathered outside. A pink slide pointed downwards to a slick of grey puddle, a squinting swing set with frayed ropes, a rocking horse left on its side. The place felt too empty, too quiet to be fully real. The barn opening out onto the yard was a rusted skeleton, crowded with neglected machinery, all spikes and blades, bundled and forgotten like rolls of barbed wire.

'What time is it?' Aleyna said.

Jack shrugged.

'I left my phone in the cottage,' he said. 'Looked like it was on the blink this morning anyway. No signal, nothing.' He shot her a glance and tried to look reassuring. 'Probably nearly three or so,' he said.

'So late?'

'We started late.' He grinned. 'When we said last night how we could walk it off come the morning, I think we were all thinking we'd actually see the morning. Why? What time did you think it was?'

Aleyna turned, looking back up the path. She felt very conscious about how their voices carried. Somewhere, she could hear the gentle hiss of the sea, the clatter and turn of pebbles in a distant tide, but otherwise it was quiet and still. She found warmth in the way Jack talked, but at the same time it felt too loud, too impolite. It drew attention in a way that made her uncomfortable.

'I don't know,' she said. 'To be honest, I'm not even sure what day it is.'

Jack laughed.

'Trick question,' he said.

'I don't know,' Aleyna said again. 'It should be New Year's Day, but how would we know? We haven't seen anyone else. We could have slept for days for all I know. Months. We woke up and it's like the world has been emptied while we were asleep.'

Jack didn't reply, but Aleyna felt his eyes on her; she felt he was studying her, looking for a sign she was joking, a hook on which he could hang a smart remark. Instead, he turned away again and sighed.

'Do not partake of the food they give you,' he said, his tone affected as though he was quoting something from memory.

'Excuse me?'

'Faeries. If they offer you food and you eat it, you become trapped in their world and subject to their whims. Don't look at me like that, I read it somewhere. In a book. So it must be true.'

'I haven't eaten any faerie food,' Aleyna said, amused despite herself.

'You had one of those scones Mrs O'Landlady left out for us.'

'Mrs Leachy is not a faerie.'

Jack shrugged. 'How would we know?'

'I doubt faeries make scones.'

Jack looked sceptical.

'I wish they would,' he said. 'I'm ravenous.'

They walked in silence for a spell, and Aleyna hugged her coat tight around her as though she could squeeze more comfort from it, even though the dampness had infiltrated it entirely. Kevin had bought it for her and it seemed so extravagant that she assumed he was apologising for something he had yet to confess to. He had never been particularly good with choosing gifts for her. On their first Christmas together, he had bought her a second-hand paperback copy of *The Siege of Krishnapur*, confessing as he did so that it had only cost him two-fifty from one of the vendors under Waterloo Bridge, and that he only bought it because he liked the cover. He made up for it with his cooking, to which he applied the same level of attention that he spent on his code. If he was an engineer in the kitchen rather than an artist, there was passion there too: he saw processes and subroutines, his ingredients subjected to functions and iterative loops, but there was love stirred in with each, binding everything together at a level deeper than chemistry.

Aleyna had grown up with good food, but Kevin's recipes still had the ability to take her by surprise. She hated to imagine how much greyer her life would be without his cooking, without him.

The coat was beautiful and clearly more expensive than he could afford. She'd brought it with her to Ireland to demonstrate how much she appreciated it, but now, as it hung heavy and misshapen on her, she wondered if she had ruined it by wearing it for the walk.

'What do you think they're doing right now?' she said.

'Who?'

'Who do you think?'

'Maybe they're back in the cottage after all. Fire lit, feet up.'

'Holding hands?'

'Kissing. Fucking.'

Beside them, the stone wall they'd been following for the past hundred yards gave way to a three-wire fence bordering a broad field that disappeared uphill into whiteness. At its distant edges Aleyna thought she saw movement again, something dark against the mist. Looking closer, she saw there were several shapes there, too dark to be seagulls; they could have been crows. They moved with a clumsy flapping motion that suggested wings, but at this distance their size was troubling. Perhaps it was only a trick of perspective, but there was something about them that felt too big for common birds, and the way they moved unsettled her: they stumbled and flustered and flapped about like the loose tarpaulin on the empty house. They rolled and blustered chaotically as they edged slowly down the field towards the fence.

'Lou's probably asleep by now,' Jack said, his attention elsewhere. 'All tucked up and content to have that cramped little bed to herself. She barely slept at all last night. Tossing and turning all the time, it's a miracle she got as far as she did on the walk.'

'Let's move quicker then,' Aleyna said.

Jack looked at her, concerned.

'Alright,' he said, and he reached out to take her hand.

She didn't look back as they hurried down the road together and Jack didn't speak, making their flight feel more urgent.

She hadn't been paying attention to their surroundings as the four of them had begun their walk. She'd been talking to Lou, the two of them planting one foot in front of the other with little attention spared for the passing landscape.

It always used to bother her that she only knew Lou because of Jack and Kevin. To begin with, she was never entirely sure if she liked her or just felt she should accommodate her for Jack's sake, but time had brought them closer, sanding down the residual prickliness between them and leaving them with a mutual respect for the fact that they were both still there despite everything. Aleyna had never been confident when it came to friend maintenance, and working from home as a freelancer had whittled her list of face-to-face colleagues down to the bone. She was grateful she had Lou there, somewhere in the background. An almost-friend was sometimes good enough.

Lou had met Jack when the company had been bought out, way back when. She had been the one hired to project manage the transition, breaking the start-up apart to salvage what worked and throw everything else out. Jack she kept for herself, not in a mercenary move, but an unexpected development, unaccounted for but worked around. That was how Lou worked. Her life was scheduled in Gantt charts and dependency diagrams. She had been the one to organise the New Year's holiday but the walk had never been part of the plan. Little wonder she'd turned back so soon.

The path felt alien to Aleyna, and while the fog had thickened since their outward journey, the road itself was new to her, the hedges and walls and fences on either side were unfamiliar; the potholes in the tarmac seemed fresh.

She stopped abruptly, forcing Jack to tug at her arm in surprise.

'What is it?' he said.

'This isn't the way we came.'

He looked about him, flustered.

'It has to be,' he said. 'There's no other way we could have gone.'

'It's wrong,' Aleyna said. 'We didn't come this way.'

Jack sighed.

'We could go back,' he said.

'No.' She pulled out the map from her coat pocket and started unfolding it. But it was too big, too unwieldy. Lines and shapes and endless place names. Already she felt the paper softening in the mist.

'Listen.' Jack squinted into the fog. 'The sea's that way, you can hear it. If we carry on downhill, we'll get to the main road eventually, and we can just walk along it to get to the cottage. We can't be far.'

'Fuck,' Aleyna said. The word sounded misshapen when she said it; like the previous night's drinking, it felt like something she should have been giving up. The map was defeating her. She crumpled it thoughtlessly, searching its hieroglyphics for the cottage, the path, the standing stone. But she couldn't engage with it, not entirely. The geography swam before her and all the labels conspired to say the same thing in different ways. A hundred places she had never heard of, a thousand places she never thought to see.

'Come on.' Jack rested his hand on the map, a gentle gesture and one that surprised her with its calmness. It occurred to her that she felt at ease in his presence in a way she didn't feel with Kevin. It wasn't a relaxing feeling, there was always a nub of sickly tension that she was doing something she shouldn't, but it felt comfortable in some other, inexplicable way; like two pieces from different jigsaws fitting together snugly even if the picture made no sense.

'I'm sorry,' she said.

'It's okay.' He smiled. 'Let's go back.'

He took the map off her and started folding it. She saw immediately he was doing it wrong, fold against fold; it bunched awkwardly in his hands, but she didn't say anything.

They set off again, downward, seaward, deep into the white. Aleyna glanced back over her shoulder, the way they had come looking nearly the same as they path they had chosen to continue down. There was no sign of movement that she could see. No shapes, no shadows, no flapping wings.

Jack reached up and pressed his hands to his head.

'My mum would appreciate this,' he said.

'The walk?'

'The fact I have a hangover. She'd say it was penance. Some sort of purgatorial state the drunk have to pass through before they earn sobriety. She'd say all that to me like she was quoting scripture, but she'd be laughing at the same time.' He grimaced. 'Catholics,' he said. 'It's all about what you deserve with them. Sadistic fuckers the lot of them.'

Aleyna could only imagine what her mother would say if she knew her only daughter had been drinking. She certainly wouldn't laugh. She wouldn't give speeches either. She'd just remain silent in that way of hers; she would quietly leave the room when Aleyna came in.

'Hey,' Jack said. He had stopped on the path some paces behind her, standing by the low stone wall, staring into the field angling down to their left. He turned back to her, grinning. 'Look,' he said.

At the end of the field, the sun was shining. A hazy amber disc suspended low in the spread of grey, punching through where the clouds had weakened. The field beneath it was oddly beautiful, even and mudded, the day's moisture hung on the too-early shoots of greenery forming a glittering path to the far side. Aleyna could see a wire fence in the distance, on the other side of which was the angular ghost of a low building, a telegraph pole, a skeleton tree.

'It's the street,' Jack said. 'That's the place just a few hundred yards up from the cottage, which means we're over that way somewhere.' He gestured airily, back and to the left.

'So we *are* on the wrong road,' Aleyna said.

'I don't know,' Jack said. 'This one probably connects eventually.'

They stood together, side by side at the wall, and neither said anything for what felt like hours. As they watched, the sun sunk imperceptibly lower and the path of light it cast broadened.

Aleyna sighed. 'We should cut across.' One of them had to say it. 'We should climb over the wall and just… just walk across.'

She sensed Jack had turned to look at her but she didn't meet his eyes.

'Farmer might have a gun,' he said. 'Might not take kindly to us traipsing over his neatly ploughed field.'

'Farmer is probably as hungover as you are.'

'True.'

Again, silence; and again, it was Aleyna who spoke first.

'I just want to go home,' she said.

She felt Jack's hand on her shoulder.

'Come on then,' he said.

> • <

The field was wet underfoot, a film of standing water reflected the subtle pleats of the clouds, but the ground itself, while spongy, was firm enough. They walked together in silence, Jack a few paces ahead and Aleyna happy to tail behind. As they walked, the mist seemed to loosen around them and the sun brightened to the extent that Aleyna could feel a trace of its warmth on her forehead and cheeks.

Ahead of them, the line of the road slowly began to come into sharper focus, and Aleyna could make out the shape of the building they had seen more clearly. It was a hunched little cottage with its back to the field, a single, tiny square window hanging tight under the roofline. They had passed it on their way uphill, and while then it had struck her as a lonely looking place, now there was a warmth to it that felt compulsive.

Jack stopped to shake the mud off his boots.

'Christ,' he said. 'It's like… it's like fucking porridge.'

He kicked at nothing, long legged and gangly, and while small sods of mud spun off his feet, the rest remained clenched around the soles and the uppers, thick and dense and solidifying.

'It's not worth it,' Aleyna said. 'You'll only get more.'

'It's the more I'm worried about.' Another kick, this one almost unbalanced him. She caught him and laughed, but he shook her off and plunged on ahead.

The mud was sticking to her shoes as well. At first it felt like she had something in her shoe, and then like she was standing on something, a rock or a tussock, something uneven that threatened to upend her. More than anything, she could feel the weight of it. She could feel the weight of the landscape, pulling at her and slowing her pace.

'I need a stick or something,' Jack was saying. 'Do you have a pen? Or some keys?'

'Just keep going.'

'How about the map? Give me the map.'

'Jack.'

But she understood his impatience with it, and when his back was turned again she set her own feet down at angles, as though she could push off the excess mud against the ground itself; but it just clung to the sides of her shoes, making them thicker and heavier still.

Her legs ached, but still she persevered.

They approached the centre of the field, but Aleyna had to look back to see where they had come from to be certain. The road ahead of them looked barely closer than it had been when they had first climbed over the wall. It was clearer, true, but no nearer. Behind her, the path they had come from also seemed too far away. It was a distant blurry line in the mist, another hint of something boundless and infinite.

It reminded her, inexplicably, of a holiday she and Kevin had taken years before to the Norfolk coast. They'd visited a beach with signs warning of riptides to the north. Aleyna had been frightened by the prospect of being caught by the currents and dragged out to sea, and yet there had been kids splashing about in the waves regardless, some barely toddlers, waddling about the surf in inflatable armbands. Their parents were lying on the beach, oblivious under paperbacks and beer bottles. Aleyna and Kevin hadn't stayed long. He was trying to work but the sun bleached out his laptop screen, and she found herself counting and recounting other people's children, terrified not just that one of them might get swept out to the horizon, but that she might be the one expected to follow, just because she had been the only one paying attention.

Now the field felt bigger to Aleyna than it had done before; it felt sea-like, oceanic, tangled with hidden currents. It was a vertiginous thought and she stopped so abruptly that her heavy feet stumbled, so she almost pitched forward into the mud.

And then I'd never get up, she thought.

What a way to start the year.

Jack was still moving onwards. He looked like a string puppet, each foot raised comically high in turn, his shoulders angling first one way then the other, his arms flailing for balance. One foot, two feet. He looked so determined, like a child learning to walk for the first time.

She wondered what would happen if she let him keep walking. Maybe he would disappear into the fog like Kevin and Lou had. Maybe the field would keep stretching and stretching to accommodate the distance between them.

'Jack,' she said. She only spoke quietly, but he turned in surprise as though she was beside him after all.

'What is it?'

He glanced around him, then without even a thought started picking his way back to her. One foot, two foot. He looked pleased with himself, as though he had traded his dignity for a way to master himself.

'There's something I need to tell you,' Aleyna said, taking herself by surprise. She hadn't intended to say anything at all. Not to Jack, not to Kevin, not to anyone. She smiled at him instead as he reached her, and he put out a hand, maybe to comfort her, maybe to support himself.

'It's alright,' he said. 'We just have to power through. We'll only get stuck if we let it.'

She looked down at their feet, facing each other like dance partners. For a moment she wondered if it was all too late anyway. She wondered if she would ever be able to move again. She felt that the mud was drawing her downwards. In her shoes, her feet were as cold as stone, water had pooled around them, green shoots rocking like pondweed.

'Jack,' she said, and there was something about the way she spoke that made him pull her close and hold her.

Across the outer edges of the field, there was the ghost of something moving. Dark shapes flickered and flapped around the grey-white fringes. Aleyna watched them over Jack's shoulder, she saw how they approached: circling, fluttering, stumbling, surrounding them.

'We should go back,' she said.

FIVE CONVERSATIONS WITH MY DAUGHTER

(WHO TRAVELS IN TIME)

1.

Carrie was six when she first told me she could travel in time.

I was sleeping on the sofa that night. Laura wouldn't let me in the bedroom, she wanted me out of the house, but I'd talked her down. I'd told her I would need time to find somewhere else to go and she'd said I could stay at Nicole-from-work's place if I liked her so goddamn much. I tried to come up with a retort that would make me sound like the grown-up, but she shut the bedroom door in my face before I could say anything at all. I waited outside and listened to her holding her breath on the other side. She was upset with me, but she wasn't going to let me hear her cry.

Carrie found me in the lounge. I'd taken some spare bedclothes from the airing cupboard and had made a fair fist of assembling a bed on the two-seater Chesterfield. I was lying there, stripped to my boxers and reading a paperback Laura had left on the coffee table, when I became aware of the small figure in the doorway.

'Mummy's sad,' Carrie said and I put the paperback down and pulled myself up to a sitting position, patting the seat of the sofa beside me.

Carrie bounded up onto it and sat there, snuggling up to me; I looped the blanket around us both.

'You should talk to her,' she said.

'Tried that, kiddo,' I said. 'She'll be okay. She just needs a bit of time.'

'She might need less time if you talked to her, Dad,' she said. 'You should never wait to be forgiven.'

And there was the slip that made me frown.

'Since when did you call me Dad?' I said. Until then it had always been Daddy, and the abbreviated term sounded alien when spoken in her six-year-old voice.

She pushed off me and looked at me seriously, and again her expression was subtler than I'd ever seen it before. Carrie was still at an age where her emotions were unfiltered, but here she was being serious, in that contrived way adults occasionally adopt when they talk to someone younger or slower.

'Probably when I was about fourteen,' she said. 'Louise O'Dowd heard me calling after Mummy in the school playground and she wouldn't let me forget it for the next two years. I'd hear much worse, but there and then I demoted you both. One syllable each, and even then only under sufferance.'

I blinked at that.

'Look who swallowed a dictionary,' I said.

She didn't laugh. She didn't pull a face. She didn't punch me in the shoulder and go 'Da-ddy', like she normally did when I made fun of her. And it struck me how the memory she'd described was already stale to her. It had been supplanted by an anecdote, polished over time so it shone brighter than the truth ever had. She looked at me, small-smiled, sharp-eyed.

'I have a secret,' she said. 'And you must promise not to tell anyone, not even me.'

'I don't understand.'

'Right now, I'm six years old,' Carrie said, 'but I'm also older. Older even that you are now. Just for now, two points in my life have converged.'

It was a game, I was sure of it. Carrie always was one for imaginative play. Little wonder since she spent so much time on her own. My work started early and ended late, so sometimes I'd only ever see her at weekends.

Ever since she could speak, she would tell us tall stories, spotted with beautiful, accidental moments of the profound and the surreal. She was a storyteller unmoored from the gravity of realism, and she would look up at us, her eyes bright.

'When I was a little girl,' she would say, and she'd point to me and say, 'You were there and you were delivering packages, only you weren't on a motorbike, you were on a dragon called Mr Spotty.' Or she'd point to Laura and say, 'You could fly. And you were still a nurse but you had wings. Only they fell off and you were sad. So the doctors put them back and then you weren't sad any more.' She'd relate what she'd done the previous day, sometimes incorporating her best friend into the narrative. 'We went to Cornwall and Leonora was there, and we played on the beach. And Leo and me built a castle out of the sand and it was bigger than the house and my bedroom was at the top and it had a garden. And the birds came from far, far away and they sang. They sang all day. And we made records.'

But they were improvisational fantasies and if Laura were to question her about what she'd already said, she'd simply make them up anew. The beach wouldn't be a beach, it would be a forest; it wouldn't be in Cornwall, it would be in Wales. They wouldn't be birds, they'd be bears...

But there, on the sofa, she looked at me patiently and repeated what she'd said.

'I'm six years old,' she said, 'but I'm also older. Older than you are now. Two points, converged.'

'Carrie—'

'I shouldn't be telling you this,' she said. 'But I'm going to need your help. Listen. In my future, we've discovered a way to travel in time, but it's limited. We can only travel back down the paths we've already forged ourselves. Unspooling our personal history until we find the place we need to go. Even then, we can only stay for a little while and only when our old self is unconscious. It's dangerous, we need to be away by the time they wake or lasting damage might occur, but it's real. And it works.'

How do you respond when your six-year-old daughter talks to you like that? I barely said anything. I wondered if I was frightened of her; my only reference point for kids sounding too adult was those horror movies where children become possessed by something violent and horrifying.

'There's something I need to change,' Carrie said, 'but I'm not going to be able to do it on my own. We need to calibrate so I can judge the right time, so I might be in and out. I'll be back later and I'll talk to you again, so if you have questions, save them. And don't tell anyone about this. Not Mum, not even me. Do you promise?'

I stared into those eyes, so sincere, so strong. She had her mother's eyes and the thought was abrasive like a friction burn.

'Do you promise?' she said again.

'Yes,' I said. 'Of course,' I said.

She leaned forward and kissed me on the cheek, then she lay her head on my shoulder and like that, I could feel she was asleep.

We sat there for a moment together. I listened to the clock ticking heavily in the lounge and the way the rhythm of her sleep-breathing seemed to fall into time with it. Then I gathered her up in my arms, wrapping the blanket around her, and I carried her back upstairs to her room.

She shifted in my arms.

'Daddy,' she murmured. A protest, a greeting, an explanation.

'Go back to sleep,' I said. 'You've been sleepwalking is all.'

2.

The phone went and Nicole answered it. She passed me the handset, a frown on her face.

'It's your daughter,' she said, and she arched her eyebrows in that way of hers.

It was one in the morning and we were both still awake. I took the handset and bundled out of bed, carrying it downstairs, held before me as though I expected it to bite. Nicole called after me, but I ignored her.

'Carrie?' I said.

'I haven't got long,' Carrie's voice said. 'I never did sleep well when you were out of the house.'

'Carrie, how did you get this number?'

'I know where you are,' she said. 'At this point Mum doesn't, but she will. I won't tell her but it will all come out and it'll be messy, but I think you know that already.'

Six weeks had passed since I'd last spoken to the other Carrie, and as the time had gone on, it had felt less real to me. My Carrie, everyday Carrie, was no different than she had been before. Maybe I watched her closer than I once had, but her preoccupations were those of any young child who engages with the trivial with the utmost seriousness.

But I caught myself willing it to happen again. I'd been meaning to move out of the house sooner, but I made excuses to hang around instead. Putting Carrie to bed at night, I'd check at the door to see if she was asleep, then I'd stay awake downstairs, listening for her delicate footstep outside.

Laura lost patience with me. She made a stand.

'I can only look after one child,' she said to me, shaking with anger. 'You either grow up, or you go away.'

I've learned the hard way that ultimatums like this are dangerously loaded. If I'd tried to assure her I really was the responsible adult she wanted me to be, she would have only heard a petulant whine, an unlicensed promise, poorly deployed.

The right answer was the wrong answer plus time to repent, even if it could only look like the wrong answer in isolation. Laura cried when I left. I held her and promised that when I came back, I'd be a better person for her and for Carrie. That gave her hope, I think.

I moved out, which was a good move. I moved into Nicole's, which was a stupid one.

'Are you going to tell me about the future?' I said to Carrie.

'No,' Carrie said. 'You don't need to know anything about it.'

'You say that,' I said, 'but some lottery numbers wouldn't hurt.'

'Don't push it, Dad.'

Dad.

I stood there for a moment, listening to the weight of her breath filtered through the receiver, trying to gauge the differences between it and the Carrie I knew.

'I don't understand how this is happening,' I said.

'It's complicated,' Carrie said, 'but the technology is expensive to run. I don't know how long I'll have the right to use it. So I don't think we should waste it.'

'You're doing alright, then?' I said and wished I hadn't. It felt so crass. 'Are you happy?' I said instead.

I heard impatience in her voice and it didn't quite fit, sounding like something childish repurposed into something parental.

'You asked me about time travel when I wasn't asleep, didn't you?' she said. 'I remember this weird conversation with you when I was small—'

'I'm sorry—'

'You promised you wouldn't talk about it.'

'I know,' I said. 'It just didn't feel real to me. You said you wanted me to help you. I'm sorry.'

'I do want you to help,' she said. 'But not yet. When the time comes I just need to know that you'll do as I ask.'

'Anything.'

There was a pause. A long pause, stretched longer by the impossibility we found ourselves in. These were not seconds gaping between us, but years, decades, more.

'Well,' I said, 'I'll be waiting for you anyway. Whenever you're back.' Dissatisfied, I risk embarrassment and reach for whimsy, 'When the clock strikes thirteen or whatever.'

'What are you talking about?'

'*Tom's Midnight Garden*,' I said. 'It's a children's book. Time travel. It's sweet.'

'I've not read it,' Carrie said.

There was another pause, this one longer, made heavy by things neither of us could bring ourselves to say.

'Can you tell me what it's like?' I said. 'Time travel.'

'Do you remember the crosswords I used to do with Mum?'

'No,' I said. 'I don't think you've started doing that yet.'

'We have,' Carrie said. 'You just haven't noticed. Anyway, there was one I remembered. The clues were something like: six across, see fifteen down. Fifteen down, see six across. Both were seven letters and there were no other clues, only the other words that crossed each of them. That's what time travel feels like. Two clues in different directions that you have to solve at the same time. Sometimes you just need to be brave enough to risk getting it wrong.'

After she hung up, I took the phone back upstairs again. I put on my shirt and told Nicole I would have to find somewhere else to stay.

She stared at me from the bed.

'You're an asshole,' she said. 'Do you know that?'

'Apparently.' I nodded. 'But I've learned to live with it.'

'You don't learn to live with being an asshole,' Nicole said. 'You figure out how to stop.'

She turned off the bedside light and let me find my way out in the dark.

3.

I found a flat down the road from the house and moved in. At the depot, I worked extra hours until there was enough goodwill among the management to allow me to rearrange my shifts with other riders, so I could spend more time with Carrie and Laura. I still saw Nicole around the office, but she didn't really talk to me any more. Even over the radio, her voice sounded as terse as a recorded message.

Laura started to ask me to babysit when she was out on call. To begin with, I was her last resort, but with good behaviour and plenty of time I edged my way up her list.

I bought a copy of *Tom's Midnight Garden* and started reading it to Carrie the next time I was over. It was a little old for her, perhaps, a little old-fashioned, but it was different and it was something of our own.

'What happens next?' Carrie said when I closed the book the first time.

'You can find out next time,' I said.

'But I want to know now.'

I thumbed to the last page and started scanning the paragraphs to refresh my memory. Carrie's hand shot out and snatched the book from me.

'You can't skip to the end.' Her expression was scandalised. 'We have to read the whole thing, otherwise it won't make any sense.'

I stared back at her, disoriented and amused.

'Well,' I said, 'we can ask Mummy if she'll read you more tomorrow.'

A few days later, Laura called me.

'I don't know what you're up to,' she said, 'but it seems to be working.'

'What do you mean?' I said.

'Carrie wants you to read to her before she goes to bed.' At first I thought she was angry with me, but I could have sworn I heard the way she smiled.

Carrie and I finished reading *Tom's Midnight Garden* over the next couple of weeks, and even before we were done, I found myself in the library, lining up something new to read her next.

'You're like Scheherazade,' the other Carrie said when I next saw her. 'Always have to keep another story in your pocket in case you fall out of favour.'

I was babysitting that night. I'd had a call from Laura saying she had to get back to work that evening because the maternity unit was short-staffed, so I went straight to the house after work, parking the bike out on the lawn where it always used to live.

I was watching the end of the news on television when Carrie came bounding down the stairs at a run. She surprised me by doing a cartwheel across the carpet, an imperfect one, all legs and arms and flying hair, but when she landed she was grinning wildly.

'God,' she said, 'I forgot just how much fun that was. I forgot I used to find them so easy to do.'

Next, she did a handstand up against the wall, laughing at me upside down through the hair that had fallen over her face. She did roly-polies across the floor and I helped her manage some semi-somersaults, my hands on her waist so she wouldn't fall. I picked her up and flew her around the lounge and she whooped with the simple joy of it.

'Won't this wake you up?' I said afterwards.

She was sitting beside me on the sofa, wearing my motorcycle leathers which looked so big on her. I'd told her she looked like she'd shrunk in the wash.

'I am awake,' she said. 'You're not going to wake her unless I go away again. It's complicated.'

She glanced at the dark window.

'Such a shame I can only come here at night,' she said. 'Maybe you should chloroform her one day and we can go for a walk. Go up a mountain. Go to the beach.' She sighed. 'I would love to run in the sand again.'

'That would be fun explaining to your mother,' I said.

Carrie's laugh faltered when she spotted the book on the coffee table. *Tom's Midnight Garden*, its spine creased and bent back. She picked it up and ran her fingers over the pages with a curious reverence.

'I remember you reading me this,' she said and smiled. 'When I was in my twenties, I was living alone in this horrible little flat and this cat adopted me. Rake thin, black fur, the most beautiful eyes. I called it Tom and everyone just assumed I was thinking cat equals tomcat and that I had no imagination whatsoever, but I called him Tom because he went out in the garden at midnight and I'd imagine him having all kinds of adventures.'

I realised I was holding my breath. That little glimpse of her life felt so precious and delicate, I felt anything I said would be clumsy enough to break it.

'Did you live alone long?' I said eventually.

'I'm not telling you anything about the future,' she said. 'I just mentioned I had a cat once. I don't think that counts. I've always liked cats, after all.'

She set the book back down on the table and shrugged off the jacket.

'I don't think you should ride bikes any more,' she said.

'It's sort of what I do,' I said. 'It's something I'm good at. Fastest motorcycle courier in the county.'

I grinned. It was supposed to be a joke but it was poorly aimed.

'Your mum and me used to ride together,' I said. 'When we first met, we'd get on the bike and we'd just take off, see how far we could get. I had this crappy little Suzuki at the time, but it got us to Cumbria and the North York Moors and Scotland. Long, winding roads, barely any traffic. We howled along them as good as flying. And when you've got two people on a bike, they have to hold onto each other for the whole trip. It's beautiful really. Most intimate way you can travel.'

Carrie made a noise that might have been a laugh had it been better behaved.

'She was holding onto you,' she said. 'You did all the driving and she was holding on for dear life. Not the same thing at all.'

I shrugged.

'Well, she seemed to like it at the time.'

'But you could get a different job,' Carrie said. 'Maybe something in an office.'

I looked at her closely.

'Is this a warning about my future?' I said, only half joking.

She gave me a dark look, heavy with irony.

'Not at all,' she said. 'You die in a terrible office-related accident and I'm just trying to hurry it along.'

I blinked at that.

'Kidding,' she said.

4.

Time passed, the years stacked up. Every day Carrie grew steadily and greedily, and I managed to forget about the other Carrie and her occasional visits because my preoccupations became exclusively with the moment-to-moment. When I thought about the future, they were specific, administrative futures. Schools, money, health. The future of the other Carrie seemed too far away to concern myself with.

At work, Nicole announced she was getting married to a man she'd met online. He lived in Colorado and she'd only met him once, but by that point she'd spent most of her career talking to the riders almost exclusively over the radio, and so falling in love over the Internet felt admirably logical to her. The day before she left for the States, she baked a carrot cake and presented pieces to each of us when we returned to the depot. Even when she saw me, her smile was so broad, her eyes so bright with excitement, I could see that any history between us had been utterly and beautifully eclipsed by a future that looked to her like a fairy tale.

A few months later, the company was sold to a competitor on the far side of the county. Most of the old management were fired, but they wanted to keep the couriers. They offered me a new bike, more routes, more distance, more long and winding roads to fly down, but I declined and took a job in the local sorting office instead where the work was dull and static, but the hours were easy and I could get home for half past six each night.

On Carrie's ninth birthday, Laura asked me to move back in.

'If nothing else, to save a bit of money,' she said. 'You're here most of the time anyway, and that flat may as well be storage for all you use the bloody thing.'

I said yes. Of course I said yes.

It became apparent to me how similar Laura and Carrie had become, or perhaps how similar they'd always been. Sometimes it felt as though Carrie was a part of Laura, an exploratory shoot, an independent growth. And I realised I had become happily dependent on having the two of them in my life. Two fixed points from which a sense of perspective can grow. Only Carrie wasn't a fixed point at all, she was two points of her own, one orbiting the other in a widening spiral, starting so close but stretching further and further with every iteration.

One night in early June, I heard movement downstairs. Laura had fallen asleep on my arm, and when I gently extricated myself from her, she shifted.

'What's that?' she said, too quiet, too drowsy to care about an answer.

'Probably the cats,' I said, pulling on my dressing gown, but she was back in her dream again and she didn't hear me.

It wasn't the cats. Carrie was in the lounge, tracing her hand over the family pictures on the bookshelves, the new ones I'd installed to carry all the books we'd collected over the years. *Tom's Midnight Garden, Charlie and the Chocolate Factory, Ballet Shoes, I am David*, so many more. I'd built the shelves a little too wide so the books were set back and the front edges had quickly filled with picture frames, birthday cards, letters and ornaments.

'Sorry it's been so long,' she said without turning around. 'Work has been stressful. Access to the machine has been difficult. It's...' Her sigh contained years. Those which had passed between us, those she could see ahead of her.

'...complicated,' I finished for her.

She shook her head.

'There you go again,' she said, 'skipping to the end before I can finish.'

Her hand stopped on a photograph of the beach where we'd been on holiday the previous summer. The small figure of Carrie ran across the sand, her delight frozen, a single moment of preserved and ageless joy.

Carrie smiled. 'I remember that holiday,' she said. 'We stayed in that cottage with the face on it.'

'Two windows for eyes,' I said. 'The door for a nose, the little garden fence like teeth.'

It had only been last summer, but the way she spoke of it was so wistful it sounded as though it was already in danger of being forgotten. It had been a tense holiday, I had only been invited to go at the last moment, but we played house together convincingly enough, and later I wondered if it had been a test by Laura to see if she wanted me around more.

'I thought it was a happy face,' Carrie said. 'I saw it smiling. It was welcoming and friendly. But you and Mum thought it was scary. I remember that, too.'

'We thought it was sad,' I said. 'Less to do with the face, more of a feeling in the place.'

'Well, if I can travel in time, who says others can't?' She turned back to me. 'Ghosts are time travellers too, after all.'

She smiled.

'You're looking well,' she said. 'The office job clearly suits you.'

'It's a warehouse, and I'm putting on weight,' I said. She didn't respond, so I tried something else. 'Is it time yet?' I said.

'So impatient. It'll be soon. Very soon.'

'Soon as in next week?' I said. 'Soon as in next year?'

She cast me a sideways glance.

'Where I'm from,' she said, 'they're not so dissimilar.'

She picked up the school photo, which had only arrived the previous month. A grey cardboard frame showing the whole of her class. She moved her finger over the line of plastic smiles.

'You know,' she said, 'I don't remember who most of these people are any more. It's terrible isn't it, how easily we push whole lives aside to make room for new faces?'

Her hand paused, and I craned across to look. A blond girl on the back row, a rabbit-in-the-headlights expression of alarm. Carrie traced the shape of her face with her fingertip, gentle as though she was afraid she might push the girl away.

'That's Leo,' I said. 'Surely you remember Leo.'

'I remember,' Carrie said. She set the picture back on the edge of the bookshelf where she'd found it, then she turned around and nearly jumped at me, taking me by surprise. She put her arms around me and held on tightly, burying her face in my chest.

We stood like that in silence for a time. I said nothing, content to just hold her there and let her speak first.

'Daddy,' she said.

5.

The phone call came while I was still at work. I was summoned to the office, where everyone looked serious and no one could make eye contact. I was told I could leave whenever I needed, so I went straight away, howling across town in the little family Punto, more recklessly than I ever had when I'd been on a bike.

Laura had been working that afternoon, so she was already at the hospital when I arrived. She saw me coming down the corridor, her eyes rimmed red, and had I any breath left to give it would have been hers if she'd asked me for it.

It had been an accident, we were told.

There was a new extension being built at the school, we'd both seen the letters that had been sent home: a new library, a new kitchen, a new play area. While the site was closed off, while dire warnings had been issued, Carrie and her friend, Leo, had taken it upon themselves to find a way inside.

Misadventure, they said. Little Miss Adventure and the daring things she does. Look at her climb to the top of the scaffold. Look at her slip, now watch her fall.

And now she lay, tiny and broken in the hospital bed that was far too big for her. Marshmallow white, it held her cupped, and I wondered if I envied the way it could effortlessly keep her secure. She was sleeping, one of the nurses told us, but we'd already been filled in on the extent of the damage. We'd seen the X-rays. We'd seen our daughter in cross-section, where there were gaps in the labyrinth of her where there should be no gaps at all.

How do you respond when your eleven-year-old daughter lies like that? I barely said anything. My only reference points were those public information films they used to screen when I was small. Overwrought reconstructions of terrible accidents, miniature horror movies warning children that the beautiful world they lived in wished them harm.

The doctor appeared in the doorway, an apologetic look on her face. Laura touched my arm and followed her, and as the door closed Carrie opened her eyes and looked directly at me, as though she'd been waiting for us to be alone all along.

'Why didn't you tell me to stop you?' I said. My worry had made me angry and I hated myself for it. 'Isn't that why you came back? Why didn't you tell me? I could have stopped this.'

She said, 'This wasn't why I came back.'

I sat heavily on the chair by the bed.

'Then I don't understand.' Sometimes, it felt as though that was all I ever said to her. 'You,' I said. 'I mean,' I said. 'You've hurt yourself,' I said. I started to say something else, but I couldn't bring myself to describe what had happened, because sometimes the past felt as clouded and obscure as the future.

'When I was a little girl,' Carrie said, her voice mechanical, dispassionate, 'there was an accident and I severely damaged my spine. Since then, I have no longer be able to walk unaided and I spent much of my childhood in a chair.'

It sounded like she was reciting the biography of someone I didn't know.

'It made me angry,' she said. 'And my anger made me fight. And if I didn't fight, I would never have been in a position to come back here to talk to you.'

She sounded so patient.

'This isn't what needed to change,' she said. 'I've seen the end of this story and *this* isn't what needed to be different.'

I stood up again, and when I stood over her, she looked like a porcelain ornament that had been dashed on the floor.

'Listen,' she said. 'Thirty years from now, there will be technology which will help me walk again. I'll walk on hills. In parks. I'll walk on beaches with the sand between my toes.'

Her smile wasn't quite convinced. It's not the same, she seemed to be saying, but I'm excited by it. The span of time felt insurmountable to me. She was eleven years old. She would have to live her life three more times—

'Don't misunderstand,' she said. 'This isn't me being a saint. This is me being selfish. This doesn't define me. It's hard. I work hard. But Leo? Leo will be alone. Leo will find it harder.'

The name sounds like a gear change. I stare at her; caught in the middle of a conversation I didn't appreciate we were having.

'You must tell her it wasn't her fault,' Carrie said. 'And you have to make her believe it. You have to tell her parents. You have to tell everyone. You have to tell me. Because otherwise, I won't forgive her until it's far too late.'

She stared at me then.

'Do you promise?' she said.

I shook my head.

'This is what you wanted me to do for you?' It seemed so small, so trivial. But her head ducked just a little in confirmation.

'But if you'd let me stop you—' I said.

'It doesn't work like that,' Carrie said. 'I told you. Two clues in different directions.'

She closed her eyes.

'I'm sorry,' she said. 'I'm tired. I'm so very tired. And it's all tangled up and strange and I don't know what's up and what's down any more and... I remember Mum and me always being close. But everything else is changing and I can't do this now.'

She smiled, then.

'But I'm happy, too,' she said. 'Because this time, you and me? Well, we had something to talk about, didn't we?'

I took her hand. It felt too cool, too light. It lay limp in my own palm like it had gone asleep ahead of her.

She smiled again. Her adult smile. It filled her for the briefest moment and then her eyes closed and I watched the expression fade. And there was the sleep-breathing sound, Carrie's sound, everyday Carrie. The rhythm so familiar to me now I could have identified it blindfold in a crowded room.

The door opened and Laura found me there. She came up to me and put her arm around my waist.

'I heard you talking,' she said. Then, incredulous, moved: 'Were you *praying*?'

It was a question that took me by surprise, but I nodded anyway because it didn't feel like a lie. After all, who do we pray to, if not the future we howl towards so recklessly? That long and winding road, along which we can as good as fly if we don't slow down to consider the way. We pray our path will be clear, we pray we do not travel alone.

Laura and I sat together by the bed. We held each other's hands and watched while our daughter slept in a way that frightened us both.

We will wait there together and we will be there together when she wakes.

WALKING TO
DOGGERLAND

(2)

The hospital was in King's Lynn and Ronnie took the coast road with the sort of clip even the local busses would have avoided. Her face was set, starkly delineated with a fury she found otherwise inexpressible. Whenever she tried to bring up the subject of Lulu and the house, she stalled, pausing to regroup.

'It's *just*,' she said.

'I *don't*,' she said.

'The *thing* is,' she said.

Penny stared at the farmland racing past the window: the patchwork fields, the braided rows of lavender, neatly combed across the shallow hills.

Eventually, Penny said: 'The dog I saw at the station, it reminded me of Oscar.'

'Who's Oscar?'

Penny glanced at her sister, and saw her concentration on the road ahead was fierce.

'Never mind,' she said. She smiled, even though she knew Ronnie wouldn't see it.

They got trapped behind a bus for a short while, and Veronica's impatience threatened to boil over. Penny studied the dusty advert on the back. It was old, advertising last season's pantomime on the Bryhanton Pier. The poster looked oddly archaic, as though the design of such things had remained static for the past few decades. The polished faces of celebrities Penny couldn't identify were superimposed on smaller, cartoonish bodies representing their characters. Even under the layer of scum from the bus's exhaust fumes, there was a bright energy to the arrangement that made Penny smile wider, although she wasn't sure why.

'What is it?' Ronnie said, shooting her a look.

'Oh, nothing,' Penny said. 'It's funny. It's just nice to be back.'

Ronnie grunted. 'Speak for yourself,' she said. The bus pulled into a layby and she took the opportunity to roar past.

> • <

Lulu was in the public ward on the third floor. They followed the directions the receptionist had given them, taking the lift next to the cafeteria, following the corridor all the way down and then turning sharp to the right.

As they approached the ward, Penny understood she had become hyperaware. She hadn't seen Lulu for so long it occurred to her that she might not recognise her at all. Lulu had never come to visit her at the order, and since she had left Lulu's plans had never aligned with Penny's holidays. The beds she passed were populated by old women, and even though she had to tell herself that Lulu wasn't *that* old, the truth was that perhaps she really was, perhaps they all were. The biggest age gap was between Lulu and Veronica and during the summers at Breakers, Lulu had been the responsible one, the sensible one, the substitute adult whose presence reassured them that everything would be alright. She'd always had a head start, perhaps, but the others were catching up. To hear Veronica talk of her boys made them sound as though they were still small, but they had grown up and older as well. They had both arrived late in her marriage to Stephen, desperate measures to plug a widening gap. Perhaps that was why Ronnie imagined they were younger than they were. Tom, the oldest, had moved out, he was living with his partner in some flat near Brixton; David, the youngest, was in his last year at university. Penny didn't remember what subject he was studying but she did remember thinking that it didn't quite sound like a real subject to her. Ronnie flustered about at home, chasing after their ghosts, the way she talked about them on the phone, anyone would think they all lived together in the same house.

Penny, always the youngest, was now past sixty herself, but having spent more than forty years in the order there was a sense she had only ever been in stasis. She didn't feel like an old woman, but the face she saw in the mirror had aged with no such dishonesty.

When they rounded the corner and passed the nurses' station, Lulu's presence was unmistakable. She was sitting up in the bed on the corridor side of the ward, staring down the passageway towards them as though she'd heard them coming. She looked older, certainly. She looked thinner than Penny remembered, too. Her hands, crossed in her lap, were clothed in softened skin, spotted with dark islands. To Penny's surprise, she looked like their mother. She had the same poised manner, the same flinty expression that indicated, without ambiguity, that her current situation was a waste of her time. If Penny hadn't seen the oxygen tank propped by the bed, she might have said her sister wore her age with dignity, but there was something shocking about the delicacy of her form; she looked as though she had been modelled from pipe-cleaners and tissue paper. Her grey hair long and bunched up about her shoulders by the pillow propped at her back. When she smiled, her face smiled with her, a whole underground map of smile lines, unearthed and excavated over the years; but her eyes remained as cool as Penny remembered.

'Well, look who we have here,' Lulu said. 'The virgin and the mother.'

'Lulu.' Veronica's tone was chiding, but Penny smiled.

'Hello, Lulu.'

'Louise, please.' Lulu's face crinkled in annoyance. 'Or Lou. I'm not twelve, for pity's sake. Lulu sounds like a twelve-year-old or a dancer in a bordello.'

'No one says "bordello" any more, *Lou*,' Veronica said, taking a seat on the edge of the bed.

'What would you know?' Lulu said. 'Ever been to one?' Her attention turned to Penny.

'Penelope.' She smiled. 'How's the outside world treating you?'

'I'm very well, thank you.'

'She has a job already,' Veronica said.

'Nothing exciting,' Penny said.

'Administration. For a library,' Veronica said. 'Apparently they love nuns. They do what they're told and keep to timetables. Amazing work ethic.'

'*Ex*-nun,' Lulu said. 'I'm glad you're out of there, Pen. I would have broken you out myself if I could have.'

Penny faltered. 'The door was always open,' she said, shrinking a little inside of herself when she heard how pompous the statement sounded.

'Well then,' Lulu said. She turned back to Veronica. 'And how are Tom and David?'

'They're fine.'

'And Stephen?'

Veronica stiffened. 'I'm sure he's fine,' she said.

'How are you, Louise?' Penny said. The eyes turned back to her and her confidence wilted a little.

'I'm also fine,' Lulu said. 'I was careless, that's all. They're just fussing, that's all they're doing.'

'They said you fell,' Veronica said.

Lulu scowled.

'I didn't fall,' she said. 'I just tried to get up and couldn't. Not the same thing.' She turned back to Penny, lowering her voice as though she was confiding in her. 'My hip. They say it just stopped responding as it should have. It's had its off days in the past but it usually rights itself. Not this time. I was just sitting on the sofa watching the television and... and then I couldn't get up again. I would have stayed there, but I really needed a piss. It's not serious. It's not that serious.'

Veronica fussed.

'You must take care of yourself, Louise,' she said, reaching for her big sister's hand. Lulu snatched it away.

'I daresay I'm fitter than you are,' she said. 'You're looking old, Ronnie. You look tired. The grey hair becomes you, but the running shoes really don't. You're really not fooling anyone, my dear. Shouldn't you have retired by now?'

'No.' The word was overextended and dangerously sharpened. 'You're the one who can't stand up any more.'

'Don't you dare patronise me,' Lulu said. 'I go for walks every day. Up to the headland, down to the beach and back.

The sea air's supposed to do you good, isn't it? Well, there's plenty of it here.'

'I've spoken to the doctor,' Veronica said. 'She told me all about your lungs.'

'They're fine. Good old set of bellows.'

'So what's that for, then?' She gestured at the oxygen tank, a plastic mask tucked over the valves like a party hat. 'You share your house with a whole city of black mould,' Veronica said. 'It's poison, Lulu. It's killing you.'

'Oh, don't be preposterous.'

'It's not preposterous. It's true. You're breathing through a tube, for pity's sake.'

'Only when I'm upset.' Lulu's eyes flickered with a familiar cruelty. 'You're not going to upset me, are you Veronica?'

Veronica flustered.

'I mean,' she said, 'that at your age—'

'I'm not that fucking old.'

'You're seventy-four and you can barely walk or breathe unaided.'

'That's nothing. People live longer these days, it's in all the papers. I could live to be a hundred and ten if I bloody well feel like it. I'll be damned if I don't outlive you both.'

Veronica took a breath.

'We've been in the house, Lulu,' she said. 'It's blindingly clear that you are not taking care of yourself.'

Lulu's expression dipped a fraction, then set hard.

'It's none of your business,' she said.

'Oh, for pity's sake. You're our sister—'

'And the house is *mine*. I bought it. It's mine. It's none of your business what I do with it.'

'You haven't done anything with it! It's rotting into itself!'

They lapsed into an abrupt silence, aware for the first time that there were others in the ward, and that their argument was not as private as they might have preferred.

Lulu turned to Penny. 'Do you see that woman in the bed opposite?' she said. Penny started to turn, but Lulu stopped her. 'Have a look when you leave. She was up all night last night demanding attention. And this morning, she just kept taking her clothes off. Sitting there on the bed staring at me with her tits out. The nurses had to keep coming in to cover her up.'

She grinned. 'This place is a madhouse. I don't think I'm in a hospital at all, they just dumped me in the sanatorium instead.'

Veronica coughed politely.

'Louise,' she said. 'In the house. The boiler isn't working.'

'I know.'

'Well then.'

'Well nothing. I've got someone coming to look at it.'

'And most of the light bulbs downstairs have blown and need to be—'

'I'm saving electricity. I'm saving the *planet*. You've got kids. You should thank me.'

'Louise.'

'It's my home, *Ronnie*. It's my business.'

'It's damp. You're breathing in spores night and day. It's not healthy. Louise, it's a squat.'

Lulu's expression softened.

'Did I ever tell you about the place where I lived when I was in Baltimore? Now *that* was a squat. I lived there with a man named Elroy. Tall and handsome, cheekbones you could hang your jacket on. He'd found a room above an old second-run movie theatre and I moved in with him for a time. It had been a flat once, but now it was storage and the current managers never seemed to realise it was there. They certainly didn't know we were. You got in through the fire escape in the alley alongside. Upstairs there was a big broad loft and no one ever went up there. We set up a mattress on the floor and we'd lie there, face to face, listening to the movies they played downstairs. Elroy had been there for so long he'd heard most of them before. They only seemed to have the same ones on rotation. He knew all the dialogue by heart and he'd mouth the words. We both would, after a while. That was one of the happiest times of my life, and to this day I still can only think of him with Bogart's voice.'

Veronica looked at her with a level expression.

'Wonderful,' she said. 'On top of everything else, now you sound senile.'

'Ronnie, do be a love and fuck off.'

'It must be lovely,' Penny said. The suddenness and sharpness of her voice surprising everyone, not least herself. 'It must be lovely living at Breakers all the time.' Her smile had always been warm and even Lulu seemed to thaw a little.

'It has its moments,' Lulu said. 'Although you've never been there during the winter. The coast can be bitter then. Grey skies, cold seas. It feels like being at the mercy of an anger you don't really understand. It feels a bit like being under siege.' She sighed. 'But there's an awe about it as well. I've always thought the sea is like a monster, and it's absurd to live complacently when you live next door to monsters.'

Veronica shook her head.

'I don't know why you bought it at all,' she said. 'It always seemed rather perverse to me.'

'Honey, you're a suburban mother with two point four children and a hatchback. Your concept of perversion is delightfully twee.'

Veronica bristled.

'Well it's alright for some, jetting off around the world—'

'If you hadn't been so eager to breed, you could have done exactly the same. I *asked* you to come with me to California that time. But no, you were more interested in handcuffing yourself to some quantity surveyor...'

'Lulu!'

'*Louise.* Honestly, Lulu sounds like the name of a wartime whore.'

'Stephen wasn't – *isn't* – a quantity surveyor.'

'He was a suffocating cunt and you were a fool to marry him.'

Veronica leapt to her feet as though she'd been electrocuted, her face was bright red, her eyes wide. Penny set a gentle hand on her shoulder. She was pretty sure Veronica had said worse about Stephen herself, but also knew how she considered it to be a privilege she had earned.

'Let's not all get upset,' Penny said. 'Please.'

Veronica and Lulu turned to her as though, in the heat of the exchange, they had both forgotten she was there. Lulu's smile was benign.

'Well look at that,' she said. 'Mum cop, nun cop. It's a different approach, I'll grant you.'

Veronica shook herself free of Penny's touch and resumed her position on the bed.

'I talked to the social worker,' she said.

'Saints preserve us,' Lulu said.

'Listen to me, because this is serious.' Veronica reached into her handbag and produced her notebook. 'If you can't get the boiler fixed, if you can't get the place cleaned up, they're not going to let you move home, because they'll say you can't take care of yourself alone there. You'll just make yourself worse.'

'Poppycock.'

The vehemence of the word set her coughing, which mostly served to exacerbate her anger. Veronica sighed.

'I'm serious, Lulu. If you can't make that house fit for living in, they'll put you in care and sell Breakers to pay for the costs. Do you have the number of someone I can call about the boiler?'

Lulu stared at her a long time before exhaling a breath theatrically.

'There's a phone book in the cabinet in the hall,' she said. 'A man named Richard... Glider? Gilder? Something beginning with G. He's a handyman but he knows tradesmen in the town.'

'I'll call him. You should also probably get someone to look at the roof. Upstairs is very damp.'

'It's the chimney,' Lulu said. 'Richard came round to look at it. There was a quote somewhere. Probably in the drawer in the living room with the other paperwork.'

Veronica spread her hands.

'Well? What happened?'

'I put it aside until I could afford it.'

'Why couldn't you afford it? What about all your photographs? The exhibitions? You were living like you were raking it in. I know how much you inherited from Father. You got more than either of us.'

Lulu shrugged. 'I bought a house.'

'It didn't cost that much, surely.'

'And a car.'

'But, still.'

'And quite a lot of wine.'

'Lulu.'

'And cocaine isn't cheap.'

Veronica stared at her.

'You don't have any money? No savings?'

'I have a pension, of a sort. It tides me over. Keeps me in soup.'

'My god,' Veronica said. 'I'm only thankful Mother and Father aren't around to see what you've become.'

'Oh.' Lulu's offhand tone was calibrated to be careless. 'I don't think they'd really care,' she said.

Veronica shook her head with vehemence.

'That's absolutely not true,' she said.

Lulu looked amused.

'Oh Ronnie, you bloody fool,' she said. 'Our mother was too busy with her bloody *physics* and our father, bless him, was terrified of her. Little wonder! She was interested in solving the world as a whole, not piece by piece. Our reality was never the one she was interested in. The longer I live, the more I think the world was a monster to her. Can you imagine how celebrated she'd be now if she'd been a man? They'd name streets in London after her. I don't blame her for any of it, but whichever way you cut it, the three of us were little more than different samples in one of her experiments.'

'Lulu!'

'Oh, don't look at me like that. You know it's true. I mean, the early years when she came here too? They were nice, they really were, but you could see how distracted she was. How impatient she was to get back. You probably don't even remember that. Even when I was six, she just seemed terribly disappointed that I couldn't discuss wave theory with her.'

She paused to regroup. Patiently regaining control of her breathing. When she spoke again, she was quieter, huskier, but no less intense.

'Every term they'd ship us off to The Immaculate Heart,' she said. 'Because that's where *she* was sent when she was a child. Every summer they sent us here, because that's where *she* went. She ditched us with Old Widow Battleaxe to play the role of whatever monster kept her in check as a girl. I told you, I don't judge her for it, but it's transparent, isn't it? We're her *Boys From fucking Brazil*.'

'Lulu that's tasteless. Stop.'

'Oh, don't be obtuse. You've heard the same stories I have.'

'Enough. I don't want to hear any more.'

'And poor old Daddy was nothing but a lab assistant really, wasn't he?'

'Oh, good heavens. Penny. Make her stop. For the love of—'

'The only thing he really contributed was his Catholicism. *Her* daddy had been devout, remember, but she had tossed it all away as soon as she could. Do you think she advertised in the papers for him? Poor man, he didn't stand a chance did he? With only his little foolish god to fall back on.'

She shot a glance at Penny.

'No offence,' she said.

'None taken,' Penny said.

'But Mother?' Lulu raced onwards. 'You know what she was studying. You were subjected to the same interrogations as I was. Taking little notes. Looking at us over the top of her glasses. Did you know they have her archive in Massachusetts? They do. I went to visit. In all those papers, do you know how she describes motherhood? *An imperfect laboratory*, she calls it. *An imperfect laboratory existing under chaotic conditions.* That's it. That's all she says! But we're all in there. Subjects L, V and P. We're just diverging lines on her silly little graphs. I'm not joking.'

'I'm not listening to any more of this.' Ronnie certainly looked flustered.

'Don't tell me you've never thought it yourself,' Lulu said. 'If it wasn't for the age difference between us, we could be twins. *Triplets.*'

'Oh! Lulu! This is absurd.'

'Ronnie.'

'Veronica,' Veronica said, her tone cold. 'My name is Veronica.'

Lulu sat back in the bed, a small smile on her face.

'Veronica,' she said. 'I'm sorry.'

Veronica was on her feet again.

'I think that's enough for this evening,' she said. 'We'll be back tomorrow. Perhaps. Come on, Penny.'

She elbowed past and disappeared into the corridor.

Penny's smile was small.

'It was lovely seeing you again, Louise,' she said.

'You too, Penelope.'

Penny stepped closer and leaned in to hug her older sister. She felt Lulu stiffen at her touch. She felt brittle and unmoving, as though she was made entirely of knots and straight lines. She smelled of carbolic soap and toothpaste. Penny held her until she softened fractionally in her arms.

'Sleep well,' Penny said, breaking away, smiling wider. 'God bless.'

Lulu smiled back, a warmth in her eyes, a viscous lens that might have been the bud of a tear. Her voice was small when she spoke, but in a curious way it followed Penny down the corridor and out into the night.

'God bless,' she said. 'God bless.'

> • <

They drove back mostly in silence.

Veronica had been waiting for Penny in the car, staring straight ahead. Only once her sister had closed the door and connected her seat belt did she say anything at all.

'It's not true,' she said. 'What she said, it isn't true.'

Penny nodded. She wasn't sure which part of Lulu's screed had upset Veronica the most.

'I don't believe she ever didn't care,' Penny said.

Veronica wouldn't meet her eyes.

'No.'

Penny's memory of her parents had always felt faintly compromised. All three of the sisters had boarded at The Immaculate Heart convent school, although Lulu had been so far ahead of them they barely saw her on the premises. The summers had been spent in Bryhanton, where Mrs Kaye was just one of a series of substitute guardians. It was perhaps no surprise, therefore, that her memory felt as though it had been edited and revised.

When she thought of her father, she thought of stilted, suited figures in black-and-white films. Figures that walked a little too fast, a little too strangely, because the films never ran at the correct speed. *Always in a hurry to be anywhere else.* That sounded about right. She recalled the distance of him more than anything else. The faint look of panic in his eyes when he was trapped by her attention. Despite what Lulu had said, their father's Catholicism had never been a defining aspect so much as a gently pencilled-in shade. For a time, she had thought of him as the attentive parent during her childhood, and it was only later that she realised her experience of him had been different from that of Lulu or Ronnie. To Lulu, he had barely been there at all. To Ronnie, he had been silent and ghostly. Penny's memories were different. There had been affection there, she was sure of it. A quiet sadness to him as he dressed the grazes on her knee, a sturdy hand on her shoulder when he collected her from school. He attended church diligently as though it was a penance, and it was he who took her to her first confession. She remembered them reciting the act of contrition together by rote as they walked down the road to St Theresa's.

She was fifteen when he died, and she had never really been told the circumstances that claimed him. Lulu and Ronnie barely missed him, and to Penny, the absence he had left felt like a privilege she didn't quite deserve. He had died, she was informed, and now she should run along and do something else. She did as she was told. She hadn't wanted to make a scene.

Their mother had been a formidable woman on her own terms, and considered together, this permitted their father to fade further into the background, an act that suited him. It was perhaps no wonder he was wary of his daughters, if he imagined they might all grow up to fill her shadow. Penny often wondered if he looked at them and saw her instead. Their mother had spent most of her life engaged in a personal war, first for the right to belong in the field in which she thrived, and then for the right to be recognised within it. She began as a fresh-faced bluestocking in Cambridge, a young woman permitted to study but not graduate. But she learned to read the tides of the early twentieth century and she moved with them, collecting qualifications from more liberal institutions until her arsenal was unstoppable enough to intimidate the unshiftable dustiness of the male academics.

'There is another world,' she had been quoted as saying in one of her speeches from the later years of her career, 'in which every door I encountered and found closed was open. *That* world looks upon this one as an experienced adult does upon a toddler still learning to walk.'

She certainly had an imposing way about her, but her parenting philosophy was one of calculated distance. In a particularly English way, she assumed they would each find their own places in the world without her interference. She'd had to make do and so would they.

She had visited Penny twice during her time in the order. The first time, Penny remembered her features broken into a grid of graph paper squares by the wrought-iron screen between them, the severe age lines drawing functions across imagined axes. The meeting had been awkward, as though she could barely see her youngest daughter beneath the uniform she had chosen on her own terms. She questioned Penny briskly, with a distant and analytical air.

'What was the point that brought you here?' she said.

Penny didn't understand.

'What decision did you make that brought you to this point?' her mother said.

'I came to see you,' Penny said. 'You came to visit.'

'But at which *point* did you make that decision? When did you know I was coming?'

'Yesterday. When we received your letter.'

'And did you decide you would agree to see me then?'

'Yes. Yes, I think so.'

'Might you have chosen not to see me?'

Penny stared at her through the grille.

'I don't know,' she said.

'Did you entertain that thought?'

'I don't know. Maybe I did? I don't remember. I don't think I did.'

'Would you have decided that then, or later? Between receiving the letter and stepping through that door, was there a point when you made that decision?'

'I don't know. I'm sorry.'

'What might you have done instead?'

'Instead of seeing you?'

'Instead of seeing me.'

'I don't know. Mother. Please.'

Her mother leaned forward in her chair.

'What might you have done?' she said.

Penny shook her head.

'I don't know,' she said. 'I might have said a prayer. For both of us.'

Her mother nodded, her smile softening.

'Does God make your choices for you?' she said.

The interview went on for another hour. She questioned the choices Penny had made during her life, the choices that might have led her not just to her current position in the building, but to her current self. Penny wouldn't have called it an interrogation, but she saw her mother take notes in a small notebook, and then she checked her watch and explained she had to go.

It transpired that she had a conference in Liverpool and that had come first; her daughter being in the same city was little more than an expedient detail. In return, Penny lost track of her mother's own commitments, something the confines of the order made blessedly simple to achieve.

Her mother had comfortably outlived her father, and when she died, Penny had been given a day to attend her funeral in a small church outside Oxford. For various reasons she didn't question, neither Lulu nor Veronica had been able to attend and Penny had arrived alone, an inadvertent ambassador for her mother's legacy.

The journey to Oxford was one of the first times Penny had been outside the order since she became a novice. The outside world seemed to have grown bigger, busier and noisier in her absence. The people on the train platform seemed closer to her, so close she could smell the breath of them. She spent the whole train journey clutching her train ticket in her hand until it warped and wouldn't work in the ticket gate.

Antonia Landry's death drew quite the crowd, buoyed by newspaper columns listing her achievements in a way they had pointedly failed to do while she was alive. Even though she was the only relative in attendance, Penny gave up her seat in the front pew and stood near the back instead, hiding within the anonymity her habit granted her.

She thought of her father. Of the funeral she hadn't been permitted to attend. She found herself searching the faces of the men in the room, in case, for some reason, it had all been a mistake and he was there after all. The idea seemed less far-fetched, but still distasteful. She bowed her head and prayed silently for forgiveness or understanding or both.

There were speeches from academics, student representatives, politicians and writers. The more they spoke, the more Penny felt as though her presence was a betrayal of whatever it was her mother had stood for. She felt unkind eyes seeking her out and sizing her up. She heard confident discussion that her mother had never had children at all, only an ongoing experiment with other Antonias from other worlds, other selves who had lived in different branches of the real, but Penny had no wish to get involved in such speculation.

She thought of the choices she had made that brought her to that very point. Tracing back the knots of causality, the choke-points and straight lines on the map her mother had imagined of the world. The last time she had seen her mother had been a couple of weeks ago. Antonia Landry had known she was dying and she said so. She looked older, wasted, as though the gap between her visits had been decades rather than years. This time, she didn't ask Penny questions.

'I had a friend,' she said. 'When I knew her, she was wild. Adventurous. She was a lot of fun to be with. And then one day, she was involved in a car accident. She wasn't injured, it was miraculous – if you'll forgive the term. The other car wasn't so lucky. Three people died. A father, his six-year-old son, and a friend of the family. It wasn't my friend's fault. It was just an accident. Nothing more. Something that came out of the blue. A lightning bolt from the heavens.

'She was never the same. She never drove again. She rarely went outside at all. She had been shaken so categorically that her worldview was reduced to a single, terrified moment.

'She told me it was as though she had been climbing a sheer cliff face. And she had stumbled, clung on by her fingertips, swinging there, a tiny figure on a blank wall. And she had looked down. And there was that moment of vertigo, the realisation of how far she had come, how much she had to lose if she fell.

'We'd worked together before. She knew that in one world, in many worlds, she had been the one who died. It was only the toss of the coin that decided she was in a world where she might survive.'

She had fallen into a silence then, one that Penny had no wish to break with a word of her own. She waited instead, and her mother continued.

'There's comfort, I suppose,' she said. 'In knowing that as you become old and tired on that cliff face, some version of you will keep going. But do any of us reach the top? Do any of us get to do that? Or is there no top to this cliff? Does everyone fall in the end?'

By the time Penny fled her mother's funeral, she already felt as though she had faded to invisibility. She decided to take an earlier train, a decision that surprised her with how right it felt. It was a moment that gave her a curious kind of confidence, and as she stood alone on the platform it crossed her mind that she could take any train, anywhere. It was the same tug she had felt as she sat on Bunker's Hill as a child, suddenly realising she could run away if she chose to.

She didn't take a different train. She didn't run away. It was a relief, in a sense, to be back in the familiar blankness of her cell.

There was less traffic on the way back to Stove Causeway, the light from the headlights formed a goldfish-bowl window on the world. A ragged hole cut out of black construction paper. Darkness blinkered everything else, and for a moment Penny could imagine that was all there was. A flickering film projection of what lay before them, a headlong race of roadside imagery lit by torchlight. It was the sort of motion picture that deserved a whirling organ score, and her imagination – in a whimsical mood – supplied something carnivalesque and carefree.

When they reached the Pinnerman, the figure emerged out of the shadows like a phantom and the shadows cast by the headlights made his grin wider, his eyes emptier. The lights were unsparing on the figure and Penny saw more clearly how ruined the statue looked. His face was cracked and his body was missing whole plate sections, exposing a skeleton of iron lattice beneath. But his smile was still broad as Veronica steered past him, and the way shadows swooped across his face made him look as though he was winking impishly at them.

Wallasey Road was like a tunnel in the dark. The headlights made the tree branches circular, reaching in and out of their peripheral vision, and at the end, the sea was obvious only by the absence of anything else. The lights made no dent in it from the road. It was a deeper darkness torn free from the rich velvet of the sky.

Veronica parked abruptly outside the Royal Coronation Guest House as though she had forgotten it was their destination all along.

'This is us,' she said.

Penny had never been inside the Corrie before. It had been a fixture of her memory of the Stove Causeway, a bright and cheerful little place with colourfully rendered walls, populated by a rotation of summer guests, some of whom the sisters would befriend, some of whom they'd avoid. Living in Breakers for six weeks each year sometimes made her feel as though she was a local. Not of the town, but of the Stove itself, the brief strip of buildings she could see when she stood with her feet in the lacework fringe of surf and turned back to see which windows were watching her. Those who stayed in the guest house were tourists and interlopers, each lasting for one week, maybe two, before vanishing again. The children they met marvelled at the fact that the sisters could stay so long each year, and in return each of the girls, Penny included, relished the perception of authority it granted them. They were the ones who knew the best places to run down the beach, the times of the tides, the best trees to climb on the headland path. They knew about the Pinnerman and his history, they could trace the stronger sea currents on the tourist map in the brochure.

'If you swim out, swim to the left,' they said. 'Go to the right and the riptides will take you all the way out to sea.'

It wasn't true, not really, but as the summers came and went they said it often enough that it had become more authentic than it was ever meant to be.

Veronica had booked two rooms, the two on the first floor, both overlooking the sea.

'Off season,' she said by way of explanation once they'd lugged their bags up the narrow stairs. 'They're just happy to have us.'

The rooms were neat, if slightly fussy, as if a carefully calculated tweeness had been employed to judge every design and furnishing decision. An embroidered sampler hung on the door in each room, detailing a lengthy list of regulations that guests were requested to adhere to. These ranged from the traditional ('No smoking'), to the oddly specific ('Do not wear Doc Marten footwear on the rug or in the en suite').

There wasn't anywhere nearby to eat on the Stove. Veronica wasn't in the mood to drive back to town, but had been blessed with the foresight to purchase a couple of microwave meals from the petrol station on her way over. The woman on the reception desk refused to let them use the guest house's kitchen, and had looked scandalised to be asked, so they retreated to Breakers instead, where the cold, gloomy dampness seemed to have consolidated during their absence.

While Veronica cleaned the microwave as best she could, Penny moved the working light bulb from the hallway so it hung in the kitchen instead, and later, while the meals were warmed according to the instructions, they sat together in the dining room, unconsciously taking their allotted seats at the table they had occupied during those long summer weeks.

They huddled in their winter coats, forking rubbery, lukewarm spaghetti carbonara into their faces from the plastic trays, warped and puckered by the microwave.

'I never thought I would miss Mrs Kaye's cooking,' Veronica said.

It might have been the earthy, damp smell of the house, but the food tasted alien and tainted. Penny finished her meal dutifully but Veronica gave up halfway through.

'Well, this is miserable,' she said, spinning the fork across the tabletop so it left whorls of sauce across the surface.

She ditched the container in the bin, and while Penny found a cloth to polish the table with, Veronica occupied herself opening each cupboard in turn, clucking her tongue.

'Here we are,' she said. 'This is more like it.'

She reached into the cupboard by the back door and retrieved a pair of wine bottles, both unopened.

'She wasn't kidding when she said she spent most of her money on wine.' She held them both up to Penny. 'Red or white?'

Penny shook her head. 'I don't really…' She stalled.

Shrugging, Veronica regarded the two bottles she'd found, judging them both without enthusiasm. She replaced the white one, closing the cupboard and rooting around in the drawer for a corkscrew.

'Let's get out of here,' she said.

Penny assumed they were going back to the guest house, but Veronica hesitated outside the door and leaned back to look up at the sky.

'Do you want to go to the beach?' she said.

'The beach?'

Veronica shrugged.

'It's a nice night. We could sit on the beach. Like we used to. Remember when we'd sneak out past Mrs Kaye's room and go out on the beach at night?' She hefted the bottle towards the door. 'Besides, I want a drink, and I don't want to incur the wrath of chintz Big Brother.'

Penny nodded in agreement, before realising it was too dark to be seen.

'Okay,' she said. 'That would be nice.'

The first few drops of rain fell before they could reach the dunes. First a drop landing on the back of Penny's hand, then one on her cheek, then, the tip of her ear. The drops felt cool and electric; they felt clean, bracing.

'Oh for fuck's sake,' Veronica said. She stared upwards, her face contorted. She turned back to Penny.

'We could go to the beach anyway,' she said. 'It'll probably pass soon enough.'

The dark sky was clogged with clouds, choking out the stars and turning the moon into a faint smear of saffron. The rain intensified with such ferocity that Penny, soaked through, found herself laughing.

She saw her sister's shoulders fall in defeat.

'*Fine*,' Veronica said.

The reception desk at the Corrie was mercifully empty, so there was no one to see the two drenched figures pick their way up the staircase. They parted company on the landing.

'Well,' Penny said. 'Goodnight then.'

Veronica nodded.

'I'll see you,' she said.

Alone in her room, Penny stripped out of her wet clothes. She hung her skirt and blouse over the slim radiators under the window. In the en suite, she turned the shower on and let it run until the water was hot and generous, filling the brittle cold of the room with a density of steam.

It was just another thing that she had started to take for granted. There had been no showers in the order, and it was only on rare occasions that there was any hot water. The washroom at the order was a small, square cell just off the main courtyard. There had been a tap at waist level on the wall and a drain in the concrete floor. A small barred window high up in the wall let in the seasons without discrimination, augmenting the running tap with a flurry of snow or a mist of rain. Her definition of luxury in those days had been a plastic bucket big enough for her to stand in. She still remembered how the sense of the water pooling around her ankles had felt glorious and unearned. When she had closed her eyes, she felt like she was a child again, the clean, sharp chill of the sea climbing at her ankles, her chilling blood fooling her into believing it was becoming warmer.

Outside the order was another world. Technology and expectation had progressed so swiftly that on some days she felt as though she had fallen into the pages of *The Eagle*. In the bathroom at the Corrie, she closed her eyes and plunged her head under the showerhead, whispering a simple prayer of thanks; of compassion to those who weren't as lucky as she had found herself to be. She felt the water spill through her, wrapping her in its warmth and filling her.

Her shower was brief and efficient. If her time at St Bernadette's had taught her anything, it was not to be wasteful. She turned off the water firmly and dried herself. A white towelling dressing gown was hung on the back of the door, and once she had pulled on her nightdress, she retrieved it and slipped it on. There was something delightful about the weight and softness of it. It felt as though the warmth of the shower was still inside her and the dressing gown was insulating it, keeping it there. She could feel the heat of it making her face turn pink.

She sat on the edge of the bed and prayed silently for a moment or two. She didn't kneel any longer, the cartilage in her knees had mostly fractured over the years. Sitting and praying still felt like cheating, but she told herself it was a minor transgression, more so now than it might have been before.

When she was done, she settled on the bed and opened the book she had taken from Lulu's house.

The Infinite Worlds of Antonia Landry.

The damp had made some of the pages unreadable, so the introduction was harder work than it should have been. It discussed her mother's academic work and published papers with an unguarded enthusiasm. It made an effort to view the work in a feminist context, citing Antonia's struggle to find acceptance in her field, her famous speech to the Royal Society, and it revelled in the scope her theories potentially afforded. It descended quickly into technical details which were made more obscure by the islands of mould obscuring the text.

Penny persevered for a few pages, before turning to the block of photographs that formed the book's middle section. Most were quite poor quality, and some seemed to be of questionable relevance. There was a photograph of her mother at a black-tie function, surrounded by uncomfortable men with glistening faces; there was a portrait of her, taken much later in her life, sitting in the armchair in her study, looking quite the prim academic. There were establishing shots of buildings she had worked in and various diagrams and models she had been responsible for. The last picture, occupying a full page, reprised the shot from the cover of the book. Penny had seen the picture maybe a hundred times as she was growing up, but unlike the cover, unlike almost all the versions of the photograph she could remember in all their various contexts, this version was uncropped and showed the picture in its entirety. In it, her mother was standing on the beach on Stove Causeway. She was wearing a pair of woollen trousers, heavy-looking boots and an overcoat that was a little too big for her. At her feet there was a dog, a Labrador, its eyes half closed, its tongue lolling as though it had been out for a particularly satisfying run.

Penny blinked in surprise. She must have seen the complete picture before. Surely she had. And yet here, there was something unfamiliar about it, something new and inexplicable.

A tap at the door startled her.

Veronica was there, still dressed and rain-sodden, the bottle of wine in one hand, a glass tumbler in the other. Veronica looked her up and down.

'It's not even ten,' she said. 'Are you going to bed?'

'I just had a shower,' Penny said. 'The rain.'

'Right.' Veronica elbowed her way into the room, closing the door behind her with a careless kick.

'Get your glass. There should be one in the bathroom.'

'I don't really drink,' Penny said. 'I'm sorry.'

Veronica sighed.

'Tonight of all nights, I'm not drinking on my own,' she said. 'I'll pour you an inch and you can bloody well pretend. And if you do drink it, I won't tell anyone. You can always clean your teeth again. It's not the end of the world.'

Penny demurred. She gathered up her clothes from the radiator and transferred them to the towel rail in the bathroom, retrieving the glass from the sink while she was there.

Veronica had made herself at home when she returned to the bedroom. She had taken up residence in the armchair beside the window and had already opened the bottle with a dull pop.

'Give,' she said, gesturing with a hand, opening and closing until Penny planted the glass in it. She filled both glasses and passed one back, holding up her own in a toast. 'To... I don't know.'

'Breakers?' Penny said and Veronica grimaced.

'Breakers,' she said. 'May it burn down in an insurance fire.' She clinked her glass against Penny's and took a sip. Her expression softening as she deflated into the armchair. 'I will say one thing about our older sister,' she said, holding up her glass. 'She has *very* good taste in wine she can't afford.'

Penny sat on the edge of the bed, holding her own glass in both hands.

Veronica closed her eyes as though she was suffering a migraine.

'God,' she said, abruptly. 'The stupid woman.'

She opened her eyes and looked directly at Penny.

'Lulu, I mean, obviously.' She shook her head. 'I don't know what she was thinking. I really don't. It's like she's just waiting there for us to tell her we're going to take care of it for her, and I'm not going to. I'm just not. And she wouldn't be grateful if I did. She'd still be as rude as you like. God. It sounds so cold of me, but I just can't. I'm too old. The boys have only just left, I want some time to myself, you know? God.'

She drank again, and Penny could see how the wine calmed her a little, how it helped her settle deeper into the chair.

'I'm not going to invite her to stay at mine,' she said again. There was something about her tone that reminded Penny of Mrs Kaye, that sense that everything she said was an attempt to head off an argument that hadn't yet been instigated.

She shook her head again as though she might clear it.

'I don't know why she'd talk like that.'

'She was upset,' Penny said. 'She's always been a bit prickly when she gets upset.'

Veronica studied her, her expression arch.

'You know,' she said, 'for someone who abdicated themselves from society for forty-odd years, you seem to think you know an awful lot about people.'

'I'm sorry, I just—'

'No.' Veronica set down her glass and flapped her hand at Penny briskly. 'I'm sorry. I didn't mean it that way.' She flailed her hands, a little stunted shrug. 'I'm tired. I'm upset as well. Upset by what she's done to Breakers. It's so sad. It's irresponsible. It's really not fair. But mostly, I'm just tired. I'm tired of being the responsible one. The *mother*. You know? As though after our childhood, *one* of us had to show it could be done properly.'

Her shoulders fell again.

'God,' she said again and reached for the glass.

Penny set her own glass down and reached out to touch Veronica's knee.

'You're a good mother,' she said. 'The boys think the world of you.'

'I know, I know,' Veronica said. 'They're not boys any more, are they? It's so strange to think of them as *men*, but they have been for years now. I love them both. It's hard to describe, it's... enormous. It grows out of you until it's... it's just impossible. I mean, they can both be little shits at times, but that's just part of how it works.'

She looked thoughtful.

'Sometimes it feels like... the *gravity* is all too much,' she said. 'It's like a science fiction movie, like a bad dream. You try to move onwards, but this black hole is just slowly dragging you back and back. The kids I teach are always the same age. Every year, they're preparing for their exams. The same questions, the same answers. As though the A-Level Physics class crawls along in its own slower time stream. Over and over, it's the same, always the same. I thought that Stephen was a way forward, if you can believe it. I always imagined that once you left school there were these stepping stones that led you onwards. A job, a marriage, a house, a kid, a dog. It was like one of those board games. Roll the dice, move your counter. One, two, three...

'But then my job was flaky. Stephen was too obsessed by his own work, it blinkered out everything else. I loved the boys, but it was just me looking after them and I was exhausted. The dog got hit by a car on the road and I had to bury it in the garden while the kids screamed behind the French windows. I called Stephen because I needed to cry at *someone* but... It was all such a farce. Like a sitcom. *Terry and June*. Only darker, because Terry and June never speak to each other any more, because June used to put the kids to bed then lie in bed pretending to be asleep when Terry got home because she couldn't bear to put on that happy mask he used to like.

'I thought it would be easier once we got divorced. I thought it would be easier when the boys left home. I thought, *finally!* Enough with the distractions! I can roll the dice again and move forwards, but it's not the same game any more. It's like someone changed the rules when I wasn't looking.

'And I kept thinking, but I'm doing the right thing. I'm doing the thing you're supposed to do. This is supposed to be the life that's expected of us. The car in the garage, the dog under the lawn, the kids getting older, unrulier, moving out completely. It all seems to work in the house across the street. It all seems to work on the TV, in adverts, in books, in the Hollywood movies you sit through at the cinema. Why the fuck doesn't it work for me? What did I do wrong?'

'You didn't do anything wrong,' Penny said.

Veronica looked at her directly.

'I envied you,' she said. 'You and Lulu. Your life seemed so simple, hers so exciting. Mine felt so… static. I was the one who had abdicated myself from life rather than progressing, not you.'

'I don't think that's true, Ronnie.'

'I know. I know. It's stupid, I'm sorry. It's just that… I feel like I spent most of my life wanting a bit of space, wanting desperately to be on my own again. And then everyone leaves and it's the worst thing I can imagine.'

She sighed.

'Like Lulu did,' she said. 'Like you did.'

Penny reached forward and took her hand.

'We didn't leave you, Ronnie,' she said. 'We were always there.'

Veronica didn't seem to have heard.

'And when I look in the mirror,' she said, 'I see this old woman staring back and I think to myself, where did she come from? How did I let that happen? The kids in school treat you differently. They don't understand ageing, not really. Everyone is old to them. Ask them what old is and they'll say *thirty* or *forty*. But you see yourself shifting from *mother* to *grandmother* like you're stuck on a conveyor belt. Already over the hill and I don't even remember climbing the blessed thing. And then, I'd keep getting postcards from Lulu. And photographs. Here she is on a beach, here she is on a yacht, a desert, a market, a mountain...'

She tailed off, her eyes unfocused. She downed the rest of her wine and topped up her glass.

'Did I tell you about Gavin?' she said.

Penny shook her head.

'I must be drunk, otherwise I'd not tell you even now. Gavin's my good news,' Ronnie said. 'I'm sorry, I didn't mean to sound all maudlin. This always happens when I drink wine. I should really stop it.'

'Who's Gavin?'

'It's still early days. He's older than I am, for Christ's sake. It's silly really.'

'It's not.'

'Oh, but it is. I feel quite foolish around him. And he's just... ordinary, really, but he's sweet. Old-fashioned sweet, but good old-fashioned. He's a widower, he lives a few streets over. We were always in nodding acquaintance, but then. Someone introduced us a good while back. I think he was just lonely. Hiring himself to cut people's lawns, do a bit of gardening and so on. I... I don't know.'

Maybe it was the wine, or maybe she was blushing.

'It's a small thing. Delicate. It's like we're teenagers again and we're tripping over each other in embarrassment.' She smiled. 'He's *courting* me, Penny. Can you imagine? I didn't even know people did that any more, I didn't even know that was what I wanted. I…' She cleared her throat.

'And then there's the boys.' She smiled. 'Insurance. I never really understood it until they both came into focus. But now I see it more clearly. You invest in your future. You gamble. Go all in. I put everything I had into those two lads to keep forging ahead for all of us. Lighting the way. It takes time and it's heartbreaking when they finally move on past you. But it's wonderful too, because maybe, once in a while, they'll turn back and see us, and smile. And my god, that's worth everything, Penny. Everything.'

A flicker of a smile played over her face.

'And I shouldn't be telling you this either, but Tom and his girlfriend Megan are expecting in… when was it? June, I think.'

'Oh! Congratulations!'

Ronnie flapped her hand as though she were putting out a fire.

'It's ridiculous really,' she said. 'They're so young. Stephen and I were so careful, we took so long. But… they didn't plan it. I don't know if they're ready or how they're going to be able to afford it. They don't even own a…' She laughed darkly. 'Oh listen to me, what do I know? Anyway, it does look like I'll be doing most of the childcare for the first few years, so that'll be my retirement. How funny, after all this time doing what I believed was the right thing wrongly, here I am with a house, a bloke and a kid after all. All those things I thought I wanted, just not the ones I planned for.'

She raised her glass ruefully.

'And then there's you,' she said, looking up to stare at her younger sister. 'What possessed you?'

'I don't understand, I'm sorry.'

'Don't say you're sorry. What possessed you to join that order? That convent? I never did understand. Lulu was just Lulu, of course she was never going to settle down; the kids were always going to move out eventually, even Steve being Steve was sort of inevitable. But you? You took us all by surprise.'

Penny smiled. She looked down at the floor, feeling her cheeks pinkening a little. She had never been good with attention, and even alone in the room with Veronica, dressed in her nightgown and the borrowed dressing gown, she felt exposed and uncomfortable. The question was one she had considered herself, of course, one she had built up and torn down a thousand times. From the perspective of innocence, from the perspective of experience, she questioned herself because the answer had always remained so uncertain.

'It just made sense to me,' she said eventually, answering Veronica's question as truthfully as she was able.

Her sister shook her head.

'You were too young,' she said. 'You had your whole life ahead of you. It was that school, wasn't it? I could murder our mother for leaving each of us there. I really could.'

'It was a choice I made,' Penny said. 'Me alone. I don't regret it, even now.'

'But the Carmelites, Penny.' Veronica looked momentarily deflated. 'Why them? If you absolutely had to join an order, why not the ones at the school? The Dominicans? Just something less severe. Somewhere else where you could have at least gone outside.'

'Anything else would have felt like a half-measure,' Penny said. 'Different orders represent different branches of the faith. My research was diligent, I promise.'

'It was absurd.' Veronica shook her head. 'Stephen considered putting the boys into a boarding school, but I wouldn't have it. Not at all. I wish I could have stopped you. It was such a waste.'

'No,' Penny said. 'And it had nothing to do with the school. I was away from that then. College, remember. And I would see them sometimes. The nuns walking down from the Catholic cathedral. They'd walk together and there was something beautiful about the way they moved. Later, I learned that the building across the road from my dormitory was home to another order. Also Catholic, but not the same one. This one was a closed order. Recluses. And I would hang by my window, hoping I might see them. They were like a ghost story. I knew they were there, I believed fervently, but… I missed lectures doing that, if you can believe it. It was something to fixate on and I couldn't look away.

'And… Dad. You know? It was something we had in common. Something I don't think you and Lulu had.

'And then one day, I summoned up the courage to knock on the door. They didn't open it, of course. So I found the local convent school and asked them to help me set up an introduction. We met and we discussed my vocation. I always thought that would be so hard, that I would have to do so much to prove myself, but… it was easier than I thought it might be. And they were just people after all, but they were kind. They were so kind. And I spent more and more time there. I agreed to become a novice with them. And then…'

She spread her arms, she shrugged.

'You were so young,' Veronica said again. 'They should never have let you commit yourself so fully. That was unkind of them.'

Penny shook her head.

'It wasn't like that at all,' she said. 'It *was* hard, but it was hard-earned. Our vow was one of poverty, isolation, silence. Do you remember when we used to have those retreats at The Immaculate Heart? I always found those so peaceful. Just me, God and prayer. Meditation. It was like that. It was never easy. We relied on the kindness of others. Shop surplus and charity. It was cold and hard, but it was *simple*. Does that make any sense to you? Not easy, but simple. Do you remember all those questions Mother used to ask us? The choices we had made that made us who we were? My life until then had been a tangle of knotted threads. There, there were no choices, my life had been combed perfectly straight. It was simple. It was *clear*.'

Veronica laughed out loud.

'Oh honey, they brainwashed you.'

'They didn't.'

'You can't blame me for believing they did, Penny.'

'I really don't blame you for anything.'

Veronica's smile was hard-edged.

'God, you still sound like a fucking saint.' She sat back in the chair again. 'Do you know what I resented most about them?'

'No,' Penny said.

'They called you "sister",' Veronica said. 'I don't think I'll ever forgive them for that. They took you away from us, but they took the word that connected us as well. It was *our* word. We were your sisters. Lulu and me. Not them. Never them.'

'Well, it's all in the past now,' Penny said. 'Maybe it's our word again. Yours, mine, Lulu's.'

Veronica's face fell. She took another sip of wine, but this time the taste of it made her grimace.

'Do you have pictures?' Penny said.

'Pictures?'

'Of Tom. Of David.'

'Of course I have pictures.' Veronica set her glass down. The remaining inch of red circled the bowl and settled. She reached into her pocket for her phone, pushing herself to her feet.

'Scootch up,' she said, flapping her hand at her sister until Penny shifted to the other side of the bed. Veronica joined her, landing heavily on the mattress. She held the phone so they could both see it. Penny could smell the alcohol on Veronica's breath, but could see how her expression had softened.

'I took this one before I drove down,' Veronica said. 'There's Tom, that's Megan. They waved me off.'

'They're lovely,' Penny said.

'There's David. My god, he's the image of his father.' There was a trace of bitterness there, but amusement too.

Veronica took control of the phone again.

'I've got the scan somewhere,' she said.

She diverted into her email, and scrolled through her messages briskly. Penny glimpsed the names in her inbox. Tom, Tom, David, Gavin, Gavin, Gavin. She jabbed open one message.

Tada!
Confirming order of one (1) granddaughter.
(I think she's got your nose.)
Love, Tom x

The screen filled with a black-and-white image. A cone of busy static hiding a tiny organic shape within the warp and weft of its noise.

Veronica passed it back to Penny, and Penny could feel the warmth of her pride.

'There she is.'

'Oh,' said Penny.

Veronica laughed. 'Yes,' she said. 'Oh! That's what I said when I first saw her. Then I had a sit down.'

She reached across and zoomed in on the image with a gesture. The picture of the foetus filled the screen, its shape no more distinct, but there was something rather beautiful about the mystery of it. It was a glimpse of life, not yet ready to be fully known.

'Do you have more pictures?'

Veronica took the phone off her.

'Not of the baby,' she said. She exited the email and returned to the photograph album, bringing up a picture of David looking startled wearing a suit and tie. She passed the phone back to Penny.

'You need to swipe to get the rest.'

Penny stabbed her finger at the phone obediently. The picture lurched but remained the same.

'No,' Veronica said. 'You have to swipe. Give it here.'

'Sorry.'

Veronica moved through the photographs with a practised gesture of her thumb. Tom and David. Tom and Megan. Sometimes Veronica, rarely Stephen. Each image sliding off to the screen to make room for the next.

'This was last week. Sunday lunch. That's Gavin.

'That's the Italian restaurant on the square. Gavin took me there for my birthday.

'That's Megan. That's Tom.'

'They're lovely.'

Not all the photographs were of the boys. There were pictures of the house, the garden, a flower arrangement that had caught her eye, a beautiful tree, a squirrel. They sat there together for another hour, Veronica commentating warmly as they slid back together, one picture at a time, into the past.

THE NEW MAN

There was a time, I think, when I used to write you poetry.

I found pages once. Folded four times and tucked snug behind the bedpost. The paper was spotted with pale grey circles that smeared and spiked the blue ink. The handwriting was mine, but the words were all his.

A memory had got to me. One of those images that nag at you until you put them to rest. The corner of a room, the dark at the back of a cupboard. The memories are never specific; they aren't of people or things that were said. Instead, they're something fragmented like the torn corner of a treasure map. The memory taunted me and I gnawed on it like a dog with a chew toy. Keeping it at bay until it consumed me. I turned the bedroom upside down until I found the pages as though they were what I had been looking for all along.

I sat next to the bed, cross-legged on the floor. When I set to reading them, I struggled. Each individual word was clear to me, but they were lost in sentences that were difficult, lines I couldn't decode at all. I read all the pages twice, my brain clouding, wandering, starting again. They were just words. They were private words written by one stranger to someone I only hoped I knew.

'You wrote that,' you said. I hadn't heard you come in, you move so quietly these days. I sometimes hear you whispering to the kids when you're alone together. I hear the light catch of your breath when the stair creaks under your weight.

I looked up from the ruin of the room. You were standing in the doorway, your arms crossed. You had always been so patient with me but today you looked away from me, suddenly quiet.

'I'm sorry,' I said.

I say that a lot these days.

You shook your head, shaking my words away. You raised a hand at me then stepped out of sight. The memories crowded. Open doors. Empty stairwells. Darkened landings and silent streets. They bristled at me; missing pieces from discarded jigsaws.

I turned to the pages, softening between my fingers, and read them again and again.

> • <

Write it down, Doctor Williams said. *Write all of it down.*

You are asleep upstairs. You and the kids in your private little rooms. I sit alone at the kitchen table. The pen in my fist. These muscles have so little memory of writing longhand. I have to force them to draw letters on the page in a way that I recognise as my own.

> • <

It was never your fault.

The choice you were given was an impossible one, even if it must have seemed so easy at the time.

I've tried to reconstruct the scene. Night after night, it plays like a TV drama. In a minimally furnished office, high above the cloud layer. The woman from the company says to you: 'Do you want your husband back?'

I imagined her using your name. A forced familiarity she'd been trained to use to reel people in.

'*Laura*,' she says. 'Laura, do you want your husband back?'

I don't think you could have stopped to consider what that might mean. For you, for us, for Ben and Carrie. I don't think the woman from the company told you everything you might have needed to know.

Two parties wanting very different things. A grieving wife who wanted her family to be whole again; a company wanting to be absolved of negligence with a calibrated act of generosity.

Maybe here, the woman from the company reaches across the table and touches your hand?

'Yes,' you say. 'I want him back. I want him back now.'

The Laura I remember would have said that.

The music rises, a synthesiser, overemphatic and cheap. The colours are all slightly off. This TV show is showing its age. Its emotional cues are obvious and trite. It was made for a simpler time.

In the early days, when we worked together in the faculty staffroom, I remember the way you would argue in precise imperatives. You would stare at your opponent with clear, determined eyes and I don't think I was the only one who would fold under your scrutiny.

I don't imagine the woman from the company would have been so soft. The touch of the hand was a device not a feeling. Instead, I imagine her gesturing to the lawyer at her side. He is bald. I'm picturing glasses, tie, a suit with razored seams. I see him pushing a sheaf of papers across the table towards you. He uncaps a pen and places it on top.

Beside him, the woman from the company smiles in a way that hindsight might interpret as predatory.

'Let me tell you what we can do,' she says.

> • <

I don't remember much about the accident.

One of the doctors tried to explain it to me. A slim young figure whose white coat looked too big for him.

'Frayed edges,' he said.

On a screen, he showed me what looked like a scribble of sound waves, many coloured lines drawn over each other like an infant's picture on a refrigerator door.

'So, this is what was going on in there.' The pencil he pointed to my head with seemed quaint in the bright starkness of the consultation room. I found myself following it, squinting, my head bobbing after its every move. It is something organic and traditional. Old-school technology in a modern world.

The doctor tucked it into his breast pocket, frowning. He looked like someone who struggled to communicate on a layman's level.

'We had to make a clean cut. Some of these straggly bits at the end might have to left behind.' The pencil was out again, this time it gestured to the screen. He gave me a shorthand smile. He didn't look like the sort of person who smiled very often.

'I doubt you'd want to remember any of that anyway,' he said. 'That's the part where you died.'

His correction, when it comes, feels artificial. 'Where you *almost* died.'

I heard what happened from others.

But first, context. Context. Doctor Williams tells me to remember the scene, then reconstruct the memory. That way, she says during our sessions, I won't get lost.

This is the scene. Unit 15 is in the north of the city's industrial district. The warehouse floor is around one and a half million square feet. There are overhead crane units that use a grid of rails set high in the suspended ceiling.

One of the cranes fell and killed me.

Almost killed me.

Killed me, but only for moments.

All of this is known. All of this was reported. But no, we need more.

On each crane, there's a control block that hangs down on a sprung cable. Again: old-school technology, an affectation that we're fond of. Once you've hooked up a pallet and hoisted it about a metre or two off the ground, you follow behind it on foot, holding the button down all the time otherwise it grinds to a halt and swings about and takes a time to get moving again. We call it walking the load.

The roof network is serviced often, but for one reason or another the last safety inspection was stopped early. This happens sometimes. It was recorded in the ledger and more time would be allocated to it later. But until then, those rusted bolts holding up the rail at section B-16 were missed.

I think you can see what happened next.

We were assembling an order of Category VI organs. Mostly kidneys, some livers. Jeff Parry was overseeing, and he had started walking the load to the collection bay for packing. Jeff's an old hand at this. It wasn't his fault. He's a bulky guy, a big bush of red whiskers and a Cheshire cat grin buried somewhere beneath.

I was using one of the mid-level pallet trucks to retrieve some materials for a different order, and I was there under B-16 when Jeff came along with that load of his and put weight on it.

These are things I *do* remember.

I remember a noise like claws tearing open a metal door. I remember a dull popping sound, like a finger being dislocated. I remember a shower of sparks, and then the load Jeff had been leading landed flat on the ground with a clatter of its own.

Only one image remains in my memory after that. The straight line of the crane cable, still taut. It must have been a fraction of a second before gravity reshaped it, but I remember seeing that straight dividing line, floor to ceiling as though the warehouse had been snapped in two.

I don't remember doing anything heroic, but they say I did.

They say I swung the truck around in a circle, sideswiping Jeff out of the way. The impact made us both fall. Jeff tumbled off to the side. He broke his ankle, I heard later, but he rolled out of the way like a big ginger medicine ball. I wasn't so lucky. The crane chassis, and most of intersection B-16, sliced down on top of me.

The truck took most of the damage, but not all of it.

People told me what the scene looked like. They told me about sirens and twisted metal and blood, *so much blood like you wouldn't believe.*

All I know is that the crane fell on the me that was, and knocked me spinning out of the world.

> • <

When I woke up, I was someone else.

They had strapped me to the bed because they were worried that if I woke unattended, I might make the connection on my own and panic. It was something crazy and they wanted to be there in person to explain it. But I knew anyway. Everything was there, but everything felt wrong. I felt as though I was wearing a set of clothes one size too small. When I opened my eyes, the view was different to what I knew. You don't think you see much of yourself unless you're looking out of the wrong face.

I was under the bedcovers, but the shape beneath it was alien. I didn't panic; I was still woozy, as good as hungover. I took it for a dream. I went back to sleep.

> • <

Context: Peveril & Mowbray Incorporated is the biggest producer of cloned and vat-grown organs in Europe, North Africa and Western Asia.

Context: I'd been working at the warehouse since the college closed down. That's where I used to work. I was teaching history to school leavers when half the community colleges in the region were put out of business due to local authority cuts. People didn't need *actual* colleges, we were told. People with limited income preferred online courses. They were cheaper, no classrooms, no transport to worry about.

The competition for jobs at the remaining IRL schools became cutthroat and I wasn't much of a fighter back then, so I took a job at P&M to tide us over while you retrained as a primary school teacher. That was eight years ago.

The company was working on new areas, they told me afterwards. They could now grow whole body clones to precise specifications. Hundreds of millions can buy you a younger self to move into when you start to feel the age pinch around the edges. They shift you across as though you're upgrading to a new mobile phone handset. You can live forever that way if you're one of the few who can afford it.

My old body had been broken beyond repair in the accident but a stubborn trace of life remained blinking off and on and off and on. With your permission, they scooped what they found out of the wreck and poured it into a new vessel, fresh from the vat.

They described it as a 'basic model'.

'Skin, eye and hair colour are unchanged,' they told me. 'Fingerprints have been rebuilt. DNA has been redirected.'

I wasn't really sure what any of that meant. I wasn't even sure if it was true. But it was about as much of the physical me as remained.

My mind, they refer to as 'content'.

'The content is mostly memories,' the doctor told me. A different doctor, this one older, a serious looking man with red-framed glasses. 'The parts between are harder to define, but if you cut and paste the memories into place along with other pertinent data, the gaps will all fill themselves in eventually. The way they work together. That sort of thing. We used various methods to ensure the correct connections were made…'

He explained more, but he lost me. I just sat and nodded at him, a dull roaring sound filling my ears.

'They percolate,' the doctor said. 'Like coffee.'

When he was certain I understood, he gave me a mirror with someone else's face in it. The face in the mirror said it wasn't me in a voice that wasn't quite mine either.

I was supposed to be forty-two. I was lanky with a skinny frame and a burgeoning gut from too many post-work beers; I had a narrow face with weaselly features, scraggy with a reddish beard. I had a crooked nose and a receding, greying hairline. Freckles. I had freckles. Not any more. The new me looked like a kid's action figure. Shorter, stockier, and shaven to within an inch of its life. It looked youthful in a way that wasn't earned. It was all muscle and symmetry and unlikely angles.

'You'll need to wear it in,' the doctor said with an all-encompassing gesture. He caught me looking at my hands. They were too big, the wrists and arms too. Like they'd been inflated with a bicycle pump.

'Think of your body as a pair of shoes,' he said. 'It'll rub a bit to start with, but it'll adapt.'

I put my hand to my stomach. It felt solid, flat, wrong.

'I'll need to drink more beer,' I said. 'I'm going to have to work pretty hard to get my figure back.'

The doctor frowned.

'I really wouldn't,' he said. 'Your new biology is very young. It'll hit you harder than you remember.'

I waited until he had gone then lay back on the bed. I closed my eyes until the noise went away. I thought of you and worried you would reject what I had become. Or maybe you would like it better? I wondered if that would be worse and fretted restlessly.

I thought of you again and – forgive me – I reached down to my groin. The length there filled my hands more than I remembered.

I thought of you. I remembered your touch. Your taste.
Let's see what content we have up there, I thought.

> • <

You had already seen what they had done to me.

You came to visit while I was unconscious and had been allowed to sit beside me while I slept. I wonder how that felt to you. Sitting by a sleeping stranger, waiting for him to become someone you once loved.

You know all this already. But Doctor Williams says that reconstructing everything is important.

'Brick by brick,' she says. 'Each one is important. Each one is part of the structure.'

Doctor Williams drives me up the fucking wall at times.

So, here's the scene: we had both been working at the college for a year or two when we first met at a function organised by the history faculty. It was supposed to be a barbecue, but the weather blackened and forced us indoors. The food was a write-off, so we drank instead. I was stuck in a conversation with my faculty head about Bertrand Russell when you pushed your way in and took over. I'm ashamed to admit I don't remember the exact nature of the argument; I mostly remember the passion and intelligence with which you defended your corner. It hadn't needed to be a fight, but you made it one and you won.

I learned later that you were a year younger than I was. You were a military brat. You'd moved around a lot as a kid but now you'd moved north because it was somewhere you'd never been.

When you came to visit me after I woke, I could see you were trying to hold yourself together when I said your name, and I wondered who was being strong for you. You kept you distance, then, but I understood. Really, I understood.

'Close your eyes if it helps,' I said, but you shook your head.

'I need to know it's you,' you said. 'I need to know that all of it is you.'

You didn't close your eyes as we talked. But sometimes you would look away from me, focus elsewhere as though you could centre yourself.

We kissed before you left. But it wasn't the kiss I remembered of you, it was a small, chaste little thing that you flinched away from, blushing with embarrassment.

'I'm sorry,' you said.

'It's okay.'

I reached out a hand, but you stepped back.

'I'm sorry.'

> • <

The next time you visited, you brought the kids.

You held them between us as though they might protect you from me. They stared at me from the other side of the room, but they too had changed since I'd last seen them. Both looked taller, and I was struck – harder than I had ever really been before – by how much Ben had inherited from me. The nose, the chin, the lopsided surliness in his eyes.

They recognised the cadence of my voice, but I could see their eyes widen when they tried to make the connection between what they could see and what they could hear. There was a disconnect between what they remembered of me and what they had been told was true.

Carrie was the first to approach me. Seven years old and driven by curiosity. She stood by the hospital bed and looked at me, fearless. I was so proud of her for that.

'Why do you look different?' she said.

'The old body had a crash,' I told her. 'This one is new. Like when we got the new car.'

She nodded as though it made sense to her and settled on the bed beside me.

'You smell different,' she said.

'New car smell,' I said. 'It'll wear off, I promise.'

She ducked her head a little and then made a decision.

'It's okay,' she said. She gave me a kiss and let me hold her for a little while. I looked over her shoulder at Ben. Three years older, there was a gulf between them. He backed away against you. He was unyielding.

> • <

After two more weeks of tests and observations, they sent me home.

Again, this was like a TV show. Stirring music – some recent ballad, maybe. Shots of the city rushing past the window. My stranger's reflection flickering in the glass, the hair on the scalp grown into a reddish crew cut, already thicker than it had ever been before.

The clouds hung low and charcoal grey as we drove down Whitehall Road. Near identical cobbled streets of small terraced houses peeled off and curled downhill like ribs on either side. Rectory Road looked the same as any of its neighbours, but somehow, I felt I was home.

The view over the city was as I remembered it, with boxy industrial plants fading into the far distance. A comb of chimneys scraped the smog layer. Further back, I could just about see the enormous glass and steel towers of The Greens, vanishing upwards, puncturing the clouds and disappearing up and out of sight.

Some of the neighbours found excuses to watch me get out of the car. I didn't know what they'd heard, and judging by their reactions, I'm not sure what they believed. I smiled and nodded to them like someone they'd never met, but it was a half-hearted greeting that wasn't reciprocated. I felt their eyes on my back as the door closed behind me.

The house was smaller than I remembered and more cluttered. My new dimensions had diminished its old ones. The doorways felt tighter, the rooms more cramped. The smell was different, and it took me a little while to realise it was the smell of the people who lived there; including the trace of the one who didn't any more. A family picture mounted on the wall above the television looked less awkward than I remembered it. The old me grinning like an idiot, you looking tolerant and amused, the kids before us, just on the edge of spinning out of control. I wondered how long the old me would haunt the place. I didn't say anything to you.

At my own suggestion, I spent the first night on the sofa in the lounge. A small room, cluttered with over-full bookshelves and mismatched furniture. It was a sideways perspective on a place which should have been familiar.

Again. Context. Brick by brick. I had bought the house when I first got the job at the college. It had been cheap, but it had been a lengthy commute through the cross-town traffic to get to work each day. Most of the people who lived nearby worked in the plants and warehouses in the industrial district, and it wasn't until I ended up there myself that they acknowledged I was there at all.

I didn't sleep well. Instead, I watched the halogen glow of the streetlamps outside, listening to the passing traffic rattle on the cobbles and the slipstream fragments of conversation from those walking past.

The following day, you went to the school for a morning meeting and took the kids to class. Alone in the house, I tried on some of my old clothes and found they no longer fit me. Too tight, too long. I looked like I was dressing up as my old self. I put them away as I had found them, so they would not look as though they'd been disturbed.

I looked at myself in the full-length mirror on the back of the bedroom door. I imagined it wasn't a mirror. It was a doorway, behind which an actor had been hired. He mimicked my movements and lip-synched when I yelled at him. He copied me when I sat heavy on the edge of the bed and sank my alien head into alien hands.

I looked up to meet his eyes and a fury took over. I jumped up and punched the fucker, but his fist met mine, and the glass between us exploded into knives and scattered across the floor.

I was still sitting, dumb and startled on the bed, when you found me early that afternoon; the light filtered through the closed curtains of the bedroom and soaked the room in a dull red-orange glow.

You looked at the broken mirror, shards still jumbled on the floor. You took my hand and traced the thin line of laceration across the knuckles, already healing over.

Wordless, you sat beside me on the bed and put your arm around my shoulders. I felt you lean into me. I felt the warmth of you. We sat there together for a long time.

This time, when you kissed me, you did not hold back. Your taste was a rush to me, and memories too long undisturbed fluttered like a stack of photographs thrown into the wind.

Yours was an exploratory kiss; a testing one. Testing to see if mine was a future you could allow yourself to accommodate.

You were silent; you took your time. You guided me to my feet, and I said nothing, but allowed myself to be led. You undressed me like a doll: arms up, you pushed my T-shirt over my head.

I felt your hand drift, whispering over my skin with only the promise of touch; you traced a path over unfamiliar contours, and still I did not move. I let you explore your new terrain, because it was yours as much as it was mine. You had known my previous shape so intimately; the sheer newness of me was strange to the both of us.

When you came to face me again, you lifted your hand away from me, and I felt the absence of you keenly.

You unbuttoned your shirt and unhooked your bra. I saw the age of you, and I found it achingly beautiful. I had the sudden sense you had left me behind and I needed to race to keep up. You took my hand and guided it to your right breast. Fingers splayed, my hand could cover it almost completely. I moved to touch you, but you shook your head fractionally: no.

Instead, you guided my hand around, so I would embrace you. You pulled yourself close and tilted your face up to meet mine. You kissed me again, then pulled away, your smile half-hidden in shadow.

'So, this is how it feels to be unfaithful,' you said.

> • <

Later, we lay together, your small body spooned in my clumsy new one. The afternoon had waned. A block of shadow edged across the room towards us.

'I'm sorry about the mirror,' I said.

'I didn't think you had it in you.'

'They replaced your husband with a caveman.'

'Don't joke.'

I could hear you smile. 'So, don't laugh.'

You pulled my arm tighter around you.

'We'll be okay,' I said.

It struck me as a rather limp thing to say, and part of me was so glad you didn't respond. I listened to you breathe instead.

> • <

It took a month or two before I went back to work, but when I did, I got a hero's reception that did not feel earned. Jeff Parry came out of the applauding crowd and pumped my hand up and down. He stared at me wide-eyed and awestruck.

'It's good to have you back,' he said. 'No matter what you look like.'

I was given new overalls, new boots, and put back on the floor. Kai Bremner had been promoted to my old supervisory role in my absence, so for a probationary period I was brought on as a day labourer until they could reinstate me in my old job. The pay was lower accordingly, but I was content to spend the time getting used to the old routine, back walking loads with the rest of them.

Ballard, the shop steward, was less than pleased.

'You're being taken for a ride,' he said to me when our lunch shift came round. 'It was their fault you nearly got killed in the first place, and their solution is to dress you up like a meathead and then demote you? That's bullshit. What's this done to your health benefits?'

I told him the company covered everything. I hadn't doubted it until then.

'Okay,' he said. 'Good. Otherwise they're taking the piss. I'm going to write some letters, you're going to sign them, you hear me?'

He sat back and looked me up and down.

'Did you hear Units 17 to 20 have had layoffs?' he said.

I shook my head.

'Automated,' he said. 'Machines. AIs. Stuff machines could never have done in the old days. More efficient, better productivity and so on. I told them: "You still got to have people to run the bloody things." And when I say that I just get these looks, you know? And they're going: "Well it ain't gonna be you, buddy." I mean, Jesus.'

He snorted in disgust and fished out his phone. It was an old model. Something dumb and simple. He'd told me once he was never going to upgrade to a new one when the old one did all it was supposed to do.

'Seriously, though.' He put the phone away in this pocket. 'If they're going to pay up proper damages like you should be chasing for – and I don't mean this fancy new skin they've flattered you with – you want to get to them sooner rather than later. Have you any idea how much money they would have given your family if you'd died?'

'No,' I said. 'It didn't cross my mind.'

'It should,' Ballard said. 'By still being here, you've made them look good and you've saved them a packet. They can dress you up, send you out the door and let you starve, and they still look like they're on the side of the angels.'

He looked like he was going to go further when a group of others surrounded us, led by Jeff. They wanted to test how capable I was now I was back. Before, I had been skinny, bookish and unathletic. The new me, unlikely though it seemed, looked more like something from the tabloid sports pages.

They cleared a table and started lining up to arm wrestle. Jeff was first, sitting opposite me with a big dumb grin on his face, his elbow on the table, his hand outstretched, palm open and inviting.

Ballard raised his hands and took a step backwards.

'All yours,' he said. 'I'll send you those letters. Don't wait to post them, I'm serious.'

I flattened Jeff's arm with little effort. The others took turns, and I took them out one by one like I was folding paper. They were giddy for it. Like they couldn't believe it. They were cheering by the time I was done. I looked up and saw Ballard standing in the doorway, watching. He raised his eyebrows, mock-impressed, then turned away, back to the floor.

> • ‹

In our home, as a family, we circled each other, searching for a new and stable orbit.

Carrie adjusted the quickest. To her, the change seemed normal. Other things changed, so why couldn't I? When I read her a story one night in the bedroom she shared with her brother, she reached up and touched my chin.

'I liked it when the other you had a beard,' she said. 'You were fuzzy. You should grow a beard.'

'I don't think I can,' I said. 'I haven't shaved for a week and all I got was some wisps up here, look.'

I touched the adolescent down edging my top lip.

In the bunk above, Ben shifted.

'You don't want to hear a story, Ben?' I said.

There was a grunt in reply, then: 'You don't read them right,' he said.

Carrie made a theatrical shushing noise.

'You're not supposed to say,' she said.

There was further movement in the bunk above, then Ben's legs appeared and he jumped down to the floor. I closed the book on my lap.

'What do you mean?' I said.

'You don't read them right,' Ben said. He pulled out the book I had read them the previous night from the box on the floor. It was a small paperback picture book. A boy comes to tell his parents there's a monster in the back garden, the parents ignore him, and when he goes out to confront the monster himself, he gets eaten.

'You're supposed to do voices for the monster and the mum and the dad, but you don't any more,' Ben said. 'It's boring.'

He kicked a stray Lego brick across the carpet. The room was cramped and small and the red wooden bunk beds took up most of the space in it. The blue-carpeted floor was strewn with paper, school books and the remains of toys which had not been tidied away.

I paged through the picture book as though it were something I had never really understood before. I tried to imagine how I might have read it in the past but drew a blank.

'I don't remember any voices,' I said.

'That's because you're not our dad,' Ben said. He said it loud like it had been growing inside of him. 'You're just some guy.'

Carrie shrieked.

'You're not supposed to say!' she said. She ran across to Ben and tried to stop his mouth with her hand. He fought her off, and she fell, howling. Papers crumpled under her, toys scattered.

'Mummy said you're not supposed to say!'

Ben was yelling back. He jumped at Carrie, who rolled out of his way, screaming.

There was so much noise, but I barely heard any of it. A dull whine had filled my ears, growing in pitch and blanking out almost everything else until you burst into the room and surveyed the scene in horror.

'Why are you just standing there?' you said to me.

Carrie ran to you babbling in a way you understood better than I did. Ben followed, also in tears. Your expression shifted. You looked at me, your expression a whirl before it settled on me, pleading.

'Just give us a moment, please.'

I backed away. Surprised my frustration now felt more like anger. It burned unwarranted, and it frightened me.

I put my hands up and stumbled downstairs so hastily I nearly fell. I caught myself on the front door handle at the bottom and pulled myself up.

'Where are you going?' You were standing at the top of the stairs, Carrie in your arms, clinging to you. I hadn't meant to go anywhere, but the idea took root. I grabbed my coat from the hook and swung the door open in a drunken gesture. I was out on the street and into the cool evening air.

> • <

I walked further than I meant to.

I walked down Rectory Road then turned onto Whitehall. I passed grey streets on both sides, separated by narrow paths which connected the back yards like links in a chain.

Further downhill the street broke up, a string of unlit shops, a closed-down bingo hall and a boarded-up church. I put my head down, and followed the road until I found myself on the outskirts of the industrial district.

The buildings here favoured function over aesthetics. They were dull corrugated boxes surrounded by wide moats of tarmac and chain-link fences. There were chimneys spotted with red warning lights, disappearing first into the darkness and then into the clouds.

The buildings sang with the nightshift. Machines spun and whirred, screamed and rumbled. I could hear the voices of workers calling out to each other: warnings, instructions, banter.

I walked on, taking left turns and right at random until I felt my head begin to clear.

The warehouses here were quieter. I didn't hear voices at all, just the low click and purr of constant machinery.

'Hey! Hey, you.'

I turned to see a man hurrying towards me from one of the factories; he flicked a cigarette stub behind him. By his overalls, I took him for one of the foremen. His movements were ungainly, and he was nearly out of breath by the time he reached me.

'What the fuck are you doing out here?' he said.

It was such a strange outburst, I almost didn't know how to respond. I didn't know what I was doing, after all. But the man didn't seem interested in a response.

'And where the fuck did you get that jacket?'

He shook his head, his eyes dangerous.

'If you don't get back on the line in the next fifteen seconds, Milburn is going to kick the crap out of you, you got that? And you better hide that jacket; he'll have that off you soon as look at you.'

I caught myself sizing him up. He was big but slow. Unfit. I imagined I could have laid him out with one blow if he was going to give me the opportunity.

I wondered where that thought came from.

'I don't know what you're talking about,' I said. I turned to leave and felt his hand on my shoulder. I turned back swiftly, fist already balled, but he was looking behind him, his own hand lowering.

'Ah, fuck,' he said, less to me than to himself.

I followed his look and saw another figure standing in the door of the warehouse, watching us. His shoulders were sloped, his face was lowered in deference, but I recognised him.

He was me. The new me. The same face, the same basic model. He blinked, and I wondered if the recognition went both ways, but there was something a little slow in his eyes, something unfocused.

'Ah, fuck,' the foreman said again. He marched off towards the warehouse door, casting a quick look back over his shoulder at me as though to confirm his mistake.

He snorted with laughter, then slapped the man in the doorway across his back.

'Come on, dipshit,' he said. 'No dawdling. The line won't run itself.'

He pushed him back inside and glanced at me again before following. I heard his laughter, a crowing noise amplified and ringing in the cavern of the warehouse. The sound of it followed me home.

> • <

For several months, the letters Ballard had written for me did not receive a reply, and there was no word about when my original job would be reinstated. Kai Bremner stopped looking guilty and started getting self-righteous instead. I couldn't really blame him. It wasn't his fault.

Our combined salaries began to look too small to cover our bills and so we began to cut corners to compensate.

Remember how our cupboards began to fill with the distinctive, no-frills packaging design of the local supermarket's 'Everyday Essentials' range? Bland tins of bland food. No added taste, little nutrition, just enough to get by.

When I finally heard from the company, the news was not what I had expected. Having considered my recent test scores and reports from Doctor Williams, they said, they had concluded that the old me had been more qualified than the new one. They suggested I applied myself a little more and tried again in the future.

'Basic model,' Ballard said when he came to visit one weekend. 'Do you know what that means?'

I shook my head.

'It's a side line. You've seen the ads for the main thing they sell? A personal clone you can move into when you get too old? Well, the basic model is for the proles. They plan to sell them in bulk. Export market. Fill 'em up with the broken, the captive, the disenfranchised? A basic chassis for a simple AI? That's their area. That's ethics for someone else to worry about.'

He smirked.

'Military contracts, private security, physical labour, sex industry and so on.'

'Sex industry?'

'Why not?' Ballard said. 'Basic model, jack of all trades. What I mean to say is, I don't think they're bred for intellect.'

He tapped the side of his head.

'If you're missing anything, maybe they couldn't fit it all in. We both work in manufacturing; we both know how it works. The punter wants to pay less, so you cut corners and then spring them with an upgrade fee when they notice. You got the basic model. No frills. No extras. Don't look so surprised, they're running a business here.'

He shook his head.

'It's funny. The way the warehouse works is part of what they're selling. *Old-school*. It's absurd really, isn't it? They could automate it soon as blink, and lay us all off in one go. But the old tech is their selling point, isn't it? Or at least it was. All those nice rich liberals who can afford the products we sell, but have all these questions about the ethics of the bloody thing. Tell them they're keeping people employed and they roll over like fucking puppies. *Hand-made*, they tell each other. *Crafted by artisans*. All bullshit ways for them to feel better about themselves, if you ask me.'

I passed him a cup of coffee and he looked at it critically.

'You used to make really good coffee,' he said. 'Guess you forgot that, too.'

He shot me a serious look, then broke and laughed.

'I'm kidding,' he said. 'Bad mood. I had advance warning of more layoffs. More automation. Robots, man. Fucking robots. Pushing back against this shit is like farting into a thunderstorm.'

He looked serious again.

'Stay strong, though,' he said. 'Whatever's left of you up there? Treasure it. Make it count.'

The following day, you were out of town visiting your mother and I managed to corral the kids into bed early. Ben still wasn't speaking to me, and was content to lock himself in the bedroom if it kept me away.

In the lounge, I pulled the family photograph albums out from the bottom shelf of the bookcase. I sat on the floor and started working my way through them, looking for things I didn't remember. To begin with, almost all the pictures sparked some outer edge of memory, but before long, wider holes began to appear: a holiday by the beach which I didn't recognise; Ben's fifth birthday party, in which the old me stood by a barbecue wearing an apron and a chef's hat. There was a family gathering which didn't seem to fit anywhere with my experience.

I went upstairs and popped open the hatch to the attic. I pulled down the ladder with a clatter and pushed myself up inside. Under the eaves were crates of things we had forgotten. I worked my way through until I found the shoeboxes and carrier bags full of other photographs: the older ones, the unsorted ones, the neglected ones.

I dropped them all through the hatch onto the landing and noticed the kids' door was open a crack, a pair of pale faces staring through it.

'Go back to bed,' I called. 'Daddy's looking for something.'

The door closed with a click and I remembered they never called me that.

They'd be fine, I thought. I slid down the ladder and carried everything downstairs to the lounge.

You came home early to find me pacing. The floor and furniture of the lounge was thick with scattered photographs of our life together.

You looked at me and there was sadness there. You reached out a hand.

'Come upstairs,' you said.

> • <

'When they first told me,' you said, 'they said you had died. They didn't believe there was any way you could have survived. And I came home and I saw the hole you had left in the house. It followed me from room to room. It stood behind me when I looked out of the window. So close, I could see it in the reflection when the light was right.'

You pushed yourself out of my arms and sat with your back to me on the edge of the bed.

'And now you're back, and you don't quite fit the hole you left behind.'

You stood up and walked around the bed and out of sight. I did not turn to watch you. I listened as you dressed. The soft hiss of fabric over skin, the stretch-snap of elastic.

'Not yet,' you said.

> • <

Downstairs, I found you picking up the photographs. I watched you from the foot of the stairs.

'What were you doing?' you said. You sounded tired.

'Looking for holes,' I said.

I started trying to explain what I had found out but you silenced me with a wave.

'You don't look at photographs to find the things you've forgotten,' you said. 'This isn't our life. These are placeholders for memories of a life we pretend we've lived.'

You slotted the photographs back into one of the shoeboxes, order be damned.

'If you want to find what they couldn't fit in that head of yours, perhaps you need to think differently. Things we didn't take photographs of. Things we hoped we could forget, but which we can't. And so we learn from them anyway.'

You shook your head and looked at a picture of the old me: one of the ones from the college, close to when we first met.

'You're so in love with the idea that *his* life — our life — before the accident was perfect. And if that's what you think, then you're missing more than you know.

'You're missing the arguments we had, you're missing those stupid fights with your family, you've lost the memory of the miscarriage and what happened afterwards, you've lost all of our dumb idiot mistakes and I hate you for it because I envy you your ignorance.'

You threw the box down.

'Do you remember the affair?'

'What affair?'

'You don't, do you?' You continued slowly, choosing your words with delicate care. 'One of us fucked around with someone else and almost blew us apart. But it means nothing to you now. You don't even know which of us it was, do you?'

I felt a heat under my ears, as though I was blushing like a schoolkid. But it wasn't embarrassment. It was that anger again; that alien fury I didn't recognise at all. I pressed it down as though I could smother it.

'So tell me,' I said. Too quiet, too controlled.

You stared at me as though I had shouted.

'If the old you thought he could forget, I don't think he'd ever want to know. It was when we were still at the college. Ben was two. The things we said to each other in front of him—'

'Laura—'

You pushed past me.

'Just... I don't want to talk about this now.'

You started up the stairs.

I didn't know what to think. So I didn't think at all.

I don't know what happened next. Maybe it was exactly the sort of memory that just doesn't fit any more.

Then, the light fitting was shaking. The pictures were skewed. There was blood on the curl of my hand, blossoming into a dull thudding pain.

A crater had opened in the wall by my side. A rosette of cracks spiralling up the paintwork.

You were standing at the top of the stairs. I thought I saw a trace of a figure behind you. One of the kids? Ben, I thought.

I opened my mouth to say something but shut it again.

'Now you're going to make a stand?' you said. 'Now you can smash mirrors to pieces and break holes in the walls, you can finally stand up for yourself?'

You shook your head, looking for a moment as though you were going to say something else. But you changed your mind and turned on your heel, crossing the landing out of sight.

❯ • ❮

There was a time when I used to write you poetry. Sometimes I'd write to you about love. Sometimes I'd just write things I felt but found no other way to express. Some poems were apologies. I used to write a lot of apologies.

But whatever part of me was able to find the words in that way just isn't there any more. I stare at a page and the page stares back. If I don't understand how to read what you find beautiful, how am I supposed to write it?

There was no room for poetry when I almost died. There was no room for poetry when you asked them to save my life.

Doctor Williams says I need closure, but I don't think she understands. If I close the door on what's missing, how will I ever let it back in?

It wasn't your fault. It was never your fault.

You're in bed now. You all are. In stockinged feet so as not to disturb you, I looked in on each of you in turn. In our bedroom, you were smiling in your sleep and I wondered if you were dreaming of him, of me, of the me as I was. I blew a kiss across the room and turned away before I could imagine it land.

It is three o'clock in the morning and I'm sitting in the kitchen. My new self doesn't need as much sleep as the old one. More hours I could work. More energy I could spend. I have a photograph of you and Carrie and Ben; it's a photo I took some years ago on that brief holiday out of the city and away from the clouds. I'm not in it but you're all looking into the lens like you used to look at me.

On the table, a sheaf of paper stares at me, a pen hovers in my stubbed fist of a hand. Ink splays. With effort, the handwriting is almost the same, but the words... the words are mine, not his. Sometimes I think I write the same thing, night after night after night. I don't know what I'm saying. I don't know if I should ever let you read this. I don't know if I'll be still here when you do.

I used to write you poetry. Today, this will have to do.

THE KNOWLEDGE

They sent you to me because you know this already. You look at me like I'm an old fool. You're not the first, but I say again: you know this. Not up here, maybe, but in *here*? It's all there, folded neat and tucked away in the chambers of your heart, waiting to unfurl and show its colours like a rosebud in the spring. Waiting to carry itself around the routes inside of you, your veins and nerves and organs and tissues. You only need say the word, and it will know where to go.

Not for you the endless hours with the *A to Z*, tracing your finger along the London roads and streets and avenues. Not for you, the tours of the city on a moped, pages torn from your blue book and pinned open before you, the late, late nights calling over the runs of the day. Not for you, the revision of points: the police stations, the theatres, the hostels, the restaurants.

No. They sent you to me, lad, because you're like us. Your interview will be rote, your exam a formality. They sent you to me because the knowledge is in your blood.

RUN 6:
LANCASTER GATE TO ROYAL FREE HOSPITAL

Hospitals are the city's hearts; all traffic departs from them, all traffic returns. Many of your fares will be taking the first or last journey of their lives. Assume this is true of everyone who hails your cab; treat them with the respect such journeys deserve.

Mark out the hospitals on your map. Use the red pen.

The driver's purpose is to tap into the veins of the city. We are the white blood cells; we carry information around the circulatory system.

Draw a circle around each of the hospitals, draw them so the circles touch but do not overlap. You are not an ambulance, but these are the places you should go to when your passengers treat you as though you are.

During times of plague, fleas found vehicles in rats. They spread through the city's secret infrastructure and carried their cargo wide. Today, we hear the argument that people are the disease and that London is sick with them; they will use you in the same way to spread their kind.

Draw a line between each pair of hospitals on the map. Do you see the shape it makes?

RUN 65:
ST JOHN'S WOOD TO BROMPTON ORATORY

Turn on the radio, adjust the dial. Music runs through our history and you can follow it like the instructions on a dashboard-mounted GPS. Listen attentively and it'll lead you back.

Stop here. Look. The celestial musician Krauncha has insulted the Sage Vâmadeva at the Indra Court. The sage takes his revenge. He lays a curse upon him: look how the musician becomes a rat! A rat as big as a mountain. Rats are unstoppable, they are relentless, they gnaw through every obstacle in their path. Watch as Krauncha lays waste to the ashram of the Sage Parâchara.

We are not alone on the city's roads, but we have advantages others cannot match. There will be those who think they can tap into the city with technology. In doing so, they believe they will understand it in the way that we do.

But to know the city, to feel it, requires much more than a simple interpretation of raw data. Knowledge and understanding are worth more than numbers and statistics. Instinct and experience are worth following above any fat, friendly arrow wheeling on a dashboard display.

Satellite technology is reactive. It determines paths to avoid obstacles which have already occurred. You will be capable of anticipating the obstacles before they exist. You will gauge the variations in the world and foresee how the passive might become aggressive.

The Sage Parâchara has invoked Ganesha to break the rat. Here he is, making such an entrance! Look at him, as he loops his pasha around the mighty rat's neck and brings him to heel at his feet. This is the moment when Ganesha takes a rat as his vehicle. He masters the creature. He makes himself light so Krauncha can bear him without pain.

Remember this when a fare complains because traffic has made progress slow across the parks. Turn the music up high and remember how we once carried gods on our backs.

RUN 113:
ROYAL COLLEGE OF MUSIC TO CROUCH HILL

Circles are preferable to straight lines. When you plan a return journey, always come back a different way so you do not erase the path you have made. Your fare will thank you for a change in scenery. No one wishes to witness what they have already seen, played in reverse as though everything they've achieved has been reeled back in.

Choose a road with a school in it. Use a pencil to trace a path through the traffic-calming scheme without marking over the lines. If you do not succeed, start again. Do you see how difficult it is to stray from a path which has already failed you?

Here is a story to teach your young: a musician is hired to rid a town in Lower Saxony of vermin. Consider that he does not drown the rats. Consider instead that he consigns them to exile in a magical land, hidden behind a door in the mountainside. Later, when the town refuses to pay him for his services, he leads their children there too and seals the door behind them.

The children find the rats have established a civilisation within the mountain. A rat utopia. What happens next? This is what happens: society adjusts. The human minority adopt the nature of their rat-like hosts in order to survive. They scavenge, they fight, they breed as fast as they can to keep their numbers strong.

And in this manner, by a different route, they come back to where they began. Circumstance turns like a wheel, evolution plays its hand, and finally, they understand.

RUN 238:
ARCHWAY TO GLOUCESTER GATE

Early in the morning, Camden High Street is bright with flayed meat. Remember to bring gloves and cleaning products. Remember to open the windows wide, and allow the air to circulate.

In seventeenth-century France, a rat is captured in the kitchen of a small country house. He is forced into servitude, made to become a coachman at the behest of the youngest daughter. In his carriage, he takes the young woman from her home to a ball at the palace. He waits in the shadows while she dances through the night and falls in love with a man who cannot appreciate anything beyond the look of her.

The music draws us when night falls.

Count the number of right turns it takes from Camden High Street to the West End. How many times will you pirouette before the lights overwhelm you?

At midnight the coachman is dismissed and given his freedom, but when he returns home, he is taken before the many-headed Rat King and put on trial for collaborating with the human enemy. He is sentenced to death and his brood set upon him. They eat him alive; they feed upon his remains.

The knowledge runs deep, it fills the very meat of him. And this is how they learn what he has already learned.

Use a green pen and mark the laybys where it is safe to stop when your fare wishes to be ill.

RUN!

The piper does not lead the rats to the door in the mountainside. He leads them to the wharf and lets them cast themselves into the tide. Rats can swim, but not when the music takes them, not when they believe themselves to be dancing.

So what does he do with the children?

To know is to understand that there is no magical land.

RUN 240:
STOKE NEWINGTON CHURCH STREET TO
HIGHGATE CEMETERY

Some fares like to be told stories as they are driven. Learn something you've heard and practise in a mirror until you are fluent.

Here's a story I heard once upon a time. A hanged man does not die. His remains are chained to a bed where he is imprisoned forever, his ragged, mouldy bedclothes a-heaving and a-heaving like the seas.

The story is not that he frightens people when they stumble on his room and find him staggering across the floorboards towards them. The story is that he missed his vehicle to the other side and he waits and waits for another to come in its place. How cruel we are to witness an episode of someone else's tragedy and colour it as a horror story of our own.

This is the last route you will learn. The route, which takes your fare beyond the hospital, beyond the city limits, beyond all else. They will not know why, but they will call on you, on us, on one of our kind.

Take your time, let them admire the view; they will have paid for this ride long ago.

And this is what we were taught all those years ago when the dread collaborator was eaten alive by his kind. The knowledge of London: the before, the after, the always. This is what he showed us. This is what we learned. The infinite threads of the world, with their knots and tangles and millions of frayed ends.

Stick with us, lad, we'll teach you the way.

MY UNCLE EFF

MY UNCLE EFF

My Uncle Eff had never been the sort of man who would simply die. He climbed too high, he saw too much. He was a man always destined to become one of his own stories.

This is not a story about how he went missing. This isn't a story about how I found him. You might not believe it, but this isn't a story about Eff at all.

I tell Carrie stories about Eff. When I do, I'm conscious that I'm digging him deeper into his own mythology, occluding the gauche simplicity of the truth with further layers of narrative. It feels right, in a way. It's all he ever wanted; the widening lie. Nothing so common as a funeral for Eff, when his elevation to legend is at stake.

I tell Carrie stories and the infection of Eff seeps like spilled water. A single incantation of 'once upon a time' and I sense him somewhere hidden, growing stronger as the words feed him. I see his fingerprints on Carrie's schoolwork. The stories Eff once told me, the stories I told her, repeated and adapted, scrawled in colourful crayon on a page of sugar-paper.

I must have been her age when Eff first told me about his mother. I was eight years old, an empty vessel ready to be filled, and from her drawings I know that Carrie's no different. There's a curious kind of horror to children's pictures. Here's the grandmother who died before I was born, resurrected on the page a generation later. A circle for a face, blots for eyes, staring upwards at the pencil-line ceiling of her downstairs room.

'She lived alone in the family house,' Eff said. 'And when she got old, she had me and your dad come by. We moved her bed down to the sitting room so she didn't have to bother on the stairs. But she didn't like the thought of all the empty rooms above her. She said she could hear footsteps in them.

'"You've got to seal it all up," she said to me. "You've got to lock it all up or the devil will move in."'

Eff said he did as he was told. He boarded up all the windows and had locks fixed to all the doors. He brought a contractor in to install a door at the top of the stairs and he set a bar against it, tight and firm.

'It didn't do any good,' Eff said. 'She heard what she wanted to hear. Her husband's footsteps in the locked-off rooms. His impossible footfall on the stair. I'd go round sometimes and find a mug of old tea left for him outside the locked landing door, teabag bobbing as he used to like it, getting stronger, colder.

'But she wouldn't be moved. She wouldn't hear sense. I can respect that, kiddo. People don't always need what's sensible because it doesn't always do you good. Everyone thinks it's the best thing, but it isn't. Not for everyone.'

When I asked what happened to her, Eff cocked his head and lit his cigarette. He was a tall, lean man, and when he sat beside me on the beach he looked as though he had folded himself up like a stepladder. His hair was long and unruly, it curtained his face and hid him from me. When he was on holiday, he never tied it back.

'Oh,' he said. I saw a smile flicker. 'She fell. In the end, everyone falls.'

My parents didn't like Eff telling me stories back then. He had a relationship with my dad that I never really understood. When he wasn't there, my dad didn't want him about; but when he was, he would never refuse him. There was something *adult* between them, which they never saw fit to explain to the likes of me.

When it came to Eff's stories, things were more cleanly cut. My parents told Eff they thought I was too young to hear the things he had to say, and the adamance of the way they said this fuelled me. It drove me to linger near Eff and wait for him to tell me what we both knew he shouldn't. And he did. He always did.

As I got older, I imagined I would never tell a child of my own the stories that Eff told me. I shield Carrie from the things I see in the news that frighten me: climate change, politics, the bloody despair and conflict caused by both – but there's something about the way a child can look at you that makes you want to raise your game for them.

'Tell me a story,' Carrie says.

And so, of course, I do.

❯ • ❮

Here's a story about where I used to live.

Years ago, before I was born, there was a man who lived in flat 913 who cheated on his wife. His name was MacNamarra and he was a miserable sonofabitch who didn't have time for anyone except the woman two floors up, who let him fall asleep in her arms while she rocked him like a baby. When his wife found out, she seasoned his Sunday steak with rat poison and opened him a beer so he could wash it down.

Rat poison doesn't kill you straight away. Not if you're as big as MacNamarra was, not if you only have a little. MacNamarra didn't have a little, but even that wasn't enough to kill him outright. He felt something seismic in his gut and it lit warning lights all the way up to his brain. He made it to the lift in the south hallway, he even managed to punch the emergency button which lit all the lights red and sent the lift directly to the ground floor.

Only his corpse made it all the way. People said he died somewhere between floors seven and six, as though that was something anyone could possibly know.

There were other lifts in the tower, but when I was small we didn't take any chances. Fuelled by sugar and superstition, all of us tower kids owned the staircases. We told each other that if you took the lift, when you passed the seventh floor, all the lights would flicker. They'd flash red and you'd catch sight of MacNamarra huddled in the corner scratching his stomach raw as though he could claw the poison away.

One summer, Beth Dooley from 812 said she saw MacNamarra's face behind the window of the stairwell door on the seventh floor. Dooley was a bit of a punchbag. We'd each of us taken our turn holding her out over the stairwell, and even though we knew she was only talking to us because she wanted our approval, we staked out the door for a good week in case we might see something we pretended we didn't want to see.

As we got older, the story grew with us. As the lift descended past the seventh floor the lights would now go out entirely, and when the doors opened in the foyer the lift would be empty, except for a sweet burning smell, like someone just put out a match. But for the passenger, the lift would keep going, deep down into the ground; down into the dark.

The Under Tower was the tower we knew reflected in the concrete and dirt which surrounded us. The primal ground in which the city had been seeded, the ground that untamed development had poisoned and corrupted. Sometimes, you could see the Under Tower in the sheets of rainwater which pooled between the broken flags, tinged dull and pink by the local clay. It extended deep into the earth, a neatly ordered hell. The corridors were endless, the walls were like red Chinese paper, and if you ever found yourself there, you would never leave.

> • <

Eff used to follow us on our family holidays during the summer. He was never invited but he used to tail behind us in his off-white VW van. Most years, we would stay in the trailer park just outside Hunstanton on the Norfolk coast, and Eff would park up on the path outside. This was how he liked it, he was part of something, but he was also separate, the travelling wise man camped outside the castle walls.

In the mornings, I remember how the side door of his van would be open and he'd be sitting on the edge with a cigarette and a newspaper.

'Kiddo,' he'd say. A one-finger salute to his temple.

He was never supposed to leave his van there – there was a sign saying as much that I swear the proprietors of the mobile home park used to move around so it was opposite our rental every year. My father sometimes had difficulty booking a place at all because they were frightened Eff might follow him. But he was never moved on. That was how people treated Eff back then. He had the sort of presence that made people take a step back, reconsider the wisdom of making any sort of fuss. Even compared with my father, who was the brother who had spent time in the army, Eff was the one who intimidated. He was a man who looked as though he stood taller than he was. He dressed slim and there was a stillness about him that gave him a strange kind of stature. I had no doubt he was the sort of man who knew how to handle himself in a fight, but it wasn't as though he looked dangerous or violent, it was more that he looked as though he didn't care. Fight me, he seemed to say, and I might bleed, but you'll get bloody and some things will never wash clean.

The last summer we spent at Hunstanton was the last summer Eff spent with us. As far as I know, it was the last time any of us saw him, and perhaps that knowledge colours every memory I have of that time. As though everything he said to us, every move he made, might have contained a hidden key that could explain where he went.

On that day, his destination was clearer.

'We going to the cliffs, kiddo?' Eff said and I nodded. We always went to the cliffs. Every year. It was like a pilgrimage. Just him and me.

Hunstanton, *Sunny Hunny*. It's one of the smaller resort towns on the eastern flank of Britain. Positioned on the north-west curve of the rump of East Anglia, it is a rare British coastal resort that looks inward across the Wash, and on a clear day, you might mistake the line of clouds on the horizon for Lincolnshire or Skegness rather than a different country entirely. The town slopes downhill to the coast, where the waterfront is spotted with the usual amusement arcades, seaside attractions, chippies and general stores decked out with postcards and buckets and spades and nets. It's perhaps a little more genteel than the likes of Great Yarmouth or Scarborough; the beach itself trails lazily westwards, but to the east it gives way to lumpen scree as it passes beneath the rise of the cliffs.

The red chalk cliffs are a jarring sight even if you're expecting them. We've come to expect certain colours to be assigned as signifiers. Red is a warning, red is an emergency, red is anger and anxiety. To the British, used to browns and greys and greens, it is an alien colour to find in a landscape. It is Mars or Australia, places the average Brit only pretends to understand. But there it is in the Hunstanton cliffs – a broad stripe of orange, a broad stripe of crimson. A bright and vivid snapshot of the mid-Cretaceous landscape; a living diagram of a hundred million years of the land itself densely folded upon each other like hardened steel. Here is history cleaved cleanly and put on display, the ages demarcated in bright colours of chalk and ore, the grit thick with Albian ammonite fossils coiled in its clay. Along the sea line, boulders are painted with green-furred moss and laid out in straight ranks, obsessively arranged by an orderly tide. Above, tube-nosed fulmars nest on the cliffside, circling stiff-winged across the water.

There is academic interest here, it goes without saying, but to the layman it's difficult to describe the landscape without resorting to the vocabulary of a butcher's shop.

Here is the meat of the cliffs: crimson as freshly cleaved pork shoulder. Above it, a layer of white fat, generous and even to counter the east coast winter. At the top, the bristling grass of the coast's hide. It is a scientific diagram stolen from the wrong textbook. Geology as biology, the earth as seasoned flesh.

With Eff's stories behind me, it is no wonder that as a child, the cliffs fascinated me: red-and-white striped like the sticks of rock you could buy on the seafront, but dense and portentous in a manner that left me unsettled. Up close, the cliffs could be dangerous. Rocks pried loose would fall and the beach was littered with the blood-coloured clusters, sea-slick and glistening in the surf like flesh bitten free and spat into the sand.

To me, a tower kid from the city, the cliffs were an anomaly. The natural landscape I knew was the geometric green fringe beyond the city limits, I saw it turn with the seasons but it was always just out of reach, dispersing with distance whenever I tried to get close to it. The colour and shape of the cliffs was at odds with how I understood the countryside, but to Eff it was the other way around.

'This is how the country is,' he once told me. 'Everything else is wrong. This is how it's supposed to be.'

Eff talked about landscape as though it was an animal. I told him he made it sound as though he thought it was alive and he just gave me an amused look and turned away.

'Used to be.' He gestured at a fissure rising up the chalk face. 'See that?' he said. 'There's a path that goes up the cliff.

Near vertical and no easy climb. The chalk is soft, fragile. You can see by all the fallen stones that it crumbles easily.

'But there *is* a path. And when the moon is right, the light of the cliffs takes on a different colour and a different shape. The shadows strengthen into ledges and steps and handholds. It can look taller than it does in the sunlight, because in that particular spectrum of light, it *is* taller. And there's a story that says, if you pick the right night and you pick the right path, you can climb to the very top of the cliff. And what's at the top?'

'The caravan park,' I said.

He laughed and shook his head.

'Not on that night, no.' He whistled, a low note of hollow awe. 'On that night, if the conditions are just so, you'll find yourself way up high, higher than the cliff, all the way to the clouds themselves, and if you look down, you'll see the corpse of Britain laid out before you as though you had crawled from the very wound that killed her.'

He lit another cigarette and grinned at me with crooked teeth.

'You believe me?' he said.

I nodded because that was how the game was played. If I questioned him he'd stalk off, irritated and bored. He needed attention, acquiescence. He nodded back and slipped his pack of cigarettes into the chest pocket of his shirt.

'Good girl,' he said. 'In the old days, ancient times, the people here built a tower on the top of the cliff. Did you know that? Well, they did. It would have been just about there, see?'

I followed his fingertip, squinting into the brightness behind the clouds.

'And the people back then knew a thing or two about places with power. They lived with the moon and they knew when the time was right just by seeing the light of it on the skin of their hands. Once a year, when it was time, the tribes of the island would send their best people here. They'd send their representatives to this very spot. There'd be a big feast. A party, you know? A festival. There'd be music and bonfires and all of that. And then, when the moon was ready and the path was clear, the representatives would climb the cliff. They'd go there to petition the gods, they said. To stop a war with their neighbours, to get more livestock in their farms, better crops, better breeding. All those things. They'd petition the gods by climbing that cliff and putting their cases to them upstairs directly.

'The tower was just for show. It marked the place where the path was, but it was mostly there so the festivalgoers could look up and pretend they knew where the petitioners had got to. And when they were gone, they set fireworks off from the top so it looked like souls being taken up into the heavens. And everyone down at the festival would go crazy because they thought the whole thing was a success for another year.

'Only of course, none of the petitioners would come back. Not because they'd gone to the gods, but because all they'd see from the top would be the corpse of Britain, lain out there as though she'd just been murdered. They'd see how the land lay. They'd see the reality of their impact on the world. They'd see their status in the universe, and when you're faced with something like that, there's not much you can do really, except lose your damn mind.'

He tapped the side of his head.

'And that's exactly what they did,' he said. 'They climbed that cliff to see what they could see. All they saw was the truth of the world, and that was it for the lot of them. They reached as far as they could reach and then they fell. All the way down. Only they never landed. Not here. For all we know, they're still falling somewhere. Endlessly falling.'

He smirked at me.

'You're probably saying to yourself, how could you possibly know? If everyone who climbed that cliff died or disappeared or went crazy in the head? How could old Uncle Eff have even the slightest idea of what they saw?'

His smirk widened and he leaned closer, his tone dropping to a conspiratorial murmur.

'Well, there was one who went up but didn't look,' he said. 'A young girl she was. Local to the area. Her papa made the fireworks they used for the festival, just as his daddy used to light beacon fires at the top in his day. But the girl knew the fireworks were a trick. Something bright and beautiful to distract the mob from what was really happening. She wanted to know the truth, and so, on the night of the festival, she followed the petitioners up the cliff, hiding in the shadows so she wouldn't be seen. She stayed a safe distance from the others and she didn't dare look down. Up she went, into the moon, into the clouds, and she nearly reached the top when she heard them screaming up ahead of her. Not screaming like her little brother screamed. Not screaming like a *person* screams, but screaming like an animal under the knife.

'Instinct told her to cover her eyes, but not before one of the petitioners, the one at the back, came stumbling down the path towards her, mad already, eyes on fire. He was yelling about what he had seen as though by shouting it, he could make himself forget. He took her for a spirit and tried to fight with her, to push her off the top, but she fought her way free until she was alone up there with the dreadful silence.

'She was there for a long time, trying to find her way down. She kept her eyes closed, but when she didn't believe that wasn't good enough, she blinded herself with her thumbs just to be sure.'

Eff held both his thumbs up to my eyes, grinning until I flinched backwards and swiped his hands away. He laughed.

'She didn't know how she got back, but she did. And when she was home she told her papa until he believed her and made a promise to set his gunpowder to the foot of the tower and send it to the gods themselves.'

Eff nodded at the cliff face, looming before us.

'That's what's at the top of that cliff,' he said. '*Perspective.* Perspective of us against the land. Perspective of how we fit into the fabric of our place. And we're just not built to understand that sort of scale. We can't take it in. You know? Because some things are just too big for little things like us to understand. It's like a parasite understanding the host beyond what it takes from it. And yet…'

He got to his feet, stretching tall. 'And yet, given the choice, who wouldn't look?'

He grinned at me, a brief gesture of inclusion before he turned away and stalked across the sand to the moat of shadow beneath the cliff. I thought I could still hear him talking, as though all through the morning he hadn't been talking to me at all.

> • <

Here's a story I wrote about my father.

We lived in flat 1109, my mum, my dad and me. We had the sun in the afternoon and a view over the multistorey and the rec grounds. You could see past the city limits and on some days it almost looked like we weren't in the city at all. The distance was green and blue and grey, the hills rolled untamed. I used to pretend we lived in an air balloon flying above a wild landscape.

We had perspective, my dad would say, and people would envy us for it. Mum said he was an idiot, she said when the lift was out, the stairs were a devil on her back. When she told her friends how we all got on like a house on fire, she meant the flat was a tinderbox waiting for a spark.

Dad considered himself born in the wrong country at the wrong time. He left the army when I was born but never found anything to replace it with. He listened to louche jazz and read Beat poetry, he taught me to roll his cigarettes and tried to show me how to swing dance, but I was too embarrassed and the lounge was far too small. He worked shifts in the warehouses south of the ring road, from which he brought home enough money to get him drunk, if not always enough to keep us fed. Mum made up the shortfall with extra cleaning work. When she thought her impatience with him would reach breaking point, she picked up late shifts in the business district offices, and in that way they could miss each other for days. She'd bring me back pencils and empty notebooks which had been thrown away. I used them to sketch cartoons. I drew Mum and Dad. I drew the Under Tower. I drew MacNamarra pulling himself apart.

When I was twelve, I got home from school to find them both standing outside in the hall, thunder brewing between them. Dad was surrounded by plastic bags, stuffed with his belongings. Clothes, books, his precious vinyl.

Mum stood in the doorway like she was guarding it. Dad came up to me and he just stood there for what felt like hours. Eventually, he dropped to his knees and told me he had to go away for a while. He looked like he was begging and I hated him for it.

I sided with my mum that day; I walked past my dad without a word, leaving him on his knees among his belongings. From the doorway, I watched as he got back to his feet and turned to look at us one last time. And I watched as just behind him, the lift in the south hallway arrived on cue to take him away.

I had half a mind to race the lift to the foyer. I could have done it at that age, barrelling down the stairs like a helter-skelter. But I didn't, I just imagined it opening passengerless on the ground floor, while my dad continued downwards into the dark.

> • <

When people asked me where my father had gone – because people did, back then – I would tell them he was in the Under Tower and that he would never come back. I would imagine him living in a flat which looked like ours, but a flat in which it was never daylight outside; where the rooms were painted in Hunstanton red and there were sounds from the rooms on either side that you never wanted to understand. As I sat alone in our flat, I imagined him alone in his.

As I got older, I'd tell people I'd forgotten about him, because it seemed easier than to explain. I grew up and moved away from the tower. I made my own life and was proud of it for a time. I fell and failed in love, I rolled my own cigarettes and learned to swing dance with boys who were both better and worse teachers than my dad ever was. I taught myself to drink; I taught myself never to drink again. I dreamed of broken rooms and ochre corridors extending and twisting and folding in upon themselves.

I met Carrie's father and we tell ourselves we're in love, but I've never fully trusted him. The men in my family go away, and the way I see him looking at our daughter some days, I know he's no different.

I found employment in a company based in a tower of its own. Out in the business district like the ones my mum used to clean after hours. Over time, I learned to ride the lift, but even then, I would watch the floor indicator numbers as though they were counting down to something terrible. Between floors seven and six, I would yawn and cover my face to hide the fact that my eyes were tightly closed.

❯ • ❮

Eff was there for the rest of that holiday. He told me other stories, but he didn't seem to believe in them in the same way as he did with the story about the cliff path and the corpse of Britain. I've come to appreciate that children sense a storyteller's faith in their narrative in a manner that adults can underestimate, and so I don't consider it a surprise that I no longer remember Eff's other stories with the same veracity.

The holiday continued in the usual unexceptional ways. The mobile home became too small for us as the week wore on. One night, Dad and Eff went to one of the pubs in town and they both came home bloody for reasons neither saw fit to explain. Both made a point of laughing about it the following morning but I didn't believe that either.

I spent a lot of time on my own. I walked about beneath the cliffs looking for fossils in the shingle, souvenirs from an earlier, mostly forgotten extinction. In the town, I spent my pocket money on a keyring in the shape of the lighthouse and a little glass bottle of red chalk. When we left, we waved goodbye to Eff and none of us ever saw him again.

It was only when I was older that I understood I had barely known him at all. I had only ever seen him intermittently as a girl and then, being young, on my holidays and easily impressed, he had burned absurdly bright in my memory. I had only ever seen the storyteller Eff, the adventurer, the wise man camped outside the castle walls. I was nearly fifteen when it finally clicked that his name wasn't even Eff; it was F for Francis, for Frank, for Frankie. My dad was out of the picture by then, so I never did get the chance to interrogate him properly. Without primary sources, Eff slipped easily into legend. A few memories of his stories stitched together to make up for the fact that the man who had told them was still a stranger to me.

I like to believe that his own story was more satisfying. He had waved us off from the campsite and I had looked back out the window to see if he was following us, but he wasn't. His stick-figure slouched out of sight behind the rise and he was gone. With hindsight, I realise that I wanted him to fade, to dissolve, as though he had been holding himself together until we were just out of sight. It was dark when we got home to the tower and the full moon was there to connect the stories I had heard with an audible click. Eff had stayed behind to climb the path up the cliff face. His wasn't a story, it was a confession. He had gone to see the corpse of Britain, because – in my mind – it was what he was always destined to do.

The more time passed without him, the truer and stronger the story became to me. It would have been compromised if he had come back to us and – to my shame – there was a part of me that didn't want that. I wanted his story to be real, and accepting that he had done what I imagined him to have done, there was only one way for the fidelity of his fairy tale to hold true.

Time passed and the story held firm enough for me to let it go and live my life.

It was the news that brought it back. Flooding in Norfolk, increased erosion along the coastline. The last nesting pair of local petrels lost in the wind. Storms and hurricanes and rising tides. At first, I closed my eyes and I primed my thumbs as though it would be better not to see.

But when I looked again, there were the cliffs, the stripes dulled on the television, but unmistakable. It was a part of my story that I wanted to be part of Carrie's. If the landscape were to disappear then I wanted her to have witnessed it with her own eyes, so she could recall it as a memory, without embellishment. I imagined she might grow up to become the person who saves it.

I don't know why I didn't tell Carrie's father where we were going. Perhaps it's because I thought he would want to come too, as though he might use our proposed trip to Hunstanton as a way to connect with my childhood and make the cord that joined us stronger than I ever intended.

I knew he read books about how to appear invested, but I wasn't having any of it.

I told him we were going to visit my mother and he waved us off. Carrie craned around in the seat to watch him diminish in stature and vanish completely as though he'd been holding it all inside.

> • <

Here's a story I wrote about my mother.

My mother never moved out of 1109. She shared it with a succession of men, none of whom seemed to fit. When we met, we did so on neutral ground. Pubs and cinema foyers and coffee shops and supermarkets.

One evening she called me, and although we spoke only briefly, I read something in her voice that I'd not heard since I was small. I cancelled my plans for the evening and made my way home for the first time in nearly twenty years.

When I reached the tower, I took the stairs. I wasn't as fit as I'd been as a kid growing up in the stairwells, and the steps felt harder and steeper than I remembered. The stairwell rang with the echoes of slamming doors, as though a message heralding my return was being passed from floor to floor. On the eleventh floor, I saw the south hallway had been repainted since I'd last seen it. The view from its strip of windows showed less perspective, more concrete, more glass. The green and blue and grey wilderness of my childhood was nothing but a thin pencil line in the distance.

Mum was wearing make-up when she opened the door. She was wearing her Sunday best. On the sofa, there was a man who looked like my dad, had my dad ever lived to be old. He had lank thin hair and liver spots; his skin had loosened into jowls. But behind the glasses were those same eyes begging to be understood.

He said my name and all at once I was twelve years old and my dad was on his knees on the landing, his every belonging strewn around him. He said my name, he reached out a hand.

Somewhere, in a distant squalid room with broken floorboards, I pictured a man sitting alone. Unshaven and rake-like, he watched hellish silhouettes dance upon the red-paper walls, his breaths rationed, fearing he might draw attention.

My father is gone, I said. My father is in the Under Tower.

Mum joined the man on the sofa as though presenting themselves to me as one might make everything alright. They sat together, hands held as though they would never part. I looked at the way they looked at me, hopeful and apprehensive. I turned away from them, out of the door and into the hall. I heard the man get to his feet but I didn't look back. Somewhere behind me, he called my name.

In the red-paper room, my father glanced up.

And the lift in the south hallway arrived on cue to take me away.

❭ • ❬

The beach of Carrie's childhood was different to the beach of mine. It was late autumn and the stretch of sand was mostly empty, the sea too cold for all but the hardiest of swimmers. I watched her run across the sand, the mittens tied to the cuffs of her sleeves fluttering around her.

Perhaps it is the same, but there are aspects of it that I'm surprised I don't remember. The smell of the sea, salt and rot and ripening weather, which I associate more with other holidays I took alone when I was older. The landscape feels softer than it did, in a way I can't attribute entirely to the reports of erosion I read about in the news. The cliffs are masked in black netting but the colours seem less vivid than those in my memory. Russet browns and umber reds and off whites. If I squint, I can still see the meat of them, but they are not what I imagine when I dream about the place.

It is only through Carrie that I see there is still magic in them. The way she listens as I tell her Eff's stories, with wide eyes and open mouth. The wonder with which she regards the layers of chalk and ore rising above us both.

I think of the world she will never get a chance to see. I think of the world I once knew but have forgotten.

That night there is a bonfire on the beach and we stay up late, past Carrie's bedtime, to join the crowds huddled around it in our coats. There is music somewhere and the coldness of the November night draws us closer as though we know each other.

When I think of Eff, I imagine his face lit by the fire in the same way that Carrie's is now, and there is something of prehistory in the immediacy of it, civilisation shrunk down to a fragile point of brightness in the vastness of the night. Faces ruddy by firelight, huddled close in hoods and hats. I think of my father, of Carrie's father, of my mother and me, and through some trick of the light we are all Carrie's age together. Wide-eyed and open-mouthed. All of us sitting around the same fire, silent in our wonder, watching the flames and seeing the stories hidden inside them. Sometimes you need to look at the shapes they make, Eff says. Sometimes that's the only way to see how it burns.

There is a sweep of wind, and as one we look up, tracing the sparks as they dance upwards into the darkness, disappearing into the vacuum of the sky. And as they blink into blackness, one by one, it is easy to close our eyes and see them thrive, unimpeded on their journey into other layers outside the limits of our perspective, dancing onwards, forever upwards, pressing forwards to petition their gods.

WALKING TO DOGGERLAND

(3)

Penny dreamed of the sea and the gods it contained. She dreamed of her parents, risking the waves in a wooden rowboat, their backs to her, their faces turned to the horizon. She dreamed she stood on the cliff at the top of Barrow Hill. She looked over the edge and imagined she saw a figure climbing up towards her. She dreamed that Sister Agnes stood beside her, the wind snatching at the surplus of her cowl and making her vast.

'What if we were to jump?' Agnes said, her voice girlish and excited. 'What if we were to fall?'

She reached out her hand to Penny and there was something glasslike in her smile. Then, in the familiar manner of dreams, it wasn't Agnes at all, it was Lulu instead. Still wearing her hospital robe, unbowed by the cold and the wind, but the smile was the same. The sense that something dangerous was laced through something familiar.

When Penny woke, it was still early and the window beyond the curtain was dark. She could see the hallway light was on outside, framing the doorway with a warm and angular halo. She tried to relax but found herself restless, lying in the unfamiliar bed, allowing her eyes to adjust to the dark and staring up at the unfamiliar ceiling. She had always imagined ceilings as blank canvasses for dreams and the stranger they were, the stranger the dreams became. Her cell in the order had a flagstone roof, perpendicular lines and intersections, the flags open and inviting like the pages of a holy book she needed the time to master. The ceiling in her flat in London was still uncomfortable. A painted expanse, the paint cracked in ways that still felt random and chaotic to her. She would lie in bed and, when she should have been succumbing to sleep, she searched the paintwork for its source instead.

> • <

The first time Penny entered the order, she had felt the world contract, and there had been a degree of reassurance in the way she left the bulk of her at the door. She saw the faces of the sisters already present, their features confined to a triangular aperture within the twist of their veils. Even then, she saw the differences between them: Sister Theresa with her round pink cheeks, Sister Francesca with her sharp nose and rulered brow. Even though the way they moved had become so similar with experience, she saw traces of their character in the way they walked, the way they turned their heads, the way they thought and acted.

She had only been a visitor then, not even a novice – she had yet to make her vows or cut her hair – but already she felt her future narrow before her. It focused intently, and the clarity and brightness of it was overwhelming. For a time she felt flushed with the sense that she had found her place in the world. Where everyone else hunted so desperately for purpose, how lucky she was to understand her path while still so young. She saw herself fitting into the prescription of her future like a simple key in an elaborate lock.

To an extent, the cell she was offered was not so different from the student accommodation she had been living in for the past three years. A narrow room with a single bed and a desk. The crucifix mounted above the bed the only concession to decoration. There was a window high in the wall which let in a bright rectangle of morning that diminished into a knotted line across the desk by midday, and when the door was closed she had a distinct sense that there was nothing on the outside, and there was nothing that needed to be.

It was the smell that took the most getting used to. The order's hallways were dense with the odour of bodies who lived without proper access to the fullness of modern hygiene. On a hot day, the undercurrent of sweat, blood and excrement was unmistakable, but when it rained, the corridors were washed through with a brisk, verdant dampness that felt so fresh and pure that Penny would sometimes stand in her doorway with her eyes closed, letting it transport her to a meadow, a mountainside, a rainforest. Sometimes, she imagined that she would open her eyes and see that Sister Agnes's neatly manicured garden in the centre of the quad would have grown rampant and overwhelmed the building, drowning it in dank greenery.

The purpose of the order, she was told, was to become closer to the grace of God through the study of His words and His deeds. She would meditate, she would pray, she would devote her thoughts to a single purpose. On that, her first day, she sat on the edge of the bed, feeling the hardness and spareness of it. Her feet were together, her hands rested on her knees, and she sat there like that for hours, barely moving. With her physical space reduced to the bare essentials, she considered how her mental world had the potential to open wide. How with patience and practice, she might become receptive to a world she had hoped for, but which she had barely imagined before.

There was a stillness to the room. A faint stuffiness to the air, a trace of damp masonry and exhaust fumes, as though nothing had moved through it for years. Outside, the city sounded as it always had done: traffic – human and vehicular – bustling against each other; engines, voices, horns. But the room felt separate. It was a bubble of a world, adjacent to the one she had known, but distinct from it. With the door closed, it was a world whose dimensions could be so simply understood they became negligible. She closed her eyes and imagined the infinite.

> • <

In her room in the guest house, Penny held her breath so she could listen to the sound of the sea outside, the gentle give and take, the asthmatic wheeze of the tide, filling and exhaling against the sand. She had opened the window a little, seasoning the lavender stuffiness of the room with sand and salt. There was something hypnotic about the sound and the smell: a secret music to it that made her drift.

'What if we were to fall?' Lulu said. Her hand was cold, her fingers too long.

It was a different noise that distracted her and snapped her back to the clarity of consciousness. The sound of soft, padding footsteps in the hallway, on the other side of her room from the window. The closeness of the sound swelled it and made it intrusive. She looked to the door and saw a shadow flicker beneath it as someone passed by, the shadows strengthened and gathered as something leaned closer.

Penny pushed herself up in the bed, afraid that if she made too much noise, she might frighten her visitor away. The next sound was a snuffling one, the unmistakable inquisitive exploration of a dog tracing a scent.

'Oscar.' It was absurd, of course, but it didn't matter. Perhaps this was still her dream; and if it was her dream, why shouldn't it be Oscar?

Penny threw off the covers and hunted in the darkness for the dressing gown she had worn the previous night. She was dimly aware that such a mundane detail grounded the experience in a cool reality. When she opened the bedroom door the dog had gone, but she searched for and found the trace of sand where it had been, a thin trail of scattered yellow gold that led back down the hallway to the stairs.

Without thinking, Penny followed. Down the stairs and through the hallway. She let the front door close behind her, not considering how she might get back in.

The night was still dense, still chilled from the evening's rain, but there was an outside light in the porch which spotlit a circle of the road and the edges of the dunes beyond. A line of footprints ran from the door across the road and Penny followed them, holding her dressing gown closed with one hand. The rain had left the tarmac wet and cool underfoot, it glittered like a dance floor under the halogen light.

The dunes were rougher under her bare feet, the grass spiky and wild, surprising her confident progress and forcing her to stumble and slow down. The detritus of the beach, wood and stone and sundry rubbish left behind by the careless, was jagged beneath her soles, but Penny plunged onwards. Most of the cloud cover had cleared to the periphery of the sky and the stars were dense like a fisherman's net heaving with its glittering harvest. To the west, she could see the speckled lights of Bryhanton, hugging the coastline beyond the edge of the cliffs. There was something coy and conservative about the colours of it, something unadventurous and afraid in the way the lights reflected in downward brushstrokes in the sea.

The beach was empty, the trace of the moon made it pale and grey. There was just enough light for her to see the line of footprints continue away from her to the water's edge. She bent low to examine them, pushing her hair back from her ear. The wavering gait of a loping dog was easy to recognise, each print four small thumbs circling a child's shallow fist. Each print scooped the sand with a hurried enthusiasm which didn't dim even once they reached the line to the tip of the tide. She thought she could make out the shadows of footprints beyond the waterline, increasingly shallow dents in the surface of the sand, straightening to flatness with each wash of the sea as the elastic of the beach reasserted itself. She stopped at the water's edge and stared owlishly into the horizon as though she might see Oscar waiting for her there.

She spoke the dog's name, but didn't shout it. The unwelcome foolishness of the situation was creeping upon her and she had no wish to acknowledge it directly, fearing it might accelerate the reality and dispel what was left of the dream.

From somewhere, she thought she heard the sound of a dog bark. A single exclamation point punctuating something impossible, somewhere out to sea. Shapes danced before her and coalesced with the shadows. She could see Oscar, then, standing out in the waves, looking back towards the land, her head cocked in benign bafflement that she wasn't being followed. Penny didn't move any closer to the sea. She stood on the beach and waved instead.

'Oscar!' she said, and then she shouted it. 'Oscar!'

The dog's tail wagged languidly.

A whistle cut through the darkness and the dog stiffened to attention.

Penny searched the horizon until she found the figure she had been expecting. A silhouette of a man, waiting in the impossible distance. The clean line of the horizon where he waited made his scale impossible to judge. The clouds slid from the face of the moon, and for a moment the man was not quite a silhouette after all. There was briefly enough light to brighten his profile, enough to let Penny see the seams of his cheekbones, the dusting of beard across his jaw, the loose-fitting clothes. She saw his face was slightly downcast as he waited for the animal he had summoned. She saw him raise his fingers to his lips once more and again the night was cut through with his whistle. A haze passed between them, and when it had cleared the figure was no longer a man, but a woman in woollen trousers and an ill-fitting coat. Her head started to tilt upwards but then the light was gone again, the figure fading with it, and Penny watched as the dog turned away from her and loped towards the blue-black horizon, dispersing into the darkness and shadows of the sea.

> • <

Two years after she had found Oscar on the beach at Stove Causeway, Penny and her sisters spent their last summer at Breakers. Throughout the six weeks there was no indication they would not be returning the following year, and even Mrs Kaye seemed unaware that they would not be back. She had waved them away on their final day with the usual rote promise to see them again the following year.

The following autumn, the owners of Breakers sold the property to a retired American film director. The following winter, Mrs Kaye lost control of her Citroen 2CV and struck one of the pines at the top of Wallasey Road. When asked what had happened, she explained that she had oversteered abruptly, momentarily believing that the Pinnerman had stepped into the road in front of her car. He had stared down at her as the emergency services cut her out of the wreckage and she could have sworn he was smiling at her in a way she didn't like at all. When she was discharged, she moved to Southbourne to be closer to her daughter and never returned to Bryhanton again.

The final summer at Breakers had been a quiet one, free of any portents of the future to darken the sisters' memories of it. The previous year, Lulu had taken a summer job at the small department store in town; here she had made a modest sum working behind the cosmetics counter. This time she had a secretarial position closer to home, but she still travelled out to Bryhanton for occasional weekends, a gesture that flattered her sisters, given that both Matthew and Faye were away for the best part of the period.

On a bright Sunday afternoon during their last weekend, Lulu had led them up the cliff path to the summit of Barrow

Hill and they spread themselves out on the brushy meadow, splaying the brittle grass into halos around them.

Penny was growing restless. She had tired of the book she'd brought for the expedition and the grass was making the back of her neck itch. She got to her feet and teetered closer to the edge. A thin rope fence demarcated a safe line to remain behind, and beyond it there was a foot or so of bulbous, bristly tussocks before the cliff plunged down to the rocks below.

The mid-afternoon sun was bright enough to force Penny to shield her eyes with her hand.

'It's a clear day,' she said. 'I can see Doggerland.'

The sea was an even grey, but in the distance, approximately north-north-east, it appeared both darker and more silvery, as though an enormous fish basked just below the surface. It felt right to her; the holiday was almost over, and this was the first time they had come to pay their respects to the undersea peninsula.

They had played Doggerland in one way or another since they first started coming to Breakers as children. Their mother had been with them those first few years, and the fact they could trace the story back to her gave it a resonance it would otherwise have lacked. She had told them about the landmass that once connected Britain to mainland Europe. They had traced it in the enormous World Atlas stored on the top shelf in the front room, finding the underwater contour lines and imaging them green and brown. Since then, it was Lulu who had deduced where it might have been located from the causeway, and some years later, once their mother had begun to stay away, it was Lulu who first saw it from the summit of Barrow Hill. The trace of silver beneath the waves did seem to be waiting for them each subsequent year, cementing the story into one that became a myth, with its own weight and depth in that curious way childhood games often do.

Behind her, Lulu grunted.

'You can't see Doggerland, Penny,' she said. 'Doggerland doesn't exist.'

'I can,' Penny said. Turning back, with consternation.

Lulu lay in the grass, a hand limp across her face to block out the sun. She had turned her head to look in Penny's direction and Penny could see her expression was sharp between the shadow web of her fingers.

'We always see Doggerland when we come up here,' Penny said. She was aware, on some deeper, intangible level, that she was sounding childish.

'Dogger *Bank*,' Lulu said, 'is further north. We wouldn't be able to see it from here, even if it wasn't underwater. It's a sand bank. Shallow sea. It's all that's left.'

Penny turned back to the view and found the silvery line once more. It was the same line that had always been there, the same line they had all decided was the shape of Doggerland beneath the water.

For some reason, she felt suddenly sad.

'I do wish it was still there,' she said.

'What?' Ronnie pushed herself up onto her elbows.

'I mean, the real Doggerland,' Penny said. 'The old one. The land that used to join us to Europe.'

Lulu pushed herself up into a sitting position, crossing her legs and snatching at a length of grass, stripping it with her fingernails.

'It wasn't very interesting,' she said. 'Just moors and marsh. Like the rest of Norfolk. It wasn't some fantasy land. No mountains and forests, no castles on hilltops.'

'I never said it was.'

'I'm just saying.' Lulu smiled at her, a benevolent expression that was both matter-of-fact and condescending in a manner that reminded her of school.

Penny shrugged. 'I just thought it would be nice to be joined to the mainland. To be able to get there without having to take a boat.'

Ronnie shook her head.

'But that would mean we were no longer an island,' she said. 'And it's because we're an island that we have the best navy in the world.'

Lulu rolled her eyes.

'For pity's sake, Ronnie,' she said, 'you sound like a textbook.'

She looked at Penny with a wry expression.

'We lost Doggerland,' she said, 'but we gained an empire instead. Isn't that nice?'

Ronnie pushed her shoulder so she rocked, first physically and then with laughter.

'If we weren't an island we'd have been invaded even more. The Spanish wouldn't have needed an Armada, they'd have just walked here.'

'The Spanish wouldn't have walked here through Denmark!' Penny said.

'Besides, we'd all be Vikings then,' Lulu said. 'The Vikings would have taken over everything already, so the Spanish wouldn't have stood a chance.'

'I just meant,' Penny said, struggling a little because she wasn't really sure what she had meant, 'it would be nice to be less… cut off from everything.'

Ronnie looked prim. 'If we weren't cut off, we'd have rabies over here, and if we had that you'd never get a dog.'

Penny sighed.

'We're never going to have a dog anyway,' she said.

Lulu got to her feet and joined Penny by the rope.

'One day you might,' she said. 'Penny and her dogs. I can imagine you with a whole pack of them. Huskies. You know? Mush!'

Penny laughed, but the comment felt faintly mean-spirited. She retreated to the grass and sat down heavily.

Lulu remained standing, staring out at the horizon as though something had caught her attention.

Ronnie sighed theatrically.

'Lulu,' she said. 'What are you doing?'

Lulu's head bobbed a little in reply. She turned back to them, her smile short.

'I was just thinking,' she said. 'That's all.'

'Can't you think sitting down?' Ronnie said. 'You're looming. I don't like it when you're looming.'

Lulu ignored her.

'I was thinking about Doggerland,' she said.

'Well, of course you were,' Ronnie said. 'We were just talking about it.'

'Isn't it funny to think what this place would have been like when there was land out there rather than water?' Lulu turned back, shielding her eyes from the sun with her hand like a sailor in a crow's nest.

'This wouldn't have been a hill then. It certainly wouldn't have been a cliff. You would have been able to set off in that direction without even checking your step. And you could keep going on and on.'

She hitched up her skirt and stepped over the rope.

Ronnie sat bolt upright, startling Penny into doing the same.

'Lulu,' Ronnie said. 'What are you doing?'

Lulu didn't say anything.

'Lulu.' Ronnie scrambled to her feet and Penny followed.

'I'm not going to do anything,' Lulu said. 'I just think it's interesting.' Despite her reassurances, she took a step forward towards the edge.

'What's interesting?' Penny said.

'That the same winds, the same waves that took Doggerland, shaped these cliffs. The landscape pushed itself together and made hills and mountains, and then the sea and the wind whittled them down until they were soft. And they're still doing it. They're doing it right now. Look! Look at the way the sea is chipping away at the edges of the land, breaking it down into sand. This is what it means to live on an island, Penny. We're constantly under siege, and I don't mean by the Spanish.'

She paused, looking up into the grey spread of the sky. For a horrible moment, Penny imagined she might lift her arms and let the wind snatch her away from them.

'Lulu,' she said. 'Please come back.'

'I'm not going anywhere,' Lulu said, as though the suggestion was ridiculous. 'But how long will *here* be here for? If I were to stay standing right here in this spot, how long would the ground be here to support me?'

She closed her eyes.

'You can almost hear it coming apart,' she said. 'You can almost hear it dissolving, like when you stand on the beach and the tide comes in to drag away the sand beneath you.'

Penny reached out her hand.

'So come back to firmer ground.' She was suddenly conscious that the gesture wasn't enough. She stepped forward boldly, stepping over the safety chain. She heard

Ronnie take a sharp breath behind her, but even though she didn't take her eyes from Lulu, she knew that Ronnie had done the same.

The silence was tender, overextended. The sun chased clouds across Lulu's expression until she burst into laughter, lightly stepping past her sisters, back to the crumpled meadow.

'I was only playing,' she said. 'The looks on your faces! My darling little saviours! Come on, Mrs Kaye will be hollering herself ragged if we're not back soon.'

She snatched up her cardigan from where she had left it in the grass and set off towards the cliff path, her movements wiry and careless, her face cast up, her eyes closed, accepting the grace of the afternoon sun.

〉•〈

The morning was dark grey with a haze of rain by the time Penny met Veronica in the breakfast room. Her sister, the only guest present, was already on her second pot of coffee and was browsing the news websites on her phone. She glanced up over the top of her glasses as Penny joined her.

'You look like you slept well,' Veronica said, and Penny assumed it hadn't been intended to sound like an accusation.

'Mostly,' she said. 'I'm not really used to soft beds. It feels a little like I'm drowning.'

Veronica snorted.

'Well, at least you avoided the wine,' she said. 'That was a mistake. Next time, tell me to leave it at Lulu's place and not bring it here.' She smiled brightly at the young woman in the starched waitress uniform who had approached their table with a notebook open in her hand. Her expression was slightly flinty, as though it was a miserable day and the sisters' presence was a burden too far.

Penny ordered a modest breakfast and watched as the waitress tried to make a mark in her notepad. Doodling a spiral in the corner to kick-start the ballpoint pen.

'More toast?'

'Please.'

'More coffee?'

'Not for me, thank you,' Veronica said. 'Penny?'

'A cup of tea would be lovely, thank you.'

'Tea.' The waitress frowned as her pen defeated her. She cast the sisters a dark glance as though this infraction might have been their fault, then turned on her heel and walked back to the kitchen.

'I've called the handyman Lulu mentioned,' Veronica said. 'I'll nip into town later and get a few more sets of keys cut. We can leave one with him and one with the social worker. She might be around later this morning. It would be good to meet her, don't you think?'

Penny nodded, only half listening. She looked at the windows and it struck her how often as a child she had walked past the guest house, past those very windows, but this was the first time she had ever been inside.

'I might go visit Louise again,' she found herself saying. As she spoke, she felt the weight of what she intended and it felt inexplicable and impossible.

She looked up to see Veronica frowning at her.

'Well, I was going to do that later,' she said. 'She's not going anywhere.'

'No, I know, but...' Penny risked a smile. 'I'd only be following you around like a lost dog otherwise.'

Their breakfast arrived, the plates hitting the table with alarming force.

'Thank you,' Veronica said to the departing waitress. She looked back to Penny. 'I could use your help,' she said.

'You have it,' Penny said. 'But I'd only be sitting there while you and the social worker talk. I'd slow you down, and the truth is...' She hesitated. 'The truth is that when you and Lulu are together, you're always arguing with each other. I never get a chance to say anything.'

Veronica gave her a look.

'Well, look who's grown her tongue back,' she said.

'Ronnie, that's unkind.'

'Well, we'd better skip breakfast then,' Veronica said, flustering to gather her wallet, her phone, her room key. 'I won't have time to drive to the hospital, drop you off, and then get back for the social worker...' She was up in her chair like a meerkat, restlessly trying to signal the waitress. Her hand rose but Penny caught it, a small laugh escaping her as she guided it back to the table and held it. It felt cool and brittle.

'I'll get a taxi,' Penny said. Again, it was a *decision* and it fell between them like something made from iron and lead. But it wasn't a sudden thing. It wasn't a spur-of-the-moment choice. It had been brewing, all through the night and as soon as the morning sun had spilled in through the window to cross her bed.

'Don't be ridiculous, Pen. I told you, you need to be more careful with your money.'

'Veronica, please stop.'

Penny hadn't meant to sound desperate; the high note in her voice was uninvited. Veronica scowled, then softened. She reclaimed her hand, and raised it to her cheek which had become rosy with embarrassment.

'I'm sorry,' she said. 'It's just...'

They sat in silence for a spell, and the ribbons of steam from the teapot curled between them.

'I can meet you in the hospital,' Penny said. 'We can drive back together.'

> • <

The hospital bustled during the daytime, the smell of disinfectant stronger, as though it blossomed in the sunlight. Penny checked in with the receptionist and listened patiently as she was given the same directions as on their previous visit.

Lulu was in exactly the same place as they had left her. She looked much the same except for the oxygen tube taped under her nose. She looked bleary, as if she'd had trouble sleeping. She watched Penny's approach with a quizzical expression.

'Where's the other one?' she said.

'It's just me,' Penny said, taking the seat Veronica had occupied before. 'Ronnie will be over later.'

'Well, aren't I the lucky one.'

'You are,' Penny said, her tone gentle but firm. 'Yes.'

Lulu gestured to the bed across the ward.

'Did you see?' she said.

Penny turned around to see the bed was circled with a curtain.

'The poor bitch died last night,' Lulu said. 'The one who kept taking her clothes off. She had a "bad night", they said. And that was that.'

'Oh,' Penny said.

Lulu nodded with relish. 'They just section off the bed like that. It's all very tasteful. Hauled the body off when they thought no one else was watching.'

'It's very sad.'

Lulu sighed.

'This is the geriatrics ward,' she said. 'All of this lot are fucking crazy up here. They're all just waiting for death, they'll all be shipped off out of sight when no one's watching. We're all past it. Over the hill.' She looked at Penny, her expression pointed. 'And you put me here.'

Penny regarded her levelly.

'I didn't put you anywhere, Lulu,' she said. 'And neither did Ronnie.'

Lulu's expression softened. She shrugged.

'It was worth a try,' she said. 'Christ, I'm not *old* enough for this. Is Ronnie upset with me?'

Penny nodded. 'Yes,' she said.

'Ronnie has such absurdly high standards for all of us,' Lulu said.

'She loves you.'

'Yes, well.' Lulu stared at her. 'Of course she does, the silly fool. What about you? Are you upset with me?'

'I don't like seeing you like this,' Penny said. 'I don't think that's the same thing.'

'Happens to the best of us, kid.' She narrowed her eyes. 'You seem... brighter than I might have expected. You're glowing.'

Penny blushed.

'The sea air,' she said. 'I'm not used to it.'

'Nonsense,' Lulu said. 'The sea air scours you. You're doing better than that. Tell me about this job you've got.'

'It's nothing special. Secretarial. Administration. Mostly filing things, really. Simple things.'

'Do you enjoy it?'

'Yes.' She smiled, faintly embarrassed. 'It's exciting in a way.'

'Good. The moment you stop enjoying it, stop doing it.'

Penny laughed.

'Oh, I don't know,' Lulu said. 'Perhaps that's not true. I kept moving, and look at me. First one thing, then another. But you know what? Your standards start hardening. You start something new and you're already looking under the hood to see how it's going to disappoint you down the line. Maybe that was lousy advice. Maybe that just means you'll never be satisfied.

'But the alternative? That's accepting the thing you dislike. Maybe that's worse. Maybe that's always been a death sentence.'

She looked up again, her expression wicked.

'You'll have to ask Ronnie,' she said.

They lapsed into silence, and Penny took the cue to reach into her bag.

'I brought this,' she said. 'I found it in one of the boxes upstairs.'

'Oh.' Lulu's face fell. 'You haven't been trawling through everything, have you? I'd really rather you didn't.'

'The box was open, I didn't pry.' Penny produced a book from the bag and laid it on Lulu's lap. It was a portfolio, bound in black and finished like velvet. A simple square frame in the centre showed a black-and-white cropped detail of a slim woman in a Louise Brooks wig, laughing uproariously in a way that was joyous, but also faintly disturbing in its theatrical excess.

'Well, well, well.' Lulu's voice was a murmur. 'This was the last one I published. The last one anyone wanted from me. Did you look inside it? I suppose you would have missed all of this.'

'I looked at it.'

'Did it shock you?'

'I think they're beautiful,' Penny said. 'It's all so beautiful. So much more so than I realised before. I've always loved your work. And I had seen some of these before. When you had your exhibition in Brighton, one of the newspapers printed some pictures and Sister Agnes got a copy somehow. She was very excited.'

Lulu laughed.

'Sister *Agnes*? Really?'

'Really.' Penny's smile faltered a little.

'There used to be a Sister Agnes in The Immaculate Heart when I was there. She was one of the older ones, and my god, she was a nasty piece of work. She must have died before you got there.'

'I don't remember her.'

'She *must* have died, she was ancient. One of the old guard.' She grimaced. 'Either that or she's still alive, somehow. God's blessing keeping her skeleton clattering along.'

'We had a Sister Asumptia. I remember she was very kind.'

'It's reassuring to think that progress didn't spare that hellhole.'

A silence widened between them. Penny coughed.

'I think...' she said, approaching the subject with caution. 'I think Ronnie is upset about what you said about Mother.'

It looked as though Lulu was about to retort, but she collected herself and nodded instead.

'Maybe I was a bit harsh,' she said.

'Is it true?'

'Does it matter?' She looked thoughtful for a moment. 'I was older than you. Older than Ronnie. There's a big old age gap between us, remember. I saw things of them that you didn't. I saw her struggle – her and Father. There were expectations of both of them.'

She hesitated, looking thoughtful.

'I hated that we barely saw her. At least I did for a while, I really did. But in the end, I didn't hate either of them, because I understood they couldn't really help it. I hated the places they put us instead. School. Here. The places Mum had already suffered through. The places she was allowed to hide us away. Sometimes I wonder if we were just hypothetical to her. Experiments. What-ifs. That sort of thing.'

She shook her head.

'I don't think she was happy,' she said. 'And it's hard to blame her being negligent when I know she didn't profit from it. Sometimes I wish I had been old enough to tell her it was alright, but—' She made a gesture, part shrug, part careless sweep of the hand. 'Isn't it unfair how we're so often too slow to forgive someone? That it takes... so long to understand their position, that it's always just too little, too late.

'And each summer while you two went about your Enid Blyton adventures, there I was, getting angrier and angrier. I was sick of being the oldest one, the one in charge.'

'I thought you loved the summers at Breakers,' Penny said.

'I loved being with the two of you,' Lulu said. 'I really did. But that place? I resented it. It felt like a holding cell. I resented *her* for abandoning us like that. But at the same time… but at the same time, I admired that independence of hers. I yearned for it.'

She sighed. 'It always struck me as the height of arrogance to forgive someone for being who they are. I admired her so much. She would have been horrified, but I think I'm more like her than she would admit. Ronnie too, in a curious way. And you? Well… you surprised us all.'

She looked at Penny intently.

'May I ask you something?'

Penny nodded.

'Yes,' she said.

'Why did you leave?'

'The order?'

'The order, yes.'

Penny hesitated. For a brief moment she felt as though she was back in the quad. She was reaching for the door and Sister Agnes was weeping.

'It's a strange thing,' she said eventually. 'I knew I wanted to join the order. I believed I had the faith to do so, to devote myself to becoming closer to God, but God is always close. That's the beauty of Him. I think, somehow, I always knew I was going to leave. One day. It was a little seed of doubt. And I still wonder if I lied to them, to myself, by denying it for so long.'

She reached across the bed and took Lulu's hand. It felt fragile, as though it had been constructed from wind-blown twigs and softened leaves.

'I realised it was the only decision I had to make,' she said. 'Every day was the same. Every day was scheduled. And it was easy, and it was hard, but all the time I knew where I was supposed to be and what I was supposed to be doing at every point. And for a time, there was comfort in that.

'It was only after Mother's funeral that I understood my only choice each day was whether or not I would stay.

'And I'd think, *tomorrow is my last day*. Then the next day, I'd think: *tomorrow*. And the day after, the day after that. It's a little thing, but each day I thought it, I knew my faith wasn't quite strong enough. I knew my vocation wasn't as firm as I had always thought it might have been. And then forty years or so had passed, before I woke up one morning and thought, *today* instead.'

Lulu smiled softly. 'It was very brave.'

Penny shook her head.

'No, I don't think so. I still have a terrible fear of choosing the wrong thing. A terrible fear of stepping off the path that's been laid for me. Every day, every moment. It's my choice now and it's overwhelming. But even then, I think it would have been braver to have stayed.'

'Will you go back?'

Penny shook her head.

'I don't think I can.'

'They wouldn't let you?' Lulu looked as if she was ready to rise to anger on her behalf.

'No, it's not that. To them, I have broken my vows, and that's a difficult thing to come back from. But even if that weren't true, and they would have me back with open arms, I just don't think... Now that I've seen the world outside, now that I've tasted it. I don't think I have the volume of faith it would take to return. The sheer force of belief to close the door on what I have seen in the knowledge that I would be doing the right thing. It's difficult to explain. It would feel like the wrong sort of faith to me. It would be betraying God a second time. Does that make sense to you?'

'I don't know,' Lulu said.

She opened the book in her lap and traced her fingers over the photograph inside. A portrait of a tall, striking looking woman sitting on a sofa, smoking. Her own eyes, dark with eyeshadow, burned into the camera as though she could see all the way through it to the eye behind.

'Why did you buy Breakers?' Penny said.

Lulu sighed.

'So I could destroy it,' she said.

'Why?'

For the briefest moment, Lulu looked lost.

'I don't know,' she said again. 'I think I came here with firmer ideas than I have now. It was an impulse thing.'

Her eyes glittered briefly with a crystal-cut memory. She closed the book again, turning it over and holding both her hands over the cover as though she could block it all out.

'Something happened,' she said. 'I don't want to go into it. I had been in New York for many years by then, and for a time – a rather glorious time – it had been a love story. You absolutely wouldn't have approved. And then...' She ducked her head to one side. 'And then it was over. A careless word and that was that. It's terrible, isn't it? Love makes you feel both stronger and more vulnerable than you'll ever be, and when it's gone – oh! All at once it was over and I felt crushingly alone. I remember sitting in the apartment we'd lived in together and I felt so terribly betrayed. As though the future we had worked to build for ourselves had been snatched away from me, and I was so *furious*. It simply wasn't fair. After all we had… how could she agree to marry such a silly, inconsequential little man.'

Her sigh fractured, leading to a cough. She reached for the plastic tube and held it tightly to her nose so she could recapture her breath.

'And so,' she said, 'I had this idea that I might be able to lash out at the past instead. I wanted to break something, *disrupt* something that had brought me to this point. Something of Mother's; something of *hers* most of all. It was a foolish thing, but these days… It was like one of those modern cameras. No one prints their photographs any more. When the memory card is out of room, we just go back and delete the oldest images, which seem so irrelevant now. They disappear without a thought so we can make room for something new.'

She sighed, leaning back against the angled support pillows of the bed as though they might fold around her and hide her away.

'But then I got here, and everything seemed so much less urgent. Impulses are hard to maintain when a transatlantic flight is required. The town was in decline, the shops along the pier were boarded up. Even the Pinnerman was falling apart. Breakers looked so hopeless and pathetic when I arrived. I could have kicked it apart and moved on, but… I don't know. Maybe I felt sorry for it after all. The beach forgets itself with every tide, perhaps I could too.'

She turned her attention back to Penny, her eyes sharpened.

'What about you?' she said. 'How did you feel, coming back into the world? Was it everything you expected?'

Penny nodded slowly.

'At first, I hated it,' she said. 'The noise of it. The smell. The sheer open space of it. The decisions we make every day were overwhelming, like a wave building on an otherwise calm day. It took time, it's still taking time. But… now…'

She paused, looking at her hands folded in her lap as though by instinct they had resorted to prayer. The image of the dog returned to her. Not Oscar, but the dog made of sand she had seen when she had arrived in Bryhanton the previous day. Something inert that looked as if it was only asleep; something that looked as if it might wake at any moment and lope off down the street.

'I think,' she said, 'there's beauty in it. In all of it. So much.'

'Beauty?' Lulu looked sceptical. 'Even this place?' She gestured to the ward.

'Even this place,' Penny said. She followed Lulu's gesture and caught herself entranced. It was true, it was beautiful. Not just aesthetic function of the space, but the movement within it, the humanity, the carefully penned ellipses of its residents' lives. She turned back to see Lulu watching her carefully. Her expression had softened again.

'There would have been a time I would have done anything to have seen like that,' Lulu said. 'I think I spent too much of my life sizing up the world through a viewfinder. I think it made me get too distanced, too jaded, too quickly.'

'I've been away for a while,' Penny said.

'I know.'

'Do you remember the hill we used to climb when we were children?'

'Barrow Hill?' Lulu smiled. 'Just above the headland?'

Again, Penny nodded.

'Do you remember how we used to take the path up the cliff? That zigzag path with the ropes and the chains?'

'They closed that down because of health and safety,' Lulu said. There was a trace of contempt in her voice, but amusement too.

'No wonder,' Penny said. 'Remember how we used to insist on climbing it with our eyes closed? We'd pull ourselves up hand over hand, feeling ahead with our feet.'

'God, I do remember that! It's a miracle we didn't kill ourselves.'

'It was because of the view, remember?' Penny said. 'When we climbed it normally, we could see the view slowly getting better and better. But if we went up to the top with our eyes closed, we could take it in all at once.'

Lulu smiled at the lightness of the memory.

'*That* was beautiful,' she said. 'It punched us right in the solar plexus. We could stand at the top of that hill and look all the way out to sea.'

'And on a clear day,' Penny said, 'we would say we could see Doggerland. Just under the waves, like Atlantis.'

Lulu laughed.

'Doggerland!' she said. 'Heavens, I haven't thought about that for years.'

They lapsed into silence for a moment, each consumed with the distant warmth of the same memory.

'They're not going to let me go home, are they?' Lulu said.

'I don't know,' Penny said.

'They're talking about an operation for the hip. They're worried about keeping me in these bloody things.' She swung a hand at the oxygen canister propped beside her. 'The house has stairs, there's that long road down to the beach. I doubt they'd trust me in the car.' She sighed.

'We're passing each other, aren't we?' she said eventually. 'You're going out, I'm coming in. Tides crossing. They're going to put me in my own little convent and that'll be that.'

'It's not like that.'

'Isn't it?' A delicate smile. 'That's good to hear.'

She turned the book over again and smoothed the cover with the palm of her hand.

'I remember telling Myra about Doggerland once,' she said. 'You would have liked Myra. She was fierce. I always thought she was fierce. I told her about this continent that used to join Britain to Europe and make it complete. I told her how it was lost during the Ice Age. Made us an island. Made us alone. I don't think she believed it, bless her.'

Penny took her sister's hand and held it until it was warm.

'I don't want to quote scripture at you,' she said, 'but there's a line about those who don't see but still believe.'

Lulu looked up, her face set.

'Do you know,' she said, 'after all is said and done, I don't regret any of it.' The familiar edge was there in her voice again, that familiar steel.

Penny smiled.

'Nor do I,' she said.

❭ • ❬

Lulu was asleep when Penny left her. She laid a gentle hand on her sister's still cheek, and in a curious way, it felt as though it had already begun to fade from her. She took the corridor by which she had arrived without looking back.

The hospital had fallen into quiet during the time they had spoken, and the wards she passed were empty, their beds clean and freshly made. There was no one at the nurses' station and no one at the cafeteria, the rich amber haze of early evening sunlight made the rooms glow with shafts of folded light. When she passed the reception desk, the only thing she could hear was the sound of her own footsteps and the echo that accompanied them.

When she reached the hospital's front door, she saw a figure behind the glass. A familiar shape from a lifetime ago. She saw it raise its hands to its face and she heard a whistle, sharp and commanding. By the time the doors had slid open on their lazy automatic servos the figure was already retreating into the distance, and Penny saw the landscape had changed. She was no longer at the hospital in King's Lynn, but on the beach at Stove Causeway, and as the figure walked out towards the horizon the sea retreated away from it, exposing the stretch of sand like an unrolling sheet of gold foil. She waited on the sand until it was almost gone and then she reached down to remove her shoes before she began to follow.

As the tide went out, it left a broken mirror behind. Slim reservoirs of lost sea collected between the corrugations the lip of the departing shawl of salt water had combed into the sand. For a precious time the evening sky, itself disparately textured with the flocked scales of cloud, reflected across the sand. And from the perspective of an observer standing on the empty beach, the translation from the sky to the earth was accented but almost perfect. The same blue-grey hessian, the same peach and vanilla bruises of the departing sun.

Penny walked barefoot across the sand. Although the illusion collapsed as she stepped inside it, she knew that from a distance, she too would appear to be doubled – one Penny connected to the other by only the soles of her feet – and the thought of such fantasy lent a lightness to her step. If she were to jump into the air, would she break the connection to her reflection? Would the other Penny fall down and down, deep into the sands of the beach, until she disappeared completely? Or were they connected by their own personal forces and tensions, a push and pull that would always draw them close.

Penny didn't jump. Instead, she walked purposefully, being vigilant to keep one foot on the ground as much as possible for fear she would lose her shadow completely. Her toes dragged in the slicks of water that were ice cold, then warm; sharp then soft. She walked onwards, a straight line away from the land like a detective tracking the path of the tide. She could still hear the sea, the low churn, the muted drum roll and cymbal crash. She could still smell the vegetable salt of it; she could hear the gulls arguing and she could see them circling, so far away they looked like a cloud of gnats on a summer's day. But the sea was distant, unusually so, as though the tide had not so much gone out as retreated. It had fled to the safety of the horizon.

As she walked, she knew she had gone further than she ever had done before. The tide had gone out beyond itself and the way it had departed seemed like an invitation. It had peeled itself back to expose the bones of a mystery it would otherwise possessively conceal. Not treasure so much as territory. Not secrets so much as scale. The landscape had transformed in a way she had never seen before, and she knew that if she were to turn back, she would see the row of houses, Breakers among them, no longer precarious along the edge of something greater, no longer manning the border between one state of being and the other, but stranded and alone, the purpose for which they had been built reclaimed and confiscated. They would look ashen and ashamed without the sea to give them weight. She did not look back. Not then.

Ahead of her she saw nothing but the vast prairie of rippled sand, reflecting the growing dullness of the sky. She couldn't see the crumpled churn of the sea that, on a more common day, was always present at one remove or another: she could not see the whitecaps or the spray. She could not see the water shift from opaque green to stained-glass blue as the light transformed it. She could only hear the percussion of it, distant but unmistakable, as it drew her onwards.

The dark had begun to gather when she found the hole. The night falling in a series of discrete veils from rich plum to blue-black permanent. Had it been any darker, she might have missed it entirely, or worse still, she might have fallen headlong into it. As it was, there was barely enough light to see how deep the hole went. It was a well of black cut into the silver of the terrain. The roughly circular circumference was hastily drawn, an atoll of ragged hills and outcrops of excavated sand. She stooped low to see better, being careful to keep a respectful distance from the edges should the ground beneath her collapse. She allowed her eyes to adjust to the dim evening light, but although she couldn't see deep into the hole, she could see the lines carved in its sides, marks made, she assumed, by something digging its way out.

She straightened and examined the border, keeping low and distant, and edging around it until she found what she was looking for. Footprints. A dog's footprints. That shallow fist, those pushed thumbs, the pencil-hole signature of the claws. On this side, the hole had already partially collapsed, and inside she could see more prints, distorted and smeared in the loosened sand.

When she stood up, she could see the line of prints leading from the hole, towards the distant horizon. A dot-to-dot line like a footpath on a map. The wavering, easy gait of the prints was familiar, the pools of water that gathered in each shone.

Penny smiled. She followed for a few paces and then stopped.

Ahead of her, the trail split, diverging into branches leading east and west and north-east and north-west. From where she stood, she could see the new branches split themselves, not once but a dozen times, the footprints racing across the sand in all directions, turning at every moment. The clean smooth surface became something busy and crowded like a punched texture on a metal plate. It extended away from her into a shimmering distance. She moved forwards despite herself, looking down to see how her own footprints had muddled the ones that had already been there before her.

A voice sounded from the shore. And now Penny turned to look back. She was surprised to see how far she had walked. The line of the shore was marked by lights which blossomed and smeared at the distance. She cupped a hand to her eyes as though it might help her focus through the darkness.

The voice sounded again.

'Penny!'

There was someone there. Someone running. A dark little figure bobbing closer by degrees.

'Ronnie,' Penny said, as though by saying her sister's name she might cement her presence.

'Penny, wait.'

She was closer now, and Penny could see she was holding a shoe in each hand, which made her gait slightly absurd. She ran barefoot, long-legged and gangly. The exertion made her grin widely, but when she got closer Penny realised she was laughing.

'Penny!' she said, fighting to get her breath back. 'I saw you weren't in the bedroom. I've been looking all over for you. What are you doing out here?'

Before Penny could answer, Ronnie hopped from foot to foot.

'Oh!' she said. 'It's cold.'

She dropped a shoe and swore.

'Sorry.'

'It's okay.'

They both crouched to retrieve the shoe and almost butted heads, which only set them both off laughing.

'Is it okay?' Penny said when they were on their feet again.

'It'll dry off.' Ronnie shook the shoe anyway. 'Where are you going?'

There was a warmth to her. Even in the dark, there was an energy to her, a glow.

'There were footprints,' Penny said. 'See?'

'A dog, maybe? So many!'

'Only one, I thought. Oscar, perhaps.'

'Oscar!' Ronnie laughed, then her laugh faltered but the humour remained. 'It can't be. Penny, you know it can't.'

Penny shrugged. A small gesture.

'I don't think that matters,' she said.

They stood for a moment, listening to the distant sea, sensing the salt of it prickle their skin. Ronnie dropped both shoes and took her sister's hand.

'Are you alright?' she said, her concern older, unexpectedly parental.

Penny nodded.

'Yes,' she said. 'Are you?'

'Yes.' Another laugh. 'Yes, I am. How strange.'

The silence grew wider before Ronnie spoke again.

'Do we follow them?' she said. 'Where do we go?'

Penny pointed out into the darkness, away from the land, away from Breakers, away from the beach and the causeway, the town and all it contained.

'I thought,' she said. Then she started again. 'I saw,' she said, but again the sentence failed her. She took a breath. 'Forwards,' she said. She had meant it as a question, but there was a simple confidence at the core of it that surprised her. She looked at her sister, and for the briefest moment she felt afraid.

But Veronica was smiling. She squeezed her hand in the way she had once done to alleviate nightmares when they were both children.

'Forwards,' she said.

TALKING TO STRANGERS ON PLANES

ARRIVALS

At the airport, the tannoy sounded for all the world like the voice of God. Aleyna heard it repeat the same phrases in different languages with the preternatural patience of a parent to a child. She heard the tone of it but she didn't hear what it said. It was as though it operated at a higher register than her own awareness. A captive countdown that spoke directly to the bones of her.

The path from the gate led in spirals through the airport, up and down escalators and staircases and through long, carpeted corridors, separated into directional channels. The windows, when she passed them, were tall, facing the runways outside. Here in London, any snow that had fallen had barely settled. The fringes of white on the grey landscape outside bore the appearance of the softened edges of photographs, carelessly torn.

The crowd rushed and Aleyna rushed with it. Any sense of companionship they might have shared over the past couple of days had already dispersed. At passport control, they clotted into zigzag queues. Around her she saw eyes, ringed with red and clouded. A kid hollered and she wondered if it was the one in the blue hat that had been on the plane, the one whose cockerel cry had kept the morning fresh all the way across the Atlantic. At one point, she had imagined the child's voice had become as familiar to everyone on the plane as it must have been to the girl's father, but now she realised she couldn't tell any more, as though the acoustics of the immigration hall had made everyone anonymous again.

She was halfway down the line when a minor commotion at the back of the hall made people turn around. A trolley was being steered around the back, forcing other passengers to stand aside. Her first thought was to imagine it was the body of the old woman who had died during the first leg of the flight, and judging by the reactions of some of those around her, she wasn't alone. Voices fell to silence, then rose briefly, only to fall again. An eddy of interest in the impatience, rapidly subsumed. The trolley jostled past. Too small for a body, too heavy and slow to steer. Something else. Equipment, maybe. *Luggage.* It passed out of view and was forgotten again.

The passport gate approached and the bud of tension that had always been there, planted deep in Aleyna's gut, twitched and grew. An aspect of the night came back to her, recoloured. It had felt fine and reasonable talking politics in the hotel. But now she knew how it was always something that gave her pause when she was travelling. Not because her opinions didn't matter, but because whenever she came under the scrutiny of national infrastructure, she couldn't shake the image that everything she said was appearing verbatim on a string of ticker-tape in some distant and hidden bunker.

The gate before her flashed green and she stepped forward. Pressing her passport onto the scanner and regarding the camera levelly while it ticked through its process.

The whole thing felt slightly absurd. A system that pretended to be technological, but felt more like a scam. A method to abdicate human prejudice in favour of the assumed impartiality of a machine. Someone was employed to compare her photo with the passport and she was reminded of the Chinese Room experiments; a device that resembled a computer but was operated by people and processes. Overall, Jack had always had more problems with electronic passport gates than she ever had. His faintly satirical default expression attracting more approbation than her patient nervous one.

Jack. She hadn't checked her phone since the plane had landed. She hadn't even thought about it. She hadn't thought of him at all.

The light flickered green again and the gate opened to let her through. It was almost disappointing, in a way. In America, when people with US passports went through passport control, they were automatically issued a brusque 'Welcome home', once their documents were approved. It was just a scripted line. Compulsory, she assumed, and no more sincere than the 'have a nice day' people had become blind to in other parts of the service industry. Perhaps that was something people would never stand for in the UK. In the same way greeters in high-street shops were avoided or ignored. A fake sentiment she understood she would probably resent, but which she missed anyway when it so pointedly wasn't there.

She stopped outside the baggage hall to turn her phone on, and notifications filled the screen like a string of white bunting.

He was outside. He was waiting for her. He loved her. Even from the briefest snippets, she could read the unctuous tone in his vocabulary; a need for approval competing with the triumphant understanding that she would owe him something.

She turned the phone off again, rehearsing an excuse. *Battery was dead. No power on the plane. I know. I'm so sorry. Have you been waiting long?*

Is that how it was going to be? She had made her decision. She had been resolute in the air, resolute in the hotel in Reykjavik. This was the end for the both of them. A new start. A way to navigate out of the dead end they'd found themselves in. One of them had to say it out loud for it to be true, and it was never going to be him.

She checked her wallet for cash and made a mental note to stop by a bank machine. She would be paying her own way home today.

There were familiar faces at the baggage reclaim already. Gathered around the conveyor apparatus, a sleeping dragon splayed across the hall. There were a few nods of recognition between people but otherwise walls had been raised again. Everyone huddled in smaller families and couples. They muttered to each other, leaning on one another's shoulders. She could hear the tiredness in them that she felt herself. She saw the singer and Redhead and spotted Baby Blue Hat and her father. Blue Hat was asleep across her father's chest. Splayed vertical as though she had been fired at him out of a cannon. The father was peering over her shoulder, paging through his own phone's notifications, a glassy expression on his face.

The conveyor remained still and so Aleyna searched the crowd instead. People were clustered close around the belt as though they might short circuit the process and get away first. There was a crackle of tension about the place, and for some reason she imagined violence might be simmering somewhere out of sight.

She saw Callum standing on his own, looking a little bit broken, a little bit run down. He was wearing his overcoat, already tightly buttoned up to his neck. His gloved hands rested on the extended handle of his cabin luggage. He looked up and smiled as she approached him, and when he spoke he did so as though they had been talking all along, without the interruption of the morning's flight.

'Do you know,' he said, 'it sounds awful, but I'm half expecting the first thing out on that conveyor belt will be Mrs Anthony, all trussed up in a shroud. Isn't that a terrible thing to say?'

Despite herself, Aleyna laughed.

'I thought I saw them wheeling her past the passport control,' she said. 'Do you think she's haunting us?'

'Poor dear,' Callum said. 'I do hope she had an easier time with immigration than I had. My passport went *bleep-bloop-blap*. I had to go and speak to one of the gentlemen in the kiosks.'

'I hope he was kind.'

'He didn't really say anything. Which might have been a kindness in itself. Sometimes I find it very hard to tell.'

It had never really occurred to her that airlines would have procedures in place for people who died during the flight. Death and planes was a very simple correlation in the public consciousness. A basic Venn diagram of people who died in accidents and people who died on planes? The overlap was easy to understand. The portion representing those who died of natural causes, who just happened to be on planes at the time, seemed like a more unexpected proposition.

'How was your flight?' Callum said.

'Comfortable. Mostly. I think I slept. You?'

'The same. The new seat was very pleasant, even if the company was lacking. Still. As far as I know, nobody died.'

'Blue Hat didn't keep you awake?'

'I imagined she was singing lullabies.'

'There's a gift to that.'

They waited. The conveyor growled to life and the crowd jolted back to watchfulness.

'Do you think her luggage is still on the plane?' Aleyna said. 'Mrs Anthony's, I mean.' She had a vision of a floral-print holdall circling the conveyor, ignored. She imagined it full of gifts for the grandchildren. Chocolate buttons and gingerbread men.

'Perhaps they'll consider it unattended and subject it to a controlled explosion.'

'Counting up or down?'

Callum smiled.

'You choose.'

The first bag appeared at the mouth of the conveyor. A black plastic shell suitcase tipped onto the belt and began its circuit like a shy fashion model. The crowd tensed, fingers itching. The pause before the next bag seemed faintly overextended, as though for dramatic effect.

She noticed that the singer was standing directly opposite her across the carousel. He looked grey in the morning, as though he hadn't slept for the past few nights or days or whichever was which. He jostled forward and grabbed the bag as it slid past him. Strutting off towards customs, checking his phone with one hand and sparing not a glance for his erstwhile audience, those he left behind.

Other bags began to process in. Drawing sluggish circles around the space. Watched first with suspicion, then relief, the suitcases and luggage were claimed, one by one, hauled out of their trajectories and onto the polished floors. The room echoed with the clip-clop of plastic wheels breaching the gaps between the tiles.

Aleyna's own bag arrived, but she waited with Callum until his showed up too, dismissing his amused warnings that it had been sent somewhere else.

'The one thing you can never predict is whether or not you'll have clean underwear at your destination,' he said, and as soon as he said it he smiled, faintly embarrassed. 'Ah, now. There she is.'

They didn't speak as they walked through the customs hall. They didn't speak when the doors opened and they stepped out into the airport's foyer. A mob of people were there, craning past them to find someone else. Aleyna didn't even look to see if Jack was among them. She walked out through the sliding double doors with Callum instead and into the tempered winter.

'How are you getting into town?' she said to Callum.

'A taxi, I think,' he said. 'I shall treat myself. I'm not as young as I used to be, and I've spent most of the past few days waiting for things to show up, waiting for my name to be called. I don't trust myself on a tube train platform.'

She offered to walk him to the taxi rank, but he demurred.

Beside her, a young boy ran past, mittens flapping on elastic at the hems of his sleeves. His mother rushed for him; stooping to snatch at his hand, she caught a stray glove instead. The elastic stretched, then snapped. The boy howled and the mother caught him up in her arms.

Across the street, a van pulled into the traffic. A discreet looking vehicle.

'Mrs Anthony,' she said suddenly and Callum looked across to her, faintly surprised. 'You said you met her. Before the flight?'

Callum nodded.

'Briefly,' he said. 'Yes. I told her she looked beautiful. I think she was offended.'

'That's not what I'm asking.'

'I know.' He winced a little. Glancing back up only shyly. 'Like gossamer, it was,' he said. 'Gossamer.' He spread his hands. 'So.'

Aleyna turned to Callum and peeled her own gloves off. The air was cool, the sweat between her fingers prickled. She extended her hand to him, holding his gaze.

'It was lovely to meet you, Callum,' she said.

He nodded, pleased, moved, but when he extended his own hand, it remained gloved. His grip was strong but light.

'You too,' he said. 'A pleasure.'

For a moment, it looked as though he was about to say something else, but he changed his mind. He released her hand and nodded at her, a single nod with a certain finality to it. He turned away.

From somewhere behind her, she heard Jack's voice calling her name.

'Callum,' she said. The old man turned back to her.

'I think your young man is looking for you,' he said.

'He's not *that* young,' Aleyna said.

'I think you have something to say to him,' Callum said. 'And you don't want me there for that.'

'I just...' She faltered. 'You never told me why you were visiting. London. You said... I don't know. I just—'

He interrupted her with a raised hand.

'I'm here to see my son,' he said. He nodded once more and cleared his throat. When he spoke again, his voice was softer.

'I'm here to see my son.'

His smile, when it came, was a delicate thing, like a wild flower that blossomed too early; ill-equipped to survive the winter. He turned from her before it had time to fade completely and walked away, his pace slow as he disappeared into the crowd.

TRANSIT

Callum couldn't sleep. The hotel room was like a box. A machine designed to hold people in storage until they could leave. Some years ago, he had read an article about the popularity of capsule hotels in Japan, where, from the photographs, it appeared that guests were kept in drawers or on shelves. The hotel room he had been assigned struck him as being only one or two steps up the ladder in terms of volume and comfort. Everything looked as though it had been engineered to fit into its allotted space with the absolute bare minimum of excess. Walls and furniture appeared to have been constructed as part of a single prefabricated unit, and between the bed, the door and the en suite, there was only a narrow L-shaped carpeted area. Everything else was occupied with being something else.

The bed was a plinth at the far end, its length the exact width of the bedroom itself. On the wall behind it, a vinyl window blind was firmly closed, showing only a neutral grey blank rectangle. Even though he suspected there would be no view to speak of on the other side, other than the airport and its subsidiary buildings, Callum couldn't move it an inch, and this exacerbated the suspicion he had been harbouring that the room had no real windows at all. It was a stranger to sunlight. It was coffin-like. It was designed for the briefest of visits; a temporary solution to keep people out of the way.

The whole room was operated by a touchscreen device that didn't seem to be working. The bearded young man at the front desk had explained that there were some problems with the heating and the shutters but everything else should have been working.

'If you have any problems, just call reception,' he said. The poor bastard must have been parroting the same phrases to everyone on the plane. By the time he got around to Callum, his words were starting to run together, their meaning lost somewhere along the way. Callum didn't want to bother him any further, and when the receptionist handed him his key card, a dead-eyed expression etched on his face, Callum took it with a grateful smile.

'Hang in there, lad,' he said. 'You're doing fine.'

There was no phone in the room, and Callum's mobile phone plan didn't include Iceland within its roaming charges. A neat little message had popped up on the screen informing him, in an oblique manner, that he couldn't afford to make phone calls here.

In the room, Callum tried to find a way to operate the lights, but failed. He tried to find a way to open the blinds and turn off the air conditioner. He tried lying on the bed with his coat over his eyes – he'd slept part of the way on the plane after all, and that had been more constricted, brighter, and considerably noisier. But the room had an oppressive quality to it. The noise and light and dimensions seemed to have been engineered for him alone. It was a very personal kind of oppressiveness, the sort he imagined American authorities employing to torture terrorist suspects in holding camps somewhere.

It didn't take long for it all to feel too much for him. He picked up his coat and his gloves and took the elevator downstairs to the hotel's reception lounge.

The lounge was darker than his bedroom had been. An irregular-shaped space filled with awkwardly placed pillars and plush burgundy armchairs. Mood lighting had been set to gloomy, the ambience of a gentleman's club you might find in a period detective serial. He found a chair far away from the draught and the light of the main concourse and made himself comfortable.

He retrieved his wallet and slipped out the photographs he kept in the identification pocket. Nora had always looked faintly sceptical in photographs. The part of her he missed most was the delicate smile she wore as she dozed in the mornings. He missed waking up and finding her there beside him. The absence of her, relaxed and huffing gently in her sleep, still felt like the cruellest loss. A way to unseat him before his day had begun.

The other photograph was of the boy. Still young and patient with his father. Crouched beside the dog on a grey line of beach.

He started drifting almost immediately. His thoughts turning from how he would respond to whoever took him to task for sleeping in a public space to a fracturing memory of the scene in the photograph, a family holiday they had once taken. The seaside. Cromer. The brittle nostalgia painted onto every wall.

The sound of someone clearing their throat brought him back into the present. He glanced up and saw a familiar face sitting in a chair a row or two ahead of him.

'You're still wearing your gloves,' she said.

The young woman. What was her name? Alice? Annie?

'Aleyna,' he said. He held up his hands, turning them. 'Yes. My wife gave them to me. Have you been here the whole time?'

'I didn't mean to wake you,' she said. 'Although you did start snoring a moment ago. I might have laughed and woken you. I'm sorry.'

'Snoring?' He got up and moved closer, gesturing at the chair opposite her. She nodded. 'It doesn't sound like me. I don't snore.'

'How would you know?'

'I wouldn't. My wife was a beautiful liar.'

He sat in the chair, the upholstery was unsettlingly cool.

'Same book?' he said, nodding at the paperback Aleyna held in her hand, her thumb marking her place two-thirds in.

'Same book.'

'I would ask if you thought it was good, but I keep interrupting you reading it.'

Her face pinched. 'It's alright. Not brilliant.' She looked embarrassed. 'I have a weakness for airport bookshops,' she said. 'Every time I get on a flight, I make time to just linger in the bookshop. I tell myself I'm going to get one of those airport exclusive editions. You know, those big paperbacks that cost the same as the hardbacks? But I never do, I always talk myself out of it. I always tell myself I can wait.'

She turned the book over, inspecting the creases that covered half the spine.

'I bought this one because… I don't know. It's about three sisters who live in a cottage by the sea. Turns out they're witches or something. It's a bit silly.'

She looked up, her cheeks bright with embarrassment.

'It's funny, isn't it? I always assume that if I'm going to read anything on a flight, then it needs to be something light and frothy. As though my brain capacity during a flight can't cope with reading something that's actually good. So, yes, I buy trash at airports. Always. *Sea witches.* Mea culpa.'

'I knew a man once,' Callum said, 'and whenever he flew, he would take a copy of *Ulysses* with him. Told me that being in a plane was the only way the thing made sense to him.'

'Very Joycean.'

'Is it though? You see, I've never actually read it. Isn't that awful? I tell people I have, of course. And I've skipped around a bit. So I have a rough idea of what's what, and where's where. Molly Bloom's affirmation and so on and so forth. But, no.' He pointed at her. 'No. God no. No. But don't you tell anyone, now. They'll confiscate my passport.'

'I haven't read it either,' Aleyna said. 'I do sometimes feel like I should.'

Callum shook his head.

'Life is too precious,' he said. 'Read Beckett instead. Now, he's your man. Funnier and much, much shorter.'

She smiled. It was a loose expression; he could read the tiredness in the frame of it and recognised the depth and weight of it. He nodded back but didn't say anything further. There was something pleasant about the quietness of the empty bar that he did not want to disturb. There was a warmth there; a shared sense of resignation at something absurd that must simply be endured.

It was Aleyna who spoke first.

'What are you doing in London?' she said. 'Do they know you're late?'

He waved a hand. 'Oh,' he said. 'I'm in no rush.'

'Administration, right?' Aleyna said.

Callum hesitated, distracted.

'The lady last night,' he said. 'She was saying it was bad luck to talk about terrorism in airports. But I was in London back in the seventies. Me and some friends from home. They'd brought a car with them and we were doing some sightseeing. Where were we? God, I don't know. What's to see around London? The M25? Anyway, do you remember what colour Irish registration plates were back then? Red. Bright fucking red. It was like driving around with a daub of paint over your car. *Unclean.*

'And we were driving out of town and we heard on the news that a bomb had gone off in central London. IRA, you see? Happened a lot, back then. They'd had the phone call, you know. Evacuated the scene and then, *bang*. The usual. And we just looked at each other and then opened a book on when we'd get pulled over by the police. Fifteen minutes. I won a fiver.'

'God.'

He waved his hand.

'This was back in the old days,' he said. 'When people in England would hear the word 'terrorist' and assume they must be white people. *American-funded* white people at that. Funny how times change, isn't it? Funny how short our memories are.'

He shook his head.

'Anyway,' he said, 'I don't know why I brought that up.'

'Bombs,' Aleyna said. 'Countdown timers.'

'You're right. That was a very adamant young man.'

'You didn't stay for the recital,' Alenya said.

Callum shook his head, his eyes widened.

'I did not, no,' he said. 'Did I miss anything?'

'He played some songs,' Aleyna said. 'He was alright. I'm sure I've seen him somewhere before, I didn't catch his name.'

'He was playing some awful doggerel when I left. I thought I should leave before he started singing *The Lass of Aughrim*.'

'I think he was singing it in your honour.'

'For me? Well, if I see him, remind me to tell him I'm charmed.'

Aleyna laughed.

'Jack used to play the piano,' she said. 'I remember he once tried to serenade me in a shopping centre. It was excruciating.'

'Jack is your... *ex*-husband, did I remember that right?'

'Partner,' Aleyna said. 'Boyfriend. Not ex yet.'

'But you were thinking of putting an end to it all. Have you thought some more?'

'Yes. Maybe. I don't know.' She sighed. 'That's the thing with time away. A business trip, on my part. When it feels like a holiday... when you realise you're not looking forward to going home?'

Callum didn't say anything, he just waited, giving her space.

'It just feels like so much effort,' she said. 'Either way. Me breaking up with him feels like a trial. Me staying feels like a trial. I'm sorry, this is probably very dull for you.'

Callum's smile flickered.

'Not at all.' He shrugged. 'And there's nothing wrong with not knowing. It's a blessing, in a way. It's not a welcome gift to see how and when everything ends.'

'I suppose not.' She set the book on the seat beside her and clasped her hands between her knees, stretching. She yawned.

'But sometimes,' Callum said, 'you really do have to burn it all down in order to earn a new way to begin. Endings are important, like I said. They let you start something new. We have to depart before we can arrive, after all.'

'Like setting off a bomb?'

'Just like,' he said. 'And some people have relationships that they've both seen counting downwards since they started them, and so...' He cocked his head. 'When it starts approaching zero and no one's getting out of the way, what do you chose to do?'

She mimed an explosion and they both laughed.

'Soon,' she said. 'Maybe? I don't know. It's odd. He's an ex in my mind, but he doesn't know it yet himself. It's like we're operating in two different versions of the same world. That's how being in transit feels, sometimes, doesn't it? As though one version of you is on hold, while the world outside waits to catch up, to fit you back into your place. Maybe all these delays are trying to tell me something, after all.'

Callum shook his head.

'Just weather,' he said.

Aleyna laughed. 'Just weather,' she said.

Callum cleared his throat.

'My son is a better flyer than I am,' he said. 'He flies at lot with his work. He's a civil engineer. I'm proud of him. He flies out to projects. Buildings, bridges, bloody great dams, you know.'

He sat back, thoughtful.

'When he told me he was going into engineering, I thought: good. Now, there's a way a man can make a living. I told him that engineers reshape the world, but I never once, not for a moment, thought he listened to me.

'But then he went to college, and then he got the job, and he would tell me about all the flying he was doing. Going about here and there and everywhere. And I thought, *that* is how I lose him. That's what happens to him. My dear boy, my beautiful child. Gone. Like that.'

He shook his head as though the thought was absurd to him.

'Do you know what the odds are of dying in a plane crash? One in five million. *Five million!* I looked it up! But it's so… *visible*, isn't it? An aeroplane goes down and it makes the news, and I'm half convinced that we all sort of expect it. We get on a plane and we sigh and go, ah well, then. If you must. The convenience of it makes gamblers of us all.'

He sighed, then smiled again. A brave sort of smile.

'He was so small when he was born,' he said. 'It's a strange thing, to hold a child for the first time. It's a strange thing to just…'

He glanced up, embarrassed.

'Listen to me,' he said. 'Foolish old man. Living in the States has made me go soft and sentimental. I'm sorry. I'm going on and on. Tell me about you.'

'Oh.' Aleyna shook her head. 'Don't worry. Really.'

'I'm old,' Callum said. 'And I must be tired. Do you know, they've offered me a new seat for the next plane?'

'No?'

'I originally asked for extra leg-room. When I booked. Normally when I fly, I try and get near the emergency door, you know. A bit more room to spread out. Varicose veins, you see. But they didn't have any seats – full flight. Now, apparently, they do. Fancy that.'

'Mrs Anthony?'

Callum clucked his tongue.

'Dear Mrs Anthony. Can you imagine the face of the person who will be sitting in the seat beside me when they realise there's *another* old biddy to cark it beside them.'

Aleyna laughed, but caught it as though it was inappropriate, mistimed.

'What happened to her?' she said.

'I think it was her heart,' Callum said. 'I met her briefly, before we boarded. She was afraid. I can only imagine the turbulence made it worse.'

'Oh, that's terrible,' Aleyna said. 'Someone should have stopped her from getting on the plane.'

'Perhaps the plane wasn't anything to do with it. Just a means to an already written end. Sometimes, it's just our time to be called. There's nothing much we can do about it other than not let it get in the way.'

'Is that why you were so calm on the plane?' Aleyna said. 'Everyone else was gripping the armrests and praying out loud, you were there beside me, singing away like you were on a school trip.'

Callum waved a hand in a dismissive gesture. 'Oh,' he said. 'Nothing was going to happen.'

There was something about his confidence that gave her pause.

'But how could you possibly know that?' she said.

'Oh, it's just something I... see,' Callum said, but then backtracked, dissatisfied. 'I'm not a good flyer, like I said. So, I make a point of meeting as many of the people as possible who will be flying with me before I get on a plane. Mrs Anthony aside, God rest her soul, everyone else seemed... very healthy. Good, long lives.'

Aleyna frowned. She thought of a dozen things to say, but they all seemed rather preposterous. 'Are you a doctor?' she said eventually. 'I have no idea why that would mean anything, given what you just said, but I thought I should have remembered if you said you were.'

Callum's face creased in amusement. 'Oh, god, no.' He settled again. 'Perhaps I just have an amateur interest.' He winced, uncomfortable, and checked his watch. 'What time is it here, anyway?'

'Don't change the subject! An amateur doctor?'

'No! Of course not.' He hesitated, trying to regroup this thoughts. 'An amateur interest in... *life*, perhaps? Other people's lives.' He sighed, a lengthy exhalation.

'Other people's?'

'Well, yes.' A short laugh. 'My own remains somewhat more mysterious to me. It's infuriating.'

At the entrance to the room, next to the shuttered bar, a cleaner had entered with a floor polishing machine. The cleaner wore headphones and didn't seem to have noticed them. The machine kicked up a mild, buttery roar that made

Aleyna glance around to see what Callum was looking at. When she turned back, there was a look of concern on his face. The dark resignation of a decision made.

'What is it?' she said.

Callum looked at her directly, his expression serious in a manner that struck her as uncharacteristic.

'Perhaps,' he said, holding up his gloved hands again, turning them one way, then the other, 'I should tell you a secret.'

STOPOVER

The mood in the hotel reception area was freewheeling and apocalyptic.

The passengers lingered around the lounge, their cabin luggage assembled at their feet. They waited for their names to be called by the airline representative, a prim young woman in a tailored uniform, who was working her way through the plane's manifest with the aid of the night manager from the hotel, a stocky gentleman with a polished scalp and a bristling goatee beard.

After being cooped up together in the plane for several hours, there was a sense that the passengers had finally found each other. They had been through the same turbulent hours: the wait for the plane to take off, the toss and turn of its troubled flight, and the further delay on the runway once they had finally been permitted to land at Reykjavik Airport. Now it was late, in a time zone none of them had anticipated. They had landed, but they were still suspended in the purgatory of transit.

Theirs was now a shared story, and as they waited to be assigned rooms in the airport hotel, the sheer dark and *nightness* of their transatlantic flight being made concrete by the hour, the chorus of voices raised to a cacophony as they interrogated each other for aspects of their nascent myth which had so far been overlooked.

'I was on a train once.' It was the young father who was speaking. The child he carried finally asleep on his shoulder; the lip of a blue woollen hat slipped over her closed eyes. 'Leicester to Edinburgh. The West Coast line. I was visiting my girl up there, then. She was Scottish. Red haired and beautiful like in that cartoon.

'I was travelling on my own, but the carriage was half full. We went past Oxenholme and there was this sudden bang and this smell of gas. Someone had left a gas can on the lines. Some kids, watching from a bridge. Figured they'd see what happened; figured they'd see if the whole train would go up.'

His audience balked. They'd each read stories about youths like that before, but the young father raised his hand. The kids, the urgency of his eyes seemed to say, were the facilitators of his story but not the purpose of it.

'Nothing happened,' he said. 'Just a noise and a smell of gas. We just got stuck on the line for three hours or so. That was all. But it was strange, you know?'

His audience nodded. They could relate. Three hours seemed quaint with hindsight, but now, more than ever before, they could relate.

'And this was before the Internet,' he said. 'Well, at least before everyone had the Internet on their phones. And there was no signal for the phones we did have, so no one knew what was going on anywhere except for what was going on in the carriage we were in at that moment.

'It was like our entire world had squeezed down to just those people in the carriage.

'And so, the first thing that happened was that everyone started talking to each other. Like we are now. People started talking. But then people started getting paranoid. They started saying things like, "What happens if it wasn't a kid like the train guard told us? What if it was a bomb? A terrorist? Or an *invasion*? What if while we were stuck there on the branch line, *something* happened to everyone else?"'

He bobbed the kid on his shoulder, an unconscious reaction. A movement fatherhood had taught him, made memory.

'It's funny,' he said. 'How people start to think when they get cut off like that. How people are when they're cut off with strangers.'

A middle-aged man in a business suit held up an expensive-looking phone.

'But we aren't cut off,' he said. The smugness in his tone might not have been something he had control over. 'We still have the Internet. It's just weather. Look. Weather. Nothing else.'

The young father frowned, then cancelled his frown.

'I know,' he said. 'I was just saying. You know?'

'Might not be weather,' someone said, a woman in a tartan hat. 'You can't trust what your phone tells you. Maybe it's what they want you to think. Everything's fine. Keep the cattle happy.'

This caused a stir, voices were raised. The woman waved her hands.

'A joke,' she said. 'I'm only joking.'

'This is no time for jokes.'

'This is the *perfect* time for jokes.'

The airline representative called out another name. A woman wearing two coats, one blue, one pink, gathered her duty-free bags and shuffled through the crowd.

'What time is it?'

'Does it matter?'

The bar had opened, and people were already holding pint glasses and tumblers. Drinking hours during flights had always been flexible, but tonight the bar felt earned. Outside, the snow was floodlit and bright. Inside, ice clinked and rattled, stirred by straws.

There was a piano in the bar, and a man was sitting at it. His fingers splayed across the keys, tentative as one who knew they would soon play and when they did, the attention of the room would be his. The singer was one of the first to be assigned a room; he was also one of the first to come back down. Showered, shaved, a new shirt from his cabin bag. He had a captive audience and he knew it.

'I can't believe they showed that film on the plane.' The woman speaking was almost elderly, her brow furrowed deep with practice. Beside her, her teenaged son rolled his eyes. He didn't want to explain to her that there were many films, that not everyone watched the same thing. He knew she still believed that in-flight entertainment was assigned and endured. Choice in economy class was not something she believed she was yet entitled to. 'It was so *violent*,' she said. 'With bombs and terrorists and fighting and things blowing up. I don't think they should show films about terrorists on aeroplanes. I was quite upset by it all.'

The young father asked what film she had seen. The woman's son answered for her. A sequel. Big budget. Big names. Adapted from an old television series. Unconsciously, his hands moved in the shape of an explosion to illustrate.

'I saw that in the cinema,' the young father said, nodding. 'They have parent and toddler screenings.' He gestured at Blue Hat with his chin. 'She slept all the way through it. I quite liked it.'

'I saw it too,' the singer said. His accent was American and more than one in the crowd thought his face looked slightly familiar. He played a few bars from the theme tune and his audience warmed to him, pushing closer. 'Very standard. Very clichéd. And it's all special effects, isn't it? None of it is *real* any more.'

'It never used to be *real*,' the man in the expensive suit said.

'But the artifice of it *was*,' the singer said. 'When you saw someone jumping off a building, there was a man paid to figure out how to do it. Nowadays it's all just ones and zeros. It's all so slick. In this film, for instance, the plane blows up and you can see all the pixels in the fireball.'

'I thought it was good,' the son said. 'Exciting.'

The young father nodded. 'Me as well.'

The singer played a few more notes. A descending scale. 'Let me ask you,' he said. 'Why is it that in films like that, all the bad guys plant bombs fitted with big red countdown timers?'

His audience blinked.

'It's a user interface,' the singer said. 'Like on a phone. Or a computer. Who is it there for? The *audience*, no one else. It doesn't make any sense.'

There was an argument, a good natured one, but the mother backed away from it. She was hurt that her concerns had been dismissed with inattention, but more than anything, the debate felt very *male* to her. A respect for the minutiae; the mechanics of violence, a category of trivia that had always alienated her.

She pushed through the crowd, her hands outstretched like fins. Ahead of her, she found a young woman standing alone, a redheaded figure in a striking T-shirt. She was looking at her telephone.

'Did you hear a woman died?' the mother said. 'An old woman. She was sitting very close to me. Only a row or two ahead of me.'

'I heard,' Redhead said. 'But I didn't hear anything else.'

The redhead had stepped away from the young father when he described the woman he once knew in Edinburgh.

'They called her Mrs Anthony,' the mother said. 'They shook her by her shoulder and said, "Are you alright there, Mrs Anthony?" And she didn't move. She didn't move at all.'

'Well.' Redhead smiled. A flinty thing, not quite fit for purpose. 'I'm sure she was very ill.'

'We don't know that.'

'Very old.'

'We don't know that, either.' The mother shook her head. 'I wonder what it was she ate?'

Another name was called. The woman in the tartan hat made her way to the front, issuing a sigh so theatrical it made people step cleanly out of her path. The hotel receptionist had started to turn pink, his movements had become jagged, like a busy chef during lunch service. At one point, his hand moved to his head as though he could keep everything from bursting out of him. His eyes looked a little wild, his professional expression pasted strangely into place.

'If I were to write a film...' The speaker was an elderly man, his suit worn, his smile warmed and softened by the crinkles of his face. '...I would have it different.'

The singer humoured him. 'What would you do, then?'

The man had taken his coat off and hung it over the back of a chair, but was still wearing his gloves. 'I would have the timer on the bomb counting up instead of down,' the man said.

The young father shrugged. 'Same thing,' he said.

The elderly man shook his head. 'No, it would be different. Quite different.'

The young father was agitated. 'Well, how would the audience know when it was going to go off? How would the hero? The guy defusing it?' He raised a hand. 'Do you know what my favourite countdown scene is?'

The singer shook his head. 'Tell us,' he said.

'*Goldfinger*,' the young father said. 'The bomb ticks down until it reads double-oh-seven before Bond defuses it. *Classic.*'

The young woman who had been listening to the conversation from a distance, a paperback in her hand, shook her head.

'Bond doesn't defuse it,' she said. 'Someone else does. Someone else saves Bond. M or Q or one of those.'

'No, they don't,' the young father said, trying to remember.

The woman cocked her head. She wasn't going to argue.

'Anyway, how would Bond know how much time he had if the counter counted up? How would the audience?'

'They wouldn't,' the singer said, his look distant, his grin self-satisfied as the possibilities uncurled for him. 'And neither would Bond. That's the point. It could go off at any minute, is what our man here is saying. It could go off at *any* minute and none of us would know. That would make it more frightening.'

The son thought about the proposition for a moment. 'That's rubbish,' he said.

The number of people in the bar had started to thin, and the energy of the room had knotted into discrete pools of conversation. The room had filtered. Those who remained had found their rooms and returned, bringing with them a calmer sense of expectation. The aeroplane company representative and the hotel receptionist could see the outer fringes of their work for the evening and their efforts redoubled, a final push.

'I think it's very bad taste to talk about bombs and terrorism in an airport,' the mother said.

The redhead was looking at her phone. 'Agreed,' she said.

'A woman died.'

'She did.'

'The poor woman. Do you know who was sitting next to her?'

'I don't.'

'What a terrible thing.' The mother fell silent until a name was called and she looked up. Beckoning to her son with a broad sweep of her arm.

'It's us,' she said. 'It's our turn.'

She danced on the spot until the boy reached her, his face pink and bright. 'No rush,' he said. 'God, Mum. Keep it down.'

The singer looked up at the elderly man in the gloves and nodded with the jut of his chin.

'You Irish?' he said.

'I am.'

'I'm Irish,' the singer said.

The elderly man smiled. 'Well,' he said. 'We do get about, don't we?'

The singer moved his hands across the keyboard, a fiddly approximation of 'Danny Boy'. Curlicues and ligatures.

'Any requests?' he said. 'I was going to play some things later. Maybe people need a bit of a show.'

'I thought the piano stool was just a comfortable place to sit.'

'The most comfortable, I admit.' When the singer grinned, there was Hollywood in it.

'Well, don't let me stop you,' the elderly man said. 'I think I might be off to my bed. I don't know what time it is, but I do think some attempt at sleep is warranted.'

'One for the road, then,' the singer said. 'Something from the old country.'

A flicker of amusement passed over the elderly man's face. 'You carry on,' he said. 'I'll get my one for the road from the minibar.'

He glanced at the young woman with the paperback, who had taken a seat next to the redhead. 'Do they have minibars in the rooms?'

She shook her head. 'I don't think so.'

'Probably for the best.' He saluted, or doffed an imaginary cap, then made his way through the crowd towards the lifts.

The singer sucked his teeth. He considered the room and determined that his audience was ready and ripe.

'Well then,' he said and began to play.

FLIGHT

I need to put an end to it all.

The more Aleyna thought about it, the more obvious it felt to her that there was something wrong with the plane. The cabin was full, a sardine can packed shoulder-to-shoulder, the engines and the air conditioning roared like miserable ghosts.

As the plane had lingered on the runway there was a hushed impatience to the passengers, a silent wish to urge things into motion, as though only a journey begun had a chance of ending. Now that it was in the air, this collective encouragement had been replaced by the low whine of unspoken resentment as the reality of economy air travel had reasserted itself. The cabin lights had dimmed, but the tensions had nowhere to go.

Jack. Dear Jack. This has to stop.

As she had sat in the waiting room, listening to the tannoy announce the latest delay, it had occurred to her that anything that happened to the flight might have all been her fault.

She had bought her ticket with a reluctance that bordered on petulance. She had arrived at the airport later than she needed to, digging her heels in like a kid who didn't want to go to school. She didn't want to be on this plane. She certainly didn't want to go home, and for a brief, beautiful moment she had entertained the idea that her own clouds of resentment had coagulated above the airport and brought snow down upon the runways.

Jack. I'm sorry.

She sat back in her chair as much as she could, the illusory plushness of the upholstery swiftly exposing the angular metal frame. The seat in front of her had been reclined, halving her legroom and making her feel like a dentist. When she picked up her book again, the pages felt rough and swollen as though she had retrieved it from a river. She read a page then set it down again. Above her, the seat-belt sign came back on and the speaker murmured something about turbulence.

The plane shook like a muted roller coaster. A lateral lurch, an abrupt downward feint that made Aleyna's stomach dip and set the baby off a few rows ahead. Aleyna craned her head to see the distinctive blue hat rise above the seat tops and the father lifted the kid up and then down as though he could counteract the movement of the plane. The child's face was as ripe and red as a polished apple. Eyes wrinkled into furious seams; the mouth a black-hole scream. Aleyna was sympathetic but set to untangling her headphones anyway.

Jack, I love you but... I thought I loved you...

'I always imagined that babies on planes were like canaries.'

Aleyna glanced to her right where the old man was sitting in the middle seat. He had been quiet for most of the flight, his gloved hands folded neatly on his lap as though he had been patiently waiting for his turn at a confessional.

'Excuse me?' Aleyna said.

'I don't mean to sound callous.' The man nodded at the bobbing, angry head a few rows in front of them. 'But whenever I'm on a bumpy flight and I see a baby like that, I always think, what sort of bastard God would do something to this plane while they're on board?'

His smile was a disarming mass of crinkles and Aleyna found herself smiling back at him despite herself. His hands were crossed over his knees, he was wearing what looked like a pair of calf-skin driving gloves.

'Forgive my language,' he said.

'Not at all.'

He nodded at her headphones, still knotted in her hands.

'And I didn't mean to disturb you.'

'Oh.' She wrapped the cable in a ball and hid it in her hands. 'It's alright.'

The man's name was Callum. He was seventy-eight and hailed from Galway. The autobiography he provided was not asked for but was recited with humour enough that it didn't feel like a burden. He told her he was arriving in London for the first time in five years, and given the sigh with which he punctuated the sentiment, he didn't seem happy about it.

'I'm taking the delays as a sign,' he said, casting his eyes at the luggage lockers above them. 'Someone up there is telling me to turn around and go home.'

Aleyna cocked her head.

'What are you visiting town for?'

He waved his hands airily. 'Oh,' he said. '*Administration*. What about you?'

'Oh. The same.'

There was an art to talking to strangers on planes, but it wasn't something Aleyna had ever mastered. In her experience, everyone flew alone. The social pressure of having to speak to people who had been placed next to you by chance was an absurdity she had no time or energy to countenance.

Once, she and Jack had flown to Scotland for a wedding. The budget airline had separated them during check-in, and neither had volunteered the premium to be placed together. Aleyna had found herself on the aisle in the middle of the plane. Beside her was a bulky man with a rugby player build and one of those all-encompassing senses of misplaced confidence that seem to come fitted as standard by the English public school system. Another woman sat on the other side of him, and as the plane was taxiing towards the runway, the man clapped his big hands.

'Right,' he said. 'Let's say we've got ten minutes to finish reading our books or our mobile phones. And then we'll talk to each other for the rest of the flight like real people.'

He beamed, bright teeth shining through a training-wheels beard.

'By the time we get to Edinburgh, we'll all be best friends.'

There was something childish in the tone, something weighted, too. A pleasantly phrased threat that made Aleyna's heart sag as though the plane was already passing through a storm. She considered gathering her belongings and shuffling up the aisle to swap seats with Jack, but the thought of having to explain herself to him, the thought of having to be *rescued* by him, made her feel queasier still.

Instead, she smiled politely.

'No, thank you,' she said. And put her earphones in.

That flight had been short, which was something of a mercy. She made a point of avoiding looking towards the man beside her, even when he jostled her for their shared armrest. It felt as if a no man's land had grown between them, a glowering resentment clouding her periphery. She had a mind that she could hear the words that were being used to describe her. Familiar syllables prickling at her like heat rash. She imagined the words they were attached to. *Stuck-up. Snob. Elitist. Uppity bitch.*

By the time the flight landed, the earphones were making her ears sting. The man shuffled out and helped her remove her bag without asking her. Her muttered thanks was tainted by the fear her rudeness had eclipsed his. She met Jack at the plane exit with a polite smile and later saw the man and the woman on the other side, tonguing each other in the baggage hall. She never did mention the incident to Jack. She told him that she'd slept for the whole of the flight.

He'd looked almost envious.

'I can never sleep on planes,' he said. 'I don't know how you do it.'

She smiled at him. She did that back then. Other people's anxiety had never been something he understood, either.

'Do you live in the US?' she said.

Callum nodded.

'New York,' he said. 'Brooklyn.' He glanced at her and frowned. 'Does New York count as the US? It always feels like its own thing to me.'

'I think it does, yes.'

Callum waved his finger, agitated. 'You see?' he said. 'That's London's problem. It's a capital. Which is always a mistake. New York, Sydney, Buenos Aires. People think they're capitals, but they don't have to deal with all that government shit. It drags a place down. They're just these big, crazy places, letting their hair down.'

He smiled, thoughtful.

'Are you English?' he said.

Aleyna tensed a little. She always did when the question of her nationality was raised.

'Yes,' she said.

'I thought so,' Callum said. His finger moved to his mouth, pointing. 'My wife was English. The accent. Manchester?'

'Salford.'

'I like Manchester. It's like Liverpool for people with anger management issues.'

'I know a good number of people who'd deck you for saying that.'

'Oh, I don't doubt it. Do you know what I love about America? When you ask where someone is from, they tell you where they're living right now. Over there, I'm *from* New York. Isn't that glorious? I'm *originally* from Ireland – that's the key, you see. *Originally*, you say. But now, I'm from New York. I like that. I like that a lot.'

She cocked her head.

'You don't think it's important where you're from?' she said.

'Well, to an extent, I suppose.' He shrugged. 'It's just all so arbitrary, isn't it? Where you're born is something you have no control over, and I think people dwell on it far too much. We mythologise ourselves, don't we? I'm guilty of that myself. We spend all our time as adults thinking back to how we behaved as children, as though we can try and understand where we ended up.'

He paused, looking thoughtful for a moment.

'And you know what? America is a country of immigrants, so every fucker has a story to tell you about where their folks came from. I mean, Christ on a bicycle. I want to take them by their lapels and shake them, you know? Say to them, look where you are now! My god! Look forward! If you were driving a car and looked backwards as much as you are now you'd have hit a tree by now.'

He collected himself.

'If you ask me – and I do appreciate that you haven't, and I'm just rattling on here, uninvited – but if you ask me, we should pay more attention to *where we end*.'

'Where we die?'

'*How* we die. Endings are important. The way a story ends is, to all intents and purposes, much more important than how a story begins. We spend so much time thinking about where we came from, that we lose sight of where we're going to end up.'

I need to put an end to it all.

She hadn't thought of how she and Jack had got together, she hadn't given it a moment's consideration for years. There had been a time, she supposed, when it had been a mythology of their own. They had worked together for the software firm. It had been her first real job out of university, and the company had been small enough and young enough that everyone was excited and naive about the prospects. They had bonded strongly as a group. Regular pub trips, parties, soap-opera-like webs of relationships. The friends she had made in that job had been ones she'd nurtured for longest. She was still in touch with Lou and Kevin, with Janet and David.

Jack had asked her out back then, but she'd refused. She remembered the drunken conversation where she had tried to put him in his place: he was management, she was most certainly not. It felt inappropriate and she'd told him so; a primed finger, a warning tone. It was only years later, when they met again by chance, that their respective statuses seemed more on a par. For the first time, she thought, she could see them as adults, as real adults, and there was something seductive in that, which facilitated the way they'd fallen so easily into place.

She'd asked herself if the past had laid some groundwork for their present. If they had not spent those important years together, in the same fast group of friends, they would never have met, they would never have found interest in the other. Their past had let them approach each other with open eyes. They had already seen each other drunk and foolish, lonely and keen. But did they have anything in common except for a shared and sentimental past?

As the years had passed, her ability to stomach the narrative had faded. Their relationship felt like a once-warm memory that outstayed its welcome. Now all she could think of was how to bring things to a close. A good ending. A clean, decisive cut. A way to move on.

'Are you alright, there?' Callum said. 'You seem quite lost in thought.'

Aleyna coughed, embarrassed.

'I'm sorry,' she said. 'I was thinking. I was... thinking I need to put an end to it all.' She looked surprised to have said the thought out loud.

Callum blinked.

'Gosh,' he said. 'Well, please don't do it on the flight or we might never get back.'

'I mean, I was thinking of ending things with my partner. Jack.'

'Ending things as in divorce, or ending things as in murder?'

She laughed.

'Splitting up,' she said. 'We're not married. Although it has been nearly ten years, so sometimes it feels like it.'

She had no idea why she was telling him this. 'I've almost done it before. Told him it's over, I mean. It's always felt... inevitable in some way.'

Callum nodded, his expression sage.

'Common law marriage,' he said. 'Or it would be. Britain is quite backwards in such things.' He sighed. 'Again, you see. We look backwards rather than forwards. What does some old, dusty book know about how we should live our life in these modern times? It's absurd. If the people who wrote those books knew that in the future we'd be capable of flying from one country to another, they'd accuse us all of witchcraft.'

The plane lurched again and Aleyna instinctively grabbed for her hand rest. Ahead of them, Baby Blue Hat started screaming, and there was a murmur of tense voices. She craned upwards for a view down the plane. Most of the in-flight entertainment screens on the backs of the chairs seemed to be showing action movies. Perhaps the same one, split and shuffled into a mosaic. People running, jumping; things exploding. The whole story taking place simultaneously across the plane.

'Bumpy one,' Callum said.

'I didn't think it was going to take off at all with all that snow.'

'Well, we're supposed to be above all of that now. Although I did hear that it was getting dicey in Heathrow, so we might have an interesting time of it.'

Aleyna's grin was becoming masklike.

'I really don't want to die in a plane crash,' she said. 'This might sound awful, but Jack would milk it so much, you wouldn't believe.'

Callum looked calm.

'Oh, it won't come to that,' he said. 'Just a bit choppy, that's all. They've flown in far worse, I'm sure.'

'I wish I could share your confidence.'

'Oh,' Callum said. 'Help yourself.'

Somewhere further up the aisle, a sharp voice was raised. There was movement, the stewards congregating, grasping the backs of the chairs as they moved zigzag with the plane's motion.

There was another raised voice. A muttered whisper. Then one of the stewards made their way towards the back of the plane. Stopping by a passenger in a neat trouser suit and whispering a few words. Aleyna watched as the passenger extricated herself from her seat and followed the steward back down the aisle.

'A doctor,' Callum said.

'Really?'

'Yes, look. They're trying to be discreet about something and they're doing a lousy job of it.'

'Oh, no. That's awful.'

'Possibly. I met a lady in the departure lounge,' Callum said. 'She was a very nervous flyer, and on top of that, I believe I saw her popping pills for her heart. I hope she'll be alright. She seemed even more terrified of flying than I am.'

Aleyna gave him a look.

'If you ask me, you seem like the calmest person on this plane.'

He shot her an amused look.

'Oh, I've been on a lot of planes. Enough, you could say, that I've fashioned a fine mask for myself. Inside, I can assure you I'm bricking it.'

The plane ducked again. A downward lurch, an upward swoop. Someone screamed. A snatched, involuntary sound prompting a crackling message of reassurance from the tannoy. The tension in the cabin remained, each jolt and bump bringing with it a collective intake of breath.

Aleyna closed her eyes.

Jack. I'm so sorry.

Beside her, Callum had started to hum a tune that, for a brief moment, seemed familiar.

DEPARTURES

Callum arrived at the gate early. He had waited in the main departure lounge, in the shadow of the information board, watching for the gate number to clatter into view. As soon as it was unveiled, he pulled himself to his feet and set off through the interminable corridors. He wasn't as fast as he used to be, but there were few places that made him feel older than airports. All distances were overstretched, and the frigid air felt as though it was conspiring to dry him out, leave him as a husk.

He wasn't the first to arrive at the gate. There was a scattering of people who had dispersed themselves with an almost mathematical evenness around the metal racks of chairs. A woman in an airline uniform was busying herself behind the desk. Callum slipped his gloves off and approached.

'Is this the flight to London?' he said.

The woman glanced up at him. Her expression a little wary, but her professional smile creeping in around the edges.

'London Heathrow, that's right, sir.'

'Oh, wonderful.' His own smile was as self-deprecating as he could muster. 'In the past I've sat myself down at the wrong gate and completely missed my plane.'

'Well… if you're going to London Heathrow, this is the right gate, so—'

'Damn near give myself an ulcer whenever I've flown since. You know?'

'As I said.'

'Even when it says the right destination, I'm always half convinced they'll move it and I'll miss the announcement.'

'I'll let you know if they do. I promise.'

'Very stressful places, these airports.'

'I don't disagree.'

Her smile was patient, her patience was slipping.

'Is there anything else I can do for you, sir?' she said.

Callum shook his head.

'Will you be flying with us?' he said and the smile flickered with a shadow of suspicion.

'Yes,' she said. 'Sir.'

He extended his hand.

'Oh,' he said. 'I'm so pleased. It was very nice to meet you.'

His hand hung there a moment before she took it. Her hand was limp, uncertain, but it was enough. Callum nodded at her and returned to the seats. The woman watched him go, a trace of amusement tempering her frown. She returned to her paperwork with a shake of the head.

It was a good start. Her thread was strong. A sturdy, confident rope, like one a climber might use to scale a cliff face. He sat back in the chair and searched the room until he found a clock. Hours. He had hours.

He checked over his hand luggage. Searching the outer pocket on his case where he kept the wallet containing all his travel documents. He pushed around with the palm of his hand, finding old receipts and train tickets and Hershey's wrappers. There was no way he could have lost it between the baggage check-in and here, surely, but it was worth checking.

Nora had always handled the documents when they had flown together. Callum had always wondered if it was something she did because, at some level, she enjoyed the minutiae of the organisation process, or whether it was simply because she never trusted him to manage it himself. Whether it was something she had been born to, or something she had come to learn, she had always seemed to relish putting itineraries in order. She told him she saw travel as an opportunity rather than a chore, and he imagined her seeing a curious kind of beauty in the ordering of numbers and tasks that he had never imagined himself owning the capacity to understand. Nora had always seen colours when she heard music and he wondered if this was the same thing.

He could imagine the look she might give him if he suggested it, and the memory of her look made him smile despite himself.

Nora's thread had been strong when they'd first met. A stiff and knotty cord, weathered like garden twine. Every time he touched her, he sensed the thread of her being, thinning imperceptibly at first, but then, increasingly, by degrees. It strummed between them like a plucked string. He always knew he would outlast her, but she burned so brightly he also knew he couldn't stay away purely on account of the discrepancy in mathematics he imagined between them.

Life, after all, was not a metric to be measured simply in two dimensions.

When she died, she had done so in the bedroom of their flat in Brooklyn. She remained vivid until the end. Her very existence packed tightly into the modest dimensions that had been allotted to her.

'You knew this was coming, you fraud,' she said when she caught him crying. Her laugh was a wicked thing even in those last days.

She'd always wanted to be buried back home in Lancashire and, considering it to be her very last journey, she had prepared a very specific itinerary. She wanted to be buried in the cemetery in Ormskirk, and when she said she wanted to be within spitting distance of her family, Callum had a mind that she meant it literally. She would be buried, she said, with a bottle of Islay whisky, a duty-free pack of Silk Cut cigarettes, and a pack of Bicycle playing cards, with the cellophane removed. These, she stipulated, should be placed in her coffin with her.

'Otherwise, I'll get mighty bored down there,' she said. 'Until you shift your arse and come join me, that is.'

Dying in America proved to be an expensive business. The staff at the funeral home were good lads, and they advised Callum that the airline and customs officials would have to do lists of their own. The coffin had to be sealed before it could be stowed on the plane and hiding liquor and tobacco inside the coffin would be considered illegal.

Callum had begged a moment to think. He'd walked down the road until he found a poorly stocked liquor store and bought a bottle of Talisker and six packets of Benson and Hedges.

'Do you sell playing cards?' he asked. The man behind the grille shook his head.

'Would you happen to know where I can get some? It's hard to credit such a thing, but it's an emergency.'

After a little negotiation, it became clear that a group of characters occasionally used the room above the liquor shop for a weekly card game. The room looked stark and uninviting in the cold light of day, but they found an opened pack of cards on the shelf by the door. Not the right brand, and well enough used, he pocketed them anyway and paid his guide a finder's fee. He hoped Nora's ghost would forgive him.

When he got back to the funeral home, he put on a good show of being theatrically distraught. The staff at the funeral home, being American, kind and well-meaning, saw only the weeping widower and not the bulging pockets which hadn't been there when he'd left earlier. When Callum demanded time alone with his wife, they gave it to him so readily, Callum felt a knot of guilt for having deceived them. When the door closed, he emptied his coat and began hiding his wife's contraband in the coffin, tucking the cigarettes under Nora's body and fitting the cards into the pocket of her favourite jacket. She had always been one for poker rather than patience, he hoped she would find someone to play with wherever she was going.

The bottle he saved for last. Wedging it at her feet, tucking it under the generous silken folds of the coffin lining. Standing back, the scene reminded him of the medieval monuments they had seen in York Cathedral. Long-faced sleeping knights with loyal dogs curled up at their feet.

'No Islay, I'm afraid,' he said, 'best I could do.'

Nora didn't say anything.

'Now, don't you give me that look,' he said as though she had.

He felt around in his pockets and found a lighter. He had never smoked, and it wasn't as though she would ask him if he had a light again. He sighed and slipped it into her pocket with the cards.

'Open a window before you start on those,' he said. Patting the full pocket neatly. 'They've got alarms everywhere on planes these days.'

He cleaned up the packaging and carrier bags as best he could and was completely, perhaps genuinely, distraught again by the time the door opened, and the funeral directors found him.

That was more than five years ago. The last time he'd been back in Europe. He'd told the story a number of times since, and it had become more hysterical with each telling. It occurred to him that Nora probably deserved a more fitting epitaph, but he also knew that if she were telling the story, it wouldn't stop there. She'd include the part when they reached the graveyard, and her American-sized coffin didn't fit in the English grave that had been cut for it. The pallbearers had bounced it a couple of times on the edge of the hole, briefly considering tipping her in sideways, before setting her aside and waiting for the digger to come back and make the grave bigger.

'She put on weight, Cal?' someone had asked him.

He'd nodded. 'Aye,' he said. 'Yankie breakfasts.' He stretched out his hands; he inflated his cheeks to signify mass.

The boy hadn't seen the funny side. He so very rarely came to visit them in New York that Callum sometimes wondered how well he knew them any more. He didn't know if he had said something that had offended him, or how a rift might have opened between them. Callum remembered the way he had scowled, and how, for a moment, Callum had felt stung, as though he had been the child and the boy had been the parent.

Since they had moved, Nora had always acted as if she had become younger, arguing that life was a bell curve. You end where you start, foolish and wild if you can manage it. The boy was still caught up in his adult phase: the elevated status granted by lived experience, untempered by the realisation that it didn't really mean anything in the end. The life he led with his polite little wife seemed to have ossified to a degree. During his mother's funeral, Callum had watched him as he had loitered at the graveside as if he was soberly ticking off a milestone in the life he imagined for himself. *Death of a parent. Tick.* Maybe it would make him stronger. Maybe it would make him relax a little, rather than making him look so stiff in his mannerisms, like a little English gentleman out of his element. They had parted like strangers, he couldn't see Callum off at the airport that time. It was, Callum decided on the flight home, alone, the saddest part of the whole bloody business.

There was activity around the desk. A tall gentleman and a slim woman had joined the stewardess who had been holding court. They talked in a low undertone. A shared and private joke made them laugh guardedly. Pilots or stewards? Probably the latter, although the uniforms sometimes made it hard to tell. He watched them talk. A rushed conversation, mid-work. It became clear that the man was about to leave again, and in preparation Callum retrieved his passport from the front pocket of his suitcase.

As the steward rushed past, Callum dropped his documents.

'Oh.' He sounded plaintive enough that the stewards stopped to help.

'Butterfingers,' the man chided, his humour buoyant, faintly inappropriate. He passed the documents back, and Callum, playing the doddery old fool, took them off him, his artfully unsteady hand brushing against the steward's wrist as he did so.

'Oh, bless you,' he said. 'Thank you.'

The thread was broad as steel rope on a suspension bridge. A youthful energy; an untapped reserve.

The young man looked impatient to be on his way.

'Have you got everything?' he said.

'I think so. Yes. Thank you.'

'Well, then. Enjoy your flight.'

'I shall.' Callum smiled his doddery old fool smile. 'Are you on the same plane?'

The amusement ripened to innuendo. 'To London? Yes. I just need to...'

'Oh. Well, don't let me keep you. I'm so sorry.'

'Not at all.'

And he was gone. Callum watched him go and slipped his documents away again. He had a long-standing admiration for those in the service industry. He knew the unfailing politeness could prove grating to some, but the commitment to the facade was impressive in itself, and the sheer predictability of corporate kindness was, on occasion, a useful asset.

He sat back in his chair and surveyed the room. The gate was filling up. More and more bodies jostling for space in the racks of metal and plastic seats. He could feel the warmth of the mass of passengers. A dense stuffiness of human sweat, curdled with tension, tempered by boredom.

Across the aisle, a young woman was sitting reading a paperback. Her expression faintly unengaged, either in the book she was reading or in the airport itself. She struck Callum as a focused point of perfect calm in a room that otherwise simmered.

Nora had been a better flyer than he ever had been. For her, taking a plane was the same process as catching a bus or a train. It wasn't her business to know how the vehicle worked or was operated. There were news stories about them when they crashed or went wrong, but you never heard about them when everything was fine. She was just a passenger, giving herself over to the responsibility of the operators.

She would tell him how she enjoyed the act of travel. The entire journey, and not just as a means to reach a destination. The sense of physical conveyance through a shifting landscape. She liked the sense that she was moving across the map, as though she imagined a line painting her route as the globe turned beneath her.

Callum was less enamoured. It always felt like such a chore to him. Something that he would need time to recover from, a hangover without the benefits of being drunk. He was not a bad flyer, exactly, more of a bad *departer.* The sluggish ritual of checking in and waiting. The hierarchy of queues and processes, any of which could slow him down, so all of which needed extra time to accommodate. *Waiting* was a waste of the life that had been allotted to him and he resented any system which demanded it of him.

He stood to stretch his legs and walked a circuit of the room. Taking his time, he lingered by the window and saw the sky had turned a bruised shade of purple he attributed to the filter of the glass.

'Looks like it's going to snow.' He turned to see an elderly woman standing beside him, gazing through the window with concern. Her face had slackened into something mournful, as though all she saw through the glass was something apocalyptic, something anticipated.

Callum beamed. 'Well,' he said. 'That time of year, I suppose.'

The woman nodded. For a moment she looked as if she might totter, and instinctively Callum reached out a hand to steady her.

She blinked at him, less fragile than he had assumed.

'I'm sorry,' Callum said. 'I thought...' He reframed his hand, palm flat, thumb up. 'I'm Callum. How do you do.'

She regarded him with a faint suspicion, as though she had addressed him, thinking he was someone else. But she was of a generation where etiquette dictated that she would take his hand anyway. It was only a matter of time.

'Mrs Anthony,' she said. Emphasising the *Mrs* and turning her hand pointedly so her ring was plain and visible.

'Are you quite alright?' Mrs Anthony asked him.

Callum nodded. His smile was braver than it should have been, and for a moment, he felt as though he should say something nice. Something earned.

'How beautiful you are,' he said. Her face lurched into the sort of anger that one of his smiles couldn't cloud over. He nodded instead and returned to his seat.

The room filled with strangers, silent to one another. The benches clogged with bodies and bags; atmosphere thickened with huffed impatience and stretched clicking of limbs and bones. There was the smell of plastic wrappings and cleaning fluid, of bodies at rest. Tired muscles, heavy eyelids, a shared knot of tension stitching one to the other.

Callum sat, consciously alone. The young woman with the book glanced up at him and caught his eye. She looked away again, returning to the sanctuary of her paperback with a frown.

Outside, it had begun to snow. A star-field of fat flakes wheeling lazily. The dotted lines of runway floodlights picked them out against the dark sky and the filter on the window painted the outside world in a soft lavender colour. There was something peaceful about the silence with which the world was being repainted.

A young father approached the window; a slim figure, shaven head and neck tattoos. He held his child aloft to see the winter fold in across the runways, crisping the tops of the waiting planes with ice-cream cornices. The girl was young, a toddler in a bright blue woollen hat. Callum couldn't hear what words they exchanged, but he could see the girl pointing to the window with a plump finger and he saw the father turn to his daughter, and the glimmer of unequal wonder they shared between them.

Callum smiled, but his smile faltered with no one to see it. When he looked away, a prick of sharpness obscured his vision. He closed his eyes, but the darkness was too much. Too many threads, tangled into too many knots. He opened his eyes and checked his bag again. Reaching for his passport, his documents; reaching for Nora, for the boy.

He sat back in his seat and sighed. He waited with everyone else.

He waited to be called.

ACKNOWLEDGEMENTS

Thank you to Helena Bell, John Clute, John Costello, Ellen Datlow, Samuel R Delaney, Geetanjali Dighe, David Edison, Fabio Fernandes, Neil Gaiman, Jennifer Giesbrecht, Neile Graham, Elizabeth Hand, Sarah Hickingbottom, Joe Hill, James Hoskins, Nicole Idar, Alex Kane, Margo Lanagan, Vicki Lloyd, Usman T. Malik, Liam Meilleur, Shannon Peavey, Bob Pomfret, Nick Salestrom, Kelly Sandoval, Allison Solano, Mike Taylor, Hugo Xiong, Neon Yang, Les Young and E Lily Yu.

Thank you George Sandison, Dan Coxon, Jonathan Oliver, Nina Allan, Gary Budden, Marian Womack, Andy Cox, Michael Kelly, Kit Calles, Aki Schilz, Jared Shurin, Donna Scott, Tim Major, Shona Kinsella and Heather Wood.

Thank you, Helen Marshall
for absolutely bloody everything.

PUBLICATION HISTORY

Eight of the stories in this collection were published previously in slightly different forms.

'We Are Now Beginning Our Descent'
First published in *LossLit* (2018), Kit Caless and Aki Schilz, (eds.)

'The Purpose of the Dodo is to be Extinct'
First published in *Interzone* 275 (2018), Andy Cox (ed.)

'Finisterre'
First published in *BFS Horizons* 7 (2018), Tim Major and Shona Kinsella (eds.)

'We Can Walk It Off Come the Morning'
First published in *Shadows & Tall Trees* 7 (2017), Michael Kelly (ed.)

'Five Conversations With My Daughter (Who Travels in Time)'
First Published in *Interzone* 261 (2015), Andy Cox (ed.)

'The New Man'
First published in *Interzone* 270 (2017), Andy Cox (ed.)

'The Knowledge'
First published in *Gods, Memes & Monsters*, Stoneskin Press (2015), Heather Wood (ed.)

'My Uncle Eff'
First published in *An Invite to Eternity*, Calque Press (2019), Gary Budden and Marian Womack (eds.)

ABOUT THE AUTHOR

Malcolm Devlin's first collection, *You Will Grow Into Them*, was published by Unsung Stories in 2017 and shortlisted for the British Fantasy and Saboteur Awards. His novella, *And Then I Woke Up* is due to be published by TorDotCom in 2022.

Falling from the UK, he unexpectedly landed in Australia and currently lives in Brisbane.